The Enchanted One

The Ravenwood Trilogy Book 1

Lora Deeprose

WCP

World Castle Publishing, LLC
Pensacola, Florida

Copyright © Lora Deeprose 2014
Print ISBN: 9781629891644
eBook ISBN: 9781629891651
First Edition World Castle Publishing, LLC, November 15, 2014
http://www.worldcastlepublishing.com

Licensing Notes

Cover: Karen Fuller
Editor: Brieanna Robertson

Dedication:

For Sharon

Acknowledgements:

I would like to thank my amazing circle of friends who have supported me and my odd choice of career and who have accepted my eccentricities as part of my charm. To Susan Dempsey and Brett Zufelt, thank you for always being there for me no matter what crazy adventures I get myself into. To Joan Beddoes, thank you for sharing your country wisdom with me. I will forever treasure the conversations and companionship we shared while sipping gin and tonics in our pink lawn chairs. Very special thanks goes out to Claire Paradise, my dearest friend and amazing writer, for taking the time to go through the first drafts of this book and lending her expertise and insights into making the story even better.

As always, my love and gratitude to my sisters: Amy, Cari, Tanya and Lisa. I am so proud to belong to this awesome tribe of women. To my beautiful nieces (the Snietches) Courtney and Breanne thank you for keeping me young, telling it like it is and making me laugh.

And with deepest appreciation, I'd like to thank my publisher at World Castle, Karen Fuller for giving this book life and to my brilliant editor Brieanna Robertson for her craftsmanship, professionalism and her unlimited patience in dealing with this writer who has a certain phobia about using commas.

Chapter One

She was going to kill him. Rage rippled through her as she stumbled out the back door of her flower shop. She could deal with everything else Ian did, the constant drinking, his temper, his inability to keep a job, but not this. He had gone too far, and this time, she'd make sure he'd pay.

It was bad enough she was leaving in the middle of a workday. Thank God Madison agreed to stay past her shift to look after the shop. Not that there would be many customers wanting flowers on a weekday in January. But she would have to find the money to cover her employee's extra hours, which was going to be even more challenging considering Ian's latest transgression.

She gritted her teeth as she slammed the heavy metal door.

Locking the deadbolt behind her, she put her keys in her pocket and started for home. The frosty air on her cheeks didn't help to cool her temper.

As she trudged down the alley, a huge grey shape came hurtling soundlessly down at her. She shrieked and stepped backwards as a Great Horned Owl swooped just a few feet over her head. It flew upwards and away from her.

Against the flint-colored clouds, the lighter grey form wheeled in the sky, its enormous wingspan apparent even from the sidewalk. The owl circled lazily one more time before descending in a graceful spiral to land on the roof of Lizzie's shop where it settled in to watch her.

She'd first noticed the owl living on Enchanted Garden's rooftop when she started working there seventeen years ago. Since then, she'd glimpsed the owl when she'd stayed late to fill orders, but it always took her by surprise when it sailed past her on wings as silent as death.

Seeing the nocturnal bird flying around during the day was odd. Unease mingled with her anger, twisting her stomach into knots.

Oblivious to the icy condition of the pavement, she strode toward the front of the street in the direction of her apartment.

She wasn't sure what she was going to say to her husband when she got home, but she had to do something to stop him. He had gone after the one thing that mattered to her and she wasn't about to let his selfishness take it away. This time, she was prepared to fight back.

The wind was stronger out on the sidewalk, and its biting dampness soon numbed her fingers and nipped at her ears. Her eyes started to water. Lizzie lowered her head against its icy breath and cursed herself for forgetting her gloves.

She remembered pulling them out of her coat pocket and putting them on the desk in the back office, but forgot to grab them on the way out. She stuffed her hands in her pockets and tried to negotiate the slick sidewalk without losing her balance.

She quickened her pace, trying to make it to the corner before the light changed. Her foot skidded on a patch of ice and she lost her balance. Struggling to pull her hands out of her pockets, she only managed to free her left one before she hit the sidewalk.

Her knees and left hand took the brunt of the impact before momentum rolled her onto her back. Out of the corner of her eye, she caught glimpses of legs as people walked past her. She remained sprawled on the sidewalk trying to catch her breath.

Her day couldn't get any worse.

Chapter Two

"Oh jeez lady, are you okay?"

Lizzie looked up into the face of a skinny young man standing over her. Dark dreadlocks peeked out from under a blue Do Rag he wore on his head, his dark eyes sharp and intelligent. Metal piercings sprouted from his face; a silver barbell lanced his eyebrow, a large hoop looped though his bottom lip, and both ears bristled with silver studs.

"I'm fine, just embarrassed by my lack of grace," she replied, slowly propping herself up on one elbow.

The young man reached out a gloved hand to help her up. She took it and was surprised at the strength behind his grip.

The stranger lifted her easily up from the sidewalk. "That was quite the header you took. Are you sure you're okay?"

Lizzie winced as she stood up and leaned against the young man to get her bearings. Her knees burned and her hand screamed where she'd scrapped it raw on the ice. "Yes, really, I'm fine," she said, adjusting her purse back on her shoulder. She took a step back from the young man and smiled weakly.

"You should probably get that hand looked at."

"Yes, yes I will." She looked down at her hand. The flesh on her palm was torn and ragged. Bright crimson rivulets flowed from the wound. She berated herself again for leaving her gloves back at the store.

"Hold out your hand."

Lizzie surprised herself when she did as she was told, holding out her bleeding hand to the stranger. The young man ripped off his leather gloves, shoved them into his coat pockets, and untied the bandanna from around his head. Before she could object, he began wrapping it around her palm.

As he worked at bandaging her hand, Lizzie caught a glimpse of a tattoo on the inside of his left wrist. Three shapes inked in dark blue—a crescent that curved to the left, a circle and a crescent that curved to the right.

A strange tingling pricked her scalp as she continued to stare at the design. A memory stirred, but as she tried to pull it forward, it curled like wisps of smoke in her mind then evaporated.

The stranger finished his ministrations and tied the makeshift bandage off neatly. "That should do until you get to a doctor."

She thought of how unhygienic the grubby piece of cloth was as a bandage, but dismissed the thought, not wanting to offend the one person who seemed to care about her wellbeing. Ironic that it was a stranger she would never meet again.

After reassuring the young man she'd go to the doctor, she turned and limped for home. Each shuffling step sent jolts of pain shooting through her knees. After her spill on the ice, she didn't dare put her hands back in her pockets, so within minutes, her fingers lost all feeling in the searing cold. With each step, her anger burned brighter.

This time, Ian had gone too far, and she wasn't going to put up with his excuses or be afraid of his bullying. Stealing from her store was the one thing she couldn't forgive.

Heartsick and in pain, Lizzie finally made it to the apartment. The four-story Victorian walk-up had once been a place of grace and charm. Now it was just a sad, neglected reminder of a more elegant time.

She hobbled into the lobby and over to the staircase, grateful for the heat blasting out of the clanking radiators. As the blood rushed to her extremities, the burning sensation of pins and needles added to the throbbing in her knees and the pain of her torn hand.

Taking a deep breath, she started to climb the stairs. She winced when her knees protested with each step she took. Halfway up, she started to overheat, but didn't have the energy to take off her heavy coat and carry it.

By the time she stood in front of her apartment, she had a pounding headache from gritting her teeth against the pain and a queasy stomach from being too hot.

She dug in her pocket for her keys. Her fingers found an old receipt and some loose change, but no keys. Gingerly, she put her damaged hand into her other pocket and came up empty again.

God, where the hell were her keys?

She remembered locking the back door, so she had them when she'd left the shop, and it was her habit to throw them in her coat pocket rather than her purse. With fading hope, she dug through her purse.

With no other choice, she rang the tarnished brass bell and waited. She could hear the cheap, tinny sound echoing in the apartment. When Ian didn't come to the door, she leaned on the bell then resorted to pounding on the scarred wood.

She knew he was home. He had been home for three months since being fired from his last job. Besides, Ian wouldn't venture out in the cold and ice even if he'd run out of beer. If he were out of booze, he would just have it delivered and charged to her credit card.

"Ian, for God sakes, open the door." She slammed her fist against the door again. As if in response to her pounding, the lights in the hall dimmed.

The door to the apartment across the hall opened. "Lizzie, dear, did you lock yourself out?"

Lizzie struggled to put a smile on her face. "Sorry, Mrs. Epstein. I must've left my keys at the shop and Ian doesn't seem to be home."

Mrs. Epstein raised her eyebrows. "Not to worry. I'll just go get the spare you gave me." Mrs. Epstein stepped back inside her apartment, her pink house slippers slapping and whispering on the hardwood floor.

Leaning against the doorjamb, she waited for her neighbor to return. Mrs. Epstein had left her door slightly ajar and as Lizzie tried to collect her thoughts, a sleek black cat slipped out into the hallway and headed straight over to her. Winding its long body in and out of her legs, it bumped its head against her shin, demanding attention.

"Hey, Courtney," she said, carefully leaning over and giving the feline a good scratch behind her silky ears. Her efforts were rewarded with a throaty purr.

The scuffing murmur of Mrs. Epstein's slippers announced her return. "Courtney, you naughty girl. You know you're not supposed to leave the apartment. Here you go." She handed Lizzie the spare key and scooped up her cat. Courtney squirmed in her arms and reached a paw out as if asking Lizzie to rescue her. Oblivious to the cat's request, Mrs. Epstein headed back to her apartment, holding the wriggling feline tightly in her arms.

Lizzie took a steadying breath, but her hand still shook as she slid the key in the lock and opened the door to her apartment.

Stepping over the threshold, she was greeted by darkness. All the drapes in the apartment were drawn tight over the windows and the weak winter light had no chance of penetrating the gloom. Sounds of grunting and the occasional, "Got you, you slimy bastard," could be heard coming from the back of the apartment.

She winced at the sound of his voice, her hands turning clammy. Pulling back her shoulders, she breathed slowly.

She took off her coat, carefully sliding her tender hand out of the sleeve before hanging her coat and scarf in the hall closet. She toed off her boots and left them on the mat by the door.

Shuffling past the kitchen, she noted the dirty dishes piled in the sink. She had rinsed the breakfast dishes and loaded them in the dishwasher before she had left for work. This was Ian's lunch mess. Her anger was fueled even more when she spied the empty beer bottles littering the counter.

She followed Ian's voice to the second bedroom that served as the home office. What it really acted as was Ian's playroom. She stood for a moment watching his back, her good hand clenched into a fist at her side.

He slouched in front of a brand new twenty-seven-inch flat screen monitor, earbuds jammed firmly in his ears. He focused on the screen where armor-clad warriors engaged in a battle fought on a digital landscape.

He wore the same clothes he had on yesterday—a green and white striped Rugby shirt that pulled tightly over his paunch and grey sweat pants stained with grease. His hair was freshly cut, though, and styled with platinum highlights threaded through his sandy hair.

The room smelled of dirty socks and leftover pizza, making her stomach lurch. Strewn about the floor were Styrofoam packing pieces, empty plastic bags, and two empty boxes—one for the new monitor Ian was currently fixated on, and the other for a new gaming computer, something the side of the box advertised as a Black Widow Phantom. His previous computer and monitor, which were only a year old, sat in the corner of the room under a jumble of cables.

If Ian wasn't watching football on the plasma TV in the living room, he could be found, more often than not, at the computer playing fantasy games with other online gamers. It seemed to Lizzie he preferred to spend his days immersed in an imaginary world of warriors and warlocks instead of living in the real one.

She planned to discuss his latest theft calmly. She hoped, this time, he would understand he had to stop spending money they didn't have. Money that wasn't his.

If she stayed cool-headed, maybe he wouldn't turn his ugly temper on her. She didn't want his rage exploding around her, or to feel the quick jab as he poked her ribs, or the eye-watering sting as he grabbed a fistful of her hair in his brutal hands.

She didn't want to see the disgust in his eyes as he stormed out of the apartment only to come back a few hours later smelling of beer and uttering promises to be a better husband. She thought about all the things she didn't want, but was unsure of what it was she did want from him or from her marriage.

"Ian, we need to talk," she said, trying to keep the fury out of her voice. He either couldn't hear her over the battle sounds of the game or he chose to ignore her.

"Turn the computer off, please," she said, raising her voice. She took a step into the room. The scene on the monitor shimmered just as Ian's avatar lowered a deadly-looking sword down on the head of a minotaur.

"What the...." Before he could finish his sentence, the game on the screen disappeared, leaving a blue field of emptiness on the display. Lizzie shifted her weight to her left foot just as the screen went completely black. Swearing loudly, he yanked out the earbuds and started fiddling with the computer tower when he spotted her reflection on the now dark screen.

"What the fuck did you do?" He spun his chair around to face her. "I was in the middle of something and you probably just fried my hard drive with your little stunt."

"I didn't *do* anything. I'm standing four feet from your computer. How could I have done anything?" She took a step back.

"Why are you here? Shouldn't you be at your precious store hovering over your stupid flowers?"

"Yes, I should be. And I would still be there, but I got a phone call from the bank saying my account's overdrawn. Turns out someone used the business's bankcard to buy computer equipment. Want to share with me how that could have happened?" She crossed her arms over her chest.

"How would I know? I don't have anything to do with your cruddy business. Maybe you screwed up and made a mistake in your accounting." He stood up and brushed past her, making his way to the kitchen.

They were doing the same tired old dance and she was sick to death of it. She followed him into the kitchen as fast as her painful knees would allow. She flicked on the kitchen lights as Ian pulled a beer out of the fridge. He twisted the cap off the bottle and flicked it into the sink where it bounced off a food-encrusted bowl and fell to the floor. Ignoring it, he headed back to the office, but Lizzie stepped in his path, blocking his way.

"We are going to talk about the missing money and all the new computer equipment I just saw in your office."

"This is so typical of you. Whenever something goes wrong in your life, you automatically blame me. I'm tired of being your whipping boy. Why don't you ask your star employee where the money went? She's the one who has access to your money, not me."

"Because I trust Madison."

"Oh that's rich. You trust that airhead but not your own husband."

"That's because she's never given me a reason not to trust her, which I can't say the same for you. You've taken money from me before without asking, you've been fired from jobs and not told me. You conveniently forgot to make the payments on our car and I didn't find out until the repo man showed up to tow it away. So yes, based on your past history, I naturally would assume you had something to do with the missing money," Lizzie blurted out. She knew she would pay for her outburst, but she was past caring.

"Shut your mouth. You just can't stand the idea that without my money, we wouldn't have this apartment so you could play in your little store all day. You're pathetic. Now move, I have to see how badly you fucked up my computer."

Lizzie stood her ground. "Your money? Your mother is the one with money, not you. Even this apartment was a wedding gift from your mother. And every time I manage to save a few pennies, I find out you've blown it on speakers for your computer, or booze, or fancy designer shirts that you never wear because you can't keep a job." Her voice quavered.

Ian turned toward her with lightning speed, his face blotchy with rage. "I was let go at Stanley and Associates because my boss was jealous of my talent. It's not my fault the guy couldn't handle competition."

She let out a hollow laugh. "You've got to be kidding me. You actually believe the lies you tell me. You were fired because you didn't show up for work half the time and when you did, you didn't actually do the work. Did you think they were going to hand you a paycheck for sitting at home on your ass all day? Or is it because you think you are better than everyone else and that you don't have to work like the rest of us slobs?"

"Yeah, well, I'd like to see how any other man could hold down a job while trying to live with you. They don't have to put up with your neediness, your insecurities."

The lights in the kitchen dimmed ominously. Ian and Lizzie ignored them.

"I want a divorce." Her eyes widened at what popped out of her mouth. She didn't mean it. She needed to take back the words, but it was too late.

"Go ahead. But don't forget, half of everything we have is mine, including the shop."

Panic gripped her chest and she fought to catch her breath. Ian shot his arm out so quickly she didn't see him move until he grabbed her bandaged hand, crushing it until she could feel the bones grinding painfully against each other. She let out a weak mewl of pain.

The light fixtures above them started to swing from their chains like pendulums, increasing in their speed and arc.

He moved his face close to hers. She could smell the stale beer on his breath. A fat vein throbbed at his temple.

"And here's another thought, you're going to be alone again," he whispered his venom in her ear. "All alone because there is no man out there who could put up with a freak like you. I should've left you a long time ago. I don't need to have my life ruined any longer just because I felt sorry for you." He let go of her hand and thumped his beer bottle on the counter with such force a fountain of foam sloshed onto the surface. "I'm going out. I expect you to be gone by the time I get back because you are not staying in my apartment."

As Ian uttered this last threat, the kitchen lights grew brighter as if a surge of electricity had momentarily dialed up the wattage. Then one by one, the light bulbs blew out with a succession of tiny popping sounds. Seconds later, ear-splitting reports like gunshots filled the kitchen as the milk glass shades simultaneously exploded, raining shards of glass down onto the faded linoleum.

Ian yelped and jumped back. A razor-sharp piece of glass slashed a red line across his cheek.

"You Goddamned cunt. Stay away from me," he screamed, backing away from her.

Glass crunched under his sneakers as he crossed the kitchen and grabbed his leather coat from the hall closet. He flung open the door to the apartment and turned to face her. The cut on his cheek wept a thin trail of blood down his face.

"I'm warning you, get your stuff and get out." His parting shot was cut short by the door slamming shut behind him.

Lizzie stood motionless in the sea of opaline glass. Her hand started to bleed again, soaking the bandana and silently dripping scarlet beads onto the shattered glass on the floor.

Chapter Three

Lizzie stood in the dark kitchen staring at the door to the apartment, listening to the sleet rattling against the windows. Her thoughts whizzed around in frantic circles. What had possessed her to say she wanted a divorce? She didn't want that. She wanted Ian to love her, to cherish her, to be her partner, and support her in her drive to make something of their lives. It stung that he had agreed to a divorce so quickly. There was no hesitation or regret in his voice, just rage and vindictiveness. A dead weight of dread sat on her chest, making it difficult to breathe.

The shrill ringing of the phone startled her. She'd completely forgotten about Madison. She'd no idea how long she'd been staring off into space. Racing to the phone, she ignored the pain in her knees.

"I'm so sorry. I completely lost track of time. I'm on my way," she said, not giving Madison a chance to speak.

"Is this Mrs. Chambers?" asked an unfamiliar voice.

"Uh, yes. Who is this?"

"Mrs. Chambers, this is Nurse Klem from the Toronto General Hospital. Are you married to an Ian Chambers?"

"Yes, what's this about?"

"Your husband was admitted to our emergency room a half an hour ago. He was involved in a motor vehicle accident and the attending doctor thinks it would be best if you came down as soon as you can."

"I'm sorry, what did you say?"

The nurse repeated what she said, her voice taking on a gentle tone that inexplicably angered Lizzie.

"It can't possibly be Ian. He was just here and he's fine."

"This number was among your husband's personal effects and was listed as his home phone. I know this is terrible news to hear over the phone, but you need to come to the hospital."

Lizzie stared at the bloodstained bandana wrapped around her hand. She focused on the crimson pattern as if it would help her make sense of what the nurse was saying.

"Mrs. Chambers, are you still there?"

"Yes, I uhm...what hospital are you calling from again?"

"The Toronto General. Is there someone who could come down with you?"

Lizzie ignored the question. "Where is Ian?"

When the nurse finished giving her directions to the ER, Lizzie hung up and hastily dialed the flower shop. An eerie calm descended over her, but her hands were shaking so badly she misdialed and had to slowly punch in the numbers a second time.

"Enchanted Garden, Madison speaking." Madison's voice sounded so normal. Lizzie pressed the receiver tighter to her ear.

She opened her mouth to speak, but had to choke back an unexpected sob. "Madison," was all she managed to say. The rest of the words stuck in her throat.

"Lizzie? What's going on? I thought you were coming back. It's almost closing."

"There's been an accident."

"Oh my God, are you okay? Did Ian hurt you?"

She'd never told anyone about Ian's behavior much less her employee. There was an uncomfortable silence before she answered. "No, no I'm fine. It's Ian. He was hit by a car and I need to get to the hospital."

"I'm on my way."

"No, hold on. I didn't call to ask for a ride. I'll take a taxi. I just wanted to tell you you'd have to close up."

"You are not taking a taxi. Wait there, I'm coming over."

"No, really, that's not necessary." She couldn't keep the annoyance out of her voice.

"We can argue as long as you want, but I'm not taking no for an answer. I'm driving you to the hospital and that's that. You can be pissed off at me tomorrow."

Reluctantly, she gave Madison her address. Lizzie hung up the phone and glanced at her bandaged hand. She needed to get rid of the filthy rag before Madison arrived. She made her way through the dark apartment and when she switched on the bathroom light, she winced as the brightness pierced her eyes.

Rummaging through the cupboard under the sink, she found the plastic First Aid kit at the back under a package of toilet paper. She pulled out sterile gauze and a gummy roll of medical tape from the kit. Removing the bandanna, now stiff and dark with her blood, her stomach roiled as she looked at the stain.

She saw an image of Ian sprawled on the sidewalk, his broken body twisted in an unnatural pose. His feet were bare. A dark river flowed from his head, spreading across the icy pavement.

Lizzie flipped up the toilet lid. Her stomach twisted painfully, but she threw up nothing but bile. She knelt gripping the cool porcelain bowl as her stomach cramped again. When her stomach had settled down, she slowly pulled herself off the floor and rinsed her mouth from the tap.

"Please, Great Mother, let him be okay." She silently prayed the way Sister Colette had taught her.

She left the water running and ignored the sharp pain in her hand as she washed the gash. She applied a fresh bandage and secured it with lengths of tape she cut with a pair of blunt-end scissors from the First Aid kit. As she worked, she glanced up at the mirror but quickly averted her eyes so she wouldn't have to examine the guilt she saw in her reflection.

When the doorbell rang, she jumped, dropping the scissors on the floor. She didn't bother to pick them up.

Leaving the bathroom light on, she traced her way to the front door, turning on all the lights in her path. Only the kitchen remained dark.

She flung on her coat, slipped on her boots, and scooped up her purse from the floor before unlocking the door.

Madison stepped over the threshold and without uttering a word, wrapped her arms around Lizzie.

She stiffened under the intimate contact. She could smell Madison's light floral perfume and her curly hair tickled her nose. She immediately pulled away from the embrace.

Madison rubbed her hands up and down Lizzie's upper arms as if trying to warm her. "He's going to be okay."

Lizzie nodded, but a cold, dark stone pressed on her heart. She knew he wasn't going to be okay, but she didn't contradict Madison's well-meaning words.

"What happened to your hand?" Madison's eyes narrowed as she spied the fresh gauze covering Lizzie's palm. She started to say something more, but Lizzie cut her off.

"I fell on the ice on the way home. It's nothing. We need to get going." She brushed past Madison, forcing her to take a step back into the hallway. Lizzie shut the apartment door and engaged the lock before heading down the stairs with Madison following in her wake.

They left the apartment with its lights blazing and headed out into the early twilight of winter. Madison had double-parked her Honda Civic with its engine running. The car's interior was warm and smelled of cinnamon from the heart-shaped air freshener hanging from the rear-view mirror.

The women rode in silence through the icy streets. While Madison negotiated the rush hour traffic and the slick roads, Lizzie looked out the passenger window, observing the pedestrians bundled up in unrecognizable shapes against the sharp wind. The light from the street lamps made the frosted trees on the boulevards and the ice-coated sidewalks sparkle. The long shadows cast from the deepening twilight transformed the familiar city blocks into a sinister landscape from a twisted nightmare.

She desperately wanted Madison to keep driving. It didn't matter where, just as long as it was away from what she knew was awaiting her at the hospital. For years, she had wished for an end to the drama with Ian, but she never wanted him dead.

I'm a liar, she thought as she swiped her hand across the passenger window to clear away the condensation. Just hours earlier, hadn't she'd wished her husband dead? Everything Ian had said about her was true. She wasn't natural. She was a freak. If she didn't want him dead then why wasn't she feeling what any normal person would feel when a loved one was hurt or feared dead—panic, sorrow, or even worry? She wasn't feeling anything but relief. Relief that her shop was safe. Ian couldn't take it away from her now.

Guilt and remorse twisted in her belly and she thought she was going to be sick again. Cracking the window open, she sucked in the bitter evening air.

Despite the road conditions, they arrived at the hospital in under thirty minutes. Lizzie dashed out of the car and shuffled toward the entrance as fast as her knees would let her before Madison had shut off the engine. Once inside, Lizzie followed the signs to the ER and made a beeline to the large, curved desk of the nurses' station.

A handful of people were lined up to speak to the admitting nurse and Lizzie had no choice but to wait her turn. With a bored air, the nurse listened while each person told her why they urgently needed to see a doctor, then handed them a clipboard and directed them to take a seat while they filled out the requisite forms.

Lizzie watched as two other nurses scurried from the admitting desk to pick up the completed forms then back to the packed waiting area where they called out the names from the clipboards.

The smell of the hospital insinuated itself onto Lizzie. She breathed through her mouth to lessen the stench, but it didn't help. The miasma of odors assaulted her—pine-scented disinfectant, vomit, blood, sickness. Underneath all that was the cloying sweetness of anesthetic. It was faint, but she could smell it.

She broke out in a clammy sweat. Being in a hospital brought back memories of another time, another hospital where she had found herself in a different antiseptic nightmare.

"Can I help you?" barked the admitting nurse. It wasn't so much a question as a reprimand.

"My husband Ian Chambers was in an accident and the hospital said I should come here."

The nurse turned to the computer at her workstation and typed a few keystrokes. "Yes, he was admitted to the ER at sixteen forty-five," she said, finally looking up at Lizzie. "You can take a seat, and as soon as the attending doctor is able, he'll update you on your husband's condition."

"Can you tell me what exactly happened? The nurse on the phone said it was a car accident, but Ian wasn't driving. He had just gone for a walk. How badly is he hurt?"

"I don't have that information. It would be in his chart, which is currently with the patient. All I have is the time and general description of his injuries from the paramedics who brought him in. You'll have to wait for the attending to ask those questions and he'll be with you as soon as he can." The nurse looked past Lizzie and Madison to the next person in line. "Can I help you?"

Lizzie opened her mouth to say something to the nurse, but Madison put her hand on her shoulder and firmly moved her away from the desk. "Let's go sit down," she whispered in Lizzie's ear.

She allowed Madison to guide her to one of the few empty seats in the waiting area. The molded orange plastic chairs were connected together by long metal rails under the seats and were bolted to the floor. When Lizzie sat down, the whole bank of chairs swayed slightly and her shoulder brushed up against the person sitting next to her.

"Sorry," she mumbled, and tried to make herself smaller.

Madison remained standing. "I'm going to get us some coffee. Is there anything else I can get you?"

"No, coffee's fine."

Madison turned to leave, already rummaging through her purse for change, when Lizzie spoke again. "Someone needs to call Ian's mother. I can't do it. I just can't." She knew it was a lot to ask of her employee, but the thought of telling Mrs. Penelope Chambers that her only son was fighting for his life in the ER was more than she could deal with.

Penelope had made it very clear early on in Lizzie's marriage that she did not approve of the match. In her eyes, Ian had married far beneath him.

For a brief moment, Madison's lips tightened into a thin line then she smiled, her eyes softening. "Sure," she replied.

Lizzie dug her cell phone out of her purse and turned it on. Although she hadn't called her mother-in-law in years, she still had her phone number in her cell's directory. She scrolled down the menu, brought up the number, and handed Madison the phone. "Thank you."

Madison nodded, plucking the phone from her outstretched hand. "I'll be right back."

As Madison disappeared around the corner, Lizzie sunk further back into her chair, hugging her purse on her lap. She scanned the crowded waiting room, wishing she had gone with Madison.

The majority of the people were focused on their own pain or listlessly watching the flickering images on the muted TV mounted high up on the wall in the room's far corner.

Where Lizzie sat, she had a perfect view of the hallway leading from the ambulance bay to the trauma rooms. Even over the noise of the waiting room, she could hear the *swoosh* of the pneumatic doors and the metallic rattle of the stretcher as it was being unloaded from the ambulance. Seconds later, she glimpsed a person strapped to the gurney flanked by paramedics. They were rapid-firing abbreviated statistics on the condition of the patient to the doctor as they raced down the hall and disappeared from view.

Three more times she witnessed this controlled chaos. Although she didn't understand what the paramedics were saying, she knew each of these people had been involved in car accidents, their injuries serious and life-threatening. The hazardous road conditions that Madison had handled so efficiently had taken other victims in their icy claws.

When she looked up at the sound of yet another gurney, she knew before they passed by her view that this person had breathed her last breath long before reaching the hospital. The paramedics weren't talking as they pushed the stretcher down the hall, their energy subdued, almost defeated. Lizzie squeezed her eyes shut.

The moment she left her body, the sensation was so subtle at first she wasn't aware what happened. She heard a soft *pop* like when her ears adjusted to a rapid change in air pressure, the sensation coming from somewhere deep inside her. She was suddenly weightless, hovering just above her body.

She watched from a distance as Madison returned holding two cups of coffee. She saw herself take a sip of the oily brew, but tasted nothing. Steamy tendrils rose out of cup, but she felt nothing against her face.

She noticed fine details of the scene below—the texture of the fresh gauze on her hand, the way the light shot gold highlights in the burnished red of Madison's curls, the hairline crack in the corner of the ceiling that looked like a crooked finger beckoning souls away from this place of pain.

It felt like her ears were wadded with cotton and she could only make out the lilt of the voices below her but not the actual words. She felt more than heard the concern in Madison's voice as she spoke. Lizzie was being told something important, something she needed to respond to, but she refused to understand what the words meant.

She let herself drift effortlessly up and away from the scene below her. She moved like mist through the concrete and steel substructure of each successive floor until she floated out into the inky night, rising steadily toward the sprinkling of stars.

What a strange dream, she thought as she ascended into the black sky. She must have fainted, but she didn't care. She far preferred this hallucination to the reality she had just escaped.

As she continued drifting higher, the wind caressed her skin and ruffled through her short hair, but she didn't feel the winter's biting cold or the staccato kiss of the sleet swirling around her.

Slowly, she became aware of another much stronger sensation, a magnetic pull coming from some far off point in the fathomless sky. It resonated like a beacon, triggering in her a longing tinged with sorrow, a deep and frantic need to follow this pulse like a heartbeat calling her home. She surrendered to her need to follow the cadence, feeling her body drift over the city. She watched detached as the city raced below her, her spirit heading west through the spiraling pellets of snow.

The longing grew stronger and her sense of urgency intensified. Her speed increased as she zeroed in on the source of the silent calling. Elation surged through her, electrifying every nerve ending in her body.

Around the edge of her consciousness, a thought began to form. When she reached her destination, an important truth would be revealed. She would finally understand everything.

An icy blast of air abruptly stopped her flight across the sky. It was like colliding with an iceberg. The cold stabbed through her. Pain, fear, and anger replaced the euphoria she had experienced moments ago. She had to get away from this presence. Danger was here.

As she retreated in the direction she came, a dark fist of energy punched through the air, engulfing her. The presence wasn't just dangerous, it was evil—ancient, slithering.

She was back in the hospital in the blink of an eye. In her dream, the speed of her arrival matched the depth of her irrational fear. She slammed back into her body with teeth-rattling force.

Gasping for air like a swimmer coming up from a deep dive, she blinked her eyes. She was surprised to find herself sitting upright still holding the cup of coffee. Looking down into the cup, she was astonished to find it empty.

When had she drunk her coffee? What had she just experienced? Was it some kind of fugue state brought on by stress?

There was no time to ponder the answer, as a doctor dressed in faded green scrubs was heading over in her direction.

She sat rooted in her chair. The doctor crossed the last few feet of grey linoleum separating them all the while looking directly at Madison.

"Mrs. Chambers?" he asked.

"No, I'm her friend." Madison stood up as she spoke.

"Sorry. I'm Dr. Lipmann. Why don't we go someplace a bit more private and we can talk about your husband," the doctor said, this time addressing Lizzie.

She stared up at the doctor, nodding in agreement, but stayed seated. Finally, Madison grasped her gently by the elbow and firmly lifted her up off the chair.

They followed the doctor down a short hallway and into a small conference room. Sitting on the edge of the conference table, he gestured for them to take a seat. Madison sat down. Lizzie dropped her coat and purse in the seat of the closest chair to her, but remained standing, clutching the back of it for support.

The doctor scrubbed his face, then rested the palms of his hands on the table. "Your husband was involved in a pedestrian vehicular accident. Unfortunately, he sustained several fractures to his legs, hips, and back and damage to several of his internal organs. He also sustained a serious head trauma. We did everything we could to save him, but his injuries were too severe. I'm so sorry to have to tell you this, but your husband died of his injuries shortly after being admitted to our ER."

"Noooo. No, not my baby."

Lizzie spun around to face Ian's mother.

She stood in the doorway, her eyes wide in her chalky face. She grasped the collar of her sable coat and stepped inside the room. Tottering precariously on her snakeskin heels, she would have lost her balance if not for her driver, who had been standing silently behind her. With quick efficiency, he stepped forward and steadied her.

A nurse poked her head around the newcomers. "Doctor Lipmann, this is Mrs. Penelope Chambers, the patient's mother."

The doctor stood up and took a step toward her. "Mrs. Chambers, I'm so sorry for your loss. We did everything that we could to save him," he said, repeating the same speech he had just given Lizzie.

Penelope didn't acknowledge the comment. Instead, she shrugged off her driver's hand and stormed toward Lizzie. "You murdered my Ian!" Her manicured hand flashed in the air, connecting with Lizzie's cheek.

Lizzie reeled back from the force of the slap.

Penelope howled like a feral animal in pain. The eerie sound made the hairs on the back of Lizzie's neck stand up.

Her mother-in-law pulled back her hand and slapped her again. Lizzie stood there, her arms hanging limp at her sides. She would have taken yet another blow, but Doctor Lipmann and the driver stepped in to restrain the hysterical woman.

Penelope struggled under the men's firm hold, tearstains leaving streaks down her carefully applied makeup. The doctor barked an order at the nurse and she scurried out of the room.

"You'll pay for this, you little witch. You'll pay for taking my Ian away from me. I will destroy you just as you destroyed him," she screamed, her eyes wild with fury.

Lizzie blinked back tears and glanced over at Madison. Madison nodded imperceptibly, scooped up Lizzie's things, and followed her out of the room.

In the hallway, they almost collided with the ER nurse, who was heading back to the room holding a syringe and a small vial. The nurse sidestepped around them and went into the conference room without looking up. She shut the door behind her, cutting off Penelope's anguished sobs.

Lizzie started down the corridor, intent on leaving the hospital, when Madison put her hand on her arm to stop her.

"Did you want me to go back in and talk to Dr. Lipmann? Arrange for you to see Ian? I mean...so you could say goodbye."

"No, Penelope wouldn't allow it and it would just make things worse, if that's possible. Could you just take me home?"

"Sure."

She quietly followed Madison out to the parking lot. She let Madison think her mute state was due to exhaustion and grief, which was partially true. Inside, she was in a state of panic. Had she finally slipped over the edge into insanity?

When Ian was irritated with her, he would accuse her of being a freak, of being crazy. That's why no one in their right mind would want her. Maybe he was right. Maybe he saw in her some deep mental defect and that was what turned him away from her and into the world of his online games.

The silence continued on the ride home. The streets had become doubly treacherous, as the sleet had turned into a blizzard while they had been inside, covering the already slick roads with a heavy blanket of snow. The fat, frenzied flakes made visibility near zero.

Lizzie kept replaying her strange flight across the sky while waiting in the ER. Maybe she had a brain tumor pressing down on her neurons, causing her to hallucinate. Perhaps she had had a psychotic break.

She caught herself up when she realized what she was thinking. Her husband was dead, his brains splattered on a cold, icy street in a heartless city, and she was sitting very much alive in a warm car worrying about her mental state. Bile burned the back of her throat. Maybe she should add narcissism to her list of mental deficiencies.

She prayed silently. Whether it was guilt or sadness, she didn't know, but she didn't try to stop the tears slowly leaking from the corners of her eyes, the salty anguish stinging her raw cheek.

As soon as they arrived at her apartment building, she opened the car door, thinking only of retreating to the safety of her home. She didn't want Madison looking at her anymore or offering her sympathetic words.

"I appreciate all that you done for me tonight."

"Wait." Madison put the car in park and leaned across the seat to look Lizzie in the eye. "I don't think you should be by yourself tonight. If you want, I could stay with you?"

"No, that's not necessary. I'll see you in the morning," she mumbled, scrambling out of the car before Madison could reply.

She let herself into her apartment and leaned against the closed door, catching her breath.

Alone again. I'm alone again.

Chapter Four

The apartment was ablaze with the exception of the darkened kitchen and reverberated back to her a silence she hadn't experienced since her early twenties. Whenever she came home, there was always the sound of the TV blaring or the muffled groans and yells as Ian played on the computer. Alone. All alone. The apartment sighed around her.

She kicked off her boots and dropped her coat in a heap on the floor. She automatically reached out to turn off the hall light, but as her fingertips touched the switch, she snatched her hand back as if she'd been slapped. Being alone and in the dark was too much. Even with all the lights on, she could still feel the dark presence coming for her. It didn't matter that the evil she felt was a construct of her unbalanced mind, it scared her. She retreated to the only safe place she could find.

As she passed by Ian's office, she closed the door without looking in. She turned quickly and stepped into the bedroom, shutting the door behind her. Digging furtively between the mattress and box spring of the queen-sized bed, she felt around until her fingers closed around a cold metal object. She pulled out the small silver key and unlocked the blanket box that sat at the end of the bed.

The simple box was made of teak, the top French polished so that its surface shone like a mirror. Once opened, it infused the room with the rich, spicy scent from the cedar-lined interior. She gently moved aside a well-worn patchwork quilt and the satin-covered wedding album with a picture of Ian and her on the cover. To anyone looking at the photo, they looked happy and in love. What a difference seventeen years could make.

She dug past a few more spare blankets and pulled out a Raggedy Ann doll. Holding the doll tightly to her chest, the smell of cedar pungent in her nose, she glanced around the room. There was no feeling of Ian in the bedroom, no poignant echoes of whispered affection, no memories of nights spent spooning in intimate comfort.

He had stopped sharing their marriage bed almost a year ago after a heated argument over losing yet another job. He had spent his sleeping hours on the pullout love seat that occupied a corner of their home office.

She tucked the doll under her arm and closed the blanket box. It closed with a sharp click. Tossing the key on the lid, she stumbled across the room, unsure her shaky legs could carry her across the scuffed hardwood floor to the safety of her bed. She collapsed face down on top of the duvet cover still clutching her doll. A strangled sob escaped her throat and she buried her face in the doll's hair to muffle the sound. She drew in a deep breath, inhaling the comforting smell of old cotton and cedar, but it didn't help.

She started to shiver uncontrollably, so she climbed under the duvet fully clothed. Lying on her back, she stared up at the ceiling as the familiar sensations of a full-blown panic attack started. A wave of pure terror began to build somewhere outside of herself. She could almost see the wave as a shimmering, rolling energy moving across the bedroom that grew more powerful as it moved closer. Her heart raced, every nerve ending in her body jittered as shocks of electricity zinged up and down her arms and legs.

When the wave finally reached her, it crashed into her chest, engulfing her in raw terror. Beads of perspiration popped out on her forehead. She was on fire, burning up from the inside. Surge after surge of fear continued to course through her, her breath coming out in short, frantic gasps.

Pinned to the bed, she rode each wave of panic, hoping as it subsided that it would be the last one, only to have another roll its powerful emotion through her.

She had never had an attack last this long. It was too strong, too big, too ferocious. She was going to burst apart into angry sparks and disappear forever.

She burrowed deeper under the covers, clinging to her rag doll for security. She needed to get herself under control. She focused on her shallow breathing and pushed herself to slow the rise and fall of her chest.

Even as the waves continued to pummel her, she forced her mind to go back to the gardens of the Priory. Back to her world when it was safe and she was loved.

The small, rounded stones under her feet crunched satisfyingly as she moved along the familiar paths. She wore shorts and a t-shirt with a white and pink *My Little Pony* prancing across the front. Her brown hair hung in two long plaits down her back.

She followed the paths around the large raised beds, feeling the warmth of the sun beating down on her head. Her breathing slowed as she conjured up from her memory the faint licorice scent of French tarragon, the peppery aroma of Bee Balm with their purple pom pom flowers alive with the fuzzy bodies of bees, the clean astringent smell of sage as she crushed the furry leaves between her fingertips.

Birds sang and the leaves of the stately oaks and maples growing outside the garden's high stone walls rustled as a gentle summer breeze blew through their branches. She summoned up the clear sound of the chapel bells calling the nuns to their prayers.

As she wandered further, past the vegetable beds and the cutting garden, the waves of panic mercifully receded. Her heart slowed and the painful fire under her skin died down. She stayed in the garden, wandering the gravel paths until she came upon Sister Collette sitting on a stone bench beneath the dappled shade of an apple tree.

Her head was bent over a small book held in her lap, her face obscured by the black fabric of her wimple. She glanced up as she heard Lizzie approach. Her clear, intelligent eyes caught sight of Lizzie and she smiled warmly. It lit up her whole face, deepening the wrinkles around her eyes.

Sister Collette put aside her book and opened her arms wide. Lizzie ran the last few feet separating them and felt the strong, protective arms close around her. She was finally safe.

She stayed in that moment until the merciful dark waters of oblivion surrounded her and tenderly pulled her down into its dreamless depths.

Chapter Five

The moment before the comforting cocoon of sleep dissolved and reality reasserted itself, Lizzie floated in nothingness. There was no pain or disappointment, only an awareness of being connected to everything and nothing at the same time.

Abruptly, her waking world intruded. The soothing balm of sleep was broken and more cruelty awaited her at the end of a ringing phone from the voice of an indifferent and demanding lawyer.

She shot up in bed, accidentally flinging her Raggedy Ann as she scrambled to pick up the phone. As the doll tumbled onto the floor, its dress flipped up over her smiling face, exposing the red candy heart painted on her chest.

She listened intently to the voice on the other end of the phone. Her shoulders sagged as she nodded in agreement, even though the caller couldn't see her.

"Yes, I understand," she said evenly, and then gently replaced the receiver. She retrieved her doll from the floor, smoothing down her dress and propping her up on the pillow. "Looks like we both had a rough start this morning."

In that brief moment before she had become fully conscious to the ringing of the phone, she'd had no memory of what transpired yesterday. The phone call from Penelope's lawyer had brought it all back.

Ian's dead.

She kept repeating the words as if their meaning would finally sink in and she would understand it was real. As real as the dull ache she felt in her knees as she wandered to the bathroom, as real the morning light filtering through the bedroom curtains. And as real as the fact Penelope was evicting her from her apartment.

Even after she had hung up the phone, showered, and dressed for the day, Lizzie still couldn't grasp that she was now widowed and homeless.

Her husband had been killed less than twenty-four hours ago and now Penelope was kicking her out of her home. Not just evicting her, but giving her only a day to get her things and get out. Although her mother-in-law had given the apartment to them to live in rent-free, it was still in her name. Legally, Lizzie had no recourse, as Penelope's lawyer had laid out in great detail. He said a process server would be around later to post the eviction notice. Lizzie didn't care. She wouldn't be around to see it.

In the stark winter daylight with all the lights still burning in the apartment, Lizzie no longer feared the nameless evil or the threat of another panic attack, nor did she feel any sadness. She was numb, encased in ice.

She craved coffee with lots of sugar, but she'd overslept, and now she needed to pack her things before going in to work. She'd have to wait until she was at the shop to feed her caffeine addiction.

She called Madison, telling her she was running late but she would be coming in. She couldn't bring herself to confess to her employee she had no choice but to go to work because she had no place else to go.

Just yesterday, she was afraid Ian was going to take the one thing that meant something to her, and now, the shop was all she had left.

She dug out her suitcase from the back of the closet and threw it on the bed. Yanking her clothes off their hangers, she stuffed them in the suitcase, adding armfuls of socks, underwear, and t-shirts from the bureau. She crammed the few pairs of shoes she owned in the outside zippered compartment of the case.

Wandering around the house, she tried to decide what else to take. In the end, the only thing she added to her suitcase was her rag doll.

Earlier, she had avoided going into the kitchen, but now she didn't have a choice. She couldn't leave the mess for Penelope or one of her lackeys to see. If her mother-in-law saw the destruction in the kitchen, who knew what conclusion she would draw from it.

She pulled back the living room curtains to let more light flood into the gloomy kitchen. Retrieving a broom and dustpan from the hall closet, she stopped short of stepping into the room.

Something wasn't right. She felt it in her bones and the way the small hairs on the back of her neck stood up.

Chapter Six

A carpet of brittle glass covered the kitchen floor. The light from the living room caught some of the jagged splinters, causing them to twinkle like stars. She stared at the spot on the floor where Ian had stood. She could see the voids his shoes left when the glass had rained down on him. It was easy to trace his path out of the kitchen by the way the glass was pushed aside or crushed into smaller fragments by his shoes.

She slowly inched her gaze over to where she had been standing. Like Ian, she too had left two clean patches on the linoleum where she had been standing. She picked out the blood drops on the shards where her hand had bled. It had dried to a deep maroon and appeared almost black in the feeble light. She gripped the broom handle tighter, but the dustpan clattered to the floor.

Again, she glanced to where she had been standing the day before. Except for the outline of her footprints, the shattered glass hadn't been disturbed.

When the kitchen lights exploded, she had been standing in her stocking feet. An electric shiver, like biting on tinfoil, coursed through her body.

She let go of the broom and dropped to the floor, frantically pulling at her wool socks. She ran her hands over the bottom of her bare feet. The soles were smooth, not a cut or even the faintest scratch on them.

The menacing glass sea winked at her as if agreeing with her wild conclusion. She had somehow managed to walk across razor sharp glass without even so much as a splinter or a puncture while wearing only nylons to protect her feet. And without disturbing the glass in any way. She shoved her feet back into her socks as if covering up the evidence would mean it didn't exist.

She couldn't explain how she managed to walk through all that glass without cutting her feet, but she wasn't going to tempt it again. She ran back into her bedroom, retrieving an old pair of sneakers she'd just packed.

The glass tinkled like ice cubes in a tumbler as she dumped dustpan after dustpan of debris into the kitchen garbage. Even when the floor looked clean, Lizzie ran the vacuum, then a damp rag, over the lino to make sure not even a stray splinter remained.

After disposing of the garbage down the chute in the apartment corridor, she returned to her unit intent on replacing the broken light bulbs. But when she stood on a stepladder examining the fixtures, she knew she'd have to leave them.

Each light was the same; globs of dull metal had fused to the inside of the sockets. There was no way she could remove them.

Instead, she scrubbed down the kitchen, did the dishes, and dumped all Ian's empty beer bottles down the garbage chute. After calling a cab, she gathered up her things and went downstairs to wait in the lobby.

She headed straight over to the bank of brass-fronted mailboxes at the entrance of the building. After slipping an envelope addressed to Penelope's lawyer containing the house and mail keys into the slot for outgoing mail, she perched on her suitcase, placing her small overnight case down by her feet. She stared out the lobby window looking for her cab. Thoughts pushed forward, demanding her attention. She pushed back harder.

She picked nervously at the edges of the fresh bandage on her hand. When she became aware of what she was doing, her hand would find its way to the cross pendant around her neck, her fingers rubbing the cool blue stone until it was warm from her touch.

Bandage, necklace, bandage, necklace. Her hand danced nervously between the two and still the thoughts kept thrusting their way forward, insisting she acknowledge them.

She had killed Ian. Somehow, she had killed him just as surely as if she had pushed him in front of a car. Her anger had brought death to another human being. She couldn't blame Penelope for evicting her. She would have done the same thing if she had been in her shoes. Knowing this didn't stop the burning panic simmering just underneath the surface.

By the time the cab arrived, her nerves were humming. Loading her cases in the trunk, the driver prattled on about the weather. One searing glance from Lizzie silenced him. She slipped into the back seat and gave the driver directions to her shop, instructing him to drop her off at the delivery entrance. Traffic was light as it was only eleven on a Saturday morning.

Lizzie paid the cabbie and waited silently as he unloaded her bags. Billows of grey exhaust swirled from the taxi's tailpipe as it disappeared down the alley, filling the air with the strangely enticing smell of gasoline. She dug in her coat pocket for the store keys. Only when her fingers came up empty did she remember she had lost them the day before.

She let out an exhausted sigh. She'd have to pay double to bring a locksmith down on a Saturday to change the locks. She couldn't bring herself to haul her suitcases around to the front, so she rang the delivery bell and waited in the cold for Madison.

She didn't have to wait long. Madison swung open the door and reached out to help Lizzie with her bags.

"It's alright. I can manage," Lizzie said, pushing past her.

Madison backed up to make room for Lizzie and her suitcases. "I'm glad you decided to stay with someone. You shouldn't be alone right now."

Lizzie said nothing as she lugged her suitcase into her small office. Pushing her suitcase up against the coat rack, she then dumped the smaller case on her desk.

Her office was the size of a broom closet. But somehow, she'd managed to cram in a desk, two chairs, an old lawyer's bookcase with glass-fronted doors, and a coat rack. Squeezed up against the wall by the door was a battered file cabinet on which sat a coffee maker, mugs, a plastic jar of powdered creamer, and a crystal bowl filled with sugar cubes.

Madison had already made the morning pot of coffee and the office was perfumed with the scent of the dark roast Lizzie preferred.

Lizzie plucked a cube from the bowl and popped it into her mouth. Sucking on the sugar, she let the thick syrupiness fill her mouth, masking the bitterness on her tongue. She swallowed around the lump in her throat.

She poured herself a cup of coffee and dropped four sugar cubes into the dark liquid. Sipping her coffee, she savored the warm sweetness. With her back to Madison, she moved to her desk, putting as much distance between herself and the sympathetic creature standing in the doorway. She didn't want Madison to hug her again or pat her reassuringly on the arm.

She sat down at her desk, leaving her coat on, and took another sip of her coffee. "So, have you had any customers today?"

"A few, not many. I did manage to get the inventory done and entered in the computer. I put a copy of the spreadsheets on your desk." Madison pointed to a neat stack of papers on the corner of the desktop.

Lizzie toyed with the edges of the papers, but didn't pick them up.

"I guess if there is nothing else, I'll go up front. If you need anything, let me know." Madison lingered at the door, but when Lizzie continued to sip her coffee, ignoring her, she left, closing the door behind her with a soft click.

Lizzie continued to stare off into space, draining her mug in greedy gulps. She got up and poured herself another, doctoring it with several sugar cubes and popping one into her mouth before taking a swallow from her mug.

She knew she should be calling around for a locksmith, but she couldn't summon the energy to even pull out the phone book. With a few weary steps, she stood before her antique bookcase. Placing her mug on its scratched and worn top, she bent down low, reaching for the bottom shelf.

Opening the door on the lower shelf, she pulled out a nondescript book. She lifted the cover to reveal a small square compartment hollowed out in the false pages and pulled out a tiny gold key.

Lizzie fitted the key into the lock of the top shelf and lifted open the glass door. Her fingers gently skimmed over the eighteen aged volumes lined up on the shelf: *Sense and Sensibility, Pride and Prejudice, Mansfield Park, Persuasions, and Northanger Abbey.* Most of the novels were contained in three volumes with the exceptions of *Northanger Abbey,* which was printed in four, and *Persuasions* in two. The book covers ranged in color and material from a deep maroon calf leather to a plain grey cloth board. The only novel missing that would have made the collection complete was *Emma.* Not that it mattered to Lizzie. It wasn't possessing the complete works of Ms. Austen that made the books special to her; it was who had owned them before. She'd kept the books in her office because she spent most of her waking hours at work and she wanted to be near them as a sort of touchstone connecting her to the previous owner.

Her hand stopped on her favorite. She pulled out the first volume of *Pride and Prejudice* and gently opened it. Holding it up to her face, she took a deep breath. The smell of aged paper and ink soothed her.

In that moment, she was back behind the safe walls of the Abbey. Had she known what life would be like outside the cloistered walls, she doubted she would have been so eager to leave. Not that going back was ever an option. The Prioress had made it perfectly clear when she had called to tell Lizzie of Sister Colette's passing. The Prioress had expressly forbidden Lizzie from attending the sister's funeral.

"I'm so scared," she whispered into the yellowed pages.

Reluctantly, she set the novel back on the shelf with the other first editions. She locked them up securely, returning the key to the book safe.

She hadn't wanted Madison hovering around her, smothering her with concern or sympathy, but standing in the office knowing she was alone with no place to call home, she desperately wanted company. She remained in her office until she had finished her second coffee and the fear of being alone became unbearable.

Moving slowly, she hung up her coat, changed her shoes, and slipped her apron over her head. These simple gestures she had done every day for seventeen years felt alien. She had inadvertently fallen out of the flow of time and now moved a half a beat behind the ticking of the clock.

Chapter Seven

Smoothing down the front of her apron, she entered the front of the store. She smiled when Madison looked up from the bouquet she was arranging at the refectory table.

It was painful to smile, her lips pulling back in a trembling rictus, her muscles tight, her cheek sore where Penelope had slapped her.

Now that she was with Madison, she didn't know what to do with herself, so she wandered around the store, mindlessly moving vases around on shelves, pinching off leaves from the potted plants, and checking the water levels in the tall metal containers of fresh cut flowers scattered around the shop.

After completing a full circuit of the store, she ducked into the large glass-walled cooler, her skin breaking out in gooseflesh from the frigid air. The air smelled of fresh green things, water from the large plastic flower buckets, and the mingled fragrance of the flowers themselves. She closed her eyes and let the sensation wash over her.

Slowly, her shoulders relaxed and she unclenched her cold fingers. She could almost hear the energy of the flowers vibrating over the noise of the cooler's fan. Some had a strong and steady pulse; others had begun to fade like a weary beating heart, slowly leaking out life.

She turned in a slow circle, keeping her eyes closed, concentrating on the flow of energy around her. She felt the different textures of the invisible vibrations brush against the skin of her face and arms. She stopped when she felt what she was searching for, a thin pulse. What she called *The Letting Go*. It was coming from a bucket of irises and although their pulse was thready, they would still be sellable for a week at least. She searched for other flowers needing her attention.

She opened her eyes and stepped toward the bucket of yellow freesias. Reaching out, she grabbed a smaller empty bucket from the corner of the cooler she kept for this purpose. Her fingers sought out the individual stems that were sending out *The Letting Go* and placed them tenderly into the empty container.

She whispered thanks to each flower and when she had taken out the last stem, she held the bell-shaped blossoms under her nose. They smelled sugary sweet with a high light citrus note reminding her of an early spring morning after a rain.

The bucket held enough flowers to make a small bouquet, which she would send over to the Dellwynne Hospice Centre nearby. The tiny yellow blossoms, the symbol of innocence and friendship, would still be good for several days.

She regularly sent arrangements and cut flowers to the hospice center. On one hand, she realized it was a little ghoulish to send dying flowers to the dying, but on the other hand, if she could bring a little color and a little beauty to someone who was in the midst of *The Letting Go,* then she would continue to send flowers.

Perhaps the people in hospice care would appreciate the irony and find some solace in the company of beauty as it went on the final journey they too would venture on much too soon.

She was adding a few slender spikes of green and white-striped beargrass to the bucket to fill out the arrangement when someone tapped on the glass door of the cooler. Lizzie straightened up and turned.

A tall, barrel-chested policeman filled the doorway. With his hat and bulky police-issue coat, he dwarfed Madison, who stood off to his right wringing her hands.

Lizzie's stomach erupted with butterflies as she stepped out of the cooler, holding the pail of freesias with both hands.

"Ma'am, I'm Constable Butler with the Toronto Police Service. I'm here about your husband's death. Is there someplace where we can speak privately?"

"Yes, we can go to my office, if you'd like." Before leading the constable to her office, Lizzie handed the bucket over to Madison. "Could you make a bouquet for the Centre with these?"

"Sure," Madison squeaked.

Lizzie noticed Madison's hands were shaking as she took the bucket from her.

"This way," Lizzie said in a clear, calm voice as she gestured toward the back of the shop.

Once they were ensconced in her office, she offered him coffee then took a seat at her desk, moving her overnight case from the desk top to the floor behind her.

The officer took a seat directly across from her in the only other available chair. His stork-like legs almost touched her desk, his bulk insinuating itself in the small space and seemed to displace all of the air. He kept his winter coat on, but removed his hat with its red band and balanced it on his left knee.

His eyes roamed around her office as he slurped from his mug. Lizzie fidgeted with her own mug, turning it around by the handle in slow circles.

"So," Constable Butler said, reaching over to place his coffee mug on her desk. His nylon jacket made scratchy whispers as he moved. "I just need to ask you a few routine questions about the day of your husband's death."

"I don't understand. His death was an accident. The doctor said it was an accident." Her throat tightened.

He sat back and pulled a silver pen and small black notebook from the inside of his coat. Flipping the notebook open with a flick of his wrist, he thumbed through the pages until he found what he wanted. "Yes, it seems that way. But we are still interviewing witnesses. It appears your husband was standing on the sidewalk at a red light when he stumbled or was pushed onto the street and into the path of the Number Ten bus."

Lizzie gasped and her hand flew to cover her mouth. The doctor had said Ian had been run over by a vehicle and she had assumed it was a car. The image of Ian being hit by a bus was just too absurd. She fought to keep a bubble of hysterical laughter from pushing past her lips.

The police officer looked up from his notebook, pinning Lizzie with a cold stare. "I can step outside for a few minutes if you need to collect yourself," he said, his voice devoid of concern.

"No, no that won't be necessary. I'm sorry, just give me a moment." She took a deep breath, but it didn't help. She still felt the uncontrollable urge to laugh. She bit the inside of her cheek. "What did you need to ask me?"

"Did you see your husband at any time before the accident?"

"Yes, I saw him that afternoon. He decided to go for a walk and that was when it happened."

"At approximately what time was that?"

"It had to have been around three-thirty or quarter to four. I'm not sure as I didn't look at the time."

"Do you always make a habit of leaving your store in the middle of the afternoon to go home?"

"No, I don't make a habit of it. I needed to speak with Ian in person about an urgent matter."

"Do you own this store, or is it owned by yourself and your husband?"

"I don't see how my business has anything to do with Ian's accident. Shouldn't you be interviewing the bus driver that hit him?"

"These are just routine questions. And the bus driver has already given his statement. The sooner you provide me with the answers, the sooner I'll be out of your hair. So, are you the sole owner of this shop?"

"Yes."

"Did your husband have a life insurance policy?"

"No, he thought it was a waste of money."

"How would you describe the nature of your relationship with your husband?"

"Why would you ask such a question? Ian tripped on an icy sidewalk and was unfortunate to stumble into the path of a bus. The streets are dangerous. I myself fell yesterday on my way home." She held up her bandaged hand for the officer to see. "And how do the intimate details of my marriage have any bearing on what happened?"

"Your neighbor,"—Constable Butler flipped back through his notebook—"Mrs. Epstein, reported hearing an argument around the time you said you were home having a discussion with your husband. She also reported hearing glass breaking. According to Mrs. Epstein, she had stepped out into the hall just as your husband was leaving and she saw what appeared to be a laceration on his cheek."

"His name is Ian."

"So what did you and *Ian* fight about?"

"That's really none of your business."

"Ma'am, it's been my experience, and I've been at this for a very long time, that your fight was most likely over money or another woman. So which one was it, money or sex?"

She folded her arms over her chest and glared at him. The overhead lights began to buzz loudly. The constable looked up, distracted by the sound.

Lizzie stood up abruptly and knocked her sore knees on the desk in the process. She focused on the shooting pain instead of her rising anger. The buzzing overhead stopped. "Constable, I appreciate that you are just trying to do your job, but I'm not going to answer any more of your questions. And unless you are going to charge me with being responsible for Ian's death, even though I was nowhere near him when it happened, I'm going to have to ask you to leave."

"Okay," he said, and jotted a few words down with his silver pen. He flipped the notebook closed and tucked it back inside his jacket. He cocked his head toward Lizzie's suitcase. "If you're planning on going somewhere, I suggest you postpone your trip. I may be calling on you again if I have any further questions."

She crossed the few feet to the door and swung it open. He took his time putting on his hat and adjusting it before he stood up and walked past her, his jacket making a horrible scratchy sound as he moved.

She followed behind him, staring daggers into his broad back as he walked to the front of the store. Before he left, he leaned into her and spoke, keeping his voice low. His fetid breath washed over her, a mixture of onions and stale coffee. "For a woman who just lost her husband, you sure don't seem to be too broken up about it. I would've thought you'd be at home grieving or at the funeral home making arrangements."

Lizzie stared up at him, too shocked by his comment to reply.

"I'll be in touch, and thanks for the coffee," he said, stepping outside her shop.

Gripping the door handle, she watched the police cruiser pull away from the curb.

"Hey, are you alright?" Madison asked from her position by the refectory table.

As Lizzie walked over to Madison, the irrational urge to laugh replaced her burning anger. Closing her eyes, she sucked in a breath, trying to suppress the sensation, but when she opened her mouth to reply, the laughter erupted. Tears streamed down her cheeks as she laughed hysterically. She clutched the edge of the refectory table, doubled over from the effort. "Oh God," she gasped between gales of laughter.

"What's so funny?" Madison asked, her lips curling up in a tentative smile.

"Nothing. It's not funny. In fact, it's horrible." She dissolved into another fit of giggles. "The cop said Ian was hit by a bus. The Number Ten bus to be exact," she said as her laughter subsided into hiccupping gasps.

Madison handed her a tissue from the box on the back counter. Lizzie dabbed at her eyes, her mood instantly turning somber.

"So he came over here just to tell you that?"

"No, he asked a bunch of questions. He said he was just doing a routine follow-up."

"That parting shot didn't sound routine. It sounded more like he was accusing you of something. I mean, where does he get off telling you how you should grieve?" Madison stood with her hands on her hips, her voice full of indignation.

"I believe Penelope's hand was all over that visit." She touched her left cheek, where it was still tender. "You heard her at the hospital. She blames me for Ian's death and now she wants to prove it."

"But it was an accident. You weren't even there when it happened."

"That doesn't seem to matter to Penelope. She is wealthy and connected and has the means of making me pay one way or another." She thought of the eviction notice that was probably posted on her apartment door by now. "I have no doubt she asked the chief of police to arrange the interview."

Lizzie dragged one of the tall work stools over to the table and perched on the seat. She rested her right elbow on the table, cradling her cheek in her hand. With her left hand, she gently touched Madison's finished arrangement of freesias.

"What are you going to do?"

Lizzie ignored the question. "You did a nice job with this. Very nice."

"Thanks. But getting back to what that cop said, you can't just let Penelope harass you like this. He was your husband, you're hurting too. She has no right to do this."

"That may be true, but she has the power to do whatever she wants and there's not much I can do to stop her."

"That's not fair. It's just not fair."

"No, it's not, but life isn't, is it?" Lizzie straightened up and looked Madison in the eye. "Would you mind taking this over to the Dellwynne?"

"Sure." Madison hesitated before continuing. "I could pick us up some lunch on the way back. You haven't eaten anything yet today, have you?"

"I'm not hungry."

"Well, I'll pick you up some soup at least. Maybe you'll feel like eating something when I get back."

When Madison had gone to the back office to get her coat, Lizzie pulled out the order book and flipped through it. During the busier months of the year, she had a steady stream of walk-ins and she took on the occasional wedding if she thought she and Madison could handle the amount of work required. But the bread-and-butter of her little business came from the floral arrangements she provided for the office buildings and businesses surrounding Enchanted Garden.

She staggered her clients' delivery schedule so the bi-weekly orders were manageable with just Madison and herself working on them. She was due to make several deliveries on Wednesday. She grabbed her spiral bound notebook and started making a list of the arrangements she would make based on her current inventory.

She jotted down the first client and was thinking of the possible flowers that would be appropriate when Madison walked from the back room buttoning up her coat. Pulling something out of the pocket, Madison held it up in her hand.

"I can't believe I forgot," she said, handing over what she was holding. "I meant to give them to you yesterday, but in the rush to get to the hospital and everything else, I guess I forgot."

Lizzie recognized the key chain immediately. It was hers.

"Thank God I haven't called the locksmith yet," she said with relief as she pocketed the keys. "Where on earth did you find them?"

"I didn't. Some guy dropped them off yesterday shortly after you left. He said he found them on the sidewalk a few blocks from here."

Lizzie remembered the young man who had helped her up from her spill on the sidewalk. "What did he look like?"

"I don't know, about my age, kinda rough around the edges with a lot of facial piercings and a few tats. Probably plays in a rock band. He had nice eyes, though, and a killer smile."

"Did he happen to leave his name?" Lizzie wasn't sure why this question made Madison blush.

"Yes, his name is Gideon." Madison blushed even harder, her cheeks flaming a brilliant red.

"Does this Gideon have a last name?"

"He didn't tell me, but…" she trailed off, suddenly finding something very interesting on the floor requiring her full attention.

"But?"

"He did give me his phone number."

She had never seen Madison like this. Despite her current feelings of anxiety over her own life, she couldn't help but be amused. She smiled. "I have a feeling this Gideon didn't leave his phone number so I could get in touch with him."

Madison gave her a startled look. "Well, even if that's what he was doing, it's not like I'm going to call or anything. You know I'm currently seeing someone." She walked over to the refectory table and picked up the freesias. "I'll be back as soon as I can."

"Don't rush. I'm just going to brainstorm some ideas for the next week's deliveries."

Cradling the flower arrangement, Madison strode to the front door. With her hand on the door, she turned to Lizzie. "If you need anything while I'm out, call me on my cell."

"Sure," Lizzie replied, not looking up from the papers as Madison left.

Alone, she tried to put her mind to her task, but her thoughts kept drifting back to the interrogation from the cop. That's what it was, pure and simple. She had no doubt Penelope had orchestrated the whole thing.

She was scared by what he had implied, but even worse than the visit was her behavior in front of Madison. She was mortified. After a few minutes of staring at the blank page, she gave up pretending to do anything useful. She closed the order book and glanced around the store.

It had been ten years since she'd bought the store. She had admired and respected Joe, the previous owner. More than that, she was grateful to him for taking her on as an apprentice when, other than working in the Priory's gardens, Lizzie had no experience in the flower business. He had taken the time to teach her everything he knew and introduced her to the people in the business. When she first moved to the big city and needed a place to stay, he had offered her the small apartment over his garage.

Yes, she owed him a great deal. When he had decided to retire with his wife, Bernie, to Florida, he had given Lizzie the first option to buy. She didn't hesitate. She also didn't hesitate to refurbish the place, to put her own style on the little shop and make it wholly her own.

She had pulled down the green plastic lattice adorning the walls, painted the entire space a soft white, and removed the harsh fluorescent fixtures in favor of softer incandescent ones. She replaced the glass shelves with plain dark wooden ones and put in a new wooden floor the same color as the shelving units. The Formica work counter that ran the length of one wall was torn out and, in its place, she installed a solid butcher block surface. She had found the refectory table one afternoon while she was poking around in an antique store and knew it would be perfect as a worktable.

She loved the feel of what she had created. The shop always felt serene and organized, yet full of life, filled with lush plants and luxuriant blooms in every color that nature offered.

This was her place, her creation. She had put so much hard work into it. It was the only place that made her feel safe, where she could be herself as much as she knew how to be. It was more her home than the apartment ever was. Ian said he was going to take it all away from her, and she had no doubt that he would have followed through on his threat. Now he would never threaten her again.

Was it worth it? Was having her shop safe worth a man's life?

She had picked up her pen during her musing and had doodled on the cover of the notebook. When she realized what she was doing, she put the pen down and examined the curious scribbles.

It was the tattoo she had seen on Gideon's wrist—a circle with two crescents on either side. Below it, she had written the words *Triple Goddess*. The strange sensation of knowing the meaning flitted just beyond her grasp.

Lizzie put the notebook aside. With a sigh born of exhaustion, she lowered her head to the table and rested on her arms.

Chapter Eight

Lizzie stirred and opened her eyes. Someone had been calling her name. She sat up abruptly, her gaze unfocused and fogged by sleep. Madison stood before her holding two large deli bags.

"I brought you some chicken soup from Bella's. Did you want to try some?"

Lizzie swiveled around on her stool, rubbing the sleep from her eyes. "Let's just eat out here. The store's dead and this way we can both eat while it's hot." She ignored Madison's look of surprise at her uncharacteristic suggestion. Lizzie had a strict rule of no food in the front of the store. She could have cared less about the food being hot, she wasn't hungry. She just didn't want to be alone.

Turning away from Lizzie, Madison opened the bags, disgorging their contents on the counter.

Lizzie leaned forward on her stool, watching Madison. "Just soup? It looks to me like you bought out everything at Bella's. Were you expecting a hoard of hungry customers to come storming in demanding food along with their flowers?"

Madison neatly folded the plastic deli bags and tucked them in the cupboard under the sink. "My momma always taught me to be prepared. When the mob shows up, I'll offer them a bite of my sandwich for every bouquet of roses they buy. But nobody better touch my brownie."

"Yes, I know. I've seen how you are with chocolate. A person would have to be insane or stupid to try to get between you and your daily chocolate fix."

"You got that right. Chocolate is the food of the gods, it cures all ills, it soothes the soul, and it tastes so darn good. In my book, it's almost as good as sex. Almost." She shook one of the bottles of iced tea and gave it a hearty *thwack* on the bottom with the heel of her hand, breaking the seal on the lid with a sharp *pop*. "Here, start with this."

While Lizzie sipped her tea, Madison busied herself placing the food out on the refectory table. She divided the bounty between them, setting the plastic cutlery on the paper napkins that were included in her order.

Pulling up a stool, she joined Lizzie at the table and immediately tucked into her sandwich

"How much do I owe you for lunch?"

"Nothing. It's my treat," Madison replied around a mouthful of food.

"It was thoughtful of you, but you shouldn't have bought so much. I'm not really hungry and it's a shame to waste all this food." She stirred her soup in slow circles.

"Don't worry about it. What you don't eat, I'll just throw in the fridge in the back and take it home for later."

Lizzie could feel Madison watching her even as her employee dug into her sandwich. Sighing, Lizzie raised her spoon to her lips and took in a mouthful of golden broth. It tasted of nothing, but the warmth was comforting. She ate another small spoonful, noticing Madison was now focused on her own food.

Polishing off her sandwich, Madison wiped her hands on her paper napkin, crumpling it into a wad in the process. She held up her right hand, examining her thumb. "Have you ever noticed that when you eat food that has mustard on it, you always end up getting some on the corner of you thumb? Why is that?" She stuck her thumb in her mouth, sucking off the mustard.

"Just one of life's little mysteries," Lizzie replied, dabbing the corner of her mouth with the edge of her napkin then placing it carefully back on the table and lining it up with the soup container. She picked up her spoon and began stirring her soup again. "I need to apologize for my behavior earlier. I can't even explain why I was laughing. I don't know what came over me. You must think that I'm a horrible person. I know I do." She pushed her soup away.

Madison stopped eating her own soup and regarded Lizzie. "That thought never crossed my mind. You're not a horrible person. I think you are a woman who just lost her husband to a senseless, stupid accident, and on top of that, you have to deal with his grief-crazed mother. That's a lot of stress all at once, and stress makes people do and say odd things. Myself, I cry when I get really angry and laugh when I'm embarrassed or someone hurts my feelings." She ate a few spoonfuls of soup and then continued. "When I was a kid, I was at my grandmother's funeral, the first I'd ever been to, and I got a wicked case of the giggles during the eulogy. It wasn't funny. I loved my grandmother and missed her terribly, but I just couldn't stop laughing. My mother eventually hauled me outside and spanked me. I stopped laughing then."

"How old were you?"

"Eight. To this day, my mother insists that I did it on purpose to embarrass her in front of her sisters."

"Do you see much of your mother?"

"As much as I can handle. She's better in small doses. After my parents divorced, she moved to Halifax with her boyfriend. So now I only have to see her every other Christmas, which works out fine by me." Madison, finished with her soup, began gathering up the trash. "What about yours?"

For a brief moment, Lizzie thought about telling her the well-rehearsed lie she told when anyone asked about her family, not that many people did. This time, she stopped herself short. She wasn't sure if it was just exhaustion, but she couldn't find the energy to tell her faerie tale one more time. Something in her wouldn't allow the lie to come out.

"I never knew my mother. She died giving birth to me," she said, replacing the lid on her soup.

"Geez, I'm sorry."

"There is no need to be. I've had thirty-five years to get over the loss."

"And your dad?"

"I have no idea who he is. My mother never told anyone his name or where he was from."

"So who raised you?"

"Nuns. One nun actually, Sister Collette."

"Wow, that's bizarre. Sorry, that came out wrong. But I guess being raised in an orphanage by nuns beats being sent off to foster care. I've heard some terrible stories about what happens to kids in the system."

"I wasn't raised in an orphanage. I grew up in a Contemplative Benedictine monastery. My mother arrived at the gates one night and asked for sanctuary. She was already in labor, so the nuns took her in. When she died, the Prioress gave me over to the care of Sister Collette."

"And you lived there your whole childhood with a bunch of nuns?"

"Yes and no. I lived with Sister Collette in a small cottage in the Priory's gardens, but I had very little to do with the rest of the sisters."

"It sounds lonely. Didn't you have any friends to play with?"

"It was definitely an unorthodox arrangement, but I never really felt alone. Sister Collette was always with me and she took really good care of me. Like any child, I had toys, dolls, paints, crayons, and books. Lots and lots of books. I had the whole gardens as my playground, and the livestock the nuns kept were my playmates. You'd be surprised how entertaining chickens can be, and I loved the cows with their big brown eyes and docile nature."

"But did you ever get to go out, you know, to see a movie or go shopping?" Madison asked, her eyes wide with disbelief, the lunch mess temporarily forgotten.

"No. The Priory is a cloistered order, and as such, it was pretty much self-contained. We sewed our own clothes, grew our own vegetables and fruit. And we raised cattle, sheep, and chickens for our meat and dairy. The honey from our apiary is actually quite well known."

"But what about stuff you couldn't grow or make, like your books, fabric to make your clothes, or chocolate? Please tell me they let you eat chocolate."

Lizzie chuckled. "Yes, we had chocolate, and I was allowed to eat as much as I wanted as long as I ate all my veggies first. For money to buy things, we sold our surplus honey, eggs, and dairy products to the locals. The nuns also made communion wafers for the Catholic churches. When we needed to purchase store-bought items, we had someone from the nearby village of St. Hyacinthe deliver the goods to the Priory. I may not have had access to shopping malls and TV, but I wasn't deprived by any stretch of the imagination. And besides, you don't miss what you don't know. Right?"

"Right." Madison was silent for a moment. "Speaking of chocolate, it would be a sin to let these brownies go to waste. Double chocolate with walnuts. Mmm." She held a brownie under her nose and gave it an appreciative sniff. "You can't possibly say no to double chocolate and nuts."

"If you say so." Lizzie smiled, holding her hand out for her brownie.

"Hah, I knew you were a secret chocolate fiend like me. You know what would go perfectly with these?"

"A cup of coffee?"

"Absolutely. I'll go make us a fresh pot." She picked up Lizzie's untouched sandwich to put in the fridge and headed to the office to make coffee.

While Madison was busy in the back, Lizzie cleared away the lunch mess and washed down the refectory table. As she scrubbed the worn surface, she pondered why she had told Madison so much about herself.

She'd never told Ian the truth. Why did she find the need to do so now, and why to her employee? And why did she feel lighter because of it?

Madison was right when she said her upbringing was bizarre, but she had been loved, and even though she felt the divide between herself and the other nuns, it never bothered her that much. Until she met Ian, she used to laugh a lot, and she remembered feeling full of excitement, that each day was an adventure, something to look forward to.

What had changed? When had she changed? Why had she held back a part of herself from her husband instead of sharing it? Would it have made her relationship with him different? Would it have made his death harder to bear?

Shortly, Madison returned, carrying two mugs and putting an end to the unanswered questions swirling around in Lizzie's brain. Lizzie finished wiping down the table, rinsed her cleaning rag, and pulled two fresh sheets of paper towel to use as napkins.

"Oh," Lizzie exclaimed after taking a bite of her dessert. "You were right. These are amazing."

"I know," Madison said around a mouthful of brownie.

A comfortable silence descended as the women focused on the delights of their brownies. As soon as Madison swallowed the last morsel of food, she picked up the conversation where they'd left off.

"You said you never knew your mother, but that's not really true. You may not have known the woman who gave birth to you, and don't get me wrong, that's really sad, but by your own description, you had a mother in Sister Collette."

"Yes, you're right, she was. I loved her very much."

"Was? Don't you see her anymore?"

"No. She died a year after I left the Priory."

"Man, I'm sorry. I can say the dumbest things sometimes."

Lizzie reached out to her, giving Madison's hand a brief squeeze before letting it go. "It's never dumb to speak from your heart."

"So, do you want to go over what needs to be done for the upcoming deliveries, or did you get it all done while I was gone?" Madison asked.

"I didn't get much accomplished while you were out. The nap interfered with my plans. But not to worry. Why don't you take off early?

It doesn't look like we're going to get any customers for the rest of today, and I can handle figuring out the arrangements by myself."

"I don't mind staying until closing. If you wanted, you could head over to your friend's place and I'll close up."

"She's coming by to pick me up after she finishes work, so I may as well stay here." Lizzie hadn't lost the gift of a spontaneous lie after all.

"Well, I guess I'll go then. But if you wanted to take some time off, I would be more than happy to cover the shop for however long you need."

"We'll see. Now get going before I change my mind and put you to work dusting all the vases in the back."

"Yes, boss." She gave Lizzie a mock salute before scooting off her stool to retrieve her coat and purse.

"I don't feel right leaving you alone," Madison said a few minutes later, standing at the door with her coat on.

Lizzie waved her hand, motioning her to leave. "I'll be fine. Go." She pulled out her notebook and pen. "See, I've got lots to do, and my friend will be here in less than two hours. I'll see you on Monday."

"See you Monday." Madison waved goodbye.

Looking out the shop window, she watched Madison dig out her cell phone, a smile spreading across her face as she spoke briefly into her phone before getting in her car.

Alone in the shop, Lizzie focused on getting her list done for the deliveries. This was a task she normally loved doing—dreaming up fresh ideas for bouquets, putting together unexpected combinations of flowers, greenery, and sometimes even herbs, using unique containers. Today, staring at the blank page and forcing herself to be creative felt like pulling teeth.

She had only gotten halfway through her list when she put her pencil down and stood up from the table. The shop was too quiet. She selected three CDs of classical music and put the CD player on random.

She always played music in the shop, and even had it piped into the cooler so the flowers could benefit from the sounds of Brahms, Mozart, Debussy, Beethoven, and Bach. She occasionally varied from her preference for classical music and threw in a CD of Gregorian chants, First Nations drumming, or Latin dance music.

She retraced her steps back to the refectory table and reluctantly sat down. Drumming her pencil on the table in time with the music, she went through her mental list of what she had in the cooler that would be suitable for her clients. Slowly, she completed her job. There were just a few flowers she would have to order from her supplier to finish off the arrangements.

She placed the call to the flower wholesaler and was surprised when a recorded voice informed her they were closed for the day. She glanced at her watch. It was ten minutes to five. The wholesaler closed at four on Saturdays and she had missed the deadline for Monday's delivery. She'd have to call first thing Monday and have Madison go in the early afternoon to pick up the flowers she needed.

She hung up the phone, making a small frustrated sound. Her wandering mind had earned her an unscheduled trip to the wholesaler on Monday and meant she and Madison would have to hustle to get the orders done in time.

It was closing time, and Lizzie hadn't even thought about where she was going to spend the night. She could just stay at the shop. She had all her things with her and the shop had a bathroom. There wasn't really a place to sleep, but she could just curl up on the floor. It couldn't be any more uncomfortable than falling asleep sitting up at the refectory table, which she hadn't seemed to have a problem doing.

The idea appealed to her. There was no place she felt more at home, and it was her business. She could sleep there if she wanted to. She could even purchase one of those fold away camping cots to sleep on.

But there was Madison. She wouldn't be able to hide the fact she was living in her shop from Madison. No, it just wasn't practical.

After locking the front door and flipping the sign over to closed, she dug out the yellow pages from her office and flipped it open to the section listing hotels.

She'd never stayed in a hotel before and the idea frightened her. She didn't want to sleep in a strange bed that countless other people had slept in. She knew that the sheets would have been laundered, but the pillows wouldn't have.

People always left parts of themselves behind—fingerprints, stray hairs, flakes of skin, and saliva. She wished she'd had the forethought to take her pillow with her when she left her apartment.

She found a suitable boutique hotel situated within walking distance of The Enchanted Garden. She reserved a suite and called a cab to pick her up, instructing the dispatcher to have the driver pick her up at the front this time. The short winter days meant the sun had set already and she didn't relish the idea of standing in a dark, deserted alley by herself.

Gathering up her suitcases, she then lined them up at the front door. She went through the ritual of securing the back door and turning out the lights, but didn't set the alarm. She cashed out, turned off the CD player, and put on her coat.

While she waited for her cab, she thought about taking her Jane Austens with her. She wanted them near her, something familiar and comforting while she stayed in a strange place. She decided it wasn't practical to transport them back and forth every day, as she wouldn't dream of leaving them lying out in her hotel room. She'd have to find out if the hotel had a safe available, but even then, the idea of not being near her precious books during the day didn't sit well with her.

Perhaps she would take just one. And just for the night. Deciding that was an acceptable alternative, she dashed to her office, took out the first volume of *Pride and Prejudice*, and after checking she'd locked up the rest of the books securely, returned to the front of the store to wait for her ride.

She hadn't noticed her injuries all afternoon, but while she paced at the front of the shop, her hand began to throb and her knees ached slightly with each step.

At least she could still feel pain. Ian didn't have that luxury. Her thoughts turned to the vision she had of him lying on the street, the scene at the hospital with Penelope, her mother-in-law's raw grief and violence.

The twinges of a panic attack began to flutter in her chest.

Where was her cab? Surely it should be here by now.

Her watch told her it had only been ten minutes since she had placed the call. As she paced, she concentrated on the pain in her knees instead of her thoughts or her mounting panic, but her chest tightened and her breathing became shallow.

Leaving her suitcases where they were, she stepped outside, hoping the fresh air would help. She kept her hand on the door handle and took in a lungful of the bracing winter air.

It wasn't snowing, but the moisture had crystallized in the air. It was like looking through a frosted veil. She had stepped outside of her Enchanted Garden into an enchanted lane. The ambient light from the office buildings added to the ethereal quality of the twilight. The streets were empty. It was as if everyone had disappeared and she alone was left to witness the beauty of the evening.

The traffic noises in the distance sounded like the muffled roar of a far off ocean. The owl hooted from his perch atop the building, perhaps calling for a mate to share the magic of the moment.

A city bus rumbled down the street, belching diesel into the air, breaking the spell. She was about to duck back inside when her cab rounded the corner and pulled up to the curb.

While the driver loaded her suitcases, she rushed to the back of the store to set the alarm then hurried out the front to secure the lock before the alarm went off. With her store locked up safe and secure for the night, she stepped into the cab and off into the unknown.

Chapter Nine

As she lay in bed on Sunday morning, Lizzie tried to come to terms with her new life. So much had happened in just two short days, she hadn't quite caught up with the reality of her situation.

Upon awaking, she had a moment of sleep-fogged disorientation and thought she was in her own bed, that everything was as it was before. Ian was still alive and sleeping in the spare room; the fight and the events following had never occurred. She was thinking about the wholesale flower market and what flowers would soon be in season—tulips, lilacs, hyacinths. When she opened her eyes, the moment of bewilderment was dizzying. She didn't recognize her surroundings. The sensation only lasted for a few seconds, but it was a helpless feeling.

The instant she remembered where she was and why, the weight of her guilt and sorrow was unbearable.

Was every morning going to start this way, the forgetting then the pain of remembering?

She reached under the covers and pulled out her rag doll. She had felt foolish bringing it to bed with her, but she needed comfort and the doll was all she had. She nestled the doll in the crook of her arm and willed herself not to cry. If the tears had been tears for Ian, she would have let them flow, but these were self-indulgent, based on her fears and guilt.

She got out of bed, unpacked her things, and stacked her empty suitcases in the bottom of the spacious closet.

Over the years, she had pared down her wardrobe to the bare essentials—two dresses, five pairs of work pants, two pairs of wool dress pants, two weeks' worth of t-shirts and turtlenecks, and a handful of sweaters. Everything she owned was either black or shades of brown.

When she had first left the Priory, she had experimented with different looks and filled her closet in a rainbow of colors. As Ian took less and less notice of her and paid even less attention to what she wore, trying to figure out what to put on each morning had become tedious, just one more thing she had to make a choice about.

With her few things unpacked, she wandered into the bathroom to wash and dress for the day. The buff-colored limestone floor was cold on her bare feet. She slipped off her nightgown, and before stepping into the spacious walk-in shower, she removed the gauze on her hand.

The wound had almost completely healed. The skin had knitted together. The only trace of the deep cut was a puckered red line. A scab had already formed along the gash, and when she touched, it was only mildly tender.

She turned to face the full-length mirror hanging on the back of the door to examine her knees. The bruises were already fading to a sickly yellow color, and when she stepped in the shower, the abrasions didn't sting when the hot water hit them.

She was a remarkably fast healer. The ability was a quirk of genetics, the same mysterious roll of the DNA dice that gave her pale grey eyes and dark brown hair. Which parent she owed thanks for this gift, or if it was the combined genes of both her mother and father, she would never know.

After she dressed, she placed a call down to room service and ordered a pot of coffee. While she waited for her coffee, she sat at the streamlined desk, opened up a sleek laptop with the Hotel's logo emblazoned on the top, and logged on to her banking site. The hotel was equipped with wireless Internet, and for a small rental fee and a deposit, the bellhop had delivered the laptop moments after she'd checked in.

She didn't bother looking at the account she shared with Ian. She knew the bank would have frozen the account until his will was read. It didn't concern her as she only ever kept a minimum balance to cover their living expenses. She was only interested in the account she had set up without Ian's knowledge. It was at a different bank and the account was under her maiden name, Lizzie Bennet.

She needed to figure out how long she could stay in the hotel while she looked for a new place to live. She didn't want to have to convert another gem from her legacy just to pay her hotel bill when she needed to finance a new place to live.

She was scribbling away on the hotel stationery, working out her budget and making a list of her preferred areas to live, when there was a knock on the door followed by a male voice announcing room service. She closed the laptop before opening the door.

As the waiter skillfully maneuvered the cart into the suite, the white coffee cup, placed upside down, rattled against the saucer.

"Where would you like to have your coffee, ma'am?" asked the waiter.

"Over there would be fine." She pointed to the coffee table beside the sofa in the living room section of the suite. He placed the tray where she indicated and poured her a cup from the silver coffee pot. The smell of rich, dark coffee filled the room.

"Is there anything else you require?" He handed over the black receipt book for her to sign.

"No, not at the moment."

"When you are done with the tray, just place it in the butler's cupboard." He indicated to a small square cupboard inset into the wall by the door. It was a unique feature in each of the suites that allowed guests to place laundry, shoes to be shined, or room service trays to be picked up without having to disturb the guest or have the unsightly mess of dirty trays littering the hallways.

After signing for her order and adding a generous tip, she took a seat on the couch and added several sugar cubes using the silver tongs. The coffee was sublime.

She decided she liked the experience of staying at a hotel despite her earlier trepidation. From the moment the doorman had held open the door and she stepped through the neo-Gothic arches, she felt at ease and more at home than she had ever felt in her own apartment.

In the hushed elegance of the small lobby, she had been greeted by courteous people whose focus was on her immediate needs. The bellhop took care of her bags, and the young lady at the front desk told her if she needed anything, no matter what the hour, she could call down to the desk and they would accommodate her.

The anonymity of it all was refreshing. They didn't know who she was, what had happened, and they didn't care as long as she paid for her room.

At first, she was unsure if she would be able to sleep in a strange bed in a strange room, or if another full-scale panic attack would engulf her like the previous night. She surprised herself by falling asleep while reading her beloved Austen. The pillow thing still bothered her even though the pillowcases, along with the bed linens, were five hundred thread count *Frette*. She'd have to do something about that.

In the meantime, she couldn't resist pouring herself another cup of coffee, this time adding a generous splash of cream. She hadn't ordered it, but it seemed a shame to waste it. While she savored her second cup, she opened the newspaper that had been folded over and placed neatly to one side of the tray. She never read the paper or watched the evening news, but now she needed a distraction from her thoughts and she much preferred reading to turning on the TV.

She skimmed through the headlines, read a few articles in the Arts and Entertainment section, then turned the page to find she was looking at the obituaries. She spotted Ian's immediately. She was surprised to find it in the paper so soon.

His photo showed a younger Ian. His cocky grin and strong air of confidence reminded her of the first time he had come into the flower shop and not the overweight, lazy, angry man he had become.

The funeral was to take place tomorrow morning at ten at Holy Trinity Church. His internment into the family crypt was to follow. The obit mentioned his attending Ryerson, but not that he never graduated. She scanned down to the list of loved ones he'd left behind, which included his mother, several of his mother's friends, relatives, and a few of Ian's friends. Nowhere did it say that he had been married or to whom. Penelope had wiped out his entire marriage. If Lizzie had had any thought of being part of the funeral, it was clear now her presence wouldn't be tolerated.

She tore Ian's obituary out of the paper as carefully as she could, folded it neatly, and placed it in her wallet.

Before heading down to the lobby, she hid her rag doll in the bureau drawer nestled in amongst her socks and underwear.

Down in the lobby, she stopped at the concierge's desk. The man standing behind the desk was in his early fifties. He wore a carefully-tailored dark suit with a white silk pocket square folded neatly in the breast pocket. His salt-and-pepper hair was cut short and perfectly groomed. On his nose perched a pair of half-moon spectacles with gold frames. As Lizzie approached him, he placed his hands together on the desk and leaned slightly forward.

"Good morning, Ms. Bennet," he said, addressing her by her maiden name. "I hope you had a pleasant evening."

"Yes, thank you." She noted his name on the brass nametag affixed to his lapel. "Frank, I was wondering if you could help me with something?"

"I would be happy to accommodate you."

"I need to find a store that carries linens." She hastily spelled out her request, hoping her voice wouldn't betray her embarrassment. She was a grown woman and had lived most of her adult life in the core of the city, yet she had no idea where to purchase even the basic necessities of a home. Ian had always insisted on taking care of such things.

"Oh, was there something not to your liking with the hotel linens?" he asked, raising his eyebrows.

"No, no. The bed is very comfortable and the sheets are so soft. In fact, the whole suite is perfect. It's just the pillows.... Well, it's just that I prefer to sleep on my own, but I didn't bring mine, so I thought I'd just go buy some new ones."

"Yes, of course. I completely understand. A pillow is a very personal thing, and if it is not just so, it can disrupt your sleep. And we all know how important a good night's sleep is."

"Exactly." She was relieved she hadn't offended him by not liking the pillows.

"If that is the only reason you need to go out shopping, I could arrange to have the pillows purchased and save you the trip."

"You could do that?"

"Why of course. Such a simple request. I can have what you need in no time."

"That would be very nice. I did have other plans today."

"Now, what kind do you prefer?" he asked, picking up a gold pen and poising it over a blank sheet of hotel stationery.

She was stumped by the question.

To her relief, he stepped in. "Do you prefer a down-filled, fiber-filled, or one of those therapeutic pillows with the memory foam or a buckwheat one? I hear those are very good if you have neck problems."

She hadn't realized there were so many choices when it came to pillows.

Early on in their marriage, when she had bought things for their apartment, Ian had always complained or made her feel like she made the completely wrong choice. She would end up taking back her purchases and buying what Ian said would be better. It had been easier for her to acquiesce to Ian's wants and preferences. She felt stupid standing there unable to decide on such a simple thing as a pillow.

"I don't really know, fiber-fill, I guess."

"What about your sleeping habits? That really is the best way to choose the most appropriate firmness. Do you sleep on your back, your stomach, or your side?"

She was relieved she knew the answer. "I'm a side sleeper," she said with conviction.

"Well, then we need to get you one that has a medium firmness. Now you should probably get two pillows so that when you read or watch TV, you can prop yourself up."

"Yes, two would be good."

As Frank was jotting down her answers on the paper, she noticed he had beautiful hands. They weren't too large or too small, the fingers were long and graceful, his nails buffed and manicured.

"One last thing." Frank turned the paper he had been writing on so that she could read it. "How much do you wish to spend?" He used the gold pen as a pointer, indicating the different price ranges he had written down.

She pointed to the lower price. "That one would be fine."

"Excellent. Now is there anything else I can assist you with?"

"No, that's all I needed. Thank you for doing this."

"It is my pleasure. Have a good day, Ms. Bennet."

"You too, Frank."

She buttoned up her coat and smiled warmly at the doorman as he held open the door and tipped his hat as she passed by.

She was a few blocks from her flower shop when she felt an icy wind pass through her. Glancing up, the Number 10 bus roared past her. Looking around at the intersection, she realized it had to be where Ian was killed.

She stopped and took a closer look at the street. There was no evidence an accident had occurred, no telltale bloodstains or broken glass from a headlight that would have shattered with the impact of hitting Ian's body.

She glanced at the road. There were skid marks that could have been made by a bus slamming on its brakes, but the road had similar marks scattered all over. She couldn't be sure this was the place where it happened, but she knew it was just the same.

When had she become such a selfish creature? Sister Collette would be ashamed of her if she could see her now. She actually was feeling happy about the new pillows and the experience of staying at the St. James with all its understated luxury and charm. She had killed another human being, and she was looking forward to getting new pillows. What was wrong with her?

Ian would never make another choice again. She had been the last person to see him alive, and what had she done? She had fought with him and made him leave the house angry. It was her fault he was dead.

And what had he experienced during the accident? Was he scared, did he have time to feel any pain or realize that he was going to die?

He died alone on a city sidewalk. That had been her final gift as his wife.

"I'm sorry, Ian," she whispered. I'm sorry I did this to you."

Chapter Ten

She had remained at the shop all day, working her way through more than half of the orders, but she wasn't pleased with the results. The arrangements were dull and uninspired.

She kept thinking of funeral arrangements as she placed the flowers into their water-logged oasis. The crunching sound as she pushed the stems into the green Styrofoam sounded like bones being crushed.

Even the smell of the flowers was suffocating. She couldn't breathe and the walls of her tiny shop felt like they were pressing in on her. By seven in the evening, she called it quits and headed for the hotel.

Instead of taking a taxi, she opted to walk the short distance to the St. James. Although night had descended hours ago, the city streets were never fully dark because of the ambient light from the streetlamps and the surrounding buildings. The night was mild and overcast, the ice had melted during the day, and the sidewalks were dry and safe again.

Before she started out for the hotel, she stood for a moment outside her shop listening for the familiar hoot of the owl. The only sound she heard was the rush of traffic. Perhaps the Great Horned was already out hunting for the night.

She passed a handful of people en route to the hotel, but she never looked up as she passed by them. Everyone seemed to be in pairs—couples going out to dinner or taking in a movie or the theatre.

If Ian hadn't chosen her shop to buy his mother flowers all those years ago, would he have found someone better suited to him, someone who would have brought out the best in him instead of the worst?

He had come into the store just days after she'd been released from the hospital and her boss had begged to her stay home. She refused to recall the reason she had been rushed to the ER. If she had listened to Joe and avoided the shop, would Ian still be alive and happy? Would he be one of the couples walking arm-in-arm enjoying a dinner out on a Sunday evening instead of lying dead in a funeral parlor somewhere?

As she strode down the sidewalk, she recalled a conversation she had with Sister Collette one summer morning when they had been in the gardens collecting herbs for the Priory kitchen.

Sister Collette had pointed out a spider web the size of a dinner plate suspended between the prickly stalks of the sunflowers planted along the edge of the garden. The web glistened with early morning dew, transforming it into a crystal masterpiece of geometry. The orb spider that created it was waiting patiently for its breakfast on one of the radial arms.

As they stood there admiring the web, Sister Collette pointed out that every living being was like the center of the web, and that actions and thoughts were like the spokes radiating out of the center connecting to the other spiraling threads of the design, connecting with other people, creatures, and events.

Lizzie had asked, if life was like the spider web, did that also mean that people's lives were already set in its design like the completed web before them? That the events and people that lay in the future were already predestined? Sister Collette said the answer to that was both yes and no. Rather than clarifying the issue, Sister Collette's answer only added to her confusion.

As Lizzie ducked into the hotel lobby, she wondered if Ian and she were destined to meet and marry. Was their coming together a part of some bigger plan she couldn't grasp and his death had been woven into the web of his life at the moment he had been born?

Even as an adult, Lizzie didn't understand the mysteries of life any better than she had as a twelve-year-old. Perhaps, she thought ruefully, life had no meaning. Maybe it wasn't like the spider web at all, but rather a series of random events and chance encounters. Maybe life was no great mystery; it was just what it was on the surface—living and dying and nothing more.

She shook her head to dislodge the annoying thoughts as she stepped off the elevator and into her suite. Ian had said she spent way too much time thinking about useless things. He had been right about that.

The maid had been through while she had been out. Although she had made the bed before she left, she hadn't made it with the skill of the hotel maid. The white coverlet with its thin black piping was smoothed down so not a wrinkle marred the pristine surface, and the pillows had been rearranged so that they were stacked one on top of the other. She knew if she pulled back the coverlet, she would find the flat sheet tucked in neatly with crisp hospital corners.

On the surface of the bed were placed two brand new pillows still in the plastic packaging they came in and two pillowslips. Folded neatly next to them were two pressed pillow cases. A note card with the hotel name embossed on the top was placed on top of the cases.

She picked up the note and read it. It was from Frank.

Dear Ms. Bennet,

I hope that these pillows are to your liking. I took the liberty of also purchasing pillowslips. If there is anything else I can do, please do not hesitate to ask. Best Regards.

He had signed his name with a flourish.

She put the note aside and pulled the plastic off her pillows. They smelled new.

She burst into tears. Holding one of the pillows tight, she sobbed into it, rocking back and forth as she sat on the edge of the bed.

"I'm sorry. I'm sorry," she wailed. If she could take Ian's place, she would do it in a heartbeat. If she hadn't been born, he would still be alive and living his full potential with someone who was worthy of his love. She was broken from the beginning, and her wrongness had corrupted him as surely as if he had drunk poison.

When her sobs diminished to sniffles, she stood up wearily and proceeded to place her pillows in their slipcovers and cases.

She felt wrung out and in need of some kind of comfort. She picked up the phone and asked room service to bring up some hot chocolate. It was her favorite childhood treat. She blamed Madison and her brownies for her sudden urge for anything chocolate. She'd forgotten how much she liked the taste and feel of it in her mouth.

She washed her face and sat in the chair waiting for her hot chocolate. She reached out and fingered the paper where she had jotted down her budget. She picked it up and scanned down what she had written. She could only afford to stay in the hotel for a month tops, then she would have to find something more permanent.

Moving out of the downtown core to where housing was cheaper made the most sense, but she had an inexplicable need to live close to her shop. She placed the sheet back on the desk upside down and moved it out of the way. That decision could wait for a few more days. She had a more pressing issue to deal with.

She picked up the phone again, this time dialing the number to the concierge's desk. The man who answered the phone had a distinct Quebecoise accent and announced himself as Georges. The sound of his voice made her suddenly homesick for the cottage at the Priory.

She asked if he could arrange what she wanted and, just like Frank, he said it was as good as done.

She went to the closet, pulled out her plain wool crepe black dress and a matching cardigan with delicate beading around the collar. It was wrinkled, so she hung it in the bathroom so that the steam from her morning shower would make it presentable for her appointment.

She placed a call to Madison on her cell phone and told her she would be taking the morning off and asked if Madison would put in the order for the flowers they would need. She told her where the list was and then hung up before Madison had a chance to ask her how she was feeling.

When the hot chocolate arrived, she poured herself a generous amount in the white bowl that came with the pot of chocolate and chocolate-dipped biscuits. While her drink cooled, she changed into her nightgown and rescued Raggedy Ann from her exile in the bureau.

Wanting to read while she enjoyed her drink, she retrieved her book from her purse and climbed into bed.

That morning, she had carefully wrapped her *Pride and Prejudice* in a silk scarf before tucking it into her purse to take to her shop. She had intended to leave it there, but as she was locking up for the night, she'd changed her mind.

She nibbled a corner of a biscuit and took a careful sip of her cocoa. Putting her drink aside, she picked up her book and began to read where she had left off the night before.

The other Lizzie, the one in the book, had just turned down Mr. Collins' proposal of marriage.

Why couldn't life be like a story in a novel? In *Pride and Prejudice,* Lizzie held out for love and in the end not only found the man of her dreams, but with her elevated status, had the means to look after the rest of her unmarried sisters.

At the time, Lizzie thought she was in love with Ian, but now she wasn't so sure. She hadn't been sure for a very long time. She really didn't get to know him before she rushed into marriage. They had only been dating a few short months before he proposed and she accepted. Was it love or a desperate desire not to be alone?

She hadn't felt alone when she first left the Priory, but that was because Sister Collette was still alive and they wrote to each other every few days. When she died, Lizzie wasn't prepared for how isolated she felt, and not being able to attend her funeral and say her final goodbyes made everything worse.

She refused to think about what she had attempted when her desperation and loneliness became too much to bear. She had still felt vulnerable and hollow the day Ian had stepped into the flower shop and into her life.

No, her life would never be like a story in a novel. She didn't deserve happily ever after, even if it did exist.

Chapter Eleven

The headstones thrust up through the snow-encrusted churchyard like jagged teeth. The penetrating sun made the snow sparkle like a carpet of diamonds. It hurt Lizzie's eyes to stare too long at the snowy brilliance. The walkways were shoveled recently, and their asphalt surface slithered like dark serpents across the blanket of white.

She glanced at her watch for what seemed like the hundredth time. She didn't want to make her way to the Chambers family crypt before the mourners did. She couldn't risk being seen. She sighed impatiently and leaned back into the plush leather of the town car's backseat.

She had asked the driver to park on one of the side roads leading into the cemetery instead of the church parking lot. She directed him to a spot where she had a clear view of the road to the mausoleum. From her vantage point, she would know when the funeral procession drove by on their way to inter Ian's ashes in the pale stone crypt.

When the driver had pulled over, he had offered her coffee from the large silver thermos he had pulled from the passenger footwell. She had declined, even though the smell of it had her craving a sip. She was too nervous as it was, and she knew adding caffeine into her already jittery system would make her feel worse. The driver gave her a polite smile and a nod of his head when she said no and pulled out a book of crossword puzzles and a pencil.

He was still working quietly on them as she watched out the side window for the procession. Despite the brilliant sunshine, the morning air was freezing and the interior of the car would have been too had the driver not kept the engine running and the heat turned up high.

Ten minutes later, she spotted two black limousines drive slowly around the curve of the road and park near the entrance of the mausoleum. The sunshine winked off the chrome fenders and grills, causing Lizzie to look away. When she glanced back over to the parked cars, her mother-in-law was already walking up the paved stones to the crypt, following the priest who led the way. Penelope's driver held her by the elbow as she slowly made her way inside. In her other arm, she cradled a large bronze urn. Behind her followed a small group of people, people Lizzie recognized from previous family gatherings she had attended—Penelope's sister and her husband, their two adult sons, and their respective wives. They walked in pairs up the sidewalk until they were lost from her view by the trunk of a large maple obscuring the mausoleum's entrance.

"I'll be back in about thirty minutes," Lizzie said as she opened the car door.

"Would you like me to accompany you?" the driver asked, putting his book of crossword puzzles aside and turning to address her.

"No, that won't be necessary. I'll be fine on my own."

Slipping her hand inside her purse, her fingers brushed against the hard spine of her book she'd wrapped inside a silk scarf to protect its worn cover. Satisfied, she zipped her purse closed and opened the car door.

She shivered as she stepped out of the warmth of the car. She'd remembered to bring her gloves this time. Putting them on, she pulled her collar up around her chin before setting off across the cemetery grounds.

The chilly air was still and the sound of her footfalls on the paved walkways sounded hollow. She followed a meandering path for a few minutes and then had to pick her way through the headstones to get close to the mausoleum unseen. The snow crunched loudly under her heels.

A few of the headstones were hidden under drifts with just the rough-hewn tops peering out of the snow; others had been tended to even in the winter so that the inscriptions were clearly visible. The few cared-for graves had plastic flowers placed at the base of the stones, dotting the white landscape with garish splashes of color.

Halfway to her destination, she veered left toward a small grove of spruce trees clustered at the bottom of the knoll facing the side of the crypt. There were patches of bare earth around the base of the trees. She stood underneath the boughs, positioning herself behind one large trunk. Reaching out, she ran her gloved hand over a low-hanging branch, crushing the needles and releasing the pungent scent of pine into the cold air.

She waited in the shadow of the trees for twenty minutes. Even with her fleece-lined boots on, her toes went numb, and every few minutes, she had to cup her gloved hands to her face to warm her nose. She wasn't sure what she was accomplishing standing in the cold, watching from a distance, not able to participate in the funeral. But she knew it would have been pointless to even try to attend. Penelope would have made sure the door was watched in case she showed up. But she felt she owed Ian at least the respect of witnessing his final journey even if it was from a distance.

She heard the squeal of metal hinges even before she glimpsed movement at the entrance of the mausoleum. She shrunk back behind the tree when a shrill cry broke the quietude. She peered around the gnarled bark of the tree to see Penelope bent over in her grief. The rawness of her pain tore at Lizzie's heart. This imperious woman, despite how Lizzie felt about her, had lost her only child, her baby reduced to a pile of ash locked away in a cold marble tomb. Tears pricked Lizzie's eyes.

Penelope suddenly dropped to her knees before her driver could catch her. Her wails of sorrow rose in the air, her despair palpable even at a distance where Lizzie stood concealed in the shadows. The priest dashed to her side. He bent over her, speaking too softly for Lizzie to catch his words of comfort. Between the priest and the driver, they managed to escort her to the safety of the limo.

The rest of the family followed silently at a distance, as if Penelope's anguished outburst was contagious. Not one of them had rushed to comfort her when she had collapsed.

Lizzie waited until the vehicles drove away before she stepped out of the trees and climbed the gentle swell of the hill toward the crypt.

From the top of the hill, she glimpsed the spires of the cathedral rising above the canopy of trees, the pale sandstone glaring white against the cornflower blue sky.

She stepped under the portico flanked by ionic columns and into the deeper shadows by the door. The air here was even colder than her spot under the trees. She was surprised to see the door ajar. In the commotion of Penelope's collapse, the priest must have forgotten to secure it behind him.

She hesitated for a moment before grasping the handle and pushing it open. The stiff hinges squeaked and in the distance, a crow cawed. She slipped inside, her heart beating a staccato rhythm in her chest.

Inky blackness stood before her, the still air saturated with the cloying scent of lilies. She reached her hand out and groped along the wall, looking for a light switch.

Ian had brought her here once to show her the mausoleum. He had boasted that not only were they one of a handful of families who had such accommodations for their dearly departed, but his father had spent an astronomical amount of money to have the place electrified.

At the time, it seemed to Lizzie such a frivolous thing to spend money on as the dead had no need for such conveniences. But stepping into the gloom, she was grateful the building had been outfitted with such an extravagance. She couldn't find the switch, so she stepped further inside and closed the door to search the other wall. She found the toggle and flipped it up, bathing the room in the soft glow from the bronze sconces mounted high up on the walls.

The interior space was much smaller than the exterior footprint, as most of the room had been taken up by the vaults covering the three walls. The floor, walls, and even the ceiling were clad in Carerra marble.

Ian's vault was to the right of the entrance three quarters of the way up the wall. His father's vault was above his and an empty one lay below, waiting for Penelope when her time came. Like all the rest, his had an oiled bronze door and a cone-shaped flower vase mounted near the handle. A huge bouquet of Casablanca lilies spilled out of the small receptacle. Ian's was the only one that held flowers.

Running down the center of the room was a narrow grey marble bench. Lizzie tiptoed over to it, the wet soles of her boots squelched on the slick marble tiles. She sat down facing Ian's vault, noticing a small nameplate was already attached to the front with his date of birth and death engraved in a flowing script.

She stared at the dates. Dead at forty. How much longer would he have walked the earth if she hadn't come into his life?

Yanking off her glove, she placed her left hand on the vault, feeling the sting of cold metal on her fingertips.

"I'm sorry," she whispered into the silence, the rest of her words dying on her lips. There was nothing she could say that would bring him back. She only hoped his spirit, freed from its earthly bonds, had found some kind of peace.

She sat motionless, her fingertips touching Ian's plaque until the cold from the marble bench seeped into the back of her legs and up her spine, making her ache with the cold. And still, she sat, ignoring the stiffness in her shoulders and the numbness of her fingertips.

She reached out with her mind like she did when she was searching for *The Letting Go,* but this time, she held an image of Ian when she had first met him in the forefront of her thoughts. His young handsome face, his laughing eyes, the sensual curve of his mouth. She conjured up the rush of elation she felt when he'd smiled at her and the love she felt when he had held her hand and bent down to kiss her tenderly. Their first kiss.

She let the delicate feeling build in her heart until she could feel it swelling under her breastbone. She continued to hold the energy in her heart, allowing it to grow stronger until she couldn't contain the overwhelming rush of love. Only then did she send the sensation down her left arm and out through her fingertips. She imagined it flowing out and finding Ian's essence. In the dim light of the mausoleum, it appeared as if a soft green light emanated from her fingers and spread across the metal door, making Ian's name shimmer in and out of focus.

She sensed a corresponding resonance moving toward her as she continued to stream her love outward. It felt like it was coming from all directions, and when it engulfed her, she cried out, her voice echoing off the marble walls.

The intensity of joy that permeated her senses was like nothing she had every experienced. It was too much. Crying out again, she pulled her hand away from Ian's vault. As she did, the pure elation she felt disappeared, leaving her cold and empty.

In the half-light of the crypt, her breath billowed out in front of her as she shivered in the cold. She stood up stiffly, removing her plain gold wedding band. It slipped easily off her frozen finger. She placed it on the bench where it clattered dully on the chilly marble.

Adjusting her purse strap on her shoulder, she slipped her glove back on before switching off the light, leaving its silent inhabitants in the dark. She stepped out into the day, shutting the door behind her.

Moving like an old woman, she shuffled out from under the shade of the portico and into the light. She cupped her hand to her forehead, shielding her eyes from the dazzling brightness.

A guttural popping and chortling filled the air. She turned to the sound, tripping over her feet and stumbling down the shallow steps onto the sidewalk. She stepped down hard, causing her jaw to snap shut painfully.

The oak tree to the right of the walkway was thick with crows. The bare tree branches swayed with the weight of hundreds of the black birds. They shifted and stretched out their wings, their cries becoming more urgent.

Then she felt it. The disquieting manifestation she'd experienced at the hospital—the Dark Presence. Its slithering specter filled the air around her with its brooding malevolence. Her blood ran cold as her heart galloped in her chest. Fear rooted her to the spot.

In one precise synchronized movement, all the birds turned and faced down the path away from her. She stared dumbfounded at the strange occurrence, and then slowly followed the birds' gaze. A man was running up the path, the tails of his long coat billowing behind him. He was headed straight for her.

She willed herself to run, but she stood immobilized.

He had almost reached her when the air erupted with the thunder of hundreds of wings as the crows took flight. They flew as one black mass between her and the man, obscuring him from her view.

The crows turned in mid-flight, circling around to fly directly at her. Within seconds, she was completely surrounded by a whirlwind of beating wings and frenzied cawing.

Around and around the crows flew, the wind generated by their beating wings whipping her short hair into her eyes. Instinctively, she threw up her arms, shielding her face.

Everything was spinning. The red thrumming of the dark evil swirled just beyond the black mass of birds. She was overcome with vertigo, and as the ground rose up to greet her, all she could hear were the rasping caws and the roaring rush of air. She fainted before she felt the man's arms close around her.

Chapter Twelve

"Open your eyes."

Someone was gently stroking her cheek.

"Come on, wake up. We have to get you out of here. There isn't much time."

Her eyes flew open. Batting frantically at the air, she pushed her heels against the pavement in a vain attempt to scoot away from her attacker, but he held her firmly by the shoulders, pinning her to the ground.

She inhaled a lungful of air, but before she could let loose a frantic scream, the man clamped his hand over her mouth. She struggled to break free, but it was useless.

"Please don't scream. I'm not going to hurt you. I'm here to help. Please, we've got to hurry."

His voice sounded familiar. For a moment, she stopped struggling and looked up at the man. The sun was directly behind his face, throwing his features into deep shadow.

The man removed his hand from her mouth and gently lifted her into a sitting position. She blinked and looked into his face again. She recognized him from somewhere. It was his eyes she remembered. His hair was different, but it was definitely the young man who came to her aid on the sidewalk.

"Gideon? What are you doing here?" Then she remembered the birds. "The crows? Did you see them?" She looked around anxiously, but they had disappeared. All of them. For a wild moment, she thought she'd experienced another hallucination.

"Yes, but they're gone. You don't need to worry about them. Now I need you to listen carefully. We've got to get out of here. It's not safe and we don't have much time. Can you stand up?"

"I think so."

He helped her to her feet, and she held on to his arm to steady herself. "I don't understand. What are you doing here?" she asked again.

"I'll explain later, I promise. Right now, you and I have to leave. You have to trust me. Do you trust me?"

"Yes," she said. She trusted him for no other reason than the sincerity in his voice.

He slid his arm around her waist and half carried, half pulled her along the path away from the crypt. He kept glancing over his shoulder as if he expected someone to pounce on them at any moment. He steered her down the path in the direction of the church. Except for the sound of their footfalls and Lizzie's ragged breathing, the air was silent.

As they started to the climb the stone steps of the cathedral, she stumbled, but Gideon tightened his grip around her waist and all but lifted her up the final few steps.

He flung open the heavy oak door and pushed her inside. Standing for a moment with his hand on the door, he looked across the churchyard, scanning the frozen landscape. Seconds later, he followed her into the sanctuary.

The church was deserted. The air was redolent with the smell of candle wax and the cloying sweetness of incense. The sun flooded through the magnificent stained glass windows, splashing brilliant fragments of colored light across the pews.

Before entering the nave, Lizzie stopped at the font containing the holy water. Out of respect more than religious reasons, she dipped a finger into the water and crossed herself, murmuring the blessing as she did so.

Lizzie stopped halfway down the nave and genuflected before taking a seat on the wooden pew. Gideon followed, sliding onto the pew beside her.

"What's going on? Who is after us and why?"

"Not us, you. And I don't know who he is. I saw a guy skulking around the gravestones and he just seemed off, so I followed him. When I realized he was following you, I circled around so he wouldn't see me. He was coming up behind you when the ravens flew at you. I think I scared him off, but I wanted to get you somewhere safe just in case," he said, scanning the church.

"What did he look like?"

"I didn't get a good look at him. Most of the time, his back was to me. When he was running at you, I was more focused on catching you when you fainted. I think he was about my height, brown hair maybe. It was hard to tell because he was wearing a baseball cap pulled down low." He stopped his constant surveillance of the entryways and finally looked at her. "Do you have any idea why someone would be following you?"

"Not a clue. I didn't see anyone, just the crows." She shifted on the pew, fingering her empty ring finger with her right hand. When she noticed Gideon staring at her hands, she clasped them tightly in her lap. "My husband died recently and…" She wasn't quite sure how to finish the sentence. She couldn't tell a stranger, no matter how kind, that she hadn't noticed anyone stalking her because she was too focused on slinking into the mausoleum like a thief.

"My sincerest condolences," he said.

She nodded, her gaze wandering over the altar at the front of the church. She swallowed hard around the lump in her throat and looked at Gideon. "Thank you for coming to my rescue again, and please don't take this the wrong way, but what are you doing here?"

"It's just a coincidence really. I was visiting my father's grave. Today is the anniversary of his death."

"Oh," she said. She shivered despite the winter coat she wore and the warmth of the church. Standing up, he took off his coat then draped it around her quaking shoulders. She pulled the lapels around her and pressed her face to the fine wool fabric.

"It's the shock that's making you cold. Is that better?"

"Yes, much." She glanced up at him.

He looked different from the first time they'd met. For one thing, he wasn't wearing the grungy Do Rag. With his head bare, she noticed he'd cut off his dreadlocks, his dark hair shorn close to his scalp. Although his ears still sported several earrings, his face was devoid of any metal decoration. Instead of jeans and a ratty leather jacket, he was wearing khakis and a fine-gauge navy cotton sweater.

"You seem to have me at a disadvantage. This is the second time our paths have crossed, and although you know my name, no doubt Madison told you when I dropped off your keys, I don't know yours."

"I'm Lizzie," she said deliberately, omitting her last name.

"Lizzie." He whispered her name. He sat back down next to her and absently rolled up his sleeves. "Just to be on the safe side, I think we should stay here a few more minutes."

His words were lost on her. She stared at the tattoo on his left wrist, hypnotized by the symbols. A faint buzzing filled her ears. She felt strongly the shapes meant something to her. Reaching out, she grasped his arm, pulling him closer.

She heard his sharp intake of breath, then he presented his wrist to her like an offering. With her index finger, she slowly traced the outline of the outward facing crescent, then the circle, then the other crescent.

The buzzing in her head got louder, taking on the rhythm of ocean waves breaking on the shore. Everything around her, including Gideon, disappeared. All she was aware of was the roaring tempo and the glowing blue shapes filling her senses. She slipped into the quiet spaces between the sounds, becoming one with the silence.

As her finger moved across his skin for a third time, she spoke. "The Triple Goddess. The three phases of the moon. The three faces of the feminine—the maiden, the mother, and the crone. So it is and so it forever shall be, by the powers of the goddess three times three. By the power of the Goddess, so mote it be."

She looked up into his face. Their eyes locked in a hypnotic gaze. The stillness stretched out into the cavernous space. The energy flowed between them, sparking the air with electricity. She felt alive and powerful. Her head spun with the intoxicating sensations.

"Who are you?" he asked. The sound of his voice broke her trance and she released his wrist. She shook her head and glanced around, clear-eyed once more.

"I'm sorry, what did you say?"

"Just that I think it would be okay for us to leave now," he said.

She rubbed her forehead. "I think I must have zoned out or something. I've been under a bit of strain lately and then the whole thing with the guy at the graveyard. And those crows, the way they came out of nowhere, that was really frightening."

"Ravens, they were ravens, not crows. They're from the same family, *Corvids*, but they're much bigger, with a wedged-shaped tale and a heavier bill."

"Was that behavior we witnessed normal? Where did they all come from?"

"I don't know. I've never seen anything like that. Maybe some animal had died nearby and they were attracted to the smell. They are carrion eaters. I don't think they meant to harm you."

It sounded plausible, but that didn't explain why they all turned in unison when Gideon had come running up the pathway. She couldn't tell him what she felt right before they had come after her. He would think she was some kind of nutcase.

Their conversation was cut short when a matronly woman with a blue rinse in her tightly curled hair entered the church from a side door.

She walked toward the sanctuary and up to the altar carrying a wicker basket with both hands. She gingerly hoisted the basket onto the corner of the altar, being careful not to knock over the heavy silver candlestick that decorated the surface. She busied herself replacing the spent altar candles with new ones she produced from the basket. She glanced over in their direction with curious eyes.

"We should get going." Gideon stood up, pulling down the sleeves of his sweater.

"Yes," she agreed, and glanced at her watch. "That can't be the time. I told the driver I'd only be gone for thirty minutes, tops. It's been over an hour. And I've got to get back to the shop so Madison can go pick up our flower order." She stood up unsteadily, handing Gideon his jacket.

"Why don't you stay here where it's warm and I'll go see to the car? Where's the driver parked?"

She easily agreed. Giving him directions on where the town car was parked, she sat back down to wait.

He shrugged on his coat, and with a promise to be back shortly, he hastened down the aisle and out the door.

While she waited for Gideon's return, Lizzie watched the old woman go about her business of preparing the church for evening mass. After replacing the candles, the woman set out fresh flower arrangements on the altar and around the sanctuary.

Lizzie glanced around. The last time she had set foot inside the church had been on her wedding day. With a sigh, she left the relative comfort of her seat and made her way slowly to the main entrance. She stopped in front of a small shrine to the Virgin Mary, tiers of votives glowing at her feet.

Only a few of the candles remained unlit. The flames from the others danced and weaved, making the red containers glow like rubies. These had been lit for Ian.

She pulled twenty dollars from her wallet, folded it neatly in three, and pushed it into the collection box before pulling out a slender wooden stick from a nearby brass container. With a prayer on her lips, she lit a votive.

She watched the flame grow tall and then waver slowly back and forth, dancing in the breeze. She prayed Ian's soul was at peace and asked again for his forgiveness.

The main doors opened, making the candle flames dance wildly as the winter air swirled around her. She turned to see Gideon step into the church.

She watched as he scanned the pews looking for her, panic in his eyes when she wasn't where he had left her. She stepped out of the small alcove and watched his features change from concern to relief.

"Are you ready?"

She nodded and stepped through the door he held open for her. He supported her arm as they negotiated the stairs down to the parking lot as if she was going to stumble or faint. She felt fine physically, her legs solidly underneath her, but she liked the reassuring feel of his hand on her arm. His touch kept her grounded in reality and stopped her from thinking about what had just happened in the churchyard.

She looked for the town car, but the only vehicle parked near the entrance was a silver SUV. Gideon answered her question before she could ask it.

"I sent him away. I thought it would be better if I drove you home. I just didn't feel right leaving you by yourself after what happened." He gently guided her over to the passenger side door of his vehicle.

When Lizzie first moved to Toronto, Sister Collette had warned her about not opening her door to strangers or taking rides from men she didn't know. The safe and sensible thing to do now was to heed the sister's advice, but she didn't want to. Gideon had come to her rescue twice, and from what she could sense, there was nothing sinister about him. She climbed inside without reservation.

Before he merged onto the 132 to head back to Toronto, he looked at her expectantly. "Where do you live?"

"I can't go home right now. I have to get back to the shop so Madison can pick up the flowers from the wholesaler I need for today. We have several orders to get out."

"I really think it would be better if you went home and rested."

"I appreciate your concern. I really do. And I am grateful for everything you've done for me, but I have commitments to my clients. Please just take me to the flower shop. I need to get those flowers and start working on the orders." She glanced at her watch and winced when she saw the time. "As it is, it's going to be tight."

"Where's this wholesale place?"

"On the outskirts of Mississauga. In the seven hundred block of Pacific Circle."

"We're not far from there. Why don't I drive us over and we can pick up your order? That way you aren't wasting time driving all the way across town only to send Madison all the way back here. This car has a lot of cargo space, and with two of us, we could get everything loaded twice as fast."

"I don't know, you've already done too much for me today. And besides, don't you have anywhere you need to be?"

"As luck would have it, I don't."

She couldn't argue with his logic. They were only ten minutes away from the wholesaler, and it would save her time. "If you really don't mind doing this, it would be a great help."

"Then it's settled." He signaled and steered the car into the flow of traffic heading toward the flower market.

Neither of them spoke about what had happened in the cemetery. Lizzie was curious about the young man who looked so different from when they first met. She wanted to talk about the ravens and their bizarre behavior. She wanted to ask him so many things, but the questions died on her lips. In the safety of the car, back in the flow of everyday life, the strangeness she experienced at the churchyard felt distant and surreal.

At the market, Gideon moved with such speed and efficiency, loading the flowers into the back of his SUV, that when Lizzie came back from settling the invoice there, was nothing for her to do.

She peered into the back of the SUV at the neatly stacked boxes, a little frustrated she didn't have a chance to inspect the contents personally before there were loaded. She resorted to a quick check on the pulses of the flowers. They all felt relatively strong and healthy. That would have to do.

She turned around and almost ran into Gideon he was standing so close. He murmured his apology and stepped out of her way. The hair rose on the back of her neck as she climbed back into the vehicle. For an instant, she'd seen something in his eyes. For the first time in their brief acquaintance, she felt uneasy in his presence.

Chapter Thirteen

Gideon and Lizzie bustled through the flower shop's delivery entrance, their arms loaded down with cartons. As they headed into the front of the store, Lizzie spied Madison on the phone.

"Hi, we're back," she called out over the stack of boxes in her arms.

Madison whirled around to face Lizzie, and when she noticed Gideon, she fumbled the phone, almost dropping it. Lizzie watched her employee's face flush a brilliant shade of crimson.

"I gotta go. I'll call you back later," Madison whispered into the receiver before replacing it on its base.

She rushed over to hold the cooler door open for them as Lizzie instructed Gideon to stack the boxes on the floor in the corner.

"Hey, Madison, how's it going?" He smiled over his shoulder as he stepped past her into the cooler.

"Good," she stammered. To Lizzie, she said, "Let me finish unloading the flowers. I just made a fresh pot of coffee if you wanted a cup."

"You're a life saver," Lizzie said. She was chilled and needed something to warm her up. She followed the two of them to the back room then zipped inside her office to snag a cup of coffee and to put back her copy of *Pride and Prejudice.*

After she'd locked her book safely in the cabinet and hung up her coat, she lingered in her office trying to imprint her surroundings into her being. She needed to ground herself in real, concrete things, normal everyday objects with weight and mass, so she wouldn't have to think about the hundreds of ravens acting strangely only to disappear in a blink of an eye.

She didn't want to spend any time dwelling on what she thought she felt in the cemetery before Gideon showed up. To put her focus there

89

would invite the craziness back in. Her moment of unease with Gideon proved to her she was overwrought, her thoughts too muddled to make coherent judgments. Gideon had been nothing but polite and considerate on the drive to Enchanted Garden. She rubbed her temples.

Her little shop seemed to be the only place that the strangeness of her current life hadn't invaded. It was the only thing that was real. It was the only thing that mattered.

She stepped out of her office at the same time Madison came in through the delivery door carrying a box of flowers.

"This is the last one," she said a little too loudly. Lizzie noticed her color was still high. She held the door open to the front of the shop then followed Madison.

"You can just put that one on the table. We can start with those orchids for the Holt Renfrew order." She cradled her coffee cup with both hands, trying to absorb the heat. "Did Gideon leave?"

"No, he just went to move his car."

"Don't you think he looks better without the dreadlocks?" she asked.

"Yeah, I guess so." Madison opened the box of orchids and dropped the lid on the floor. She picked it up and placed it on the back counter. "How was your morning?"

"It was...long."

"You went to Ian's funeral, didn't you? I read his obit in Sunday's paper," Madison added, answering Lizzie's question before she asked it.

"Yes," she replied.

"If you needed to go home, I can do the orders. I don't mind staying late to get them done."

"No, I appreciate the offer, but I need to keep busy. My girlfriend, whom I'm staying with, works all day, and I don't want to be alone with nothing to do."

"I understand," Madison murmured, then turned to unpack the flowers.

Lizzie noted with approval at what Madison had done while she was gone. Madison had prepared the flower oases by soaking them in water, placed a selection of containers and vases in a neat line on the back counter, and laid out the list Lizzie had prepared the night before on the table.

Lizzie popped into the cooler to pull the rest of the flowers and greenery she needed for the first order when Gideon returned through the front door. Both women looked up from what they were doing as he came in.

He was carrying a cardboard tray from Starbucks with three to-go cups nestled in the compartments in one hand, a paper bag in the other, and an old biscuit tin under his arm. Lizzie stepped out of the cooler as he placed the tray, bag, and the tin on the refectory table. He removed his coat and draped it over one of the stools.

"I figured we could all do with a little treat. For you, fair lady, a grande mochachino with chocolate sprinkles," he said, pulling out the first cup with a flourish and handing it to Madison.

"Oh, my favorite. How did you know?"

"It's one of my many hidden talents. I can tell just by looking at people what their favorite drink is. I'm still trying to figure out a way to translate my gift into a better paying career than a barista."

Madison giggled and took a sip of her drink.

"For myself, a Chai latte." He pulled his drink out of the tray, placing it on the table. "And for the Queen of the Enchanted Garden, I present you with a steaming cup of hot water."

"Well, I'm sorry to tell you, but your powers of beverage perception have failed you miserably. If the hot water is for tea, I'm going to pass. I have a cup of my favorite drink right here," she said, holding up her coffee cup.

"I already figured you for a coffee drinker, but I just happen to have with me my mother's proprietary blend of restorative tisane guaranteed to help soothe frazzled nerves. In fact, I always keep a stash of it in my glove compartment."

From the tin, he removed a bag of loose herbs and a small metal tea ball. He filled the tea ball and lowered it by its chain into the cup of hot water. He slowly dunked the tea ball, turning the water into a bright apple green. The two women watched transfixed by his graceful movements.

When he was satisfied the herbal tea had steeped long enough, he removed the metal ball and handed the drink to Lizzie. "Trust me. This will help." The light joking tone in his voice was gone. He looked squarely in her eyes. "Please, Lizzie."

She took the cup from his outstretched hand, never breaking her gaze with his. She put down her coffee mug and took a tentative sip of the steaming tea, being careful not to burn her tongue. The taste surprised her. The hot liquid filled her mouth with a burst of refreshing lime with just a hint of peppermint and left a sweet honey-like aftertaste. She took another sip. "This is surprisingly good. It doesn't taste at all like straw or dirty socks."

"I'll make sure to let my mother know you like it, but I think I won't mention it's because it doesn't taste like someone's smelly socks." He chuckled. Emptying the tea ball, he dried it off with a paper towel, and carefully packed everything back in the tin.

"What's in the bag?" Madison asked, eyeing it with a hopeful look. "I'm trusting you're as good at guessing what kind of treats people like as you are with drinks."

"I don't know," he said, opening the bag and handing it to her. "Why don't you tell me?"

"Chocolate chunk cookies," she squealed with delight. She handed out the cookies and they all sat around the refectory table for a few moments enjoying their repast.

Gideon wasn't kidding when he said the tea had restorative properties. As Lizzie drank the green liquid, she began to feel herself relax and the tight muscles in her shoulders and lower back finally release the stress that had strung them tight. A warmth spread through her core, making her feel slightly disconnected and fuzzy in a pleasantly dreamy way.

She listened to Gideon and Madison talk over their drinks, content to sit back and let them do all the talking.

Gideon said something amusing and Madison laughed, throwing her head back and clutching her stomach. The phone rang. Lizzie started to get off her stool to answer it, but Madison sprang off her chair to pick it up before Lizzie had even stood up.

"Enchanted Garden, how may I help you?" She spoke brightly. "Oh... I'm sorry. No, I didn't forget. It's just that Lizzie came back and I had to help her unload an order." Madison listened intently, her face clouding over with an emotion Lizzie couldn't quite name. "Yes, I know I said I'd call you right back, but it took longer than I thought. I'm sorry, I didn't mean to make you wait." Madison turned her back to Lizzie and slowly wandered as far away from the refectory table as she could. "Please don't be mad at me." Her voice took on an urgent pleading quality that made Lizzie's stomach drop.

When she finished her phone call, Madison returned to the table clutching the phone to her chest. Her eyes were shiny and she blinked hard. She replaced the phone on its charger and set about putting together an order.

Lizzie and Gideon exchanged looks, but neither said a word. She moved their drinks and half-eaten cookies over to the far counter away from where Madison was working.

"So, ladies," Gideon said with strained lightness, "what's next on the agenda?"

Lizzie was going to thank him for his work and send him home, but she didn't want him to leave just yet. Although he knew nothing about flower arranging, she really could use an extra pair of hands. And after what had happened at the cemetery, his presences made her feel safe.

"Are you sure you don't have somewhere else you need to be or something more important you need to be doing rather than hanging out in a flower shop?"

"Nope, nothing pressing on the calendar. Besides, what could possibly be more enjoyable than spending time with two charming women like yourselves? Put me to work, boss lady, I'm all yours."

"Well, first you can hang your coat up in the office. Then you can fill up the water buckets and put the flowers we just unloaded in them." She turned to Madison. "Would you mind showing him where the buckets are and how to re-cut the flowers before he puts them in water?"

"Sure," she replied. She was still subdued, but a smile flitted across her face as she led him into the back.

The three of them worked well together. Gideon set to work in the cooler unpacking boxes and carefully re-cutting the flower stems with a small knife. At first, he worked slowly, concentrating on making the cuts at the perfect forty-five degree angle like Madison had shown him. However, he was a quick study, and it wasn't long before he had all the flowers unpacked and trimmed, and the cardboard cartons flattened and taken out to the dumpster in the alley.

While Lizzie and Madison put together the arrangements, he retrieved whatever flowers they needed next. At first, Lizzie would point out which flowers she wanted, but Gideon surprised her by knowing them by name and heading to the right flower bucket as she called out what she needed. As each order was completed, Gideon placed them on the back shelf of the cooler and even answered the phone when Lizzie was dealing with one of the few customers that had come in while Madison was busy in the back.

Halfway through the afternoon, Madison changed the Brahms CD to an energetic salsa. The music was infectious. Soon, Gideon was humming to the music and Madison moved her hips to the beat as she worked at the table. Even Lizzie found she was tapping her foot to the rhythm.

When he and Madison crossed paths heading to the back counter, he playfully grabbed her around the waist and began dancing around the store.

Lizzie watched Madison move across the floor with sensual grace. Her sexuality crackled on the surface of her skin as Madison matched Gideon's rhythm and movements. She attracted male attention without even trying, even sparking interest from the few male customers who came in to buy flowers for their girlfriends.

It wasn't like Madison dressed provocatively. She wore the same uniform everyday—jeans, a t-shirt, and a black work apron, but what she wore didn't matter.

When they worked side-by-side at the refectory table, Lizzie felt like a shadow of a woman, a vague outline with no distinctive features to catch and sustain a man's gaze. At twenty-one, Madison's skin was as luminescent and smooth as alabaster. Time had not etched its wisdom and pain around her eyes or creased her brow with disappointment.

Lizzie turned up the corners of her mouth in an approximation of a smile, pushing her tongue hard against the back of her front teeth as her cheek twitched irritatingly. A familiar ache swamped her heart, an emptiness that was all sharp corners in a darkened room. She shifted her focus away from the dancing couple.

She was appalled at herself. He had to be at least ten years younger than she was. She had just said goodbye to her husband and here she was mooning over a mere child of a man.

She slipped away to the bathroom while Gideon and Madison continued to move in more and more intricate patterns across the floor.

In the bathroom, she waited for the water to run cold then splashed handfuls of bracing water on her burning cheeks. The shock pushed down her aggravation, clearing her thoughts.

Gideon was a nice young man that fate or just dumb luck had brought to her aid on two occasions. That was all. She was alone as she deserved to be and the only things she needed to concern herself with was her shop, where she was going to live, and staying as far away from Penelope as she could.

She blotted her face dry with the paper towel from the wall dispenser, squared her shoulders, and went to join the others.

They were no longer dancing and the music switched back to Brahms. They were leaning against the back counter shoulder to shoulder. Their heads were almost touching as they bent over his iPhone, intently focused on whatever was on the display screen.

"Hey, guys, it's four o'clock, and seeing as we've made great headway on the work today, why don't the both of you head home? The last few orders will be a breeze to finish off tomorrow."

"I don't mind staying for the last hour. And if you want, I could drive you to your friend's house," Madison said, looking up from the phone.

"No, my girlfriend's swinging by after work to get me and I insist you take off early. You didn't get a proper lunch and you've put in a full day's work. Go home while the sun is still out. And Gideon, I'd like to pay you for your time today."

He put his phone in his back pocket and took a half step away from Madison. "That's generous of you, but I can't accept. I stayed to help out because I wanted to, and I can't take your money when I've had so much fun."

"Well, if you won't accept my money then please accept my sincerest gratitude. Really, without your help, we would have had to stay late and it still would have been tight trying to get everything done on time."

"Now that I will accept. And you're welcome."

"I'll go get our coats," Madison said as she proceeded to the office, leaving Gideon and Lizzie alone.

"Are you going to be okay by yourself?"

"Yes, I'll be fine. Thank you for what you did for me at the cemetery. I don't know what would have happened if you hadn't showed up."

"You're safe now and I'm here. We're both okay." He closed the distance between them until he was standing only inches away from her. He reached out and gave her a reassuring squeeze on the shoulder. "There's no need to be afraid."

Returning with the two coats and her purse, Madison plunked her purse on the table before passing Gideon his coat. "Here you go."

Lizzie took a step away from him and busied herself at the table.

"Let me help you with that," he said, putting his coat down on the stool. He came behind Madison, held her coat open, and waited for her to slide her arms in.

She was facing Lizzie, and as he guided her coat over her shoulders, she gave her a wide-eyed stare. "*Oh my God*," she silently mouthed to Lizzie.

Lizzie had to bite her lip to keep from laughing. Seeing them together, she had to admit they made a cute couple. It was too bad Madison was seeing someone already.

They exchanged goodbyes, and after extracting a promise from Lizzie that she wouldn't stay late, they headed out the door.

"I'll walk you to your car," he said, holding the door for her. Madison hesitated for a brief moment before walking through the door with a huge smile on her face. As the two of them passed the plate glass window, they waved at Lizzie. Then Gideon said something to Madison that resulted in her giving him a playful punch on the shoulder.

Yes, they did make a good-looking couple.

With the shop to herself, Lizzie finally let her exhaustion take center stage. It had been crouched on the periphery of her consciousness all day, but she'd kept pushing it down. She had forced herself to focus on her work and be sociable with the two of them when all she longed to do was curl up in a ball in the corner of her office and hide.

As she finished putting away the tools scattered around the back counter, she could feel the fatigue creeping into her muscles, weighing down her limbs as if she were encased in lead. She moved slowly, putting everything back in its proper place when she noticed Gideon's tea tin. It had been shoved behind a watering can. She'd have to call him tomorrow and let him know he'd forgotten it.

Discovering she had a reason to see him again made her surprisingly happy.

As if summoned by her thoughts, the door swung open and Gideon stepped in. The cold air swirled around him like an invisible fog.

"Are you looking for this?" She held the tin out to him.

"I'd gotten all the way to my car when I realized I'd left it behind," he said, closing the gap between them.

He reached out his hand as if to take the tea, but instead, he closed his fingers around her wrist. He whispered something under his breath too low for her to hear. Lizzie's hand relaxed and her fingers lost their grip on the container.

Her head filled yet again with a buzzing of a thousand bees. Gideon was talking to her, asking her questions, but as hard as she tried to make out his words, they were lost in the roar in her head. She felt her lips move, but she had no idea what she replied.

Then just as suddenly, the sound of humming stopped and she was clear-headed once more. He was smiling at her, seemingly unaware of her brief fugue.

"I'm so glad I remembered this before I got all the way home," he said in a cheerful voice, holding up the tea tin. "Since it's only fifteen minutes before closing, why don't I help you clean up? And if you want, I could drive you home."

She had every intention of turning him down and was shocked when the complete opposite popped out of her mouth. "That would be nice," she said in a voice she didn't recognize. Although she hadn't meant to say yes, she was pleased nonetheless. She shocked herself even more when she let the truth spill from her lips. "I'm not actually staying with a friend. I've booked a room at the St. James for reasons I don't really want to get into right now. It's just around the corner, but I would feel better if you drove me there."

"I'd feel better about it too."

When everything in the store was put to rights with Gideon's help, he waited at the front while she went through the routine of closing up and setting the alarm. He held the front door open for her as they left the darkened store. While she engaged the deadbolt, he aimed his key chain at his car parked at the curb and the engine roared to life.

Instead of driving directly to the hotel, he circled around the downtown, carefully watching in his side and rearview mirrors. Only when he was sure no one was following them did he double back toward the St. James.

Lizzie didn't question what he was doing and was reassured that he had thought to take the extra precaution. Since they had left the cemetery, she hadn't once felt the Dark Presence. Still, she was grateful for his vigilance.

It wasn't until they arrived at the hotel that she realized she had forgotten to take her copy of *Pride and Prejudice* with her. She felt a flutter of panic knowing she'd be without her book through the long night. But she'd just have to deal with its absence as she couldn't possibly ask Gideon to take up any more of his time to head back to the store over a book. It was just for one night. She could do without her book for one night.

Gideon wasn't content to just drop her off at the doors of the well-lit lobby with its uniformed doorman and insisted he accompany her right to her suite.

"Goodnight," she said, opening the door with her key card. "Thanks for the ride."

"You're welcome. Just make sure to engage the extra security chain, and if you're going to order room service, ask the waiter to show you his hotel ID just to be on the safe side. Whoever that guy was at the cemetery he hasn't followed you here. If you do notice him again, or anyone else that makes you feel nervous, don't hesitate to call me, okay?" He pulled out his wallet from the back pocket of his pants and slipped a card from the billfold. "Here's my number. Program it into your cell." He held it out to her in between his index finger and thumb.

Her fingertips brushed against his briefly as she plucked the card from him. Her skin tingled from the contact. She longed to feel the whisper of his skin against hers. She wanted him to hold her.

He lingered in the hall, and as Lizzie was about to step over the threshold, he spoke. "So, how's your hand? I noticed you aren't wearing a bandage."

"Oh, it's fine. See." She held her palm toward him, showing him the thin red line that was all that remained of the gash on her hand. "I heal fast."

"So it seems." The silence stretched out between them. "I should go," he finally said. "If for whatever reason you need to call me, don't hesitate no matter what time it is. Okay?"

"I will. I promise."

He waited for her to close the door, but it was her turn to hesitate. "Do you mind not telling Madison about where I'm staying? I don't want her to know. Not yet anyway. I—"

"No need to explain." He held up her hand to stop her. "Your secret is safe with me. I've been told I'm good at keeping secrets. Goodnight, Lizzie."

She smiled. "Goodnight," she said, stepping into her suite and closing the door.

Chapter Fourteen

Lizzie started upright in bed. Her heart slammed in her chest as she fumbled with the switch on the bedside lamp. Someone was pounding on her door. Whoever was stalking her at the cemetery had found out she was at the hotel. And now he was at her door. Scrambling over the bed, pulling at the sheets entangling her legs, she reached for the phone, intent on calling the front desk for help.

Just as she grasped the receiver, her hands slippery with sweat, the pounding on the door stopped. Someone called out her name. A man's voice, urgent and full of worry. She held the receiver to her chest and cocked her head. She heard him again. It was Gideon, she was sure of it.

Her first thought was that something had happened to Madison. Why else would Gideon be at her door in the middle of the night? Slamming the receiver back into its cradle, she stumbled out of bed. She snatched her housecoat lying across a nearby chair and hastily put it on as she raced to the door.

"Open the door," she heard him call out, hammering the solid door. "It's me, Gideon. There's been an emergency at your shop. Wake up, Lizzie." He pounded on the door hard enough to make it rattle in its frame.

His words stopped her in her tracks. It wasn't Madison who was in trouble, but something to do with her shop. She lunged for the door. When she tried to swing it open, the security chain stopped her from opening it more than a few inches. Swearing under her breath, she slammed the door closed and yanked at the chain. With her shaking hands, it took her two attempts to slide the chain over and unhook it.

She swung the door open and Gideon stepped inside.

She stood in the middle of the room clutching the collar of her terrycloth robe tightly around her throat. "My store," her voice wavered. "What's the emergency?"

"Enchanted Garden is on fire. I've just come from there. The fire department is already there fighting the blaze and Madison is there too. I couldn't get her to leave."

"But I don't understand. Everything was fine when we locked up." She swayed slightly.

Holding her firmly by the shoulders, he spoke calmly in a reassuring voice. "I don't know how it started. But Madison was frantic when she couldn't reach you. She didn't know what else to do, so she called me instead. I told her I knew where you were staying, but she wouldn't leave. We can call Madison and get an update. Then you can tell her to go home."

Spiky waves of energy rolled off her as she tried to make sense of what Gideon was telling her. The small hairs on the back of her neck rose as the crackling frantic pulses rolled through her.

"No, I'm going down there." She tried to break free of Gideon's hold.

"Lizzie, there's nothing you can do by being down there and it's not safe. It's best if we let the firefighters do their job and not get in the way."

"My store is on fire and I'm going down there and there is nothing you can do to stop me. Now let go of me." Placing both her hands on his chest, she tried to push him away.

The lights in the suite dimmed then brightened.

"Okay, okay," he said, loosening his grip on her shoulders. "But I'm coming too."

She nodded wordlessly. He finally released her and she scurried on unsteady feet to the bedroom, throwing off her robe before she reached the threshold of the door.

She blindly grabbed at the clothes in the wardrobe, flinging a sweater and pants on the unmade bed. Whipping off her nightgown and leaving it in a heap at her feet, she threw on her clothes. She cursed as her fingers fumbled over the button on her pants. It only took her a few minutes to get dressed, but it seemed to take forever.

When she emerged from the bedroom, Gideon was standing over by the desk, her cell in his hand. He turned when he heard her approach, placing the phone back down on the desk.

Scooping up her coat from a nearby chair, she reached out to open the door when he stopped her.

"You forgot your socks and shoes." He pointed to her naked feet.

She held onto his arm as she bent down and stuffed her bare feet into her winter boots. Once she had her boots on, Lizzie raced out the door and down the hall, heading for the stairs. Gideon followed, snagging her purse as he went and making sure the door was secure behind him.

Outside the hotel, the scream of sirens filled the darkness of the early morning. The sound reverberated off the office buildings, making it impossible to pinpoint where they were originating from.

Gideon narrowly avoided colliding with her when she stopped suddenly and looked up into the black sky. He swooped past her, opening the SUV's passenger side door.

"Get in," he ordered, all but stuffing her into the car.

As he raced the car down the empty streets, Lizzie leaned forward in her seat, her fingers gripping the edge of the leather upholstery as if doing so she could make him drive faster. The air in the SUV crackled with her erratic energy bouncing off the interior like rubber balls.

In the few minutes it took to drive to her shop, he told her the details of the fire in a calm, low voice.

"From what Madison told me, when the fire started, the alarm company immediately called the fire department and then tried to get a hold of you. They couldn't reach you at the numbers you'd left them."

"But they had my cell number. Why didn't they try me on my cell?"

"They probably did, but it's dead. When you were getting dressed, I noticed it on the desk, so I checked. You'd left it on and forgot to recharge it before going to bed."

As he turned down Bloor Street West, he had to stop the car several blocks before Lizzie's store. Two police cars were stationed perpendicular to the road, blocking his progress. Their flashing emergency lights bathed the pavement in alternating swatches of blue and red. Farther down the street, three fire trucks were being employed to battle the blaze that lit up the night sky in an artificial dawn.

The sight of the flames licking into the sky tore a horrified cry from her throat. Flinging open her door, she raced toward her shop. Gideon followed at her heels.

A uniformed police officer stepped from the side of his vehicle, intent on stopping her from getting any closer to the blaze. He had started to say something, but as she ran past him, he stumbled back against the cruiser as if he had been pushed.

Gideon caught up with her just as a fourth fire engine pulled into the streets, its wailing siren announcing its arrival. As soon as it was in position, the vehicle disgorged several firefighters, who raced in efficiently orchestrated movements toward the burning store.

Large canvas hoses were unreeled from the engine, and a team of firemen rushing to connect it to the nearby hydrant. The captain headed over to a man who seemed to be in charge of coordinating the efforts to extinguish the blaze.

Wooden barriers were set up around the perimeter of emergency vehicles and the fire. Even at two in the morning, a small knot of onlookers gathered, watching in morbid fascination at the destruction taking place.

Lizzie ran blindly toward her store. She was several feet away from the entrance when the heat of the blaze engulfed her. The intensity of it made her stumble. Gideon grabbed her by the arm and pulled her back.

"Lizzie," someone shouted, the voice barely audible over the din. "Over here."

She turned to see Madison frantically waving her arms in the air. She stood a few feet from the onlookers, her face a mask of desperation, tears staining her face.

She took a step off the curb to go to Lizzie, but Lizzie was already running over to her, Gideon at her side.

Madison held out her arms and the two women hugged, fiercely clinging to each other for reassurance. They remained arm in arm, silently watching the spectacle before them.

From their viewpoint, Lizzie couldn't see many flames, just oily brown smoke curling out from under the eaves. It laced the air with an acrid chemical smell, taking her breath away even at a distance. The smoke puffed out of every crack and crevice in the siding and appeared to retract back into the interior of the building only to pour more of its toxic fumes into the air.

The interior of the store was darkened as the smoke continued to roil against the glass like an angry spirit looking for a way to escape its confinement.

A team of firefighters worked on the top of the building, using axes to cut a hole through the roof. Small tongues of orange fire appeared as the opening grew wider.

All around them the air was filled with the sounds of the fire alarms from the buildings on either side of Enchanted Garden, set off by the smoke-filled air.

There was an increased flurry of movement. Orders were being shouted as three of the ladders and hoses that were aimed at Enchanted

Garden were repositioned to concentrate on the two buildings on either side of the burning structure.

"My books," Lizzie whispered, realizing why the firemen were now focused on the other buildings. "My books, my books, my books." Her voice rose with hysteria.

An urgent shout from the fire chief had the firefighters scrambling to pull back the ladder suspended near the roof of her building. For one crazy moment, it looked like the plate glass window was breathing as the glass moved outward against the heat, then exploded, spraying deadly shrapnel into the street.

The fire that had been visible through the hole in the roof disappeared as the entire conflagration had been sucked into the center of the building. A muffled boom came from inside and seconds later, flames reappeared through the opening in the roof with a new ferocious energy. With more oxygen feeding the fire, the flames stretched higher through the hole in the roof.

An unearthly groan filled the night as the charred rafters of the building finally gave way. The crash that followed shook the ground and the flames surged angry and hungry into the sky. The firefighters moved forward again to continue their efforts to hold back the fire.

Lizzie pulled herself free of Madison's embrace and started toward her shop. With preternatural swiftness, Gideon grabbed her by the shoulders and whirled her around to face him. He tightened his grip on her upper arms as she struggled to break free.

"Let go of me. You don't understand, my books are in there. I need to save them. Please," she begged, tears clogging her throat.

Simultaneously, ever firefighters' walkie-talkies sent up a high-pitched squeal. Everyone within earshot of the piercing feedback covered their ears against the painful noise.

Below the shriek of static another sound began, too low for most to hear with all the other noises filling the night, but one Lizzie felt and recognized immediately.

The streetlights flared, bathing the scene below in vivid washes of lurid orange light. Some of the bystanders looked up, puzzled by the sudden brightness. A few backed away from the barriers, unsure of what was happening around them.

Gideon held firm, keeping Lizzie trapped. The air pressure around the two of them changed dramatically. She could feel the weight of it pressing against her chest, making it difficult to breathe.

"Lizzie, you've to get control of yourself. Your books are already gone. There is nothing to save."

"No," she cried, pulling against his vise-like grip.

"You need to stop what you're doing right now or you're going to endanger the lives of everyone here. You are going to hurt these people who are trying to help you." The air pressed down and around them so that his last words came out in gasps.

She felt her powers spinning out of control. She couldn't stop it. She looked up at him, helpless to stop what she'd unleashed. But he wasn't looking at her. He focused past her shoulder.

She opened her mouth to tell him she couldn't stop what was happening when she saw him give a curt nod of his head. Something hot and biting stung the back of her neck and she yelped in surprise. Her eyes widened and she tasted something metallic at the back of her throat. Then everything went black.

Chapter Fifteen

Lizzie stood in the middle of the wooden trestle bridge, looking down at the river below. The water churned around the large boulders protruding along its banks. Despite its depth, the water was so clear she could see the rocky bottom even as the water rushed by. It filled the air with the roar of its progress, blotting out even the sounds of the meadowlark perched on a tree nearby. The sun warmed her shoulders, infusing the air with the astringent smell of creosote from the timbers under her feet.

She wondered how cold the water was. If she climbed down off the bridge, crossed the moss-covered rocks along the bank, and dipped her toes in it, would it be icy cold like the dark heart of a mountain? She longed to cup her hands into the stream and taste the dark primeval places that gave birth to this river. But she didn't have time to make the climb or to even linger any longer watching the beauty of the stream. She needed to get going. Reluctantly, she pulled her gaze from the river and briskly crossed the bridge.

She followed the gravel road as it wound along the side of a mountain. She was having trouble keeping track of time. It seemed to expand and contract with each footstep so she couldn't determine whether she had been walking for twenty minutes or twenty hours.

The sun was behaving curiously, too. It kept shifting positions, one moment peeking over the eastern ridge of the mountain, washing the boughs of the trees in the soft glow of morning; the next moment, it would be overhead, shrinking Lizzie's shadow to a pool at her feet. When she would glance up again, the sun would be tipping over the tops of the trees to the west, turning the sky a pale lavender. Night never fell. The sun kept dancing from east to west, then back again.

Her pulse quickened as she came upon a fork in the road. She was almost there. Taking the new path that veered to her right, she headed downhill. Through the trees, she glimpsed the blue of a lake and the brilliant flashes of light as the sun sparkled on the water's glass-like surface.

The road leveled out and she stopped when she realized it branched out in four directions. She stood at the crossroads, unsure for the first time which direction she was supposed to take.

In front of her, to the north, the road ended abruptly at the lakeshore. The roads heading east and west looked identical—unpaved, dusty tracks curving through a thick forest of cedar, pine, spruce, and hemlock.

She closed her eyes and, with her arms outstretched, she spun in a circle. Faster and faster she turned, keeping her eyes tightly closed, laughing as her feet spun around on the gravel. Stopping suddenly, she opened her eyes. The trees spun crazily around her and she stumbled drunkenly. When her inner ears had found their equilibrium and the landscape settled back into place, she smiled broadly. Directly in front of her stood the road heading east.

East, the direction of new beginnings and journeys. She liked the sound of that.

Admiring the purple and pink lupines growing wild in the ditches, she skipped down the path like she did when she was a little girl back at the convent chasing butterflies through the flower gardens.

The feeling of coming home was so strong she broke out into a run for the last few yards.

The sun's position sped up, its strange progress causing the shadows to flicker and change direction. Everything around her strobed pink, orange, and lavender like a series of tinted pictures flashing across a screen.

She was out of breath by the time she reached the white wrought iron gate, but she didn't wait to catch her breath. The gate swung silently on well-oiled hinges and she walked up the drive, following it as it curved through the trees. Two hundred feet up from the gate, the trees fell away as the road ended in a circular loop in front of a stone cottage. She stopped short of following the drive up to the house and lingered within the shadow of the trees.

The sun had stopped its erratic dance across the sky and for the meantime, remained in a position of high noon, throwing the cottage into a bright, clear light.

The house was like the cottage she grew up in, constructed of rough-hewn stones laid in a random pattern of shapes and sizes, although the color and type of the stones were different. The proud little house before her was built with grey stones, ranging from a very dark slate to a soft dove grey and all the shades in between. The dark, glossy leaves of climbing roses covered most of the stonework on the first floor. Their trailing branches obscured all but the windows and front door. The roses were in full bloom and she could smell the sweet scent of the abundant pink blossoms from where she stood under the trees.

The cottage's slate roof sprouted two chimneys of charcoal grey stone perched equidistance across its steeply pitched expanse. Everything about the cottage was perfectly proportioned and balanced. The bright blue door was positioned in the middle of the house. The four mullioned windows on the main floor were echoed above on the second story, along with the black-painted shutters. It had a pleasing countenance.

She was about to cross into the sunshine heading for the cottage when she heard the distinctive sound of footsteps coming up the gravel drive. She didn't want to wait to see who it was. She wanted to go inside her cottage. Stepping out into the light, the smell of roses was even stronger in the warmth of the open driveway.

The footsteps were getting closer. She hurried up the wooden porch. Her hand touched the doorknob, the metal warm to the touch.

"Lizzie, wait."

But she didn't want to wait. She wanted to go inside where it was safe and quiet. She knew, behind the door, it would be dark and cool.

"Please, Lizzie, just stay where you are, just for a moment."

She hesitated with her hand still on the brass knob. "Who are you? How do you know my name?" She left her hand on the knob, but turned to the woman who stood just inside the shadow of the trees. She squinted in the bright sun, trying to make out the woman's features.

If the stranger wanted to come in, she would say no. She didn't care if she was being rude. This was hers, hers alone, and she wasn't going to share it.

"We've met very recently, although I doubt if you remember me."

Lizzie remained on the porch, still unable to clearly see the woman's face. "You're right, I don't. Now go away. I didn't invite you here," she shouted.

"I know you're tired and you just want to go lie down, but I've come such a very long way just to talk to you. Please, just a few minutes and then you can choose to do what you want."

"Okay, I'll listen to you, but you can't come inside. I don't want you here."

"Fair enough."

"Just a few minutes and then you'll leave, right?"

"Yes, as you wish. Now, why don't you come over here with me in the shade where it's nice and cool? It's much too hot to be standing out in the sun."

Lizzie looked longingly at the pretty blue door and then back at the women. "Oh all right, but make it quick," she said, then stomped off the porch. "Who are you?" Lizzie demanded as she joined the woman in the dappled shade of the trees.

"I'm Vivienne. You know my son, Gideon," she said.

"Gideon?" Lizzie furrowed her brows.

"He helped you up when you slipped and fell on the ice and he came by the shop to return your keys."

"Yes, I remember him now. He looks an awful lot like you."

"Yes, there is a strong family resemblance." She moved toward Lizzie as she spoke, stepping into a shaft of sunlight filtering down through the boughs.

"Oh, you're so beautiful," Lizzie exclaimed, clapping her hands in delight. "You're all pink and blue and purple. And shimmery. You look like you're covered in sparkly faerie dust."

"So do you. Take a look at your arms."

"Oh, you're right. Ha. We look like butterflies." Lizzie moved her arms, making the colors shift and glisten in the little pool of sunshine. "You want to take me back, don't you?" she asked, a frown replacing the captivated look she had moments ago.

"No, I'm here to help you get back if that is what you choose."

"Well, I choose to stay here. It's nice here. There are flowers and trees and a delightful little cottage. Why would I want to go back to that other place? There's nothing for me back there."

"But you're wrong. You must fulfill your destiny, and you can't do that here."

"What destiny?"

"Only you will know what your path is. What I do know is you are a rare individual possessing a very powerful magick."

"I don't want to talk about that."

"If it's because you are afraid of your gift, I could teach you how to control it so that you don't hurt people unintentionally."

108

"You would do that for me? Why? What do you want in return?"

"Nothing. I want to help because that is what I do, it is what Gideon does. We help women like you who are special. It is our sacred duty to help gifted women be free and safe."

"But if I stay here, I'll be safe. So why should I leave?"

"Right now that might seem like a wonderful alternative to what awaits you if you go back to the mortal plane, but this place isn't real. You'll be trapped here if you remain much longer. You won't be able to follow your destiny as your soul intended, nor will you be able to return to the one true home that awaits us all when our physical bodies die. You will be stuck here for all eternity. Haven't you noticed, other than me, you are alone here? Do you want to spend the rest of eternity alone?"

"I don't mind. Besides, I'd be alone if I went back with you and I'm tired of feeling that way. Here, at least, I'm alone by my own choosing."

"But you are not alone back at the hotel. I'm there, and so are Gideon and Madison. You have three people who care very deeply about you."

"That doesn't count. You just said you're only here because it's your job, same with Gideon. Madison just works for me. She doesn't care about me."

"Yes, she does, as do I and my son. If you doubt my words, take a look at yourself again."

Lizzie held up her arms. They were still covered in a sparkling light, but the colors had changed to a clear bright green. "What does this mean?"

"It means that Gideon and Madison are sending you something. You're completely surrounded in that beautiful light that comes from them."

Lizzie glanced down at her legs and torso. She was encased in a cocoon of clear, apple green light. "What are they sending me?"

"You tell me. Close your eyes."

She did as Vivienne suggested and immediately, she felt it. She opened her eyes wide with amazement. "It's love. From both of them. I can feel it flooding in all around me. I can feel their desire for me to come back, to be with them," she said incredulously.

"So you see, my dear one, you are not alone. Nor will you be if you come back with me. You need to decide what you are going to do. And you need to decide now. I can't remain here much longer."

"Because this is my creation, not yours, right?"

"Yes, you catch on quickly. So what shall it be?"

Lizzie turned to look back at the cottage. A part of her still desperately wanted to walk through the door of the quaint little house and lock the door securely behind her. She pulled her gaze from the house and stared directly into Vivienne's eyes. "You promise that if I go back, you can make sure I don't hurt anyone?"

"Yes."

"And that you, Gideon, and Madison will be there so I'm not by myself?"

"Yes."

"You promise what I'm feeling, what this is"—she held up her palms, turning them slowly, causing the green glow surrounding them to catch the light—"is really coming from the two of them? That they really do care about me?"

"I give you my solemn oath that they really do love you."

"All right."

Lizzie resisted the urge to take one last look at her beloved cottage. She could still feel the pull to remain, and if she looked, she was afraid she would change her mind.

"Now you need to follow exactly what I say. Here, hold my hands and close your eyes." Vivienne held out her hands. "Can you sense my energy?"

"Yes, it feels warm. I can see it too, even with my eyes closed. It looks like a beam of bright white light."

"Good. Now in your mind's eye, can you see the light heading off into the distance?"

"Yes."

"You need to picture yourself riding that light back to where it starts. When you start moving, don't stop. You may feel dizzy, but don't open your eyes and, whatever you do, don't let go of my hands. As we move forward, picture the hotel room. See Gideon and Madison. Let their love guide you back "

"Okay." She tightened her grip on Vivienne's hands.

"Are you ready?"

"Yes."

"Let's go home."

Chapter Sixteen

Lizzie jolted upright, her head whipping forward. Trying to catch her breath, she stared at the familiar white cotton duvet covering her legs. Lizzie felt a pair of firm hands on her back, holding her up in a sitting position.

"Oh my God, Lizzie, you're back. Are you all right?" Madison's voice sounded in her left ear.

"Give her a moment to catch her breath." A woman's voice came from her other side. "She's been on quite the ride." Lizzie realized the voice was not new to her. Her name was Vivienne. She was the one who had brought her back.

She slowly raised her head and looked at the three people ringed around her on the bed. Vivienne had been telling the truth. Gideon and Madison had been waiting for her. Smiling weakly, she tried to speak, but her teeth were chattering so hard she couldn't form the words. She was so cold and everything hurt.

She looked about the room. It was her hotel suite, but the room was aglow in candlelight. Fat white pillar candles were arrayed on every flat surface in the suite. Through the mellow candlelight, she saw the walls glowed with an ethereal iridescence.

"What's wrong with her?" Madison asked.

"She's experiencing the after effects of coming back from the *In Between*. Her body is having difficulty adjusting to her soul re-inhabiting its systems. It needs to reset itself." To Lizzie, she said, "We're going to get you warmed up as fast as we can, just hang in there. Remember, you're safe here. You have people around you that love you."

Still unable to speak from the convulsive shivers wracking her body, Lizzie nodded her understanding.

"Gideon, would you please run a hot bath? I think a balancing elixir and the herbs in the yellow pouch would be just the thing. Madison, stay with her. Your own body heat will help until we can get her into the tub. I'm just going to pop into the bathroom and get it prepared."

Vivienne settled Lizzie back down on the bed, tucking the comforter up around her quaking shoulders. Madison snuggled down next to her, wrapping her arms around her cold body.

Lizzie had never been this cold in her life. Despite the blankets and Madison's warm embrace, she couldn't stop shivering. No wonder Vivienne had failed to mention what it was going to feel like to come back. If she'd know it was going to hurt like this, she might've chosen to stay at the cottage.

Despite the pain, feeling Madison's arms around her gave her some degree of comfort. She lifted her head off the pillow and the room spun in a stomach-turning circle. She tried to tell Madison how grateful she was, but she couldn't get the words past her chattering teeth. Her jaw ached from the effort.

"Don't try to talk right now. Just lie still." Madison snuggled closer to her and rubbed her warm, stockinged feet over Lizzie's.

Lizzie's head fell back on the pillow. She heard running water coming from the bathroom and smelled sweet herbs floating on the steam of the hot water.

She watched a swirling fog of pale colors move lazily above her head on the ceiling. It reminded her of the faerie dust that covered her and Vivienne back at the cottage. She wanted to ask Madison what the beautiful mist was doing on the ceiling, but she didn't have the energy to get the words out.

She was so tired, but the spasms shuddering through her body made it impossible to drift off into the sweetness of sleep.

"Come now, it's ready." Vivienne appeared at Lizzie's side of the bed.

She allowed Madison and Vivienne to assist her into a sitting position on the edge of the bed. With each of them supporting her, she shuffled to the bathroom.

As they passed by Gideon, Lizzie looked into his dark eyes and attempted another shaky smile.

"I'm glad you decided to come back to us," he said, his voice thick with emotion.

"Me too," she whispered, her words coming out in a hoarse croak as the two women guided her into the bathroom. He gave her one of his brilliant smiles then shut the door behind them.

Fragrant steam filled the room, fogging the mirror and mingling with the iridescent vapor draping the walls. Flower petals and herbs floated on the surface of the water and four amethyst crystals had been placed around the edge of the tub.

Lizzie's feet were like blocks of ice as she shuffled across the cold marble floor. With their help, Lizzie took a seat on the closed toilet lid.

The short distance from the bed to the bathroom had sapped her strength. She craved the heat of the bath, but she wasn't sure she had the energy to remove her clothes, much less climb into the enormous soaker tub. Her fingers fumbled with the edge of her sweater.

"Here, let me help you," Vivienne said.

Like a child, she dropped her hands to her sides as Vivienne pulled off her sweater. Lizzie had been in such a rush to get to the fire, she hadn't bothered putting on a bra. She instinctively wrapped her arms around her bare breasts and looked down at a spot on the floor to hide her embarrassment at being naked in front of strangers. She heard Vivienne utter a small sound of surprise, but when she looked up to see what was wrong, Vivienne's face was serene.

Using Madison as support, she stood up and allowed Vivienne to remove the rest of her clothes. They helped her into the tub, and as she slipped into the deliciously hot scented water, a small sigh escaped her lips.

She lay back in the water, resting her head on the lip of the tub, her earlier embarrassment at her nakedness forgotten as the hot water slowly seeped into her cold limbs and the uncontrollable shivering subsided. With her eyes closed, she luxuriated in the feeling of being warm again.

"The elixir I placed in the water should be taking effect soon. Do you feel any better?" Vivienne asked.

"Yes," she said, opening her eyes and slowly pulling herself into a sitting position. It was just her and Vivienne in the bathroom. She hadn't heard Madison leave. She drew her knees to her chest, wrapped her arms around her legs, and rested her cheek against her knees as she turned to look at Vivienne. "I'm not cold anymore and the pain's almost gone. What exactly did you put in the water?"

"Just a few essential oils and herbs that assist the body and spirit to reintegrate, helps to absorb the physical symptoms too." Vivienne picked up a nearby loofa, a fresh bar of soap, and began gently scrubbing Lizzie's back in slow circles.

"That feels so good," she whispered, closing her eyes again.

"Oh, child, you are too thin. This life has been hard on you, hasn't it?"

Ian used to complain all the time that she was too thin, his words laced with contempt and disgust. Vivienne's words were different and they pierced her heart, unleashing all the sorrow she had kept bottled up for so many years.

"Yes," she said, choking back tears.

"It's all right to let it out. It would be an honor if you allowed me to witness your pain."

"I can't. You know what happens when I get upset, and you haven't shown me how to control it yet."

"I will in time. Right now, you do need to allow your emotions to rise up and out of you. That's been part of your problem with your gift getting out of control. You needn't be afraid of your emotions in here. The crystals and the Elementals"—she gestured with the loofa to the mist veiling the walls—"will help absorb your energy. But you must promise to remain here as you release your feelings, no matter how much it hurts. No slipping off *In Between*, okay? I don't think I can handle going back and getting you twice in one day." She continued to scrub Lizzie's back.

"Okay." She allowed a few tears to slip silently down her cheek, but kept a firm grip on the deeper pain that wanted to rise to the surface. "Elementals. They are the spirits of air, fire, water, and earth, aren't they?"

"Yes. You've studied about such things?"

"No, not really. The woman who raised me, Sister Collette, used to talk about how in nature there are energies that exist in the garden that help the plants grow. She said they came from the four elements that are a part of every living thing."

"That's an apt description." Vivienne put down the loofa and dipped her fingers in the water. "The water's cooling a bit, did you want more hot water?"

"Yes, please."

Vivienne reached over and turned the hot water tap on, letting it run until the water level just reached the overflow mark. She picked up the loofa and resumed scrubbing Lizzie's back in slow circles. "Your powers, when did you become aware of them?"

"About five or six years ago. That's when bad things started to happen."

"Was there any one incident that triggered it?"

"No. It seemed to happen when I was really upset. I don't mean for it to happen and I don't want to hurt people, I really don't."

"So earlier this evening, at the fire, what triggered it?"

"My books," she whispered. "When I realized all my books were gone."

"You weren't upset about your shop?"

"No. I mean, yes, but I can rebuild the store. My books were first edition by Jane Austen."

"But surely you had such valuable things insured?" Lizzie nodded her reply. "Couldn't you use the insurance money to rebuild your collection?" Vivienne put down the loofa and, using a washcloth, rinsed the soap from Lizzie's back.

"Yes, but it was those particular books that were important to me. They can't be replaced." Her voice faltered. "They were my mother's," she whispered. "I only had two things of hers, her books and this," she said, fingering her necklace. She rested her forehead on her knees and kept her eyes closed as she spoke. "I know nothing about my mother, not what she looked like or where she grew up, or even what her favorite color was. She gave birth to me at a cloistered abbey where she sought sanctuary. I know those books were very important to her because she arrived at the abbey gates with just the clothes she was wearing and her satchel of books. Nothing else. When she knew she was dying, she made Sister Collette promise to give them to me. She wanted me to have them. Her necklace and those books were my only connection to her." Her tears came unbidden behind her closed lids, and with them, her despair. She hugged her knees tighter to her chest. The water in the tub rippled when she moved. "Now her books are gone forever." Her last words were lost in the sound of her sobs.

Vivienne placed her hand on her quaking shoulder as her keening echoed off the tiled walls. Lost within her grief, Lizzie didn't notice the iridescent vapor of the Elementals had changed into a brilliant wash of moving colors as they absorbed and transformed her pain. The bathroom walls had become an exquisite moving painting of her grief.

Chapter Seventeen

Lizzie climbed out of bed and threw on one of the hotel's white terry-cloth robes. The clock on the nightstand read four o'clock. With the curtains drawn, she had no way of knowing if it was four in the morning or afternoon.

She padded over to the window. She was about to draw back the curtains when she noticed the shimmering presence of the Elementals flowing across the fabric. They were still in her bedroom, moving along the walls, ceiling, and floor. So she hadn't dreamed the events of last night. The fire, the cottage, Vivienne bringing her back; it was all real.

She reached out her hand and held it a few inches away from the Elementals. A warm surge of energy entered her palm, catching her by surprise. She thought it would feel cold and wet like fog.

"You're still here," she whispered.

"Yes. We are here." The voice sounded like hers, but came from all directions at once. The colors in the vapor flared brighter as they spoke.

She gasped and snatched her hand back from the curtain. What she had experienced since the fire could only be described as bizarre. Having an ethereal mist communicate with her in her own voice was too much for her to handle.

She watched the pastel colors of the Elementals shift and merge only to separate and mingle again, forming ever more beautiful patterns.

Even though a part of her felt foolish doing it, she took a step back from the window and addressed them. "I know you've been protecting me and the others from my powers until I learn to control them. And you've been helping me stay grounded, keeping me safe. I just wanted to say I'm truly grateful for all you've done for me."

"You are welcome. It is our pleasure to assist you."

She was moved by their reply, but it was disconcerting to hear her voice echoing back to her in surround sound.

A knock on the door startled her.

"Come in."

Gideon's face appeared through the open door. She felt a warm glow of pleasure spread through her chest.

"Good, you're up. The breakfast I ordered you is here. I know it's almost dinner time, but I figured since you've just gotten up, you'd probably want to eat eggs instead of a steak or something. Are you hungry?"

"Yes, I am. Surprisingly so. I can't believe I slept all day."

"Actually, you've been asleep for three days. It's Friday afternoon." He stepped further into the room.

"Three days. That can't be."

"It is. You needed to sleep and regain your strength. How are you feeling?"

"Rested and strangely calm considering the circumstances. But I have to tell you I'm having some trouble processing everything that's happened. I mean, I just finished holding a conversation with Elementals. If you weren't here, I'd think I'd lost my mind. I feel a little like..."

"Like you just fell down the rabbit hole?"

"Yes, exactly like Alice."

"If it helps, I'll answer any questions you might have. But why don't we do that over breakfast?"

"Okay, as long as you promise me that there isn't going to be a Dormouse in my coffee pot. You did order coffee, didn't you?"

"Yes on both counts," he said, wheeling in the room service cart.

She shut the door behind him then followed him across the room to the small table in the corner. Sometime while she had slept, someone had put the table back into its proper corner and removed all the spent candles. Only the Elementals remained in their places from three days ago.

She took a seat as Gideon arranged the plates, pots of jam, cutlery, cups, and the coffee pot on the table.

"Where are Madison and Vivienne?" she asked, placing a linen napkin in her lap.

"It took some doing, but I finally convinced Madison to go home to get some sleep. Man, she's stubborn."

She noticed the amused look on his face. A stab of jealousy pricked her heart.

"She's been by your side the whole time and only agreed to leave if I promised not to let you out of my sight."

Remorse instantly replaced her jealously. She wasn't sure she deserved Madison's loyalty or friendship.

"As for Vivienne, she had to take care of a few things, but I expect she'll be back shortly to start your training." As he spoke, Gideon removed the silver domes covering the plates, revealing a mushroom and asparagus omelet, side orders of toast and crisp bacon, and a bowl of fruit salad.

As hungry as she was, she ignored the food, instead giving into her craving for coffee. She reached for the pot, but Gideon snatched it up first.

"Here, let me."

She picked up an empty cup and leaned forward, her robe falling open as she moved. She watched the steaming liquid fill her cup, eagerly anticipating her much-needed caffeine fix. She waited for Gideon to stop pouring, but when the level reached the rim of the cup and was in danger of spilling over, she looked up at him. He was staring at her exposed throat instead of paying attention to what he was doing.

"That's more than enough."

"Sorry." He thumped the pot down, the porcelain lid clattering against the rim of the pot.

She set the cup down, sloshing the coffee over her hand and onto the table. She yanked her hand away from the hot coffee.

"Did I burn you?"

"No, I'm fine," she said, dabbing her hand with her napkin. "Did I suddenly grow a second head or something?" she asked with a smile.

"I don't mean to be rude, it's your necklace. It's a very unique piece. May I?"

She couldn't see a reason to say no, but felt odd as she lifted the cross up by its chain for him to look at. He reached out as if to touch it then hesitated. He looked up at her, waiting for her permission. She nodded her consent.

Gingerly, he traced the outline of the cross with his finger. His hand accidentally brushed against hers, sending a curious frizzle of electricity up her arm.

"The silver work's amazing. I've never seen anything so intricate," he murmured, leaning in to take a closer look.

His breath tickled softly against her neck and she could smell the clean scent of his hair. She closed her eyes and reminded herself of the age difference between them and the obvious signs of attraction she'd seen between him and Madison. The closeness of him had her heart racing.

She opened her eyes when she felt him pull away and let out a breath she'd been holding.

"So, how did you come by it?" he asked, still staring at her necklace.

"It was my mother's."

"Any idea what kind of stone it is?" He sat back in his chair, but his eyes remained locked on the cross around her neck.

"No. I've a friend in the Diamond District and he thought it might be some kind of sapphire, but he'd never seen one quite this color before. He said if I wanted to know for sure, he could send it off to a colleague who had more experience with sapphires. But I never took him up on the offer." She hesitated before telling him the rest. "Entrusting it to a stranger wasn't something I was comfortable with. My mother wore it around her neck. It touched her skin. I know it sounds silly and sentimental, but it's the only intimate connection I have with her. And parting with it, even for a short while, would be unbearable."

"Do you ever take it off?"

"No, never." She placed her hand protectively over the cross.

Gideon finally looked up at her. She couldn't read his expression. It was a strange mix of curiosity and confusion.

"If Vivienne were here, she'd be appalled at my manners. I'm keeping you from your breakfast. Dig in while it's still hot." He stood up abruptly from the table and pulled out his cell phone. "I need to make a few phone calls before Vivienne arrives. I'll be in the front room if you need me."

Alone, Lizzie added four sugar cubes to her coffee before taking a sip. As she ate her breakfast, she puzzled over his fascination with her mother's heirloom and his abrupt departure from the table. The fact that she hadn't asked Gideon a single question hadn't even occurred to her.

* * * *

After polishing off breakfast, Lizzie took a long, hot shower and tried to forget the pleasurable feel of Gideon's breath on her bare skin and the way her heart raced when his hand had accidentally touched hers. She needed to focus on the more practical aspects of her current situation.

She had to call her insurance company, but it would have to wait until Monday, as the office was closed this late on a Friday. Madison would need some money to tide her over until the shop re-opened. That she could do today. Most importantly, she needed to go to her shop to assess how bad the fire damage was.

Vivienne arrived just as Lizzie was getting dressed and mulling over her to-do list. Vivienne called out to her through the closed bathroom door.

"I'll be out in a minute," she answered. She quickly ran a brush through her wet hair and went out to meet her.

Vivienne had placed two chairs in the center of the room, facing each other. A circle of small quartz crystals surrounded them. She smiled at Lizzie as she stepped out from the bathroom.

Vivienne was wearing a crisp white dress shirt neatly tucked into a pair of wide-leg chinos. The toes of her white Keds peeked out from the pant cuffs. Hammered silver disks dangled from her ears and a large sliver and turquoise cuff encircled her delicate wrist.

Lizzie was dressed in her usual uniform—black dress pants and a black turtleneck. She had forgone makeup, and except for the cross hidden beneath her sweater, she wore no jewelery.

"How are you feeling?" she asked, gesturing to Lizzie to take a seat in one of the chairs.

"Pretty good, I guess." She sat down and curled her toes into the thick carpet. She absently watched the Elementals' pastel vapors eddy and swirl around her feet.

"Do you feel up to working with me for a couple of hours? I thought we'd start with some basic breathing exercises and meditations so as not to overwhelm you."

"Sure. But, before we start, would you mind if I asked a few questions about what's happening to me? I meant to ask Gideon over breakfast, but we got talking about something else." She picked at invisible lint on her pants.

"Of course. Ask away." She took a seat facing Lizzie, crossing her ankles and resting her hands in her lap.

"What's wrong with me? Am I mentally ill?" she blurted out, finally looking up at Vivienne.

"No, you're not sick, far from it. You have a natural ability, a talent. It's really no different than being born left-handed or double-jointed."

"If I was born this way then why haven't I noticed this so-called ability until recently?"

"Last night you'd mentioned you began to experience your powers a few years ago. How did they manifest?"

"At first, my wrist watches would stop working or I'd fry the battery on my cell phone, then computers would crash if I was around them when I was angry." She carefully omitted what happened the day of Ian's death.

"So your strong emotions were affecting batteries and electronics. What about other things, like lights?" Vivienne asked, as if reading her mind.

"Yes, that's happened too."

"Have you ever come to physical harm because of your powers?"

"No, but others have." Lizzie thought about the cut on Ian's cheek from the exploding light fixtures and how she hadn't been hurt even when she walked across the glass-strewn floor in only her stockings. Her scalp prickled. "The night of the fire, did I... Was anyone hurt?"

"No, when you and Gideon first arrived at the fire and he realized you couldn't control your powers, he called for backup. And when it became evident you may accidentally harm the people around you, he gave the order to sedate you."

"I didn't faint?" She remembered feeling a hot sting at the back of her neck before she passed out.

"No, one of our guardians shot you with a tranquilizing dart."

She'd been tranquilized like a dangerous, out-of-control creature. "Why haven't I been hurt by my powers?"

"I think you were given a talisman as a child that contained your powers and protected you from being accidentally harmed by them."

"My mother's necklace." She laid a hand at her throat, pressing the cool stone under her sweater against her skin.

"Yes," Vivienne replied.

"That's why Gideon was so interested in it. He knew it was charmed."

"No, he didn't know about the charm. His interest was academic. He remembered reading about a necklace similar to yours in the Order's archives."

Lizzie sat up straighter. Could Gideon have found a clue to who her mother was? Her chest tightened and she fought to catch her breath. Vivienne's words washed over her in an incomprehensible sea of sounds.

"The color of the stone and the intricate silver filigree matches the description found in the archives, but the text mentions two strands of Dragon's Tears, twelve stones to be exact, that was part of the setting, whereas yours is just the cross. The setting could have been broken up, sometime in the past, but we have no way of knowing. If your cross is the original and not a copy, it's not a sapphire or an aquamarine or even a blue diamond."

Lizzie snapped back to attention.

"It's a Faerie stone," Vivienne continued. "It's extremely rare and special."

"How so?"

"The necklace belonged to the royal house of the Enchanted Ones. But they withdrew from our world over six hundred years ago. How your mother came to have it in her possession is intriguing to say the least."

Lizzie shifted in her chair. Placing her hands under her thighs, she rocked forward. "You speak of Faerie stones and Enchanted Ones as if they actually existed. I've seen some crazy things lately that have stretched my concept of reality, but believing in Tinkerbell is just pushing it a little too far."

"Unlike James Mathew Barrie's Tinkerbell, real Faeries don't need you to believe in them to exist. But I'll respect your reluctance all the same."

Lizzie swallowed hard, pushing away her irritation. "Do the archives mention any names that could help me trace who my mother was?"

"No, I'm sorry. No names were listed. But Gideon will keep searching."

Lizzie glanced down at the carpet. Her vision doubled and she blinked furiously to stop the tears that wanted to spill.

"If the archives hold any clue to the identity of your mother, Gideon will find it. But you're forgetting, we already know one thing about her. She was a talented, wise woman."

"Because of the charm she put on the stone," Lizzie said, her voice hoarse.

"Yes. A very powerful charm, one I've never felt before. I suspect your mother did it to allow you to grow into your powers without hurting yourself inadvertently. To weave that kind of spell, she would've been a very powerful woman in her own right and in possession of some very ancient knowledge."

"It's not much to go on."

"No, but it's a start."

"So if this charm is supposed to contain my powers, why are they able to break through it?" she managed to ask, finally looking back up at Vivienne.

"My best guess would be your age is making you stronger. Adding to that, you don't allow yourself to fully express what you're feeling and your energy breaks through the spell. The charm contains a safeguard, like a pressure valve. She made sure if the stone couldn't absorb your excess powers, it would release them so you wouldn't be hurt. You bottle everything up, push it down. Am I right?"

Lizzie nodded.

"You need to understand emotions are energy, like an electrical charge. Our bodies and our minds are designed to feel all emotions, the good and the bad, and then release them. Holding onto them causes a build up of energy the body isn't designed to store. When you do this for a long period of time, the body either starts to break down, causing illness, or it leaks out in inappropriate outbursts or, in your case, as a violent explosion. Part of what I'll teach you, starting tonight, is how to allow those emotions to come up, to feel them fully and allow them to pass through you. It's quite a simple process, really."

"And my age, why is that a factor?"

"You're thirty-five. Women enter the beginning of their most powerful phase of their lives around forty. You are just on the cusp of that. It's sort of like entering puberty."

"You mean, this thing is only going to get worse."

Vivienne chuckled. "It's not something to fear, simply nature's design. All of us go through this change. It's just that women like you step into a much more powerful state of being than the rest of us."

"Women like me. There are others like me?"

"No, there is no one quite like you. Instead of elaborating, Vivienne removed the silver cuff from her left wrist and turned her forearm toward Lizzie. "Do you see anything?"

Lizzie leaned forward and peered at the distinctive tattoo, one she'd seen before. "It's a tattoo of two crescents with a circle in the middle."

"Gideon mentioned you could see his. As I said, there is no one quite like you."

"I'm sorry, I don't understand."

"This tattoo is a mark of initiation into a special group made up of individuals who dedicate their lives to the protection and nurturing of gifted women. These sacred symbols represent the Triple Goddess, and we are her champions. We are a secret society. When a new member receives this tattoo as their final induction into the order, a charm is placed in the very ink used so that no one but other members can see it. But you can. How do you suppose that is possible?"

"I don't know?"

"I don't know either. But I do know you are not a member of our order and no one within your circle of acquaintants is either. So the fact you can see something you are not supposed to see means you are unique among the women we have sworn to protect. And I've worked with hundreds of these special women over my career, so I would know."

"So this is your job? Working with women like me?"

"More like a calling than a job. Our society has existed as long as civilization has and we continue our sacred duty even in a day and age where magick and the powers of the feminine have largely been forgotten or dismissed as irrelevant."

"So Gideon belongs to your group too. It's not just for women?"

"No, our society is made up of both men and women. My husband was also a member. He crossed over five years ago," Vivienne said.

"I'm sorry for your loss."

"He was a good, kind man. I look forward to being reunited with him when my time comes. I was pleased when Gideon chose to become a guardian. He showed a natural talent for magick and, for a man, he has developed powers that are quite exceptional." Vivienne slipped her bracelet back on her wrist.

"For a man?"

"It's all about DNA. Magical abilities are expressed in the female chromosomes. Like most men, Gideon has a glimmer of natural magickal talent because all embryos start off female. The wash of testosterone in the womb waters down their powers. Men who practice white magic are never as strong as women and have to work long and hard to perfect what little abilities they do have. My son has a bit more than most. There are, however, men who wish to be as powerful as we are and they choose a different path. These warlocks gain their power by aligning themselves and feeding off dark and negative energies."

Lizzie shivered "So you're a witch?"

"In another time and place, I probably would've been labeled as such."

"This sounds so outlandish." Lizzie rubbed her brow as if this small gesture would make all the strangeness disappear. "I'm sitting here surrounded by Elementals, talking to you about magickal powers, Triple

Goddesses, and ancient societies as if we are talking about the weather. I don't know what is real anymore."

"Reality is subjective. There are many layers of existence. You've been to another one yourself very recently."

"About that. I know you told me it's called the *In Between* and it's a sort of dream plane."

"Yes."

"What did you mean that if I'd stayed there, I would've been trapped?"

"I was here when Gideon brought you to the hotel. When you didn't wake up, we'd thought we'd given you too much tranquilizer, but when I checked your energy, it became apparent your soul was barely attached to your body. Had you stepped through the cottage door, I'm afraid you would have severed the connection to your physical form."

"What would have happened then, to my body, I mean?"

"It would have expired," Vivienne said matter-of-factly.

Lizzie swallowed hard. "What exactly was that place with the cottage? Why did I end up in that particular location?"

"You didn't recognize it?"

"No."

"But you must. That cottage and those woods are a construct of your own memories or desires. On the dream plane, it is the dreamer that creates the environment."

"But I've never been to a place like that, nor have I ever imagined something like that, not even in my daydreams," she insisted.

"This is curious. What were you thinking at the moment before you went *In Between*? Do you remember?"

Lizzie thought back to the night of the fire. "I wanted to escape from what was happening. I know it doesn't sound rational because I had nowhere to go, but I just wanted to go home."

"Perhaps you've just blocked the memory of the cottage. May I?" Vivienne reached out to place her hand on her knee. "I just need to check something."

"Sure."

Keeping her hand on Lizzie's knee, she closed her eyes. A surge of energy flowed up Lizzie's leg at the moment of contact. She again felt love and warmth radiating from Vivienne and flowing up and into her whole being. Lizzie shut her eyes, immersing herself in the now familiar and comforting feel of Vivienne's energy.

Too soon, Vivienne pulled her hand away and the cocoon of good feelings went away with it. She could still feel the subtle loving energy Vivienne radiated, but she longed for the intense connection to come back.

"You definitely haven't repressed the memory and you're telling the truth about not knowing the location. Unless it's a place that you've been to or imagined, I'm afraid I don't have an answer."

"You can tell whether people are telling the truth just by touching them?" She was intimidated by the implications of such a talent.

"No, not quite like this. I can read people's subtle gestures and changes to their auras that indicate someone isn't being forthcoming, but not like with you. Because of our time in the *In Between*, you and I are now energetically connected. A bit of you has rubbed off on me and vice versa. It's a side effect of going after you and pulling you back."

As she pondered Vivienne's words, a truth emerged, whether from her own thoughts or from their linked energy she wasn't sure—this woman sitting before her could have died bringing her back from that place.

"You'd never done that before, have you? Gone to someone else's dream plane and brought them back. You could have just as easily been trapped there forever. You risked your life for me." Tears burned her eyes. She blinked to clear her vision.

"And I would do it again in a heartbeat."

"But why? You don't know me. I'm a complete stranger to you."

"Because you needed my help and you aren't a complete stranger. No one is. We are all related to one another because we all come from the same source. In helping you, I help us all. And isn't that the whole point of this fabulous ride we're on?"

"I don't know. I don't know about anything anymore. But I am grateful for what you did. I don't know how I'll ever repay you."

"Have the courage to be yourself. That would be repayment enough."

"I promise I will."

"So, do you have any other questions for me?"

"I do, a million of them, but right now my head feels too full. Could I ask them later when I've had some time to process what you've told me so far?"

"Yes, of course. We'll take this as fast or as slow as you want."

Lizzie relaxed her shoulders and sat back in her chair.

"Now, let's begin with the first lesson, shall we?"

Chapter Eighteen

For three hours, Vivienne worked with Lizzie, showing her how to slow her breathing, focus her energy to create a sense of inner calm, and keep herself grounded in the moment.

Some of the techniques Lizzie already knew from her time with Sister Collette. She just hadn't used them since she'd left the convent. This unexpected connection to her past brought up long forgotten memories and, with it, a poignant sadness of missing Sister Collette and her charmed and protected childhood.

When Vivienne sensed her grief rising to the surface, she used it to teach her how to let it come up into her consciousness, to give the emotion time to be felt, and to watch as if from a distance as the feelings and energy associated with it dispersed from her being.

The experience left Lizzie breathless and astonished when the sadness passed without any violent aftereffects. When she realized the feelings of loss were no longer inside her, she glanced at the Elementals. Their colors didn't intensify, but remained pastel-toned, their movements serene.

Even though she had slept for three days, after hours of intense practice, her energy and enthusiasm were flagging. Her bed called to her, but she didn't want to disappoint Vivienne. She bit down on the inside of her cheek to stifle a yawn.

"You're a quick study. I knew you'd be an excellent pupil."

Vivienne glanced at the alarm clock on the nightstand. It was a little after nine.

"I think that's enough for your first lesson. Besides, Madison's been here for an hour and, judging by what I'm sensing of her energy, I don't think I can hold her off any longer. She's eager to see how you're doing."

Lizzie suppressed another yawn. As tired as she was, she wanted to see Madison too. Vivienne replaced the chairs around the table and placed the crystals in the four corners of the room as Lizzie opened the bedroom door.

"Lizzie," Madison called out, rushing over to her, her arms held wide to embrace her. She crossed over the threshold into the bedroom before Lizzie could even take a step toward her.

This time, Lizzie didn't shy away from Madison's affection. She stepped into her waiting arms and wrapped her arms around her lithe frame. She held on tightly, relishing the warmth of the hug. It was Madison who finally stepped away, still holding Lizzie by the arms.

"Man, you scared us. Don't ever do that again." She tried to keep a stern look on her face, but she kept breaking into a smile.

"I promise I won't," she said sheepishly. Their previously formal relationship had slipped effortlessly into this new friendship, and Lizzie found she was happy by this unexpected turn of events.

She'd never had a girlfriend before and had always wondered why women put such a huge importance on their friendships. Looking into Madison's eyes, she finally understood.

If asked to define it, she probably couldn't put the sense of belonging into words. She just knew, when Madison rushed over to hug her, that to this other person, she mattered. The thought pleased her immensely.

Madison grabbed her hand and led her over to the bed. She plopped herself down on the edge, pulling Lizzie down next to her. Vivienne and Gideon joined them, Vivienne perching on the opposite side of the mattress. Gideon dragged over a chair, placing it close to Madison before taking a seat.

"How are you feeling?" Madison asked.

"Fine, a little tired, but other than that, I'm okay," she replied.

"Oh, I almost forgot. I brought you a few things." Madison sprang off the bed and disappeared into the other room. She returned moments later carrying a large shopping bag. She sat back down next to Lizzie, plunking the bag on the floor between her feet. "Gideon says you have to stay here for a while until it's safe, and I thought these might help pass the time." She dug into the bag and pulled out a handful of fashion magazines and a selection of tabloids.

She spread the glossy magazines on the bedspread as she continued to unload her treasures. Next came five paperback novels, which she handed over to Lizzie one at a time for inspection. They were all romance novels featuring damsels in tight bodices and men with exposed six-packs and bulging biceps. Lizzie ignored the pang of despair that tightened her chest. Dwelling on the loss of her beloved books wasn't going to bring them back.

She forced a smile. "This was very thoughtful," she murmured, placing the novel she had in her hand down with the rest of the reading material.

"And let's not forget the most important thing, a choice selection of Bernard Callebaut chocolates," she said, presenting Lizzie with a peach-colored box.

Although it was a small box, Lizzie knew the hand-crafted Belgium chocolates didn't come cheap. Madison probably easily shelled out twenty dollars for this treat. Opening the box, she broke the seal and peeled back the matching peach foil, exposing rows of tiny, glossy chocolates. She passed the box around.

While everyone was eating the chocolates, Lizzie slid off the bed, intent on retrieving her purse. She wanted to write Madison a check to cover her lost wages until the insurance came through. She was halfway to the door when Gideon jumped from his chair, blocking her way.

"Is there something I can get for you?"

"No, I was just going to get my purse from the other room."

"It's okay, I'll get it. You really shouldn't leave the protection of the Elementals." He zipped out of the room before she could say anything.

She returned to the bed and looked at the pile of magazines and books strewn across it. She appreciated Gideon's concern, but she didn't like being told what to do, or the claustrophobia that was sitting just on the edge of her nerves.

Moments later, Gideon returned, handing over her purse.

"How long do you think I have to stay in this room?" She glanced from Gideon to Vivienne.

Vivienne answered her. "At least a couple more days. There are still a few more tools I'd like to teach you, and then there is the question of who or what is tracking you."

"Who or what?"

It was Gideon's turn to step in. "Our seers have been working to trace the source since whatever it was found you in the cemetery. I don't know if you picked up on it, but the same presence was at the fire. Although it means it can locate you whenever your energy spikes, it was also a break for us. Every time it shows up, the seers try to get information on its location. It could be a very powerful warlock, one we've never encountered before, or...." He looked over at his mother.

"Sometimes a warlock can bind an energy force similar to an Elemental to do his bidding. The difference being that an Elemental would never cause another being harm while what a warlock gets his hands on is usually something much darker," Vivienne said.

"But what if these seers can't find out who's after me? What if it takes months? I can't stay here indefinitely." She stared at Vivienne. She knew she was hiding something from her. Using the techniques she'd just been taught, she silenced her own thoughts and focused on Vivienne's instead. She caught a snippet of words and a few jumbled images, but they weren't clear. She concentrated harder before feeling a painful jolt, something akin to a slap. A hard blank wall came down on Vivienne's thoughts.

"Please don't do that. We may be linked energetically, but it's not polite to snoop into another's thoughts uninvited," she said, her smile softening her reprimand.

"Sorry."

"We're not trying to deceive you or keep anything from you. It's just that we really don't know how long it's going to take. It's unusual for us to be taken by surprise like this. We normally know who the players are."

"That's not all, is it? If there is someone out there that wants to hurt me, I have a right to know everything."

Vivienne sighed. "Under normal circumstances, if one of our charges needed to get away from an abusive situation or just needed a nurturing place surrounded by people like themselves to learn about their powers, they would be taken to a safe house. We have them all over the world. We asked for clearance to take you to one and we were denied. So for right now, until we can figure out a better solution, this room is the best option we have."

"Oh," Lizzie said.

"I know it sounds harsh, but our society has to protect all of the women and girls who seek refuge with us. As special as you are, the Order can't open themselves to an attack from an aggressor we still know nothing about. At this time, they can't risk it. It's too dangerous. Instead, we have several of our best guardians on surveillance around the building.

"So, even here, with the Elementals and guardians protecting me, I'm not completely safe."

"No, I'm afraid not."

Up until that moment, the seriousness of her current situation hadn't sunk in. She had just bobbed along on the strange currents of the past few hours because if she stopped to think about whatever was stalking her, she'd dive under the bedcovers and not come out until it was over. Knowing some stranger wanted to hurt her and that Vivienne's own group, whose mission was to protect people like her, couldn't help sent a bolt of terror through her.

The horribly familiar sensation of an impending panic attack made her heart race. She started to hyperventilate, all of Vivienne's earlier teachings forgotten.

In a flash of movement, Vivienne's hands were on her shoulders. Her soothing presence wrapped around her, momentarily distracting her from the intense wave of fear racing toward her.

"Lizzie, look at me," she ordered. "Remember what I taught you. Breathe from your core. It's okay to feel scared, just let it come up, don't fight it."

"Okay," she stuttered, trying her best to follow Vivienne's instructions.

"That's good. Keep breathing. There now, better?" She cupped Lizzie's chin in her hand and lifted her face so she was forced to look her in the eyes.

"Better." She was still shaking, but the intense fear and the accompanying sensation of being out of control had been reduced to a dull throb at the base of her skull. She pushed herself further onto the bed until her back rested against the upholstered headboard and she pulled a pillow onto her lap. "Sorry, I'm just a little overwhelmed by all this," she said looking at the three people ringed around her. She turned to face Madison, trying to keep the tremor out of her voice. "I don't want you here. I couldn't live with myself if something happened to you because of me. I can't thank you enough for all that you've done for me, but please go home."

"No, I made a promise to Vivienne and I plan on keeping it. Besides, you're not the boss of me." She slid across the bed, moving closer to Lizzie.

She ignored Madison's attempt at humor. She would not be dissuaded. "Please, I really want you to be as far away from me as possible. Didn't you hear what Vivienne just said? This is dangerous."

"Sorry, you're stuck with me. This is my choice and I know exactly what I'm getting myself into. I've been talking with Gideon while you were sleeping and I know the score. I'm thinking about joining the Order. In fact, I've an interview with them on Monday."

"You're what? Gideon, you can't possibly let her make such a rash decision." She didn't give him a chance to reply. "Madison, I can only imagine that the past few days have been a dramatic change from working in the flower shop, but this isn't a game or a plot in one of your romance novels. You could get hurt or worse."

"I'm not a child and I'm not stupid," she said, crossing her arms over her chest. "I know this isn't some kind of game. I want my life to mean something. I need to be more than a shop girl.

Don't get me wrong, I've really liked working for you, but even if you decide to rebuild Enchanted Garden, I don't think I'll be coming back to work for you. It's not enough for me now. When Vivienne asked me to help get you back, for the first time, I felt I was part of something bigger than myself."

"She knows nothing about what you do," Lizzie pleaded with Gideon. "She isn't prepared to deal with all this." She gestured to the Elementals, who had remained silent and shifting through the whole exchange.

"You're not listening. I've talked to Gideon. I know what he does, how the Order works. I realize I have to go through interviews and a screening process, plus years of training before I'll be able to do what he does, but I've finally found what I've been waiting for my whole life. This is it. I feel like it's what I'm supposed to be doing. I know it doesn't make sense to you, that it's not rational, but look around you, Lizzie. Rationality isn't playing a big part in what's happening to us right now."

"So, you've made up your mind then?" Lizzie wouldn't admit it, but she understood too well exactly what she meant by wanting to belong, about feeling lost in a life that didn't quite fit.

"Yes, I have. Instead of being afraid for me, be happy. It would mean a lot to me if I had your blessing and support."

Lizzie placed her hand on top of Madison's. "I still wish you wouldn't be involved with me, but if you want my support, you have it."

"Thanks." Madison leaned over and pecked her on the cheek. Bouncing on the bed like a child on Christmas morning, she said, "We need to celebrate instead of cowering in the corner. None of us have been harmed, we're here together, and whatever badass is trying to get to you, he hasn't been able to. I'm not going to be scared. Isn't that what warlocks and dark forces want us to do? I, for one, am not going to give them the satisfaction."

"You're quite right. Fear only breeds more fear. And we can't have that," Vivienne said from her place on the bed.

"Champagne would be just the thing, and it would go great with the chocolates. I think I saw a bottle in the mini bar." She jumped off the bed and went in search of a bottle of bubbly.

"I'll go hunt up some glasses," Gideon said, following Madison into the other room.

"Do you really think Madison joining you is such a good idea?" Lizzie asked Vivienne when they were alone.

"What I think is irrelevant. It's not my place to interfere in her journey. But I do think she'll be an excellent guardian, and we'd be honored to call her one of our own."

"But she's too young. She could get hurt."

"There isn't an age limit on fulfilling your destiny. And you of all people should understand that life doesn't come with guarantees; heartbreak and loss are part of the balance of things."

"Well, I think it's about time the balance shifted in our favor."

The sound of clinking glasses announced Gideon and Madison's return moments before they stepped back into the room. Gideon carried four champagne flutes upside down by their bases, their delicate stems threaded through his fingers. Madison held a split of champagne under her arm, her step light and carefree.

Looking at the two of them, Vivienne smiled. "I think they already have."

Chapter Nineteen

A few days of seclusion in her hotel room turned into a couple of weeks. Lizzie's days had fallen into a routine of sharing breakfast in her room with her three new friends, learning her lessons with Vivienne, a quick break for lunch, then back to her lessons until dinner time.

Vivienne and she would spend the last few hours of the day reviewing what she'd learned and then, exhausted, Lizzie would climb into bed only to turn around and do it all again the next day.

Just like her days, her nights took on a repetitiveness. Every night, the same dream or a version of it plagued her sleep. She would wake up with the image of the grey stone cottage still vivid in her memory. She had even given it a name—Rose Cottage. She never went through the door of Rose Cottage, always waking up just as her hand curled around the doorknob. All day, a sense of longing dogged her thoughts. It was driving her to distraction.

When she told Vivienne about the dream, she was surprised by the puzzled look she gave her. She came to rely on Vivienne as her source of knowledge about what was happening in her life, and she found it disconcerting when she discovered there were things even Vivienne didn't know.

Vivienne's only suggestion was that it could be a temporary side effect of the time Lizzie spent on the dream plane and that, in time, the dream's frequency would lessen.

On a more practical note, Lizzie wondered how she was supposed to stay hidden and confined to her hotel bedroom when it would arouse suspicion if she didn't allow the maids access to change out the linens and clean. And how would they explain to the cleaning staff the existence of the swirling colorful mists of the Elementals? Her questions were answered one day when a knock at her door interrupted her lesson with Vivienne.

Without concern, Vivienne opened the door and invited the maid into the room. To Lizzie's astonishment, the maid didn't show any reaction to the current ethereal state of her bedchamber and addressed Vivienne by name. Lizzie didn't need to see the maid's wrist to know there would be a tattoo of the triple goddess inked there.

Uncomfortable with a guardian cleaning up after her, Lizzie relieved the maid of the clean linens and the caddy full of cleaning supplies and fresh rags. After collecting the used towels from the bathroom and stripping the bed herself, she handed over the soiled linens to the woman.

Vivienne had mentioned she was being protected by extra guardians, but she had no idea to what extent the Order was able to move their people into the hotel with such ease.

Other than the maid's regular visits, her three companions had become her conduit to the outside world. Madison continued to bring her magazines and paperbacks; Gideon supplied her with the daily newspapers and an iPod loaded with all of her favorite music.

Madison took charge of getting in touch with Enchanted Garden's regular clients to let them know about the fire, and through emails and a notice in the paper, all of Lizzie's customers knew about her fate.

Her trio of friends made sure that all her needs were met, and if she wanted something, all she needed to do was ask and either Gideon or Madison would bring it to her. She knew her current situation was for her protection, but her confinement was beginning to chafe. She'd never wanted adventure in her life, never had a desire to travel and see the world, but finding herself living her days out in a twenty-by-twenty room felt like a prison. She couldn't even open a window to let in fresh air.

To make matters worse, she had called her insurance agent just days after the fire, and he informed her that the Fire Marshall was still investigating the cause of the fire. She'd immediately called the Fire Marshall demanding answers. He'd been evasive when she pressed for information and never came right out and said the word "arson," but the implication hung in the air during their conversation.

Despite Vivienne's assertion she shouldn't push her feelings down, Lizzie concealed her growing agitation. It only flared up once when she had asked if it was possible to venture out just for a little while to check on the fire damage to her store. She had snapped at Gideon when he told her no even after she pushed the point.

The day after she'd lashed out at Gideon, she fumbled over her lessons with Vivienne and finally asked for a break. Hiding in the bathroom for half an hour, she cried, stifling her sobs of frustration in a towel she stuffed in her mouth.

It was true what she had said earlier, about not caring about the building. She didn't. But she did care about her business. She'd assumed the Fire Marshall would have determined that faulty wiring or some other accident of fate was the cause. Without the Fire Marshall's report, she couldn't get the building released to start rebuilding her shop and start her life again. Without her flowers and her customers, what did she have left in her life?

After three days of Lizzie's distracted moodiness, a compromise was finally reached. Madison and Gideon had gone to the site with a promise to report back every detail. Although they weren't allowed to cross the red fire department tape cordoning off the entrance, they took pictures of the store using Madison's cell phone.

Back at the hotel, Lizzie had scrolled through the tiny photos, shocked at the damage to her shop. It was hard to tell from the angles of the photos, but it looked like the roof was completely gone, a fact Madison confirmed. At least someone had had the presence of mind to nail plywood over the shattered plate glass window, but it would do nothing to stop the damage from the snow coming in from above.

She had held out a small ray of hope that to get her store open, she would just have to restore the gutted interior. Madison's photos showed it was going to take a major reconstruction if she had any chance of seeing herself surrounded by her flowers again. Without a word, she had handed Madison back her phone. She hadn't asked to leave the room since.

Instead, she threw herself into her new training. Vivienne put her through her paces, every day for eight hours, pushing her when she felt it was necessary and giving her words of encouragement when she sensed Lizzie's confidence flagging.

On the fourteenth day of her seclusion, Vivienne didn't have to employ either one to get Lizzie to give the lesson her full participation. When Vivienne arrived, she announced a different type of exercise.

"I have a theory about why we haven't picked up so much as a ripple from our enemy since the fire. It's been fourteen days and not a glimmer."

"I thought it was because of the Elementals."

"No, they can't mask who you are, they can only convert and contain your excess energy when it gets out of control. They would also be able to alert us as soon as there was an attempt from the Presence to locate you, kind of like an early warning system. Whoever is tracking you possesses a great deal of skill and power themselves and would more than likely know certain spells that could break through the energy field of the Elementals to pick up on where you are. They'd only get a faint hit, but I'm guessing that would be enough."

"So why haven't they?"

"It's because you went *In Between*."

"And when you came and got me, a little of each of us rubbed off on the other."

"Yes, you see where I'm going with this."

"Of course they can't track me because my energy signature is different now. It contains a bit of you and they'd have no way of knowing this."

"Exactly."

"So what are you planning?"

"I think it's time to change positions in the game of cat and mouse. Instead of sitting around waiting for them to make the next move, we go after them. And you shall become the cat."

"Me? But you're much more skilled than I am. Wouldn't it make more sense for you to try?"

"No, because you've made intimate contact with it before, not me. You know exactly what the Presence feels like and can detect it faster than I would be able to. It might only be a few seconds, mind you, but that would give us an advantage, and we need to capitalize on even the smallest thing that's in our favor."

"I'm not sure I can do it," Lizzie said, tugging nervously on the hem of her sweater.

Vivienne smiled. "I'll teach you everything you need to know and there will be others from the Order helping us. Are you willing to give it a try?"

"Yes, I'm sick of hiding, waiting for something to happen. But you have to promise me that if anything goes wrong, your first priority is to get Madison out of here."

"You have my solemn vow."

It took three more days before Vivienne was satisfied Lizzie could handle what was expected of her. At midnight, the three of them bundled up and headed to the rooftop of the hotel. Lizzie didn't ask how they managed to get access to the roof, but had stopped being surprised about what the Order could do.

Even though she knew there would be other guardians waiting for them, along with a handful of seers, it still astounded her when she stepped out into the night and saw what had to be over two hundred men and women ringed around the perimeter of the roof.

Gideon and Vivienne proceeded ahead of her and she hesitated at the sight of all the people waiting silently for her to do something she wasn't sure she was capable of pulling off. She had practiced the steps of what she had to do with Vivienne, but the not the actual doing. She had one shot to get it right.

Beads of perspiration appeared on her brow despite the cold night air. She reached out her hand and felt the warmth of Madison's slim fingers wrap around hers.

The guardians nodded as she passed by them and she let out a start when she walked past Frank, the concierge of the hotel. He touched his fingertips to the stylish fedora perched at a rakish angle in acknowledgment. Lizzie smiled in return.

Together, Madison and Lizzie walked past a maze of metal airshafts and heating and cooling stacks, stopping in the center of the roof where a handful of seers stood in a circle.

The air was still, but Lizzie could smell a hint of ozone lingering in the crisp night. Snow was probably only hours away from sprinkling the sky.

Reluctantly, she let go of the safety of Madison's hand, taking her place in the center of the circle of women. The seers ranged in age from their early twenties to their sixties. A grey-haired woman, who looked like she could be someone's kindly grandmother, spoke to her.

"You'll be fine, my dear. Not to worry."

Lizzie nodded, unable to find her voice.

Gideon and Vivienne stood just outside the circle of seers in Lizzie's direct line of sight.

"Whenever you're ready. Take your time," Vivienne said.

Lizzie unclenched her hands and let them fall to her sides. She took three deep, slow breaths, just as she had practiced. She imagined herself as pure energy—bright, powerful, and eternal. As she felt her field of being expand beyond her physical self, she recalled the feeling of the Presence she had first encountered in the ER waiting room and then later at the cemetery and the fire.

She focused on the how it felt, the dark, cloying sensation as if being surround by sticky tar. She turned her attention to what Vivienne referred to as her third eye, the area just between her eyes. She concentrated her energy there, letting it build, then sent it out into the night like a powerful search light. She imagined it soaring out into the sky, up past the low clouds that obliterated the stars.

Her consciousness rose with it, higher and higher. She imagined her energy spreading out and widening in ever-expanding circles.

The energy fields of every living thing buffeted and surrounded her, but none was the one she was searching for. She kept pushing her energy further out, but she felt nothing of the Presence, not even a flicker of recognition. A thin slice of fear penetrated her concentration and, for a brief second, her focus wavered, causing a ripple in her energy.

She refocused on seeking the Presence. Farther and farther her energy went out, and still nothing. She remained in that expanded state, probing the swirling ether for the one energy signature that was her goal. It remained elusive.

Her strength began to flag. Doubt and fear crept in as she weakened. She pushed on, trying to keep her energy from slipping back to where she stood on the roof.

Then she felt it. One minute nothing, the next it was almost upon her. Startled, she contracted her energy away from the pulsing energy. The air around her became heavy, and although she knew her physical body was safe back on the roof surrounded in the protective circle of the seers, the sensation of not being able to breathe was overwhelming.

All the instructions Vivienne had given her flew from her thoughts. Only the throbbing prickling of fear remained in her focus.

"I can't do this. I can't," she screamed into the void. Whether it was just thoughts in her head or actual words, she couldn't tell. She scrambled to pull her energy back to the rooftop. In that moment, she didn't think about all the people down below counting on her, she didn't think about the other women who the Order protected. Her only thought was to run, to get as far away from the Presence as possible.

One moment Lizzie was part of the swirling mists of energy, and the next she was on her hands and knees back on the rooftop. When she heard Vivienne's voice calling out to her, despair filled her heart. She had failed.

Lizzie blinked to focus her vision. It was snowing. Staring at her hands, she watched the tiny delicate flakes land on her skin and melt into pinpricks of water.

She couldn't look into faces of the people she'd let down. She wanted to be back in her hotel room away from everyone.

Gideon stepped through the circle of silent seers and gathered her into his arms. Her face and hands were numb from the cold. She pressed her forehead against his chest.

"Was it enough?" she asked, looking up at him. "Did the seers find out who it is?"

The look on Gideon's face told her everything. "No, I don't think so," he whispered.

They were joined by Vivienne and Madison as they filed across the roof and into the warmth of the hotel. Lizzie held back her tears of frustration until she was safely back in her bedroom, the door secured behind her. No one tried to follow her as she shut the door.

She kicked off her boots, but left her coat on. She curled up on top of the duvet cover, hiding her tear-stained face in her pillow.

Her friends, waiting in the other room, and all the people on the roof, had risked their lives to protect her, and the one thing she could have done to help them she had not only failed at, but miserably so.

Vivienne and Gideon had been misguided to put their faith in her. She had let her fear enter into the process and her weakness had ruined everything. She wasn't powerful, she wasn't unique. She was stupid, useless. She'd screwed up. And now her fear had cost the Order dearly.

Chapter Twenty

The next day at the breakfast table, Lizzie picked at her food, moving it around on her plate. Vivienne was absent from their morning ritual as she had been called to the Motherhouse to give them a full report on the results of last night. The failure of last night.

Madison made up for Vivienne's absence by chattering on about her apprenticeship with the Order. Her interview with the Order's selection committee had been several weeks ago and her first day of her new career would start this very afternoon.

She kept asking Gideon questions about the Order and trying to engage Lizzie in the conversation, but Lizzie couldn't get her words past her clenched teeth.

Madison's overly bright manner and the gentle compassion she saw in Gideon's eyes made her want to push both of them out the door and bolt it so she could be alone. It would have been far better if they had told her they were disappointed in her or even if they had acknowledged the utter waste of time the whole fiasco had been. No one brought up last night and that made Lizzie feel even worse.

Breakfast finally ended. Madison offered to spend time with her before she headed off to the Motherhouse, but Lizzie wanted to be alone, or as alone as she could be with her guardian and friend hanging out in the next room. She feigned lingering exhaustion from last night's late hour and said she needed to lie down.

Madison cleared the table and Gideon wheeled the breakfast trolley out of the room. Alone at last, Lizzie crawled back into bed, pulling the duvet up under her chin. She lay on her back and stared unseeing at the undulating luminous mists.

She felt hollowed out and worse than she had when she had been first brought back from the *In Between*. She couldn't keep the image of the stone cottage and how it felt to be there out of her thoughts. After all that had happened, the pull to be in that place where everything was blissfully uneventful was strong. The only thing keeping her from going back there was the promise she'd made to Vivienne.

Having spent so many hours with Vivienne, she had developed a deep respect and admiration for her. Failing her hurt the most. She couldn't go *In Between* because she knew Vivienne would go after her and try to bring her back again.

But she desperately wanted out. She wanted her own space and her own life back.

Even though she had come close to the Dark Presence during the attempt on the roof, Gideon had said the seers hadn't picked up anything, and there was no reciprocal move on its part to follow her back. It seemed to her she was still untraceable. If that was the case, she saw no reason why she needed to be hidden away wasting everyone's time. Whatever small danger might remain, it wasn't enough to make her want to stay trapped any longer.

Although she had shown everyone she wasn't as powerful or talented as they thought she was, she had proven she didn't need to fear her emotions triggering her abilities to explode. She knew how to control them now. Even now, as upset as she was with herself, channeling her powers had become second nature to her, like breathing. She was no longer a danger to those around her.

Unlike Madison, she felt no pull or calling to immerse herself any further into Gideon and Vivienne's world.

She wanted a routine and mundane life among people who had never heard of the Order or believed in powers, or Elementals, or magick. She longed to be surrounded by her flowers and knowing the most pressing thing she had to do in her life was to create bouquets and arrangements.

It was late afternoon when Vivienne finally knocked on her door, and by then, Lizzie was firm in her resolve to start her life again without the involvement of the Order.

She opened the door and invited Vivienne in. Her mentor was wearing a black cashmere sweater and wool dress pants. Around her graceful neck she wore a Hermés scarf in burnt orange and gold tied in a crisp knot. She carried a Birken bag in the same autumn shade as the scarf. Vivienne gave her a warm hug and, when she looked into her eyes, Lizzie couldn't hold her gaze.

"Sorry I wasn't here this morning. I can only stay for a few hours. There are still some things I need to attend to back at the Motherhouse."

"That's okay. I really needed to rest." Lizzie wandered over to the bed and nervously ran her hands over the duvet, smoothing out the wrinkles. "How did it go with the director?"

"As good as I'd hoped. Along with updating our attempt to contact the Presence last night, I also needed to check in with a few of our apprentices."

Lizzie continued to run her hands over the silky cotton bedcover. "Are there going to be consequences because of what I did? Or I guess I should say because of what I didn't do." She stopped fussing with the bedspread and sank down on the corner of the bed. She stared at her hands in her lap, not sure she wanted to hear Vivienne's answer.

"If you're concerned our lack of progress last night in some way means I'm in hot water with the director, you've misunderstood me."

Vivienne's use of the word *our* made Lizzie's stomach lurch. That she was willing to take the blame for what happened when the failure rested on her shoulders alone made her feel worse.

"The director isn't upset, nor does she blame anyone for not being able to identify the source of the Dark Presence," Vivienne continued. "It just presents us with a question of what to do next. That's what we were discussing. Besides, I do have some good news. The seers did manage to pull just a brief flash from your contact with it. So we are further ahead at tracking it down than we were even a day ago."

Lizzie shifted her gaze from her hands; a tiny flutter of hope gave her courage to meet Vivienne's eyes. "They know where it originates from?"

"We know for certain it's somewhere in North America."

"But there are hundreds of millions of people living on the continent. It doesn't seem to be all that useful." She was crestfallen.

"It's a small victory, I'll give you that, but a victory nonetheless. We've at least narrowed it down to one area of the world. Also, we're pretty sure you still managed to slip under its radar. We've a place to start looking and you're safe. To me, that's significant progress."

"So what now?"

"The director and the elders, including myself, haven't yet agreed on what the best course of action should be. We may just have the seers continue to monitor any unusual energies, or we might try another attempt at having you connect with the darkness directly. But only if you choose to. Of course, we wouldn't try such a thing until you and I have worked a little more at fine tuning your powers. If we do this again, it will be much more dangerous for you as we've lost the element of surprise. You'll probably need to make closer contact, and it may be able to follow you back, making you open and vulnerable again."

And you too, now that our energy is linked, Lizzie thought. Vivienne's words only made her more determined to follow her new course of action.

"But that is in the future and no need to worry about it for now," Vivienne said. "In the meantime, I have some more good news. After a few more days to confirm the threat of danger to you is minimal, you can leave the hotel and move into one of our safe houses. I can assure you they're much more spacious than your current accommodations."

"I can leave the hotel? Leave this room?"

"Yes, I'll give you a list of safe houses and you can choose which one you want to go to. I imagine, after having all of us in your back pocket for over a month, you must want to have some personal space back. Gideon will still be your guardian, as you will always represent a threat to others who practice dark magick, so for your own safety, you still need protection. And you and I will continue with your lessons."

"Do I have a say in my future?" Lizzie's earlier resolve wavered. It sounded so safe, to be taken care of, to stay cloistered.

"Of course you do, you are not our prisoner. You can do what you like."

"Then I'd like to go it alone." Her mouth went dry, her tongue felt fat and clumsy. "I don't want to continue with our lessons," she blurted out. "I don't want to live in a safe house either."

"Oh."

Lizzie saw the lightning of anger flash across Vivienne's face before her features returned to their normal calm semblance. She felt it too. A quick shiver of heat in the middle of her chest and then it was gone.

"I've been thinking a lot about what it is I want and if, as you say, I have a right to choose, then I choose for my life to go back to being normal. I miss my shop, my flowers." Her throat burned and she swallowed hard around the lump she felt there. "I just don't have what it takes to be a part of your world. I'm not like Madison. I don't feel any calling to belong to the Order. Please don't be disappointed in me," she whispered.

Vivienne opened her mouth to speak, but Lizzie held up her hand to stop her.

"Don't deny it. I can feel it in you. As much as I hate letting you down, it still doesn't change the fact I want my life to go back to the way it was."

Vivienne raised her eyebrow. Sitting down next to Lizzie, she balanced her purse on her knees. She placed her cool hand on top of Lizzie's. It was soothing on Lizzie's hot skin.

"Yes, I'm a bit disappointed, but only because you show such great talent. You are exceptional, and I looked forward to seeing you step fully into you power. But if you feel your truth lies in finding 'normal, then I wish you all the best."

"Thank you for understanding." Relief flooded through her, making her legs feel weak. She was grateful she was sitting down.

Vivienne spoke softly. "Living on your own makes you more vulnerable. I'd ask that you just consider keeping Gideon as your guardian. He'll keep his distance so you won't even know he's there, but he'll keep you safe."

"I'll agree to keep Gideon." Blood rushed to her face, burning her cheeks. "As my guardian. And I'd like to stay in touch with both you and Madison. As friends."

Vivienne squeezed Lizzie's hand, then opened up the heavy metal clasp on her purse. "If you change your mind and decide what you're seeking isn't back among the way things used to be, I'd be happy to resume our work." She pulled out a slim silver case from her bag. Plucking a business card from the case, she handed it to Lizzie. "But for now, as you say, friends we shall be."

The card was a heavy cream stock with a fine linen finish. The only words printed on it were Vivienne's first name and a phone number.

"Here's my cell number. Call me anytime day or night, even if all you want from me is to talk."

Lizzie placed the card carefully on the nightstand. "That means a lot to me."

"Well, you are very dear to me, and not just as a student or a woman who is unique among our group."

Lizzie beamed her a smile. "Would you like to stay for tea?"

"I would love to."

While Vivienne stored her bag, Lizzie picked up the phone to order tea, a selection of sandwiches and a tray of *petits fours*.

She didn't have to consult the room service menu. She had been staying at the hotel so long that she had the menu memorized. She was going to order enough for all four of them, but Vivienne reminded her that Gideon and Madison were at the Motherhouse for Madison's orientation and wouldn't be back until much later. In her preoccupation with breaking her news to Vivienne, she'd completely forgotten Madison's big day.

"I haven't told Gideon or Madison of my decision. Would you mind if we kept it to ourselves for now?"

"Of course," Vivienne said, pulling out a chair at the small table.

Lizzie didn't relish telling them her plans, but she wouldn't be dissuaded even if it meant disappointing the two other people in her life she cared deeply about.

Chapter Twenty-One

She had intended to tell both Gideon and Madison about her plans for the future over dinner. Like ripping off a bandage, she wanted to do it quickly, deal with their disappointment and disapproval at the same time and then move forward. But she wasn't to get her way.

When Gideon arrived to take his turn watching over her, he'd come alone, carrying a stack of books with antique-looking leather covers.

Coming into her room to say hello, he told her Madison wouldn't be joining them for dinner. She and a couple of the new apprentices of the Order wanted to go out for drinks to celebrate their first day before their training started in earnest.

During dinner, she picked at her food, waiting for Gideon to finish the strawberry shortcake he'd ordered for dessert before she broached the subject, but he beat her to it.

"What's up? You've been somewhere else all through dinner. Got something on your mind?" he asked, putting down his fork.

"I've made a decision about my future. I've already told Vivienne, and I'll let Madison know when she gets here."

"So, are you going to let me in on it?" A playful smile curled the corners of his mouth.

"I'm not moving to a safe house. I want to reopen my shop and be what I was before."

His smile faded. "You realize you're still in danger? If not from the Dark Presence, then from others who would be threatened by your power."

"I know, but I'm willing to take that risk. I want my old life back."

He looked down at his half-eaten dessert then slowly pushed the plate to the side of the table. "So, where does that leave us?" His dark eyes searched her face.

"Us?" Her heart skipped a beat.

"Me, as your guardian. Because of who you are, what you are, you need to be protected, watched over in case anything happens."

"Yes, I know. Vivienne told me you'd continue on as my guardian if that's what I wanted. And I do, Gideon. To know you are still watching out for me means a great deal to me." On an impulse, she reached out and took his hand in hers.

"And I will. For as long as you want, I shall watch over you. You are very special, you know that, don't you?" he said, staring at their joined hands.

"You and Vivienne keep saying that, but I don't know what that means. My powers don't make me feel special, only strange and afraid. Even before the fire, before Ian's death, I've been afraid of what I am." She withdrew her hand from his and clasped it with her other in her lap. "I'm tired of feeling this way. As soon as Vivienne says I can leave the hotel room, I'm going to start my life anew and never use my powers again. All I want is a normal life."

"I hope you find what you're looking for in that kind of life. I also hope in time you will also embrace the uniqueness of who you are." There was a sadness in his eyes that hadn't been there before. "Now, if you'll excuse me, I have some pressing research the director requested." He stood up and pushed in his chair.

He left her at the table and settled on the couch in the other room. Lizzie could hear him leafing through the books he'd left on the coffee table as she stared down at her untouched food.

It was after nine that evening before she had the chance to talk to Madison. They exchanged hugs and Lizzie congratulated her on her first day as an apprentice before settling into their nightly routine. They were both sitting cross-legged on the bed, drinking hot chocolate, and flipping through the latest pile of gossip and fashion magazines Madison had brought for Lizzie.

"So, tell me more about how it went at the Order this afternoon. Gideon said it went well," she said, putting aside the copy of *Vogue* she was looking at.

"Oh. Lizzie, it was so much fun. I mean, it's overwhelming, all the things I have to learn. It's kinda like being back in high school except I'll be learning things that really interest me, not sitting in some stupid math class or memorizing dates for history. There are ten of us, and some of them are my age but some of them are a lot older, closer to your age."

"I'm sorry, dearie, I didn't quite catch that last bit. I must've turned off my hearing aid," she croaked, cupping her hand to her ear.

"You know what I mean," Madison laughed, swatting Lizzie playfully on the arm with a nearby magazine. "Oh, before I forget. You can have this back. Turns out I don't need it." She pulled out the check Lizzie had written her from her jeans' pocket and held it out to her. "No, take it. I really don't need it," she said. "The Order is such a way cool place. Not only do they train us, but they pay for all our living expenses and they have a comprehensive medical and dental plan."

Lizzie took the check from her friend and placed it on the nightstand.

"Anyway, Vivienne told me you'd be able to move out of the hotel soon. If you picked a safe house near the Motherhouse, we could see each other as often as you want. We could arrange to have lunch together just like we do here."

"I'm not moving to a safe house."

"What?"

"I've decided to focus on the things that are important to me—rebuilding my flower shop, figuring out where to live, that sort of thing."

"But you have to be a part of the Order. Vivienne said you were exceptional. You can't possibly turn your back on who you are. It's where you are supposed to be."

She didn't need to be energetically linked to Madison to see the disappointment in her eyes. "But that's not who I am. Don't you see? I'm just Lizzie Bennet, floral arranger and shop owner. I don't want to be anything more. I am happy for you that you've found your place in life, but being a part of that world isn't mine." As soon as she spoke the words, a vision of the little stone cottage flashed before her eyes. She shook her head to dislodge the picture from her mind.

"Does Gideon know about your decision?"

"Yes, I told him over dinner."

"And what did he say?"

"That he understood my choice. He'll still be my guardian, and I want to see you and Vivienne as often as possible."

"I'd like that too. Are you sure I can't persuade you to change your mind?"

"No, my mind is made up."

"I don't have to like it, but I guess I'll have to accept it. So, when can you start rebuilding the shop? Did the Fire Marshall file his report? Do we know what caused the fire?"

"No, I haven't heard anything and I think he's avoiding me. Every time I call his office, his receptionist keeps telling me he's not available and there is no one else in the office who is willing to answer my questions. Something's up."

"Something or someone by the name of Penelope."

Lizzie nodded. "Yes, I'm afraid it does have her vindictiveness written all over it."

"So, what are you going to do? You just can't let her stall the Fire Marshall. That's illegal. It's not right."

"No, it's not, but as far as I can see, there's nothing I can do but wait it out. Penelope can't delay it forever."

"I bet if we asked Vivienne and Gideon, they probably could help. The Order have people everywhere. They probably know someone who could pull some strings and get this thing done. Or better yet, we could ask Vivienne to cast some wicked-ass spell on that bitch. Maybe turn her into a toad or a snake or something."

"As tempting as that idea is, I'd rather not ask the Order to step in. After all they've done for me, I couldn't possibly ask them for help. And as appropriate as it would be to have Penelope spend the rest of her life crawling around on her belly eating small rodents, I can't stoop to her level. It would make me like her, and I won't go there."

"I hate when you're right, but come on, not even a little spell, maybe make her hair fall out or her skin turn blue?"

"No, not even blue skin."

"Fine. So, where are you going to live?" Madison asked, changing the subject.

"That's something I need to get started on right away. It needs to be close to the shop. An apartment or condo, I think would suit. I guess I should get in touch with a realtor tomorrow."

"Why not start right now? It is the twenty-first century, Lizzie. You have high-speed in the hotel and your laptop is sitting in the other room. No need to wait for a realtor."

Madison scooted off the bed and out the door before she could even reply. As she watched Madison glide out of the room with steps light with excitement, she felt a twinge of sadness.

Although she meant what she said about being Madison's friend and staying in touch, she knew better. Once Madison was fully immersed in her new life and given a charge to watch over, her days and life would be filled. There would be no time for people from her old life. She could see that even now. She would have to enjoy the time she had left, however short-lived it would be.

"Let's find you a place," Madison said, holding up the laptop. She motioned for Lizzie to make room on the bed, and settled down next to her.

She flipped open the laptop and powered it up. "So I know the area you want, what about price and amenities?"

"I could probably go as high as three-fifty, and I really don't need anything more than a one-bedroom and a bath."

"Okay, let's see what we got," Madison replied as she typed in the requirements into the MLS website.

Lizzie found she was holding her breath as she waited for the search results to come up. Now that she was actually doing something to regain control of her life, she felt the lightness of excitement fizz through her.

"Oh."

"Oh, what?" Lizzie's excitement disappeared as she looked at the screen. "There are only three places available?"

"Yeah, I guess it's a seller's market right now. How about this one, it's listed for two hundred and fifty thousand, but it's a studio." Madison pulled up the particulars of the unit.

Lizzie peered at the pictures on the laptop. One was of the front of the building and the other one was of the suite. She felt the edges of disappointment creeping in. The building looked like a concrete bunker, the faded blue awning over the entrance tattered and frayed at the edges. The unit for sale didn't look any better. It was painted an acid yellow, the carpet a dirty beige. The current owner had the four-hundred-square-foot place crammed full of stereo equipment, a bookcase made of cinder blocks and boards, and a large bed with a velour bedspread with the image of a wolf in the center. A sagging Canadian flag hung limply across the one small window.

"Euw. That's gross. You are not living there. I don't care how close it is to work. And not for that price."

"Show me the next one."

"Right." Madison clicked on the next listing.

It was a one-bedroom just outside the area that Lizzie wanted, although the price wasn't much lower than the first one. She asked Madison to click on the details.

The interior of the apartment was a vision of pink. Dusty rose carpet, wallpaper with large pink cabbage roses exploded on the walls, pink countertops in the galley kitchen and bathroom, even the bathtub and toilet were pink.

"You can just smell the old lady smell from here. I bet her favorite perfume was rose water." She scrolled down the page. "Look, it's an estate sale. I wonder if she died in her apartment."

"Madison!"

"Sorry."

"Why don't we look at the last one?"

She obliged Lizzie and clicked on the last entry from the search. "This one's in your price range and just a few blocks from the shop. I have a good feeling about this one. It's listed as a heritage building. I bet it will have hardwood floors, plaster moldings, and lots character," Madison said as they waited for the picture to download.

They stared silently as the images of the Lizzie's old apartment appeared on the screen. All the furniture had been removed, and the empty spaces made the apartment look larger than it actually was.

Madison clicked on to the MLS homepage without waiting for Lizzie to say anything. "Why don't we expand the search?" she asked, her fingers poised over the keyboard, ready to enter the information.

"No, I think that's enough for one night. Maybe I'll look through tomorrow's paper and see what's available to rent."

Ignoring Lizzie, Madison started typing in another website. "What about this place?"

A sleek glass and steel high-rise appeared on the screen. She moved the cursor to the side menu and selected one of the model units to look at.

"The name of the condo development is called Chocolate Truffle?" Lizzie asked.

"It's an adults' only condo catering specifically to twenty-and thirty-something professional women, and they thought the name would appeal to that target market." She clicked on a thumbnail picture of the model suite. "See, the units are one and two bedrooms, nicely appointed kitchens, polished concrete floors throughout, laundry facilities in each unit, spacious balconies, a doorman for security, underground parking, a workout room, a pool that has a sauna, and steam room. What more could a girl ask for?"

"You sound like a marketing brochure. How do you know so much about this place?"

"My boyfriend works for the developer, and he says this building is a solid financial investment and will only increase in price. It's a little farther out of the area you wanted, but the subway is within walking distance and the buses to the downtown core run pretty regularly. Or you could look into buying a car."

"Wow, they're a bit pricey," Lizzie said, after glancing at the base price for the unit. "I don't know if I could justify spending that kind of money on an apartment, especially when I have no idea how much rebuilding Enchanted Garden is going to cost or whether or not my insurance will cover any of it. And I don't know if I can see myself taking the subway every day. No, it's too expensive."

"Well, it just so happens I know someone who lives there that is looking for a roommate and I know for a fact you'd get along with her."

"You?"

"Yeah. I have a two-bedroom so you'd have your own room."

"I will always be a target according to Vivienne and Gideon, and I don't want to put you in the path of that no matter how slim the chance."

Madison waved a dismissive hand in her direction. "I'm with the Order now. I can more than take care of myself. I know you're a private person and, after living here for so long, you probably are craving some personal space, so just consider the offer as a temporary solution until the market opens up and you can find something that's a bit more suitable than those two hideous places we looked at."

She knew there was no way Madison could afford to live in a place like that on what she made as her assistant in the shop. She had an idea of whose money bought the condo and she wondered what strings were attached to that transaction.

"It's a very generous offer, but I don't know if I could impose..." Madison's cell phone rang, cutting off Lizzie's protests.

Madison glanced at the call display on the phone. A shadow of worry fell across her face. "I have to get this." She handed the laptop to Lizzie and shimmied across the bed until she was sitting on the edge with her back to Lizzie before she flipped open her phone. "Hi. I'm sorry."

Madison's shoulders slumped as she bent her head to listen to the caller.

"Yes, I know your time is important," she replied, her voice becoming small and soft.

Lizzie's scalp prickled. She recognized the appeasing quality, the pleading aspect of Madison's body language.

"You're right, I'm being selfish. It's just—I didn't realize how late it was. Yes, yes, I know. You're right, I need to be more considerate. Please don't be mad. I'm leaving right now. She ended her call, keeping her back to Lizzie for a moment longer, then turned to face her. Her eyes were glistening with unshed tears. She cleared her throat. "I'm sorry to cut our visit short, but I forgot I was supposed to meet Richard tonight." She hurried off the bed and began to gather her things.

"Not to worry," Lizzie replied. She closed the laptop and set it aside on the bed.

Madison buttoned up her coat as she scurried to the door. "No, don't get up." She gestured to Lizzie. "I'll see you tomorrow for dinner. Think about my offer, okay?" She disappeared through the door, closing it behind her before Lizzie had a chance to reply.

Moments later, there was a knock on the door.

"Come in," she called out.

Gideon popped his head through the door. "What's up with Madison? She dashed out without saying goodbye. I didn't have a chance to give her a book on white magick she'd been hounding me for. Is she upset because of your news?"

"No, she got a call from her boyfriend and then she said she had to go."

"I hope nothing's wrong."

"So do I, Gideon. So do I," she said, trying to ignore the sense of dread that settled in the pit of her stomach.

Chapter Twenty-Two

Lizzie thought once she had set her mind on rebuilding her life, things would just fall into place. She had made a list of what needed to be done and she believed all she had to do was go down the list and tick things off, and away she'd go. It's how she'd always accomplished things in the past, and she'd always been able to get things done just by a steady focus, determination, and hard work. But this time, it wasn't working. This time, every step forward she encountered another road block in her way.

The cause of the fire still hadn't been determined. Hoping to move things along, Lizzie contacted her lawyer to see if there were any legal routes she could take to force the Fire Marshall's office into releasing the report. He'd said he would call her if he had anything, but she hadn't heard from him in a week.

After spending hours online searching for a place to live and scouring the newspaper's classifieds, she'd finally broken down and called a realtor. She didn't have any good news there either. Echoing Madison's words, the realtor told Lizzie there wasn't much on the market that fit what she was looking for. Still, she had set up an appointment for later on in the week to see what properties were available.

In the meantime, she had reluctantly agreed to move in with Madison. She hadn't wanted to take advantage of her friend's munificence, even if it was a temporary solution, but she didn't have any other alternatives to remaining at the St. James.

At least today, she was checking out of the hotel after a month of confinement. Being able to leave was a step forward. Something she could finally cross off her list.

Her bags were packed. She'd spent the morning cleaning her hotel room and gathering her magazines and books in neat little piles.

She was eager to go, but had to wait for Vivienne to arrive and release the Elementals from their duty of watching over her.

Sitting on the corner of the bed while she waited, she could hear Gideon moving about in the other room collecting his books and papers he'd been working on.

Watching the pearlescent mist swirl gracefully over the walls, ceiling, and floor, she felt a small pang of sadness. She'd become so accustomed to their presence, and although they had communicated with her only once, she felt not just gratitude for their protection, but a deeper connection. They were as much a part of her new circle of friends as Gideon, Vivienne, and Madison were.

She took a deep breath to clear her thoughts and allowed her energy to flow through her body and down through the soles of her feet, grounding and centering herself. Reaching out with her mind, like she did when she was checking her beloved flowers for the *Letting Go*, she searched for an energetic connection with the Elementals.

It happened instantly. In one breath, she was Lizzie sitting on the bed, separate from them; the next moment, she was a part of them. She was still aware of her own physical self, but at the same time, another part of her, a deeper part, became absorbed and moved with the Elementals as they continued their languid dance around the perimeter of the room.

For a few moments, she let herself enjoy the experience and the sensations of complete and utter bliss that came with it. It wasn't like connecting with Vivienne and feeling her unwavering love and compassion. Being with the Elementals felt like being connected to everything that ever existed. She felt the ancient knowing and complete contentedness of existing in only the now.

As she continued to immerse herself in the experience, she heard a low humming. The part of her that was still connected to her physical body and sitting on the bed could hear the incessant noise in her ears. She tried to ignore it, but the more she tried to block out the sound, the louder it became. The words came next, as if someone was whispering them in her ear.

She stirred from the bed and stood before the east-facing wall. Keeping her elbows close to her sides, she raised her hands with her palms facing up in a gesture of supplication.

"To the Guardians of the East, home of Air and Sylph, I thank you for your protection. I release you now from your duty and bid you a fond farewell."

As the words fell effortlessly from her lips, she raised her left hand and using her index and middle fingers, she quickly drew the shape of a star in the air, moving her hand from right to left. As she drew her hand down sharply, completing the shape, she felt the Elemental containing the energy of all that was air recede from her consciousness. The pastel yellow that once mingled with the other mists disappeared from the room.

She turned to the south wall, her elbows at her side again, her palms facing up. "To the Guardians of the South, home of Fire and Salamander, I thank you for your protection. I release you now from your duty and bid you a fond farewell." Again, she raised her left hand and drew the ancient symbol to release the Elementals.

The rose-colored mist evaporated.

She turned again. "To the Guardians of the West, home to Water and Undine, I thank you for your protection. I release you now from your duty and bid you a fond farewell." When she completed cutting the shape in the air, the mist of softest blue dissipated. She turned finally to stand facing north. "To the Guardians of the North, home of Earth and Gnome, I thank you for your protection. I release you now from your duty and bid you a fond farewell."

As the final mist, the color of fresh green leaves, dissolved, she tilted her face up to the ceiling and closed her eyes.

Each time she had spoken the words releasing each Elemental, she had felt their energy disconnect from hers and as they each disappeared, she felt her own power getting stronger. Her energy pulsed and thrummed through her body. She felt so alive. So strong and powerful. The high-pitched buzzing in her ears became louder.

"Gracious Goddess and the Ancient Horned One, thank you for your continued blessing and assisting with my rite. Farewell." With her eyes still closed, she pointed her left hand down at the floor and turned slowly in a counter-clockwise circle. "The Circle is open but unbroken and the blessings long remain." As she completed the circle, she spoke again to the empty room. "Merry meet and merry part and merry meet again. Blesséd be."

Every cell in her body seemed to be singing with a bright, clear energy. Then the buzzing stopped. She opened her eyes to see Vivienne and Gideon standing in the doorway. Vivienne looked pleased. She gave Lizzie a warm smile. Gideon looked bewildered and glanced at his mother for an explanation.

Lizzie smiled back at the two of them. "I hope that was okay. I know you were supposed to do that, but I just felt drawn to be the one to let them go. It was like I couldn't stop myself."

"It's more than all right and you saved me the trouble of unpacking all my paraphernalia," Vivienne said, putting a heavy silver travel case containing her crystals, herbs, and candles on the floor. "I've never seen anyone close a sacred circle without at least using an athame to perform the ritual. You are full of surprises."

"It must have been our combined energy that allowed me to do it without using anything. I'm sorry I linked with you without your permission, but I didn't realize I'd done it."

"No need to apologize, we weren't linked."

"But..." The smile died on her lips. "The words. How did I know what to say if they weren't from you, if I didn't pick them up from your thoughts?"

"Perhaps you know more than you realize. How did it feel as you were doing it?"

"Exhilarating, amazing. I feel so alive."

"It can be a rush, can't it?"

"Most definitely," Lizzie said. She took a moment to look around the empty room at the stripped bed and her suitcases sitting neatly in the corner by the door. "It's so different without them here. I know that I carry a part of each of them in me, as does every living thing, but I miss them." She wandered over to the window now unfettered by the mists. She touched her fingertips to the cold glass and gazed outside for the first time in a month. It was a bright, cold day. She squinted into the glare to the bustling street below.

She heard Vivienne quietly ask Gideon to take her bags down to the car, but she kept her focus at the world outside the window. She waited for Gideon to leave before she spoke.

"It seems like I've been away from that world for so long." She tapped on the glass as she watched the people and cars go by. "I know I said being a part of all that again is what I want right now, and I still do, but it feels strange." She laughed. "I can't believe I just referred to everyday life as strange, as if what I've been through this last little while was the real normal."

Vivienne came to stand next to her at the window. She placed her arm around Lizzie's waist. Lizzie leaned into her friend and rested her head on her shoulder, keeping her gaze focused on the outside world. "You can change your mind at any time."

"No, it's not who I am or what I want. I'll take my chances back out there even if I feel afraid. I promised myself I wouldn't let fear stop me from going after what I want any more."

Nor would she put her friends in harm's way. She knew, for all of them, belonging to the Order would mean they would always come up against evil, but she didn't want to be the one responsible for bringing it to them. Releasing the Elementals would be the last act of magick she would do. Selling flowers and forgetting her gifts would be the safest for all concerned.

"There's no reason to be afraid. Gideon will be watching over you, and I'm only a phone call away."

"Knowing that helps. It really does."

Releasing the catch on the window, Lizzie slid it open, letting the brisk air caress her face. It smelled of car exhaust and the gritty metallic tang of smog. A car horn blared, a bus rattled by belching diesel exhaust, its brakes squealing as it stopped at a red light. Someone shouted a curse down below on the sidewalk.

She lifted her head off Vivienne's shoulder. "If I wasn't linked with you, how did I know how to release the Elementals and open the circle you cast? Was it the Elementals? Were they telling me what to do?"

"No, it wasn't them. You somehow tapped into your ancestors' collective memories. I'm pretty sure your mother was a gifted, wise woman, based on the charm she placed on your necklace, and she would have had to learn her skills from someone, most likely her mother."

"Collective memories?" She turned to face Vivienne.

"You carry with you the knowledge of all those women who have come before you in the very cells of your body."

"Like an imprint?

"Yes, exactly."

"Is it the collective unconscious that Carl Jung wrote about?"

"No, he was referring to a collection of thoughts that exists separate from your physical body on an energetic plane similar to the dream plane. It is like a library containing all the experiences of every soul that has ever incarnated. What I'm referring to is more specific to you as a person. Your ancestors' experiences and knowledge are encoded in your very DNA.

"We in the Order have known this for centuries. When scientists recently mapped the human genome, they discovered a section of the double helix containing coding for nothing relating to the creation of your physical being or the functioning of your body's systems. They don't know why it's there or its purpose, so they have termed it 'junk DNA.' So like science to dismiss what they haven't yet discovered as junk. How you tapped into it, I don't know."

"So, by accessing this part of my DNA, I unlocked the knowledge of how to open the circle from my ancestors?"

"Yes, but being able to do that all without the aid of any tools or preparation is a talent unique to you. I know you crave being ordinary, but even you must realize that you are far from it. You can't change who you are."

"No, I can't, but it doesn't change what I want for myself. We should go," she said, closing the window, cutting off the street noises and any further discussion.

"Yes, it's getting late. And I have a plane to catch." Vivienne glanced at her watch. "Would you mind gathering up those crystals?" she asked, pointing to the quartz crystals in the corners of the room.

While Lizzie collected the crystals, Vivienne leaned down and snapped open the catches on the case at her feet. She removed four empty black velvet bags and laid them aside on the bureau. One at a time, she handed the crystals to Vivienne, who placed them in the bags then packed them in the bottom of the case.

"Is that it then?" Lizzie asked.

"No, there's one more thing that needs to be done. When you first arrived here, Gideon laid a line of salt over the threshold of the door and windowsill for added protection. Once we'd brought you back from *In Between*, he replaced the salt with a stronger charm called a ward while I attended you in the bath. We just need to remove the wards and then we're ready to leave." Vivienne snapped the claps shut on the case and stood up. "Did you want to try your hand at it?" She gestured to the window.

"No, I'd rather not. I don't know how to do it."

"I think if you just tapped into your genetic history like you did with the Elementals, you'd remember how to undo the ward quite easily."

"No, I'd prefer you do it. I'm feeling a slight headache coming on," she lied, trying to ignore the humming in her ears. She stood back as Vivienne approached the window. Vivienne held out her hands, palms facing toward the glass. With her back facing Lizzie, she stood silently for a few moments. The humming in Lizzie's head got louder. It sounded like a thousand voices singing the same clear, high note. Where once Vivienne stood before an ordinary transparent window, there was now a web of purple-colored light extending over the surface of the glass and all the way around the window frame.

A blinding blue-white light flowed out from Vivienne's palms and into the center of the web covering the glass. As soon as the energy from her hands reached the web of light, the web began folding in on itself. First the spirals of violet light spun backwards toward the center, and then the radial arms retracted into the hub and with one bright flash of light, like the twinkling of a star, the web disappeared.

Vivienne lowered her arms and looked over her shoulder at Lizzie. She gave her a conspiratorial wink, moved over to the doorway, and cleared the protective ward off the door. As with the window, the sparkling web of light energy pulled itself into its center until all that remained was a pin dot of purple light. Then that, too, winked out of existence. The singing in Lizzie's head stopped the moment the last ward was broken.

"There, now I think we can go," Vivienne said, dusting off her hands.

Lizzie scooped up the two pillows she had bought during the start of her stay at the hotel and followed Vivienne into the front room. She put her pillows down on the console table so she could retrieve her coat from the closet. She slipped into her coat as Vivienne did the same.

"Do you have the cell phone I gave you yesterday?" Vivienne asked.

"Yes, it's already in my purse. And fully charged." She smiled at her mentor. The smartphone was not only untraceable, but encrypted so any calls could not be listened in on.

Lizzie put her hands in her coat pocket to pull out her key card, but instead of the hard plastic, her fingers touched a soft, yielding object. She pulled it out and opened her palm to reveal a small leather pouch.

The leather was butter soft and the honey color of deerskin. An intricately beaded spiral decorated one side; the other side was unadorned. It was tied securely at the top with a rawhide thong. Manipulating it gently with her fingers, she could feel several hard objects in the pouch.

"What's this and how did it end up in my pocket?" She held out her open palm for Vivienne to see.

"By the style and design of the beading, I'd say it's one of Gideon's medicine pouches. He must have slipped it into your pocket when he first met you. It's for protection."

"I should probably give it back to him. I don't really need it anymore."

"No. Although he gave it to you without your knowledge, in a way, it's a gift and it's now yours. It's best that you keep it. It and the magic it contains belong to you now."

She put the medicine pouch back into her pocket, slipped her purse in the crook of her arm, and clutched her pillows tight to her chest as Vivienne held open the door for her.

Down in the hotel lobby, Lizzie made for the front desk to settle her bill, but Vivienne stopped her.

"The bill's already been taken care of by the Order."

"I can't possibly allow the Order to foot the bill, especially since I'm not going to be a part of it. It doesn't feel right."

"The Order doesn't attach strings to their gifts or generosity. Please just accept it in the spirit in which it was given."

She wanted to continue arguing the point with Vivienne, but Frank had left his post at the concierge's desk and was making his way over to the two of them.

"Good afternoon, Mrs. York, Ms. Bennet," he said, making a little bow to the women.

"Good afternoon, Frank," Vivienne said.

"Hello," Lizzie replied.

"I thought this may be of some use." He pulled out a folded carrier bag from under his arm. It was a glossy white with the hotel insignia printed on the side in gold. He placed it on the marble floor of the lobby and held his hands out for Lizzie's pillows.

She handed them over and he neatly stuffed them into the bag. He handed the bag over to her by the thin braided handles.

"Thank you. That's very thoughtful. And thank you for everything else, for taking care of my needs and for being there on the roof that night." Lizzie held out her hand and Frank grasped it in both of his. His hands were exceptionally soft and warm.

"It's been my pleasure. I hope that in the future, if I can be of service in any way, you would do me the honor and contact me. You know where I work. We at the St. James take pride in the fact that we take care of our guests even after they have checked out." He gave her a knowing smile. "But you must excuse me, ladies. Duty calls." He released Lizzie's hand, and with another curt bow, he turned and headed back to his desk, where a couple stood waiting for his help.

With no reason to linger, Lizzie picked up the carrier bag and led the way out of the hotel. Out on the city street, she hesitated. The noise and movement of the traffic, the smell of the city, and the cold assaulted her senses, making her head spin. Vivienne held her by her arm, steadying her.

The SUV was idling on the curb in front of the hotel. Gideon leaned on the passenger side door, his hands in his coat pockets. When he spied them stepping out of the hotel, he straightened up and held out his hand to take the bag containing Lizzie's pillows.

Placing it in the back seat, he held open the passenger side door. Before she stepped inside the vehicle, she turned to Vivienne. "I guess this is goodbye."

"Just for a little while. I should be back in the country in a couple of weeks. I'll give you a call when I'm back in town."

"I'd like that very much," she said, the words catching in her throat. She threw her arms around Vivienne and held her tight. Vivienne returned the embrace. The calm, steady love that was as much a part of Vivienne as her eye color enveloped her. In that brief moment, the prospect of being alone was too much emptiness for her to bear.

She felt Vivienne's gentle hands slowly breaking the hug. Vivienne held her at arm's length. "If you just remember to follow your own wisdom, you'll be more than okay."

She nodded, not trusting her voice to not betray her sadness at saying goodbye.

"This is not goodbye, just farewell until we meet again. And it will be soon, I promise."

"Farewell, then," she said in a voice that sounded small. She stepped back from the woman who had given her so much, who had risked her life to bring her back, and who taught her how to control her powers, who showed her how to feel again. She owed Vivienne so much that a simple embrace and well wishes seemed inadequate.

Allowing Gideon to help her up into the SUV, she sat staring at her lap as he shut her door. A few stray tears dropped into her palms. She glanced out the window to watch mother and son say their goodbyes. They hugged and Vivienne kissed her son on both cheeks.

Although she couldn't hear what they were saying, she didn't need to in order to know the love and pride Vivienne felt for her son. Maybe it was because she was linked to Vivienne, or her love for her son was so strong, but she could feel it from inside the vehicle. If she reached out with her gifts, she knew she would see waves of soft green light emanating from both of them. The energetic color of love.

She continued to watch as Gideon escorted his mother over to a black town car parked behind Gideon's SUV. The driver of the car had gotten out and was coming around to open the door, but Gideon beat him to it. He waved to his mother as the town car pulled away, then got behind the wheel of his own vehicle.

He smiled at Lizzie as he turned over the engine. "Where to?"

"I want to go see my shop."

"I figured as much. Are you sure you don't want to do something a little more cheerful on your first day of freedom? We could take in a matinee, or go to the museum, or grab a bite to eat at a café."

"No, I need to see for myself how bad the damage is. If you don't mind chauffeuring me around, I also need to stop at my bank and visit a friend in the diamond district before we meet up with Madison. I've already called him, so he'll be expecting me. Maybe we'll go to a movie another time."

"Yes, another time then."

As he drove the few blocks to what remained of Enchanted Garden, she had to work at keeping her nerves under control. Within minutes, she would see first-hand the ruin of what had been such a huge part of her old life.

She kept her eyes glued on the road ahead, tapping her foot on the floorboards of the SUV when they had to stop for a red light. They turned the corner and, soon enough, the charred remains of her shop came into view.

Gideon was right; this wasn't such a good idea. The despair hit her in her solar plexus; the icy fire of adrenaline flooded her system. She closed her eyes, taking a few slow, deep breaths to calm herself down as much as she could. It was even worse than how it had looked on the tiny display screen on Madison's cell.

He parked the car in the front of the building. The red caution tape that had been strung the width of the storefront was now gone, but the plywood nailed to the door and window remained intact.

She flung open the passenger door before Gideon had turned off the engine. Even after so many weeks exposed to the elements, the acrid smell of ash and smoke still lingered heavily in the air, taking her breath away. Her worst fear was realized as she squinted against the too bright sun, her eyes still unaccustomed to the intensity of the natural light, to gaze up at where the roof should have been. A few naked rafters charred black from the fire greeted her gaze.

An official notice from the fire department was posted on the impromptu plywood door, warning people the building had been condemned and was unsafe to enter.

"No," she moaned softly.

Gideon came to stand by her side and when she started to pry the plywood from the doorframe with her bare hands, he dashed back to his vehicle.

"Here, let me try," he said, holding up a crowbar and hammer. She stood aside and waited as he moved with quick efficiency. The nails screeched in protest as the wood came away from the doorframe.

She couldn't wait for him to take the plywood completely off the door, and as soon as there was enough space, she slipped through the opening.

"Hey, wait for me. You shouldn't go in there alone," he called after her, but she ignored him, stepping into the blackened destruction.

Sunlight filtered down through the gaping hole in the ceiling, but the charcoal-encrusted interior absorbed the sunshine, keeping the shop in an artificial gloom. The water used to extinguish the fire had frozen, coating the wreckage in a thin coat of ice. In the half-light, everything shimmered like black diamonds.

She didn't recognize anything that once had been her bright little shop. Dark, hulking shapes of broken things, burned black, offered nothing as to what they had been. She stepped further into the building, broken glass and ice crunching menacingly under her boots. For one heart-stopping moment, she was back in her kitchen standing in fear as she watched Ian walk across the shard-covered linoleum and to his death.

She yanked at her left glove. With her bare hand, she sought her necklace through her heavy wool coat. She pressed her fingers against the reassuring shape of the hard, stone cross under her sweater. The stone warmed to her touch. She slowed her breathing down and let the moment of panic pass through her.

She glanced down at her boots. The glass littering the floor was from the vases that once stood in rows along the display cabinet. The heavy wooden cabinet was face down on the floor directly in front of her. Its once-rich stain was now blistered and bubbled from the intense heat of the fire.

She jumped when Gideon placed his hand on her shoulder.

"We don't have to do this right now."

She looked up into his face. He had such beautiful eyes. In the shifting shadow and light of the burned out building, they looked sad to her. She caught herself from placing her hand on his cheek to reassure him she was all right, to take away the regret she saw there.

"Yes, I do. I need to see this."

"Then we do this together." He took her hand in his and gave it a gentle squeeze.

Carefully, they picked their way past the cabinet, stepping cautiously through the rubble. They stopped only when a heavy beam that was once a part of the roof blocked their progress. Lizzie's eyes burned from the acrid air. Everything was blackened and, at first, she didn't recognize the pieces of wood lying under the broken rafter.

"Oh, the refectory table." Letting go of his hand, she stepped toward what was left of the table. Her toe caught on a shattered bit of pottery, causing her to stumble.

Gideon caught her around the waist and pulled her in to him. "Careful," he said, drawing her in even closer.

She turned to face him, keenly aware of how perfectly her body fit against the muscled contours of his own. Her hands sought his chest through the open lapels of his coat. Leaning her forehead against the thin fabric of his shirt, she breathed in the scent of him, her pulse quickening as she took in the clean, spicy fragrance of his skin. His heart pounded a staccato rhythm against the palm of her hand.

She yearned to slide her fingers over the contours of his bare chest, to feel the heat of his skin against hers. A blue light sparked between her fingers, dancing to the ends of her fingertips like ball lighting.

Drawing in a sharp breath, she clamped down on the tumult of emotions, forcing her energy to flow down, away from Gideon, and out through the soles of her feet. The blue sparks died out instantly.

"Are you okay?" Gideon said, his lips brushing against her hair, sending a delectable shiver down her spine.

She pushed away from him and turned to the wreckage on the floor, trying desperately to regain her composure. "Yes, it's just a little hard to see this in person." She blushed at the huskiness she heard in her voice. "That table was such a beautiful piece. So much history contained in it, and now it's not even good for kindling."

"Have you seen enough?"

She sighed. "No, I'd like to see my office. Maybe there's something that's still salvageable."

"By the looks of things, we'll have to try the back door. There's too much debris in the way and the wall by the cooler looks like it's leaning."

She nodded and followed him back to the SUV, keeping a careful distance between them. As Gideon drove around the block to the back of the building, the scent of destruction clinging to their hair and clothes permeated the interior of the car.

He parked in the alleyway parallel to the door. Its metal surface looked undamaged by the fire.

Lizzie climbed out of the SUV. As she strode to the service door, she put her hand in her coat pocket to dig out her keys, but instead pulled out Gideon's medicine bag. She unfurled her fingers, revealing the soft leather pouch sitting in the palm of her hand.

"Oh, I slipped that into your coat the night I drove you to the hotel. I completely forgot, otherwise I would have told you about it. It's a protective charm." He came to stand inches away from her, too close for her comfort.

"Yes, I know. Vivienne told me. She said because you gave it to me, it's a gift. And it would be okay if I kept it."

"Yes, a gift. I'd like you to have it." He placed his hand under hers and curled his fingers over, covering the bundle in their enclosed hands.

The air crackled in the few inches of space between them. Lizzie thought she saw the blue sparks dance briefly before her eyes. Blood pounded in her ears as she looked from their entwined fingers to his face.

He leaned in and, as their eyes locked, she thought she saw a question in the depth of his chocolate brown eyes.

An air horn blasted mere feet from where they stood. Lizzie shrieked and jumped back as Gideon turned toward the sound in one fluid motion, throwing up his hands at the driver of a delivery truck parked a few feet behind the SUV.

He whispered a hurried incantation and the air began to shift and bend, distorting the buildings around them.

The man was leaning out of the driver's side window, shouting at them to move their vehicle blocking his way, when Gideon's spell hit him. Slumping back into his seat, his eyes glazed over, his baseball cap falling over his left eye.

Gideon lowered his hands and turned to Lizzie, his expression a mix of frustration and embarrassment. "Did you want to go in? I can hold him enthralled for as long as you need."

"Is he going to be alright?" She gestured to the truck driver still immobilized in his seat.

"Yes," he replied. A flash of irritation crossed his face. "He'll be no worse for wear when I release him."

She glanced at the door of her shop then back at Gideon, his face unreadable.

There would be nothing in her office that remained unscathed from the fire. Even if the flames hadn't managed to eat their way through the aged oak bookcase, the heat would have fractured the wavy glass fronts, leaving the soot and water to finish the destruction of anything that remained.

Her books were just things, just things. They never were her mother and she had been a fool to put so much store in the power of paper, ink, and old leather to create some tangible link to a woman she would never know.

She had real flesh and blood people in her life now that cared about her. That's what mattered.

She clutched the medicine bundle tightly in her hand and slipped it back into her pocket. "No, there's nothing in there for me. Let's go."

Chapter Twenty-Three

As they pulled away from the alley, Gideon released the trucker with a few quick words and a flick of his wrist, not even looking behind him as he negotiated his vehicle back into traffic.

At the next red light, he asked if she wanted to go to the bank or the diamond district next. He was back in guardian mode, professional with no hint of his earlier attraction to her. Lizzie wondered if she'd imagined the whole thing.

"Neither. I don't feel up to dealing with any of that right now. I want to be where there is laughter and noise. I don't want to think anymore. I want to be around normal everyday things and people."

"I know just the thing."

She pulled out her new cell phone and rescheduled her visit to Saul for later in the week.

As they zipped through traffic, heading out of the downtown core, Lizzie lowered her window to let the cold air play across her face. It didn't matter that the frigid air made her eyes water, she relished feeling the movement on her face. To be released from her confinement, to go wherever she wanted whenever she wanted.

She pushed the lever on the passenger side door, bringing the window down all the way. Pulling off her remaining glove, she put her hand out the window, letting the air buffet against her palm. When she lost all feeling in her fingers, she finally pulled her hand in and shut the window, leaving it open just a crack to let in a trickle of winter air.

She pressed her frozen fingers against her cheeks to warm them.

"Gideon, can I ask you about the day we met?"

"Sure," he said, glancing over at her before focusing back on the road.

"You looked so different that day you picked me up off the sidewalk. Your hair and piercings, I mean. Then just a few days later, you showed up looking like you do now. I was wondering, do you have a closet full of disguises and wigs?" It was a small detail that had niggled in the back of her brain, but now that she asked the question, she felt foolish.

Gideon chuckled. "After all you have learned and seen over the last month, why do you think my drastic change in appearance has to do with something as mundane as a wig and costumes?"

"You used magic?"

"Yes. It's called a glamour. It's quite simple really."

"You changed your physical appearance with a spell?"

"Not quite. I changed how you and everyone around me perceived my appearance."

As he spoke, the air around him shimmered, surrounding him in mist. Lizzie screwed up her eyes, trying to put his image into focus, but she couldn't.

"Much easier than wearing a disguise, don't you think?"

Gideon appeared as he had that day—a battered leather jacket, long dark dreadlocks, a bandana around his head, and as he turned to smile at her, his piercings winked in the light. He even sported a scruffy five o'clock shadow.

"I suppose. Why this particular look?"

"You mean my rocker dude persona?" He shook his dreads, making Lizzie laugh. "Why not? It's as good as any other. I'd been following you for months before I picked you up from the sidewalk, and did you even once notice me in the crowded street?"

"No, I didn't."

He gave her a sideways glance and the air around him rippled. Instantly, he returned to his normal self—short hair, clean-shaven, wearing his navy winter coat.

His demonstration brought up another disconcerting thought. "So is this how you really look, or is it another glamour?"

They had stopped at another red light and Gideon took the moment to look at her fully. His deep brown eyes bored into her, all traces of light-heartedness gone. "This is what I really look like. There is no need for me to hide who I am from you now. I would never disrespect your trust like that."

She heard the hurt in his voice and she regretted asking the question. She thought about the medicine bundle in her pocket and the look in Gideon's eyes before the trucker had blasted his horn at them.

The light turned green and he focused back on the road.

She reached out to him, touching him gently on his forearm. "I'm sorry. It's just this is still all new to me. I don't know the rules or how it all works."

He visibly relaxed and gave her the smile that made her heart ache with a longing she'd never experienced before.

"To be honest, I don't either. I've never had this kind of relationship with a charge before. Usually, I'm protecting them from a distance, and in the cases where I've been given the go ahead to make contact, I'm only with them for a short while until they are taken to the Motherhouse or to a safe house, depending on who I'm watching over. With you, it's different."

His last words lingered in the air between them, confusing her even more.

"What kind of spell did you cast back there?" she said, trying to steer the conversation onto safer ground.

"A thrall. It requires a great deal of concentration and not every guardian can perform one. I can thank my genetics for that little talent. But, it wasn't my finest hour as your guardian. I overreacted because I was distracted." A boyish grin spread across his face. "*You* can be very distracting."

She returned his smile, cursing her fair skin for betraying her feelings as a rush of heat rose up her throat, burning her cheeks. She looked out the window, waiting for the warmth in her face to die down.

"So what other magickal tools do you have up your sleeve?"

"Well, the most common tool all of us guardians use is a memory fog. In time, even Madison will be able to cast it. It's a simple charm that's easy to maintain, less concentration than a glamour. If I've come in contact with someone and I'm concerned about my identity being revealed, a memory fog makes it impossible for that person to remember the exact details of what I looked like or what I said. The downside of the charm is it can only be directed at a specific person. It doesn't work on groups of people. You have to have several guardians all casting the spell in unison to do it on a crowd."

"Have you ever used it on me? I mean, before we met on the sidewalk."

"No, just the glamour," he said, turning the SUV into a parking lot. "We're here."

She looked out the passenger side window, following his gaze. "A strip mall?" She was silent for a moment. "While I appreciate you taking me somewhere to cheer me up, I'm not really in the mood for shopping."

"Oh, we're not going shopping. We're going there." He pointed to the far end of the mall where a large red neon sign flashed.

"Bowling? You're taking me bowling?" She turned from looking at the Family Fun Bowl-O-Rama back to Gideon.

"Yup." His smile faltered when she looked at him. "You asked to be around laughter and noise, and I can definitely guarantee we'll find both in the bowling lanes, especially after you see my technique. But if you're not into bowling, we could go someplace else."

She threw her head back and laughed. "It's not that. It's just that I don't bowl."

"If you don't like bowling, we could do something else."

"Oh, no that's not what I meant. I've never bowled before because I've never had the opportunity, but I've always wanted to try. This could be fun."

"Well, what are we waiting for?"

She answered him by hopping out of the SUV. As she crossed the parking lot, she lengthened her stride in anticipation of what awaited her inside the concrete building. She was delighted at the thought of learning something that had nothing to do with magick or using her newfound abilities.

She smiled broadly as she swung open the door and was engulfed by the thunder of balls rolling on hardwood, the crash of pins, and the babble of a crowd of voices raised in laughter and sociable chatter.

Yet again, Gideon knew exactly what she needed.

Chapter Twenty-Four

Their time at the bowling alley went by too fast and before she knew it, Gideon's cell phone rang, ending her afternoon of pleasure. Madison called to say she was done for the day and was on her way home. They were to meet her at her condo.

Like a child being told it was time for bed after a long day of fun, Lizzie felt herself dragging her feet as she returned the funny little bowling shoes to the counter.

They walked arm-in-arm through the parking lot, still laughing about how horrible they both had been.

As she settled into the cold car, the sky already dark, the reality of her situation reasserted itself. Gideon turned on the seat warmers and Lizzie snuggled deeper into her seat, welcoming the warmth after the chilly walk across the parking lot. She closed her eyes as a familiar weariness descended on her. She stifled a yawn.

"We'll be at Madison's shortly and then you can rest. I shouldn't have kept you at the lanes so long."

"I'm fine. I guess after a month of doing nothing, I'm a bit out of shape, but I had so much fun this afternoon. I wish we could've stayed longer." She let out a jaw-cracking yawn, covering her mouth with the back of her hand.

"You're not sleeping well, are you?"

"No."

"Still having the dream about the cottage?"

"Yes. Vivienne had hoped in time it would stop, but it hasn't. Every night it's the same thing and I always wake up with a start just before I can turn the handle on the door and step inside."

"I could call Vivienne. Maybe she could recommend another tisane to help you sleep."

"No, please don't bother her. I've tried all the ones she's already given me and they didn't work. Besides, it's just a dream, not a nightmare or a night terror. It's more annoying than anything."

That wasn't quite true, the dream haunted her even during her waking hours, but she didn't want to worry Gideon. She hadn't suffered a night terror since Ian's death, but the dream disturbed her in a way her night terrors never had, although she couldn't put her finger on why.

When they arrived at Madison's condo, Gideon parked out front and hurried to the back of the vehicle to retrieve her suitcases. Lizzie grabbed the bag containing her pillows from the back seat and waited for him to join her on the sidewalk.

Her first impression of the Chocolate Truffle condo was revulsion. Menacing steel buttresses inset with glass sprouted off the front of the building to form the street level awning.

She craned her neck to get a better glimpse of the rest of the building. It seemed to loom over her. The building felt nothing like the name implied. It didn't call to Lizzie's mind anything remotely sweet and comforting. The only thing it had in common with chocolate was the dark brown of the exterior.

Only a few lights dotted the structure, even though it was approaching the dinner hour. Maybe people who could afford to live in such a place worked long hours to pay the mortgage, or maybe the rich just ate later in the evening.

She just couldn't imagine why Madison would want to live here. That wasn't true; the answer was obvious, but Lizzie didn't have time to ponder what kind of influence Madison's boyfriend exerted over her friend because at that moment, Madison opened the lobby door and waved them in.

She was wearing a pair of black, hip-hugging skinny jeans accentuating her extraordinarily long legs. On her feet, she had donned black patent ankle booties with lethal-looking stiletto heels. She topped off her outfit with a deep purple cashmere sweater with a plunging neckline. Her hair fell loose around her shoulders in a cascade of auburn curls.

Lizzie tried not to stare as she gave Madison a brief hug then stepped further into the cavernous lobby to allow Gideon to follow in behind with the suitcases. The coldness of the building was even stronger inside.

She moved to stand under a massive white metal chandelier. It was festooned with frosted glass squares, adding to the already arctic decor. From under the chandelier, she watched Madison glide toward Gideon. He asked Madison a question in a voice lowered so only she could hear, Madison replying with equally hushed tones.

No doubt they are discussing something to do with the Order, Lizzie thought as she moved farther into the lobby to give them some privacy. A childish spurt of jealousy made her turn her back to the two of them and survey the rest of the enormous lobby.

Every surface was white, from the pale marble floors, to the walls, to the furniture grouping. The lobby had a curved concierge's desk made of a high-gloss laminate also in white. Even the thin reed of a man who sat behind the counter looked pale and washed out. He didn't look up when they'd entered.

The only pop of color was a fluorescent orange sculpture rising from one corner of the space. Against the blizzard of white, the intense orange burned into her retinas. Like the building, it was all jutting angles and dangerous-looking points.

Lizzie had never been a fan of modern art and she had no idea what the piece was supposed to represent, but to her, it looked like the artist had captured the very essence of insanity.

"Shall we go up?" Madison said, raising a questioning eyebrow at Lizzie. Her voice echoed in the space.

Lizzie nodded, not wanting to shout across the lobby. She turned her back on the sculpture and rejoined her friends, her wet boots squeaking across the polished marble.

"I did everything you requested. You can check if you want," Madison said to Gideon.

"No, that won't be necessary. I trust your skill and…" He gave his watch a cursory glance. "I need to get going. I have some business to attend to. Will you ladies be able to manage the suitcases?"

"Of course we can," Madison said, taking the handle of the rolling suitcase from him.

"Perhaps you can show me your place another time," Gideon said.

"Sure, we'll have you over for dinner. But I'm afraid the food isn't going to be as good as the hotel's. My skills are limited to phoning for take-out." She laughed nervously. "Lizzie, can you cook?"

Lizzie hesitated. Her eyes shifted between the two, wondering if she was imagining the tension between them. "Not to worry. I'll be in charge of the cooking. You can handle the wine." Shifting her purse and hotel bag to her other arm, she reached out to take her small carry-on from Gideon. "Thanks again for this afternoon. I had so much fun."

He bent down and kissed her cheek, his lips brushing gently over her skin. "It was my pleasure," he whispered in her ear before straightening up. "If either of you sense anything out of the ordinary, call me right away. I'll be close by." He made it all the way to the door and swung it open before he stopped and turned to back to Lizzie. "Lizzie, you're perfectly safe. The wards Madison placed around her condo are just standard operating procedure, nothing more." He gave a wink.

She nodded and returned his smile. The tails of his coat swirled out behind him as he turned on his heels and stepped out into the dark street.

"Well, shall we go up?"

Lizzie could still feel the strain coming from her friend, but she hadn't a clue what was bothering her. "Sure."

She followed her to the elevators. Madison's high heels clicked loudly on the hard surface.

As they passed by the concierge's desk, the pasty man finally looked up, but only raised his eyes high enough to give Madison's backside an appreciative look.

Once they were inside the condo, Madison hung up their coats in the hall closet and left Lizzie's luggage just inside the door. She led Lizzie down a short hallway and into the main living space.

It looked just like the pictures on the website, even down to the furnishings. Lizzie wondered if this had been the show suite. It wasn't as big as it looked from the photos, but because of the enormously high ceiling, it felt very open and spacious. And cold.

"At the Chocolate Truffle, we offer three different floor plans to fit your lifestyle—a bachelor suite, a one-bedroom and a two-bedroom. My unit is a two-bedroom and quite spacious at eleven hundred square feet."

Lizzie tried not to stare as her friend morphed into some strange kind of spokes model for the condo developer.

"All the units have concrete floors polished to a high gloss finish that is both durable and compliments the overall look of the modern minimalist aesthetic of the building."

As Madison continued her spiel about the suite, Lizzie nodded politely, all the while wondering where her laid-back, sweet, fun-loving friend had gone.

The kitchen was a cook's dream with stainless steel appliances, dark wood cabinets, and a professional-looking gas range. The black granite counter tops were completely bare with not even a stray fingerprint marring the mirror finish. Lizzie couldn't see a coffee maker or toaster, for that matter.

A small island with the same black granite as the kitchen counters divided the kitchen from the living room. Placed exactly in the middle of the island was a stainless steel bowl of Granny Smith apples.

In the living room, a low, modern white leather sectional sat on a white shag area rug. A curved Lucite coffee table was positioned between the couch and a large flat-screen TV mounted on the wall.

"And here is the *pièce de résistance*." Madison picked up a remote from the Lucite table and pointed it at the floor to ceiling blinds, making them silently retract. The wall of windows revealed a panoramic view of the city skyline. "Isn't it stunning?"

"Yes, indeed."

They stood for a moment admiring the view.

"Over here is your room. You probably want to get settled in." They stepped over to one of two doors to the right of the living room. Madison flung open the door and motioned to her to step inside.

The room was a bit on the smallish side, only big enough to fit a twin platform bed, a nightstand, and a small dresser. The bedroom set continued with the minimalist style of the rest of the condo with its clean lines and lack of embellishments. Everything was white.

"You can use the dresser for your things, and I moved my summer clothes into my storage locker in the basement so you have the whole closet."

"I wish you hadn't gone to all that trouble. I really don't have that many clothes."

"Oh, it's no problem at all. Besides, I want you to feel at home here. And just next door is the bathroom. Feel free to leave your stuff out in there. I don't really use that one. I have an en suite in my bedroom."

"Okay. Sounds great."

Madison stood in the doorway. She restlessly twisted the hem of her sweater and Lizzie feared she was going to stretch the fine cashmere out of shape.

"Well, I guess I'll go get my things."

"Sure." Madison stood blocking the doorway, her fingers twisting her sweater even tighter.

Lizzie took a seat on the corner of the bed. The mattress was so firm it didn't move under her weight. "Is there something bothering you? You seem a little on edge."

"God, is it that obvious?" Madison flopped down on the bed next to her. "It's just that there're some things I have to tell you, and I don't want you to think that you're not wanted here because you are."

"What is it?"

"First, because my apprenticeship with the Order must be kept secret from people who wouldn't understand—you know, ordinary people like my boyfriend, Richard—I've been given a cover story to explain where I go every day."

"Yes, I know. Gideon told me on the way over. You're going to college to become a legal secretary. I have no problem keeping your real activities secret. It's important to your safety and that of the Order. I understand completely."

"The other thing is, Richard works very hard for the condo development company. His job is full of deadlines and he's under so much pressure, so when he comes here, it's like his sanctuary, his place to unwind. It's very important to me he feel completely relaxed while he's here."

"You didn't tell him I was coming to stay before I accepted, did you?"

"No."

"And he wasn't thrilled with the idea, was he?"

"Not exactly, but not because he doesn't like you...it's just like I said before, his down time is very precious to him and he's a very private person."

Lizzie wondered how Richard could even form an opinion about whether he liked her or not, seeing as they'd never met. "I don't want you to feel uncomfortable in your own home, and if this is going to cause tension between you and Richard, that's the last thing I want. I'll find a place to stay first thing tomorrow."

"No, that's not what I meant. I really want you here. It's just that I have a big favor to ask."

"Ask away."

"Well, Richard and I sorta have a routine. He comes over Tuesday and Thursday evenings and he likes it to be quiet, just the two of us, and if you don't mind…"

"If I made myself scarce those two nights?"

"Yes, just between six and ten. I know it sounds horrible. I ask you to stay with me and now I'm telling you that you can't hang out in the condo two nights a week."

"Don't worry about it. I'm sure I can find something to occupy my time for two evenings a week. This will be good for me to go out after being cooped up at the hotel for so long."

"Thanks for understanding." Madison sprung up from the bed, the sudden movement barely registered through the stiff mattress where Lizzie sat. She became more like herself as she strode to the door, the tension gone from her shoulders and face. "It's your first night here and I've already forgotten how to be a good hostess. You probably want to settle in. I thought I'd pop down to the sushi place on the corner and pick us up some dinner while you unpack. Unless you wanted something else?"

"No, sushi would be just fine. Gideon and I pigged out on junk food at the bowling alley."

Madison stopped in her tracks, her head tilted in Lizzie's direction. "Bowling?" She smirked, but the smile didn't extend to her eyes.

"I know, isn't it ridiculous? But I've never had so much fun."

"So you two were on a date then?" She stepped back into the room, crossing her arms over her chest.

"A date. God, no. Gideon was just trying to cheer me up. We'd just been to see the shop and it was all so depressing. Besides, he's way too young for me and he's my guardian." Her words sounded false to her ears.

"You're right, he's your guardian. We're not supposed to engage in romantic flings with our charges. It's against the rules." Her eyes narrowed. "But of course we know that wasn't his intention."

Lizzie pushed down a sudden flash of anger.

"He was just being thoughtful," Madison continued, her tone holding a hint of condescension. "I can't imagine Gideon bowling."

"He was as bad as me. We both looked absurd. But I had so much fun and we laughed so hard my sides still hurt," she replied, attempting to lighten the mood. "If we go again, you'll have to come with us."

"Sure, if I'm not too busy with my studies. I'll let you unpack then." Madison spun on her heels and left the bedroom.

Lizzie heard the door to the apartment open and close, but she stayed seated, poised on the corner of the rock-hard bed. She knew she hadn't mistaken the coldness in Madison's parting words. She had an inkling Madison's prickly behavior toward her had nothing to do with herself or Gideon, but stemmed from something far more disturbing.

The weariness returned and settled deep into her bones. It wasn't from the longing of being somewhere she knew didn't exist, but in confirming her fears that there was a darkness in Madison's life, one she was very familiar with.

She had seen it in Madison's eyes and heard it in her voice whenever Richard had called her—the fear, the panic to smooth things over before annoyance turned to rage. Yes, there was a darkness looming over Madison no magic or charms would protect her from.

Chapter Twenty-Five

Living with Madison proved to be nothing like Lizzie had imagined. It was a strange and stilted dance between them during the mornings and evenings when they were both together, except every Tuesday and Thursday, when Lizzie made herself scarce as promised.

The first morning Lizzie had made them both breakfast, wanting to make herself useful and as a way of thanking Madison for offering her a place to stay. Her reaction to the table being set and Lizzie busy in the sleek little kitchen making French toast was as bizarre as her reception the night before. The relaxed atmosphere and easy conversation they had enjoyed when Lizzie was stuck in the hotel was replaced with a coldness that left her confused.

She realized too late her attempts to show gratitude were received as being too familiar and taking liberties in Madison's pristine apartment. They ate in silence and Madison barely thanked her for breakfast before excusing herself to get ready for her apprenticeship at the Order.

Lizzie cleaned up the kitchen and thought she had put everything back in its place the way she had found it, but when she had come out of the shower, she found Madison wiping down the clean counters with furious swipes of the dishcloth.

From that point on, breakfast consisted of little plastic pots of yogurt and pre-packaged breakfast bars. At Madison's suggestion, they took their meals at nearby restaurants or ate take-out from the containers they came in.

The only thing Madison would allow to be prepared in the kitchen was the morning coffee, which she made herself. When they finished their coffee, Madison would clean the mugs and the coffee carafe in the sink, never using the dishwasher. Storing the coffee maker back in the cupboard, she would dry out the sink with a dishtowel before she left every morning.

Madison's radical change in behavior and her strange habit of coming home after her day at the Motherhouse to change out of her jeans and t-shirt and into tight-fitting clothes, painful-looking shoes, and a full face of makeup even on the evenings she wasn't spending with Richard bewildered Lizzie. She wanted to talk to someone about it, but she had no one to confide in.

Gideon was out of the question. He was friends with both of them and she didn't want to change the dynamic of the relationship by complaining about Madison.

She'd thought about talking to Vivienne, but she realized pestering her mentor about how Madison liked to keep her apartment or how she dressed seemed churlish.

Madison was entitled to live her life the way she chose. Even if she didn't like it, it really was none of her business. Having too much time on her hands to fixate on her friend's mannerisms wasn't healthy either.

For the next few weeks, Lizzie set about finding her own place to live and moving forward on the rebuilding of Enchanted Garden. The first thing she did was retrieve another ruby from her safety deposit box at the bank. From there, she took a taxi to the diamond district, exchanging the precious gem for a certified check she anticipated would cover the down payment on an apartment and resurrecting her shop from the ashes.

She met with a property management company specializing in downtown accommodations and spent consecutive afternoons looking at prospective places, but with little success. Everything she looked at was either overpriced, in terrible condition, or too far away from her flower shop.

She also spent hours meeting with her lawyer to force the Fire Marshall to release the findings on the investigation, but no headway was being made. The lawyer's most recent letter sent off to the Fire Marshall and City Hall resulted in a tersely worded reply informing them the evidence samples collected from the fire scene had been inadvertently stored in the evidence locker instead of being sent for testing.

The Fire Marshall couldn't—or wouldn't—give a timeline as to when the samples would be tested, as there was an unusual backlog of evidence, and as far as the office was concerned, it could take up to several months until the results came back.

Her lawyer told her legally there was nothing more they could do but wait for the tests to be run and the report filed. He assured Lizzie he would stay on top of what was happening and as soon as he heard anything new, he would be in touch.

To date, the only results of her lawyer's efforts were a bill for his time and a phone call informing her that a private detective had called his office requesting Lizzie contact him immediately.

Lizzie didn't bother to write down the number, as she had no intention of calling Penelope's henchman back. The police had ruled Ian's death an accident and no amount of money or harassment on her mother-in-law's part would change what was in the police report.

On Tuesdays and Thursdays, she would meet with Gideon and they would go for dinner, take in a movie or a play, and once they enjoyed an evening at the symphony. Being with him was the only part of her life she looked forward to, although even that had changed.

Embarrassment lingered when she recalled what had happened between them during their visit to her burned out shop. In the moments before the delivery truck driver blared his horn at them, she was certain Gideon had felt the pull of attraction and had been on the brink of showing her just how much. But now, she wasn't sure.

On the surface, he was still the thoughtful, funny, sensitive Gideon she had come to know and admire, but there was a part of him not available to her anymore. This subtle pulling back on his part made her question if she had misconstrued his thoughtfulness as something more.

Even if she possessed the courage to broach the subject, she hadn't the words to express what was in her heart. She cherished her relationship with him too much to risk losing him, as she feared was happening with her and Madison. Her attraction to him was still there, but she carefully cloaked her desire, disguising what she felt in the warmth of a platonic friendship.

At the end of their evenings together, Gideon always walked her to the door of the condo, but never came inside. After a friendly embrace and a chaste kiss on the cheek, he would wait until she'd closed the door and latched it securely behind her.

On tiptoe, with her eye pressed up to the security peephole in the door, she would watch Gideon trace his way down the corridor, his figure distorted by the magnification of the glass, until he disappeared from sight.

She didn't know why she performed this little ritual every time he dropped her off or what she was hoping to see. She would regard him through the tiny sphere of glass as he grew smaller until he was nothing but an ill-defined figure receding in the distance. He never once stopped to look back at her door.

Except for those two nights a week, she spent her time alone, trying to get her life back on track. Much to her chagrin, she discovered the loneliness more difficult to deal with than her month-long confinement in the hotel.

On a bleak afternoon in late February, wandering aimlessly along the streets near Madison's condo, she stumbled upon a remedy for her melancholy.

Lizzie had spent the morning sequestered in her bedroom with her laptop—a recent purchase—researching building contractors and design ideas for her shop.

Although she still hadn't heard anything from her lawyer, she decided to be proactive and have everything in place so, when the building site was officially released, she would be able to start construction right away.

At first, she had tried to make herself comfortable in the living room, but she couldn't relax. She sensed Madison's disapproving eye, making her feel like she was spoiling the pristine white living room by just being there.

Shutting herself in her bedroom with a cup of coffee, she began her research. She had a growing list of trades people, contractors, and names of suppliers for the new display cabinets she had envisioned.

After four hours of sitting on the too firm bed, her back ached and the walls of the small bedroom felt like they were closing in on her.

She rolled her head from side to side to relieve the kink in her neck. With a sigh, she turned off her laptop. She figured a brisk walk would work out the stiffness in her back and refresh her tired brain.

She had bundled up for the cold weather and set out aimlessly, her only goal to walk and clear her head. What she hadn't anticipated was the sense of separateness was even stronger out on the crowded sidewalk.

When she spied a flower shop up ahead, she crossed the street. The memories of hustling furiously to get out deliveries, working with her hands to create living works of art, and marking life's joys and sorrows with her flowers left her aching inside.

Picking her way carefully across the slick street, she thought about the day Gideon had picked her up off the sidewalk. She was several blocks away from where it happened, but the memory of that moment came to her in vivid detail.

Her vision blurred and she stopped to swipe her tears away with her gloved hand. She had mastered her feelings and knew how to control her power as easily as she drew breath, but it didn't stop the pain of the emotions as they emerged from the dark corners of her heart. Glancing up, she noticed she'd stopped in front of an old brick church.

She began to climb the steps, needing to find solace in the familiar scent and welcoming quiet of the sanctuary, when a fluttering movement to her right caught her attention.

A mother with a small child in tow was approaching the adjacent building. The woman wore a cheap-looking winter coat, the fabric too thin to stave off the chill of a February day. The hem and sleeves were frayed, revealing the dingy grey lining underneath. She wasn't wearing a hat and her stringy brown hair was raggedly shorn, exposing her ears, which, like her nose, were bright red and chapped from the cold.

What initially caught Lizzie's eye was the multitude of plastic grocery bags slung over both the woman's arms and clutched in her gloveless hands. Her shuffling movement and the breeze blowing down the street made the bags rustle like the beating wings of crows. The bags were creased and dirty like the woman's coat and looked stuffed with things other than groceries.

The child with her appeared to be between the ages of five and six, but Lizzie couldn't be certain because the girl was dwarfed by a coat that was easily two sizes too big for her scrawny frame. The sleeves were rolled back and the coat billowed around her, swinging like a bell as she struggled to keep up with her mother. Her small, red-mittened hands clutched the folds of the woman's coat for security. The little girl's long dark braids peeked out beneath the orange knitted hat. Her eyes were huge and dark in contrast to her pale skin and appeared too big for her pinched little face.

The little girl looked up to where Lizzie stood on the church steps as her mother struggled to open the door of the nondescript building. The little girl's eyes widened, a radiant smile spreading across her face.

"Look, Mama, an angel," she said, pointing her mitten at Lizzie.

"Hush, Maria," her mother said, not glancing up as she struggled to open the door.

"But Mama, look, she's all sparkly." The little girl tugged on her mother's coat to get her to look.

"Here, let me help you." Lizzie scrambled down the church steps and held the door open. The aromas of soup and strong coffee emanated from within.

"Thank you," she replied, her voice surprisingly deep and melodious.

"You're welcome." Lizzie smiled down at the child who stood rooted to a spot on the sidewalk even as her mother stepped across the threshold.

"You're pretty." The little girl reached out to Lizzie's hand that was holding open the door and touched the sleeve of her coat.

"So are you. I like your braids."

"My momma did them for me, I don't know how. Where are your wings? Angels always have wings. Do you have them hidden under your coat? Can I see them?"

"Maria, stop pestering the lady and get in here." To Lizzie, she said, "I'm sorry, she likes to talk and, once you get her going, she'll chatter on for hours."

"You daughter's lovely."

"Yes, she is." For the briefest moment, the harried look dissolved from the woman's face as she considered her daughter. "Maria, they're already serving lunch, and if we don't hurry up, they'll run out of the little crackers you like." She stepped farther into the building, the plastic bags crackling as she moved.

"I'm coming." The threat of not getting her favorite crackers seemed to be enough to disengage her from Lizzie. "Bye, angel lady." She waved to her as she followed in her mother's wake.

"Bye." Lizzie smiled and waved goodbye before letting the door close on the mother and child. That's when she noticed the simple bronze plaque mounted to the right of the door. The Sisters of Mercy Sanctuary for Women announced the building's purpose.

It took Lizzie only a moment's hesitation before she swung the door open and stepped inside.

Chapter Twenty-Six

It was near the end of March before Lizzie had a chance to catch up with Vivienne since her ordeal in the hotel. Vivienne was only in town for a couple of days before she was to set off again, this time for South Africa, so they decided to share a late lunch at the *La Petite Chou* on Young and Bloor.

They were seated at a small table tucked into a quiet corner of the restaurant, away from flow of the wait staff coming and going from the kitchen and the constant stream of patrons.

Over tender green salads tossed with herbed goat cheese and a raspberry vinaigrette, poached halibut, and tender white asparagus stalks, Lizzie listened in rapt attention as Vivienne talked about Paris—its architecture, people, and culture.

Vivienne couldn't talk about the business of the Order that called her to the City of Lights, but she could describe the beauty of the place and its people.

Lizzie shared her only good piece of news. She had found an apartment and would take possession on the first of April. It was a little farther from her shop than she would have liked and in need of a few repairs, but her desire to have her own home far outweighed the negative aspects of the place.

Lizzie relished sharing a meal with her friend with whom she also shared a special gift. To any casual observer, that's all that appeared to be going on, but to Lizzie's delight, their energetic connection made their conversation open and crystal clear. She could feel Vivienne's emotions behind the words she spoke and her tender compassion that was as much a part of her as the warmth of her smile and the kindness in her touch.

After weeks of skirting around Madison's uptight behavior at home and the growing silence between them, talking with Vivienne was such a welcome respite. The tension she'd been holding in dissolved and she felt herself relax into the moment. Sitting at the table with Vivienne in a crowded restaurant, she felt she was home. The relief was so complete it brought tears to her eyes.

She flicked the tears away with the tips of her fingers, not wanting to make a scene in the bustling restaurant.

"Things aren't what you expected living with Madison."

It wasn't disconcerting anymore the way Vivienne hit right to the heart of what was bothering her.

"No, they're not. She's so different than the way she was at the hotel or even the way she behaved when she worked for me. Now she's morphed into this person I don't recognize. There's something wrong with her and she won't open up to me. She was there for me when I needed her most and I can't understand why she won't let me do the same for her."

Vivienne dabbed the corner of her mouth with her linen napkin and placed it on her lap. "In becoming part of the Order, she's embarked on a journey that resonates with her true path, but some aspects of her current situation run counter to her destiny. Soon, she'll have to choose between the two. Deep down, she knows this, and the fear of it makes her act in ways that are not loving or kind."

"But I want to help her."

"I know you do, but she needs to do this on her own. Your job is to be there when she makes her choice and it's coming sooner than she thinks. Be there for her then. Right now, just be silent."

"It's her relationship with Richard, isn't it?"

Vivienne nodded. "Yes. But it's not just Madison that's causing you to look so tired."

"No, it's a big part of it, but I'm still struggling to get things moving forward with my shop. My former mother-in-law has managed to stall the process of releasing the building. To make matters worse, she's even hired a private eye who tracked me down. The other day, I spent two hours being grilled about the night of the fire. He was grasping at straws, but he intimated he thought I was guilty in some manner for both the fire and Ian's death."

"I thought the official police investigation ruled Ian's death an accident."

"It did, but Penelope has a lot of friends in high places and she's not going to stop until she has destroyed my life as she thinks I did to Ian."

"We can help with this."

"I appreciate the offer but I'd prefer to work through this problem on my own. Despite Penelope's money and influence, I still believe in the legal system and, being innocent, I have the law on my side."

"We could at least help with your legal costs."

"You don't need to worry about my money situation. I have resources, too. Maybe not as endless as Penelope's, but I'm not struggling in that department at least."

"But you're still struggling with sleeping through the night."

"There's no point in lying to you, is there?"

Vivienne smiled warmly. She reached behind her and snagged her purse from the back of the chair. "This may help. It's a new elixir I've been working on for you. Just put six drops into a cup of hot water and take it before bed." She handed Lizzie a small amber vial.

"Now this kind of help I will accept. Thank you." She slipped the vial into her purse. "At this point, I'm willing to try anything."

"Any new thoughts on the origins of your dream?"

"No, none at all. I was driving myself to distraction trying to figure it all out, but I couldn't come up with anything. For now, I'm not going to obsess about it anymore. I'd rather focus my energy on moving forward in my life and spending time at the Sisters of Mercy women's shelter."

"Ah, you're volunteering there."

"Yes, I came upon the place by accident and before I knew it, I'd signed up as a volunteer. I work a couple of days a week serving dinner, doing the clean-up, and some minor prep work in the kitchen for the breakfast service. It's the most amazing place. It isn't just a soup kitchen or a shelter. They have counselors and retraining programs to help the women get back on their feet. And the nuns that run it aren't anything like the ones I grew up around. They're open and non-judgmental and a real source of comfort to the women of the shelter..." She trailed off as she watched Vivienne nodding in agreement as she described the shelter. "But you already know all this because the Sisters of Mercy belongs to the Order. I don't know why I should be surprised."

"Does it bother you that you've unwittingly connected yourself to our organization after you've taken steps to distance yourself from it?"

"No," Lizzie replied.

"I can't say that it's surprising that fate has drawn you back to us."

"I don't believe in fate, it was just a coincidence. The Order probably runs several shelters in the area."

"No, the Sisters of Mercy is the only one in the Greater Toronto area that's affiliated with us. Yes, we have many safe houses, but only the one women's shelter downtown, and you seem to have found it like a compass needle seeking out true north."

Their waiter appeared at their table, asking if they wanted to see the dessert menu, effectively cutting off any further philosophical discussion on fate and destiny.

When the desserts arrived, Lizzie dipped her spoon into the delicate chocolate mousse and took her first taste. "Oh," she said, as the light-as-air mousse melted on her tongue.

Before she had met Vivienne and Gideon, she'd never had an appetite; eating seemed to take so much energy that she'd always fall back to drinking pots of coffee and crunching on sugar cubes. During her confinement in the hotel, she had shared almost every meal with Gideon, Madison, and Vivienne. She discovered, much to her amazement, the simple pleasure of sharing food with people she cared about.

Lizzie took one more spoonful of the chocolaty bliss before laying down her spoon. "I'd better not finish this. I've gained so much weight over the last couple of months I had to donate most of my clothes to the shelter because they didn't fit anymore."

"I've so enjoyed this," Vivienne said, gesturing with her hands to encompass the table and Lizzie. "It's a rare treat to take time out just to do girlie things like having lunch with a dear friend. The time has flown by and, sadly, I must leave for my next appointment."

"We'll have to do this more often whenever your schedule allows."

"Yes, I'd really like that, but before I head out, I want to update you on what we've gleaned so far about the location of the dark entity that was stalking you."

Lizzie shuddered as a chill crept up her spine. She didn't want to talk about that part of her recent past. If she didn't discuss it then it didn't exist.

"The seers worked around the clock since our attempt on the rooftop and they came up blank."

Lizzie let out a sigh of relief.

"However, just over the last couple of days, they've sensed an unusual increase in dark magick originating from California. These occurrences might be linked to the Dark Presence, so the director has sent a team of watchers to investigate. Even if I'm not in town, I'll make sure to call you if we know anything more."

Lizzie looked down at her half-eaten mousse. She poked at it with her spoon as she struggled to get her panicked heart to slow down.

"Lizzie, this is good news."

A muscle in her cheek twitched as she smiled at Vivienne. "I know. This person, or whoever it is, can't be allowed to continue trying to hurt me or anyone else for that matter. I mean, I've been the only target up until now, but without knowing his agenda, who's to say he won't go after someone else?" She laid her spoon down, took a deep breath, and continued. "That being said, the coward in me just wishes the whole thing would go away."

"I'd probably feel the same way if I were in your shoes. I was born into this life. You were thrust into our world in a very short time."

"It's not just that. If you manage to catch this person, what then? I know I said that I have complete faith in the legal system, but I don't think the Crown would be open to prosecuting someone accused of remote stalking using black magick."

"The Order would handle the matter internally."

"Do I want to know what that means? The Order doesn't sanction things like torture, do they? Without a doubt, he needs to be put away for life so that he can't hurt anyone else, but I couldn't live with myself if the Order executed him."

Vivienne reached across the table and put her hand on Lizzie's arm. "The Order doesn't operate that way. He won't be harmed, but we would ensure that he couldn't use his powers ever again. I can't give you the details, but I hope my word counts enough to reassure you."

The smile came easily to her lips this time. "Yes, it does."

"Now, as much as I'd love to stay longer, I really must get going."

"Yes." Lizzie glanced at her watch. "I should get going too."

"Why don't I run you over to the shelter? It's on my way. I assume that's where you're heading, and then we can extend our girl time just a little longer."

"I'd love that."

Vivienne insisted on paying the bill and the two women strolled out of the restaurant, arms linked in comfortable companionship.

Lizzie was the happiest she'd been in months.

Chapter Twenty-Seven

Lizzie swung open the door to the Sisters of Mercy, energized with a sense of optimism after her lunch with Vivienne. After hanging up her coat and depositing her purse in the staff lounge, she headed into the kitchen.

Donning a hair net then tying a white apron over her street clothes, she called out to the cook. "Hi, Miss Sweetie."

"Hey, Miss Lizzie, what brings you in so early? I didn't expect you for a couple more hours," said the tall man dressed in a white cook's jacket peeling carrots at the prep counter.

Along with his white jacket, he wore a matching cap over his smooth, bald head. His skin was the color of caramels and his startling green eyes spoke of his mixed heritage.

His exotic almond-shaped eyes had such an abundance of thick, dark lashes they looked like they were lined in kohl. He smelled of red licorice because of the lip gloss he applied constantly from a small tube he kept in the breast pocket of his chef's whites. Small diamond studs winked on his earlobes.

Miss Sweetie put down the peeler and gave her an inquiring look.

"I was already out and didn't feel like going back home. By the looks of things, it's good I decided to come in early." She washed her hands at the sink and stepped over to the prep counter, eyeing the mound of carrots piled high to one side.

"That's not even half of what was donated today. There's another two bushels in the cooler. Thank heaven they store well. I thought I could steam some of them for dinner, I've started two batches of spaghetti sauce they can go in, and then I'll use the rest for carrot cake. I figure we could make about six cakes, use one for the menu tonight and put the rest in the freezer for later."

197

"Sounds like a plan." Lizzie grabbed another peeler.

"Before you get elbow deep in carrots, Carlotta Jenkins left you something. It's over on the counter by the phone."

Lizzie put down her peeler and walked to the far end of the kitchen. On the counter below the wall-mounted phone were an envelope and a small package wrapped in blue paper with silver stars. She opened the envelope first.

It was a thank-you card from Carlotta, the woman with the grocery bags she had met the day she had discovered the Sisters of Mercy.

Carlotta, like many of the women who found their way through the doors of the shelter, had been hanging on by a thread, and when the thread finally snapped, she had no family to turn to.

Hers was a story familiar to the inhabitants of the shelter—an alcoholic husband who when she needed him most not only took off with her best friend, but also cleaned out what meager savings she has managed to collect, leaving her and her small daughter to fend for themselves on the streets.

The day Lizzie had met her, Carlotta had just been evicted from her apartment. A social services agent had sent her to the Sisters of Mercy while her welfare application was being processed.

One day, when Lizzie had shared a coffee with her in the dining room, Carlotta had mentioned she'd been applying for waitressing jobs, but hadn't been called for even one interview.

Lizzie had convinced her to hold off and take advantage of the job counseling programs before taking another dead-end job. Even working fulltime, Carlotta would still be part of the growing ranks of working poor.

When Lizzie discovered Carlotta shared her passion for flowers, she immediately contacted the owner of a flower shop whom she respected and proposed the perfect solution. She put the owner in contact with the nun who ran the retraining program at the shelter, and before long, Carlotta was employed as a florist in-training.

If it worked out, and from all accounts both the flower shop owner and Carlotta were thrilled by the arrangement, Carlotta would be able to move out of the shelter in as little as three months into an apartment of her own again.

Lizzie put the thank you card aside and turned her attention to the gift. She slowly removed the tape and carefully peeled back the gift wrap. Folding the wrapping paper, she smoothed out the wrinkles before lifting the lid on the cardboard box. Nestled in a mound of white tissue paper was a small ceramic figurine.

Letting out a delighted laugh, she held the small figure of a faerie up to the light to examine it more closely.

She recalled Maria saying her grade one class had been on a field trip to a paint-your-own pottery studio a couple of weeks ago.

The faerie wore a short pink dress and was crouched on a lime-green toadstool, her face uplifted. Maria had painted the faerie's skin a light opalescent blue, but the hair and eyes matched Lizzie's coloring.

She held up the figurine for Miss Sweetie to see.

"Is that from Carlotta's little one?"

She nodded.

"She certainly has an eye for color."

"Yes, she does, and she also seems to think I'm a faerie. The first time she met me, she called me an angel, but when she saw I wasn't hiding any wings under my coat, she actually apologized to me for calling me an angel when I was so clearly a faerie. You see, according to Maria, faeries don't have wings, only angels do."

"Is that why she didn't paint the wings?"

"That would be my guess."

"With the blue skin, it makes you look kinda of like a Smurf faerie."

"So it does." Lizzie chuckled.

She knew the reason Maria painted her with blue skin, but she chose not to share it with Miss Sweetie. As Vivienne had taught her, it was simply because Maria could see auras, as most young children could before they were old enough for their rational minds to close off the perception. Maria saw Lizzie's energy field mostly blue, so she painted what she saw.

"Well, I think she's right about you. You're her mother's faerie godmother, especially after what I heard you did, getting Carlotta working for that flower shop."

Lizzie blushed. "I didn't really do anything. I just made a phone call. It's Carlotta and her hard work and talent that have made the arrangement work out so favorably."

As she returned the ceramic figure to the box it came in, she noticed writing on the base.

To My Favorite Faerie. Love, Maria had been painted in black glaze in a flowing perfect hand, no doubt done by Maria's teacher.

Lizzie rewrapped the figurine in the tissue paper, tucked the neatly folded wrapping paper on top, and carefully closed the box.

She picked up her vegetable peeler and turned her attention to the mountain of carrots, humming a tune as she worked.

Later, while Lizzie was setting tables, Carlotta and Maria returned to the shelter for the evening and wandered into the dining room. Maria ran over to Lizzie, her braids bouncing behind her.

Lizzie knelt down and scooped up the little girl in her arms. "Thanks for the faerie. It's the most beautiful present I've ever received. I'll cherish it forever."

"Really? I painted it myself. It looks just like you. 'Cept for the stupid wings. I wanted a faerie with no wings, but they didn't have one. It's okay, isn't it?"

"It's more than okay. I love it."

Carlotta came up behind her daughter, a smile spreading across her face. Lizzie hardly recognized her as the worn out, desperate woman she first met at the shelter doors. Her hair was recently cut and styled in soft waves, and she wore just a hint of makeup to flatter her brown eyes.

Lizzie relaxed her gaze and sent her energy out toward Maria's mom. She saw golden sparks of light surrounding her aura of soft pinks and blues. She felt confidence and love emanating from Carlotta.

A soft warm hand touched Lizzie's cheek. She pulled her energy back and looked at the child in her arms.

"Faerie lady," she whispered in Lizzie's ear, and giggled.

"Maria, why don't you go wash up and help Ms. Bennet set the tables?"

"Okay, Mommy." Lizzie put her down and she scooted off to the washroom.

"How was your day?"

"It was wonderful. I don't remember a time in my life when I woke up excited to go to work. I can't thank you enough for the opportunity."

"You already have. Just seeing you happy and at peace is the best thanks I can get." She gave Carlotta a hug. Since she had left the convent and the warm affection of Sister Collette, she had led a life that was void and sterile. Since meeting up with Vivienne and Gideon, hugging people with open arms had become as easy as walking.

"Oh, I really am happy. Josh is such a wonderful guy to work for. I never thought my husband running off with my best friend and stealing all my money would actually be a blessing in disguise."

"Life can be delightfully strange, can't it?"

With Maria and Carlotta's help, she had the dining room set in no time and went back into the kitchen to give Miss Sweetie a hand serving the food.

With the help of three more volunteers and two of the nuns, the dinner service went without a hitch. The carrot cake with cream cheese icing was a hit and many of the clients at the shelter came back for a second piece.

By seven, the dishes were cleared away and Lizzie was serving the last round of coffee before the kitchen closed. Her feet ached and her lower back was tight from standing on her feet for five hours, but she still felt a warm glow of happiness from how her day continued to bring her so much joy.

With a fresh pot of coffee in hand, Lizzie approached the newest member of the shelter's family. She had come in two days ago, a look of bewilderment in her pale blue eyes.

According to Miss Sweetie, her name was Mrs. Hetherington.

She was in her late seventies, but her stooped shoulders made her appear older. Wisps of her snow white hair had escaped her carefully arranged coif, and her perfectly manicured fingers kept trying to smooth them away from her heavily powdered face. She wore a smartly tailored suit of peach silk and on her wedding finger was a large diamond.

"More coffee?"

"Yes, dear, that would be lovely. I don't sleep much anyway these days, so what would a little more caffeine hurt?"

Lizzie refilled her cup and put the pot on the table. "Would you like some company?"

Mrs. Hetherington looked up from her coffee cup, her watery eyes searching Lizzie's face.

"I don't want to pull you away from your work."

"It's no problem. Everything is basically done in the kitchen. I wouldn't mind getting off my feet for a few minutes and I'd welcome the company."

Mrs. Hetherington motioned for her to take a seat.

"I'm Lizzie," she said, sticking out her hand.

"Dorothy, pleased to meet you."

They shook hands across the table. Lizzie was surprised at how firm the old lady's grip was.

"Are you settling in okay?"

"Yes, the sisters have been most accommodating. I've been put up in a nice single room. The bed is comfortable and the room is clean."

"But you're having trouble sleeping." Lizzie recognized the look of sleep deprivation in the dark smudges underneath Dorothy's eyes and the slow blink of her heavy lids.

"I'm not used to sleeping alone. I'm just recently widowed."

"I'm sorry for your loss."

"I miss him terribly. We'd been married almost sixty years. He was my life, and now I don't know what I'm going to do. You see, he took care of the money and I took care of him. We never felt the need to have children, so now I'm all alone. It wasn't until his death that I found out we didn't have any money left. I know I should be angry that he didn't trust me enough to tell me how badly we were doing financially, but I'm not. My Henry was a loving man, but he had a lot of pride. It would have hurt him terribly to admit to me that he had lost all our money."

"You'll be safe here until you figure out what to do. The shelter has an amazing staff of counselors to provide you with whatever you need to start again. And if you just need someone to talk to, I'm here every Tuesday and Thursday evening."

"That's very kind of you."

"I can't take away the pain of your loss, but I may have something that will help you sleep. I'll be right back."

Lizzie zipped into the staff lounge and retrieved the vial Vivienne had given her earlier. She stopped into the kitchen and snagged a cup of hot water.

As she approached the table where Dorothy sat nursing her coffee, she watched the woman's expression soften, a wistfulness replacing the sorrow. Lizzie followed her gaze. A young mother sat at a table with her little boy on her lap. He was drinking milk out of a sippy cup and mangling an Arrowroot biscuit.

Lizzie made a mental note to ask Sister Agnes, who was in charge of the daycare, to see if Dorothy might be a candidate to work there.

She took a seat back at the table and put several drops of the tincture into the hot water.

"This is an all-natural mixture that may help you sleep. Let me know if it does and I can get you more." She handed the mug over to Dorothy who took it gratefully.

"You're very kind."

"It's the least I can do." She stood up from the table and pushed her chair in. "And besides, isn't that what life's all about, helping each other? Reminding each other that we aren't alone?"

On an impulse, Lizzie leaned over and kissed her lightly on the cheek. Dorothy's face lit up with a smile.

"You are an angel."

Lizzie chuckled. "I'm flattered, but actually, I'm a faerie. There's a little girl staying here who'll swear I am." She picked up the coffee pot, heading toward the kitchen, when a tight fist of fear hit her in the solar plexus, taking her breath away. The coffee pot slipped from her fingers as she doubled over in pain. It shattered on the tile floor, splashing hot coffee and broken glass everywhere.

Intense fear engulfed her and pain pummeled her on her shoulders and face. Reflexively, she raised her arms to shield her face, but there was no one there to defend herself against.

She glimpsed Miss Sweetie rushing out of the kitchen at the sound of the exploding pot before she doubled over again with pain.

"What's going on?" he asked. She heard him rush over to her side. She felt his large hand on her shoulder to steady her. "What's wrong? Are you sick?"

She struggled to look up into his face. Her words came out in gasps. "It's not me." She doubled over again as the pain increased. "It's Madison. She's in trouble."

Sweetie frantically scanned the dining room. "Madison? Where is she? Is she a new resident?"

"No, no, she's not here." She didn't have time or the strength to explain who Madison was. "I need to get home. My keys. They're in my coat pocket in the staff lounge."

Miss Sweetie hesitated.

"My keys. Get them now," she said with as much force as she could muster.

Miss Sweetie ran to the lounge. By then, Dorothy had made her way to Lizzie's side and guided her to a nearby chair where she collapsed.

Drawing in a ragged breath, she forced herself to concentrate on pulling her energy around herself in a protective shield.

"Is there anything I can do?" Should I call nine-one-one?"

"No, she said through clenched teeth. "I need to get to Madison, she needs my help..." Her words were cut short by her scream of agony. It felt as if someone had hit her hard in the ribs. It hurt to breathe.

Miss Sweetie returned with her coat and purse. He held her coat out to her, but when she tried to stand, a shooting pain on her left side stopped her.

Dorothy stepped out of the way as Miss Sweetie knelt down in front of Lizzie. "I think we need to get you to the hospital. I'm calling an ambulance."

"No, just give me my cell. It's in my purse. Please hurry."

Miss Sweetie reached over and dumped the contents of her purse on a nearby table, grabbing her phone from the jumbled pile of things. She snatched it from his hand before he had a chance to give it to her.

She jabbed at the speed dial for Madison's home number, her vision blurred by tears of pain.

"Pick up, pick up, pick up," she chanted as the phone continued to ring. When the voicemail clicked in, she tried Madison's cell. Again, the phone rang until it went to voicemail. She screamed in frustration, throwing the phone back on the table.

She closed her eyes, desperately trying to pull herself together and push down the physical pain so she could get to her friend. It was impossible for her to think past the throbbing sensation across her face and the searing pain she felt in her side every time she drew breath.

She heard small feet fast approaching from across the room.

"Maria, get back here, young lady," Carlotta said.

Lizzie opened her eyes when she felt the weight of two little hands on her knees.

"You got boo boos, faerie lady. I can help." She climbed onto her lap, causing Lizzie to wince in pain. "Sorry," the child said as she nestled into Lizzie's lap. "I'll take the ouchies away."

Carlotta caught up with her daughter, but stopped short of pulling her off Lizzie's lap. She opened her mouth to say something, but snapped it closed when Lizzie looked at her.

"Close your eyes," Maria said.

Lizzie did what she was told and immediately felt the warmth of little hands gently touch her lids, her cheeks, and the bridge of her nose.

The darkness behind her closed eyes transformed into a shimmering white light, as if someone was shining a powerful flashlight in her face. She had to resist the urge to open her eyes to find the source of the light.

Maria's hands moved from her face to her left shoulder, stopping where Lizzie felt the most pain. She felt the lightest of pressure as delicate fingers probed her shoulder. The light behind her lids brightened. From there she felt Maria's hands slide down to her ribcage. She flinched as the little girl's fingers sought the location of her pain. A kaleidoscope of lights as brilliant as a supernova burst behind her closed eyelids.

"All better now." Maria clapped her hands.

She slowly opened her eyes. Maria was still kneeling on her lap, her face just inches away from her. She could smell milk on the little girl's breath. She took a deep breath. The pain was gone. "Thank you."

"You're welcome." Maria held Lizzie's face in her hands, her eyes taking on a seriousness and wisdom beyond her six years. "You must hurry now, there isn't much time. Get to Madison as fast as you can."

Lizzie nodded, too shocked to speak.

Maria clambered off her lap and ran over to her mother. "Mommy, I'm ready for bed now."

Carlotta picked up her daughter, holding her child's head tight to her breast. Maria squirmed uncomfortably as her mother tightened her grip. Carlotta looked at Lizzie for the briefest of moments before turning her back and carrying Maria swiftly out of the room. In that fraction of a second, Lizzie saw fear in her eyes.

She didn't have time to run after Carlotta and explain that she needn't be afraid of her, that what she'd witnessed had come from Maria and was a gift, not something to run away from in revulsion.

With a sweep of her arm, she scooped the contents of her purse back inside her bag and threw on her coat.

"Shouldn't we be calling the police? If your friend is in trouble, I think that's the best thing that should be done," said Dorothy. She was standing against the far wall, putting as much distance as she could between herself and Lizzie. She wrung her hands; the immense diamond on her ring winked in and out as it caught the light.

"No, no police," she barked. The old woman winced as if she'd been hit.

Lizzie turned on her heels and raced out of the shelter. She was so focused on getting to Madison, it wasn't until she bolted out onto the dark street that she noticed Miss Sweetie had followed her. He kept pace with her as she ran down the block toward the condo. She glanced over at him as she sprinted down the sidewalk, her unbuttoned coat flapping behind her.

"Whatever danger your friend's in, I'm not letting you go in there alone." The vapor from his breath plumed out into the frigid night air as he spoke.

She was too winded to speak. Instead, she nodded her head and kept running. She was grateful to have him with her. She was afraid of what she might find once she got home.

When they had to stop for a red light, Lizzie bounced impatiently on the balls of her feet. It was only Miss Sweetie's large hand wrapping around hers that stopped her from rushing out into traffic to get to Madison.

When the light changed, she sprang forward, forcing Miss Sweetie to let go of her hand. Even though his stride was longer than hers, he struggled to keep up with her as she raced down the final few blocks to the high rise.

She arrived first, flinging the main door open with such force it narrowly missed hitting him in the face.

They raced across the lobby to the elevators, the concierge only giving them a bored look before returning to his evening paper he had strewn out across the reception desk. The elevator to the far right opened as soon as Lizzie hit the button.

As they rode the ascending elevator, she placed her hand on the console and willed the machine to continue up to Madison's suite without stopping. She felt the moment her energy engaged with the machine and within moments, the door opened on the right floor.

Racing down the carpeted hallway, she dug her keys out of her coat pocket and flew to Madison's door. She felt a power surge emanating from the door, but before her brain registered what it was, she had already started to put her key in the lock.

It felt like hitting a brick wall at a full run. The ward Madison had placed around the door to protect Lizzie pushed her back with such force it flung her off her feet and into Miss Sweetie, who had been standing directly behind her. They fell in a tangle of arms and legs onto the floor.

"What the hell was that?" Miss Sweetie raised himself onto his elbows.

Lizzie scrambled off him and struggled to her feet. "I'll explain later." She ran a few steps and scooped up her purse where it landed when she fell. Digging out her cell, she quickly dialed Gideon's number. If she had been thinking clearly, she would have called him back at the shelter when she first sensed what was happening to Madison. He answered on the first ring.

"I don't have time to explain. I'm at the condo. Madison's in trouble. Get here as fast as you can." She hung up without waiting for Gideon's reply. She faced the door, contemplating her next move. "The keys. Where are my keys?"

"Right here," Miss Sweetie said, sweeping them up from the carpet where they fell.

"Open the door. We don't have much time."

"Are you nuts? I'm all for helping your friend, but didn't you see what just happened? I think we should call the police."

"No, we can't. I have help on the way, but we need to get to her. There is a ward on the door to protect me from danger or violence. Just me, do you understand? The ward won't let me in because of what's going on in there right now, but it will you. It'll take me time to remove it and we don't have time. Please, trust me, it won't hurt you. Use the gold key. You need to get in there now. It may already be too late."

Miss Sweetie glanced at the keys in his hand then up at her.

"Please, I need you to get to Madison while I remove the protection from the door."

Miss Sweetie selected the gold key from the ring and slid it into the lock. He squeezed his eyes shut in anticipation of being shot across the hall like Lizzie had. When nothing happened, he opened his eyes and quickly unlocked the door.

In the seconds it took for him to insert the key, Lizzie had already begun to remove the ward. With her arms outstretched, her palms facing the door, she reached out with her mind until she felt the web of energy surrounding the doorframe. The now familiar buzzing filled her ears, the sound intensifying as the colored web of energy became visible to her.

The heavy steel door insulated any sound inside the apartment from penetrating into the communal hallway. As Miss Sweetie swung open the door, they heard Madison scream in pain.

Miss Sweetie bolted over the threshold, following the sounds of Madison's shouts. Lizzie stood by helplessly as Miss Sweetie disappeared down the hall toward Madison's bedroom.

She heard shouts—two male voices. One she recognized as Miss Sweetie's, then a crash as something heavy hit the floor. Never before had she felt so helpless. Her old nemesis, a panic attack, took the opportunity to make its presence known. It flitted on the edge of her perception, building as her frustration grew.

Her concentration faltered. The purple web of energy momentarily flickered out of her vision. She shook out her hands, drew a breath, and blocked the terrifying sounds coming from the depths of the apartment.

Her left hand shook as she reconnected with the energetic spirals of the ward and drew it back into itself. It took less than thirty seconds to remove the spell, but to Lizzie, standing helplessly on the other side of the apartment, it felt like hours had gone by until the web blinked out of existence and she was free to enter.

She dashed down the hall and stepped into chaos.

Chapter Twenty-Eight

As she ran into Madison's bedroom, she was hit with the smell of expensive perfumes clogging the air. Shattered glass from several perfume bottles, pots of face cream, and jewelry lay strewn across the polished concrete floor where someone had swiped them off the dressing table. A nightstand was tipped over and a crystal table lamp lay broken in half on the floor, its linen shade squashed flat.

Madison cowered in the corner, her knees drawn up to her chest. She was naked. Her left arm dangled at an unnatural angle from her shoulder and she used her undamaged right arm to cover her breasts.

Her left eye was swelling shut. Blood poured out of her nose and split lip, painting the lower half of her face crimson. Her one good eye was huge with fear, her gaze riveted on the bed where Miss Sweetie and Richard were struggling.

"Stop it, stop it," she screamed from the corner of the room.

Richard was straddling Miss Sweetie on the bed, his hands digging into the flesh of the black man's thick neck. He was shirtless and his large biceps bulged as he throttled the cook.

Miss Sweetie's face was the color of ash; his eyes bulged horribly and his mouth gaped open as he tried to breathe. He clawed ineffectually at Richard's arms as he struggled for air. One of Miss Sweetie's white chef shoes had come off and his stockinged heel drummed a tattoo on the edge of the bed as his body fought against the deprivation of oxygen.

Lizzie saw the horrible tableau from a heightened perception. She hadn't pulled back her energy after she'd removed the charm from the entrance, so she saw everyone overlaid with the color of their auras.

Madison's injuries appeared as a sickly avocado green, her fear and anger shot through as sparks of bright red.

Miss Sweetie was awash in a dull grey color that moved sluggishly as his life force pulled deeper inward. Only a small spark of clear, bright light remained over his heart. Even as Lizzie watched, it had begun to dim.

Richard's energy signature turned her heart to ice. His was black and writhing with white snake-like tendrils. Instinctively, she knew what she was seeing. Richard was high on something.

As she stepped further into the room, Richard looked up at her as he continued to choke Miss Sweetie. His eyes were cold and hard. He smiled at her, showing perfectly straight white teeth. Then he winked. "You're next, bitch," he said.

Lizzie let out a roar of anger, throwing up her arms, palms facing Richard. Two streams of blue light shot out from her palms directly at him. They hit him in the head, throwing him off Miss Sweetie and sending him crashing into the headboard.

Flecks of paint and plasterboard littered the pale blue silk bedspread from the impact.

She advanced into the room, keeping the connection with Richard. Narrowing her eyes, she focused her rage through the light and around his throat. It was his turn to gasp for air. He clawed at his throat, raking bloody tracks in his skin.

Using the light streams, she slowly forced him up the wall until his head was just inches from the ceiling.

He thrashed against the wall where she'd pinned him, the heels of his tasseled shoes gouging divots into the wall.

Her fury drew a curtain of red over her vision. She vibrated with the release of her bottled-up rage. Richard wasn't Richard anymore. In her altered state, he morphed into every man who had ever raised a hand against a woman. She let out a scream that contained the fury of all the women who had experienced pain from the hands of cruel men. Their voices boomed and echoed off the bedroom walls.

She heard a distant scuffle of movement, voices raised in concern, but she paid them no mind. She felt someone tugging at her pant leg, but she ignored it.

Instead, she watched in satisfaction as Richard's dark energy faded, the writhing snakes of white pulling back into his body. He'd stopped clawing at his neck, his arms dangling limply from his sides. His feet had stopped beating against the wall. His head drooped lifelessly to one side and droplets of blood from his self-inflicted neck wounds pattered softly onto the concrete floor.

"That's enough, Lizzie," Gideon said from behind her. His calm voice cut through the haze of redness surrounding her.

She had no intention of obeying him and continued to pour her anger at Richard. She wouldn't stop until she'd squeezed all the life out of his body.

She could feel Gideon step in closer to her until his hands rested on her shoulders, his broad chest touching her back.

"That's enough," he repeated. "You're killing him. He's not worth it." From his position at her back, he gently placed his hands on her forearms and firmly pressed down.

She resisted his efforts. Richard deserved to die.

"If you kill him, you will be just like him. That's not who you are. Let him go." His breath tickled her ear as he whispered to her. He firmly gripped her forearms and continued to apply a downward pressure.

A warmth spread through her back, engulfing her in a feeling of safety and love. The red mist surrounding her abated even more.

With supreme effort, she closed her eyes. She let out a sigh as she broke the energetic connection to Richard. Her arms dropped to her sides and she leaned back into Gideon for support. She kept her eyes closed as he wrapped his arms protectively around her.

As soon as she'd broken the contact with Richard, he dropped to the ground like a stone. She heard the thud as he hit the floor. She squeezed her eyes shut even tighter and turned into Gideon's chest.

She heard several pairs of feet scurry past her, heading in the direction of Richard's prone body. Lifting her head from Gideon's chest, she looked over his shoulder into the corner where Madison had been. She wasn't there.

"Madison?"

"It's alright, she's right here," Gideon said. He stepped slightly away from Lizzie, but still held on to her. He nodded down by her feet.

Madison was lying less than a foot away from her curled in a fetal position. She was crying silently, tears slowly leaking out of the eye that wasn't swollen shut.

Two women knelt next to Madison. The taller of the two was in her mid-thirties with long blond hair that fell straight down her back. She was dressed in khakis and a pale pink twinset and looked like a soccer mom. When she pushed up the sleeves of her cardigan to get them out of the way, Lizzie noticed the now familiar tattoo of the Order on her inside left wrist.

The other one was much younger, closer to Madison's age, and was dressed entirely in tight-fitting black leather. Her dark hair stood out from her head in spikes like an angry porcupine, each tip dyed a bright blue.

The blue-haired girl flipped open the hard-cased trauma kit that lay between the two women.

One of them had covered Madison with her coat. Judging by the conservative style and camel color, Lizzie guessed it belonged to the soccer mom.

Lizzie sank to her knees. "You're going to be okay." She reached out and touched Madison's foot peeking out from under the coat.

Madison snatched her foot away from her, the sudden movement causing her to wince in pain. "Don't touch me. You killed him. Murderer." Her words came out garbled, her split lip and injuries to the side of her face making it difficult to form the words. "Get out of here. Get out, get out." Madison tried to push farther away from Lizzie, but her injuries prevented her from moving more than a few inches.

Lizzie wanted to tell her friend she was wrong about her. That she was just trying to protect her from Richard, but the look of undiluted hatred in Madison's eyes dried up her words before she could speak.

The blond, who had been trying to splint Madison's left arm, looked up at Gideon for direction.

He lowered himself on his haunches, putting himself directly in Madison's line of sight. "You're badly hurt. Samantha and Lauren want to help you. I need you to be calm right now. Can you do that for me?"

Her good eye widened and she nodded.

He placed his hand on her forehead and intoned something under his breath. Lizzie didn't recognize the language, but it sounded like clear water rippling over round black stones. She saw the words he spoke as patterns of energy that floated in the space between Gideon and Madison. She instantly knew their meaning.

When he removed his hand, Madison's eyes were closed and her breathing was slow and even.

"She's ready," he said to the two women. They slowly lowered her onto the floor and returned to administering first aid.

With a dancer's grace, Gideon stood up in one liquid movement to stand next to Lizzie. He touched her lightly on the elbow. "Let's go."

Something in his voice snapped her back into the moment. She spun her head around looking for Miss Sweetie.

He was sitting up on the edge of the bed being looked after by two more women. They were dressed in white paramedic's uniforms, and like the two who were working on Madison, they had a kit of medical supplies open on the bed. One of the women held her hands to his throat.

Lizzie could see the healing energy flowing into his neck. She was surprised at the strength of his life force. It was slowly flooding back outwards from his heart.

She took a step toward him and he looked up as she approached. He gave her a weak smile and reached out his hand to her. She took it in her smaller one, grateful for the contact. "Are you okay?" she asked.

He nodded, unable to speak from the damage done to his throat, but the look in his eyes reassured her. She knelt down in front of him. With her free hand, she cupped her hand against his cheek. The paramedic who was working on his neck withdrew. "I'm so sorry, this is all my fault."

Miss Sweetie slowly shook his head in disagreement. Even the small movement caused him pain.

"You are so brave. You saved her life," she whispered.

He leaned forward and rested his broad, smooth forehead against hers. They remained that way, foreheads touching, for several minutes until she couldn't tell where her energy began and Miss Sweetie's ended.

Even though he had come very close to dying, his aura was already returning to its original bright, clear appearance, the pulse of his life force regaining its vitality even as she assessed his condition.

When their spirits touched, a small sigh escaped her lips. Miss Sweetie's true being was extraordinary in its purity and in the depth of his empathy and sensitivity. He was the most exquisite being she'd ever encountered.

"May the Blessings of the Goddess be upon you for now and forever more," she whispered so only Miss Sweetie could hear. When she sensed his strength returning to normal, she slowly withdrew her energy and opened her eyes. She kissed his hand before releasing it. He rewarded her with a wide smile.

She rocked back on her heels, but found she couldn't stand up. Before she could ask for help, Gideon was at her side lifting her to her feet. The room swam dangerously around her. She leaned into Gideon, grateful for the support.

"Come, we need to leave the healers to do their work and you need to rest," he said, leading her out of the bedroom.

She hadn't once looked over to the corner of the room by the headboard where Richard lay to see if any healers were working on him or if he was dead. She didn't care if he'd survived, and a part of her hoped he hadn't.

Chapter Twenty-Nine

Gideon deposited Lizzie on the white leather sectional in the living room then disappeared into her bedroom. The rest of the apartment was untouched from the violence contained in the master suite.

As she sat staring off into space waiting for Gideon to return, she caught a flicker of light energy coming from the front door. She turned her head, dimly aware her neck ached and she had the beginnings of a migraine throbbing at her temples.

The energy belonged to two men standing guard at the door. They were shorter than Gideon with black hair worn in the same slicked back style and were dressed in identical dark suits, complete with sunglasses. They had the same stern set to their jaw and stood with their arms crossed over their chests.

They were facing her, standing sentinel at the doorway, but because of their dark glasses, she couldn't tell if they were looking at her or staring off into the distance.

What intrigued her most were their energy signatures. They were exactly the same. She focused on the flow of emerald green and gold swirls eddying around their bodies, intermingling where the edges of their energy fields touched.

They were twins.

Gideon appeared from the doorway of Lizzie's bedroom, carrying her suitcase and carry-on. He left the suitcase, but took the carry-on with him into the adjacent bathroom.

Moments later, he rejoined her in the living room with her cases. He took a seat next to her on the couch. "You're way too open. You have to pull your energy back in a little and ground yourself."

She nodded wordlessly, but her headache had worsened and she couldn't do what he asked. She closed her eyes to ward off the pain jabbing behind them. A wave of nausea washed over her.

"Here, let me help." He placed his hand on her knee and instantly, her headache abated and her stomach settled down. With Gideon's energy strengthening her, she pulled her life force back inwards and pushed her energy down through the soles of her feet.

When she opened her eyes, Gideon's aura was gone. And when she glanced over at the two men at the door, their signatures were no longer visible either.

"I'll be right back. I just want to check on Madison. Wait here," Gideon said.

He was only gone for a few minutes, and when he returned, his face was an unreadable mask.

With Gideon's help, she slowly stood up from the couch. At that moment, the two women who were treating Miss Sweetie exited the bedroom. Although she'd left Miss Sweetie sitting up on the bed, he was now being carried out of the room on a back board. His eyes were closed and he appeared to be sleeping.

It was strange to see two women easily carrying a two-hundred-pound man as if he weighed no more than a feather. She knew magick was involved in managing this feat.

With her perceptions returned to normal, she couldn't see anything, although she could feel the charm as a change in air pressure around the three of them. She looked at Gideon in alarm.

"He's fine. It's just easier to transport him when he is calm," he said.

One of the sentinels at the door opened it to allow the healers to pass through.

"It's our turn." He put his arm around her waist to support her and nodded at the guards at the door. The twin on the left came over to Gideon, slung Lizzie's carry-on over his shoulder, and pulled out the handle on the rolling case.

"No, wait, I want to stay with Madison." She tried to pull away from Gideon, but she lacked the strength to break his hold around her waist.

"I know you do, but that's not what's best for her right now. Let the healers do their work and when she's rested and feeling better, you can see her. I'll take you to her myself."

She searched his face for reassurance, but found none. What remained unspoken tore her apart. Madison didn't want to see her. Her sorrow tore a jagged hole in her heart where her love for her friend resided. Madison blamed her for what happened, and she was right. She'd only meant to stop Richard from hurting Miss Sweetie and Madison, but she'd let it go too far. She still didn't know if Richard had survived, and now she was too terrified to ask.

"Yes, of course, that would be best," she said.

Gideon escorted her out of the condo with one of the silent twins following behind carrying her luggage.

There were six more members of the Order standing at intervals down the hall leading to the elevators. Lizzie kept her head down and followed the patterns on the carpet until they stepped into the elevator. The air in the hallway was thick with magick.

They entered the elevator and descended in silence. There were several more guardians waiting for them in the marble lobby. They had spaced themselves out evenly from the bank of elevators to the main door.

As Lizzie and Gideon walked through the protective gauntlet, the spell was even stronger than in the upstairs corridor. There was no one manning the concierge's desk, only members of the Order were in evidence.

When they stepped out onto the street, Gideon steered her toward his SUV.

Two unmarked white vans were parked directly in front of the entrance and she watched as the two women healers loaded Miss Sweetie into the back of one of the vans. The healer who looked like a soccer mom climbed in the back with Miss Sweetie while the leather-clad girl jumped into the driver's seat.

"Where are they taking him?"

"To one of our facilities. He'll receive better care there than at a regular hospital, trust me."

She did. She trusted Gideon with her life and trusted Miss Sweetie would be looked after.

When Gideon had settled her in the passenger seat, stowed her luggage, and the twin guardian had taken a seat in the back, Gideon pulled out into traffic.

"You can spend the night in one of our safe houses, or I could take you to the St. James."

Now that the adrenaline rush had dissipated and she wasn't strengthened by her magick, Lizzie barely had the capacity to answer him.

She shook herself out of her stupor. "No, take me back to the shelter, please. I'll spend the night in the employee lounge."

She was grateful he didn't try to argue with the sensibility of her choice. She looked out the passenger window during the short drive back to the shelter, not really seeing anything.

When he pulled up to the shelter, she was about to tell him to call the night supervisor to unlock the front doors when she noticed the time on the dashboard clock. The shelter locked down at nine every night and she assumed it had to be much later. The early twilight of winter made it impossible to judge the time. To her amazement, it was only a little after eight in the evening.

The terrible unfolding of the evening's events had occurred in less than an hour from the time Lizzie first felt Madison's injuries.

Sister Abigail was seated at the reception desk when they stepped into the shelter. Lizzie had spoken to the nun on several occasions and liked her open manner and her sense of humor.

Lizzie and the guardian stood off to the side as Gideon went over to speak to the nun. Sister Abigail smiled in recognition as he approached her, but her manner became business-like as he explained what had happened. She glanced over at Lizzie and nodded her head in response to something he said. When he left her to rejoin Lizzie, the nun picked up the phone and placed a call.

The shelter had taken on the sleepy hush of a household settling into the evening routine of quiet pursuits and getting ready for bed. There were very few women and even fewer children in the lounge watching TV and only a handful of teenagers in the games room.

The familiar smells of wood polish, the lingering aroma of dinner, and an indefinable commingling of scents from a home occupied by women created a welcoming atmosphere. The strain on Lizzie's nerves eased as they walked farther into the one place that felt more like home than any other she'd lived in as an adult.

The trio walked silently through the deserted dining hall toward the employee lounge, the kitchen dark and closed down for the night. Lizzie wondered who had finished cleaning up the kitchen and turned off the lights.

She staggered into the employee lounge, stopping only long enough to flick on the light before collapsing onto the futon. While being back at the shelter brought her some level of comfort, it did nothing to alleviate her exhaustion. She sank into the lumpy sofa, grateful for the small relief it provided.

The guardian wordlessly deposited her suitcases just inside the door and left just as quietly.

Draping his coat over a nearby chair, Gideon sat down next to her, close enough that their thighs touched. When he put his arm around her, she sank into him, resting her head on his shoulder.

"Your fellow guardian, the one that just left, does he ever talk?"

"Oh, Gerald. Only when absolutely necessary."

"As a guard for the Order, did he have to swear a vow of silence or something?"

"No, he's just really shy. So is his brother, Jerald."

Lizzie sputtered, a hysterical bubble of laughter escaping her lips. She instantly felt guilty for laughing. She leaned back into his arm, sober faced again. "Is he going to stand out there all night?"

"No, I'll drive him back to the Motherhouse when I leave. He needed to come with us to help me maintain the cloaking charm until we got here."

"Oh."

Although her body was demanding her to rest, her mind couldn't stop replaying the scene at the condo—Madison broken and bleeding, Miss Sweetie struggling to breathe as Richard throttled him, and the rage that filled her as she turned her powers on the pathetic excuse of a man. She did the right thing; she saved two people. She did the right thing.

"Why didn't I call the police?" she whispered to herself.

"Why didn't you?"

Turning her head to rest her cheek on his shoulder, she looked at him. "I don't know. I can't explain it. When I felt her pain, I wanted to call the police, but something stopped me. All I kept thinking was I needed to get there, to stop what was happening. Even if I had been thinking clearly, I don't know if I could have called nine-one-one."

"Sounds like she reached out to you. You couldn't call the police because she didn't want you to."

"But how did she make such a strong a link with me? The only other person who can do that is Vivienne and only because of the time we spent together in the *In Between*."

"What were you doing before you felt her?"

"Nothing unusual. Dinner service was over and I was serving coffee to the few remaining women in the dining room."

"What was your mindset?"

"Pardon?" she said, sitting a little forward.

"How were you feeling? Where you sad, angry, happy?"

"I was...happy I guess. Maria, a young girl who is staying here with her mom, gave me a ceramic faerie that she hand-painted. I was touched by her gift." She thought more about the moments leading up to linking with Madison. "In fact, I was feeling so much peace at being here in a place where I felt connected, where what I do makes a difference. I felt blessed."

"Then it wasn't so much that Madison had the power to inhabit your energy, but that you were very open because of how you were feeling. You've seen how a normal aura sits about three feet around the body."

Lizzie nodded her understanding.

"The feelings you described opens you up and sends your aura out farther than it normally rests around the body," he continued. "Madison sent out an energetic distress call and because of who you are, and how open you were, you not only picked up on it, you took on her emotions and physical pain. You saved her life."

"And now she doesn't even want to see me. I didn't mean to do that to Richard." She couldn't even say the exact words for what she'd done. "I just wanted to stop him from hurting Miss Sweetie and Madison." She put her head in her hands. She just wanted everything to go away. She wished she was back sequestered in the hotel with Madison and Gideon rallied around her. Madison had become like a sister to her and now she'd ruined everything. She'd no idea their friendship was such a fragile creature, and she'd surely smashed it to dust by not controlling her rage.

"Lizzie," he said, gently pulling her hands away from her face. "You can't take what she said seriously. She was in extreme pain from her injuries. Let her heal and you'll see. She'll come around in time." He ran his thumb over the side of her hand. His touch sent pleasant shivers up her arm despite her distress.

"I hope you're right."

"Did you know he was married?"

She looked down at their joined hands. His thumb had stopped stroking her hand.

"Yes."

The silence grew, filling the space with words neither wanted to speak.

She had an inkling as to why Madison hooked up with someone who was emotionally unavailable, someone who thrived on control and cruelty. Madison and she were more alike than she'd imagined. She had suspected about Richard's temperament the moment she had watched Madison talk on the phone with him. She had known for certain after one day as her houseguest. And she had done nothing to help her friend until it was almost too late.

"You've had a long day and you need to get some sleep," Gideon said, filling the uncomfortable silence.

"Yes, I suppose you're right."

"I can stay if you want."

The timbre of his voice made her look up from their joined hands and into his eyes.

"I'd like to stay," he said, his gaze direct.

Exhaustion had eroded her reserve. She didn't have the strength to push down her feelings for him, what she'd felt about him from the moment he'd rescued her at the cemetery and had sought sanctuary in the church.

She inhaled sharply, the air crackling between them with the kind of tension that made her heart race in anticipation and the hairs on the back of her neck rise in a delicious shiver. There was no mistaking his intention this time.

She reached out and touched his cheek, her eyes searching his. He answered her silent question by leaning in and kissing her.

His kiss was soft at first, gently seeking her permission. She responded with a passion that rose up, shocking her with the intensity of her yearning. She had been hungry for this fire, this all-consuming heat between them. She let go her restraint, matching his desire with her own.

He drew her in closer, threading his fingers through her short hair. Her arms snaked around his neck, their bodies touching, sparking a heat that threatened to undo her completely.

Flashes of red, orange, and blue danced before her closed eyes as she opened herself up to him. She ached to feel him hard and naked against her own bare flesh.

As if reading her mind, Gideon's hands fumbled with the lapels of her coat, desperate to shed the layers of clothing between them. Her eyes fluttered open as he clumsily pushed her coat down over her shoulders. His eyes were hooded with desire, his breath coming in shallow gasps, matching hers.

In a distant part of her mind, she heard the knock on the door, but it wasn't until she felt another's presence in the room that she pulled herself away from Gideon's embrace. Looking over Gideon's shoulder, she saw Gerald standing in the doorway. He stood with his hand out holding his cell phone, his mouth open as if to speak. He was still wearing his sunglasses, but even without seeing his eyes, she could read his displeasure by the sharp turn of his head as the dark lenses of his sunglasses pointed in her direction.

"What is it?" Gideon asked, his voice husky. He swiveled around on the futon to follow her gaze.

It was Gerald who answered. "It's the Motherhouse. The director tried calling you, but you weren't picking up. I've got her on the line right now," he said, holding out his phone to Gideon.

"I'll take it outside."

Gerald stood for a half a beat before backing out of the room and closing the door.

Gideon turned to Lizzie, his jaw set and his lips drawn in a thin line. All remnants of his desire had disappeared from his dark eyes. He began to speak, but she frantically placed her finger to his lips to stop him. If he spoke, all would be lost, the spell broken. She shook her head, silently pleading with him not to utter the words that would break her heart. She searched his eyes for even a glimpse of the desire that was there mere moments ago. All she saw was sorrow and regret.

He gently removed her finger from his lips, carefully placing her hand in her own lap. "I have to go. I can't keep the director waiting."

"No, please stay." She clenched her hands into fists against her thighs. He'd reduced her to pleading, but she didn't care if it meant he would stay. She would grovel at his feet if it would stop him from walking out.

"I can't. I shouldn't have done this. I don't know what I was thinking." The pain in his voice pierced her soul. In one swift movement, he stood up and snagged his coat from the chair. He draped it over his arm as he backed toward the door. "I've crossed a line, and I'm so sorry, Lizzie. You deserve better than this." He spun on his heels and vanished out the door.

She remained seated, scarcely breathing for fear she would shatter the tenuous hold she had on her emotions. She shivered slightly as she drew down around her the familiar numbness like a shroud.

She stared at the closed door as if by the sheer force of her thoughts, she could bring Gideon back, but he didn't come and the door remained closed.

She wouldn't allow herself the release of tears. To feel nothing was far better than allowing her heart to feel her dark despair. Her hand crept to her throat, seeking comfort in the cross around her neck. It felt heavy and cold against her skin.

Chapter Thirty

For hours, she sat like a stone staring at the door of the employee lounge. Only when her body gave in to exhaustion did she lower herself onto the futon. She curled into a protective ball, pulling her coat over her cold shoulders.

She found no respite in the dark hallways of her dreams. As it had been since her journey to the *In Between*, she dreamed of her Rose Cottage, for that is how she had begun to think of the little stone house in the woods.

As she eagerly made her way up the gravel driveway, the sense of the cottage patiently waiting for her to enter grew stronger. As her hand curled around the doorknob, the anticipation, a sharp-edged sensation, heightened the color of the blue door against the grey stones. The smell of pine and cedar was sharp in her nostrils as she willed the door to open this time. But it would not obey her desire and the handle rattled unyielding in her hand.

Her eyes flew open and she stared at the ceiling in frustration. Her coat had fallen to the floor during her restless dreaming. Shivering, she sat up slowly, her back and neck stiff from sleeping on a lumpy futon in the cold room. The clock on the far wall said it was only four-thirty in the morning.

There was no point in trying to get back to sleep. Even if she managed to, she knew the dream would be waiting for her. She wanted to talk to someone. But the only person left in her life who she could call was Vivienne. For one brief moment, she considered the idea, and just as quickly, realized the folly of it.

What would she say to her mentor? "Hey, Vivienne, I've had a horrible night. I think I might have killed a man, my best friend won't even look at me for what I've done, and oh yeah, I'm in love with your son and because of me, he broke his sacred vow to the Order."

She gave Vivienne a great deal of credit for understanding the foibles of human nature, but she didn't think she would welcome the news of Gideon's disgrace and Lizzie declaring her love for her young son.

Despite what Vivienne had said about Lizzie's talent, she knew the truth about herself. Everyone who came too close to her was poisoned by her touch. Under Vivienne's tutelage, her power was more dangerous now because she knew how to control and focus it. She may have magick inside her, but it was dark and twisted.

Wearily, she pushed herself off the futon.

Although no one but the night supervisor would be up this early in the morning and the kitchen staff wasn't due in for at least an hour, she decided to head to the kitchen and do what she could to help prep for the breakfast service. It was the least she could do, seeing she had put Miss Sweetie in harm's way and now the staff would be running short one cook.

She opened her suitcase to pull out a change of clothes, and when she threw back the zippered lid, she got another painful reminder of the man she loved.

Even though Gideon only had a few minutes to pack her suitcase and didn't have time to take all of her clothes, he'd managed to pack the appropriate things—pants, a change of underwear, socks, shirts, a warm sweater, and her flannel pajamas. But it was what was nestled on top of her grey wool sweater that settled another layer of pain over her heart. He'd packed her Raggedy Ann doll.

Her throat tightened, but her eyes remained dry. She had no more tears to shed. She pulled out what she needed and dropped the lid closed. Clutching her carry-on Gideon had filled with her toiletries and her change of clothes, she crept quietly through the sleeping building toward the communal bathrooms.

After a hot shower, she managed to banish the chill from her bones but not from her heart. She padded into the dark kitchen, moving slowly and quietly so as not to stir the sleeping occupants on the floors above her.

Switching on the kitchen lights, she squinted against the harsh glare from the bank of florescent lights hanging from the ceiling.

She set about preparing the industrial urns for the morning coffee and hot water for tea. After she checked the posted menu for the day, she retrieved the mushrooms and peppers for omelettes. Cutting thick slices of homemade sourdough bread for French toast, she fought with the unwelcome tides of her emotions.

She resorted to focusing on what her hands where doing in the moment and repeating in her mind the task at hand. *Now I'm slicing mushrooms. In this moment, I am washing the peppers. Now, I'm walking over to the cutting board. Right now, I'm...*

Only then could she move through the morning without the threat of losing her center to the tempest swirling under her breast.

By the time the cook and the two volunteers ambled in for the morning shift, she had done all the prep work for the breakfast service. While the volunteers set the tables, she slipped quietly out of the kitchen and wandered into the library to avoid the residents who had started to trickle into the dining room and the inevitable small talk she would have to engage in.

In the early hours of the day, the library was the one room in the shelter that would be empty of people. Because it was situated at the back of the building, the room benefited from a row of clerestory windows. The lemon-colored light streaming through them hinted that winter was finally giving way to spring. It was bright enough for Lizzie to negotiate through the short stacks of books, so she kept the lights off. The soft lighting and grey shadows suited her mood.

There were several books lying on the reading tables and scattered on the end tables that were tucked into the corners of the library next to comfortable reading chairs. Lizzie hauled over the metal library cart and started to stack the books neatly on the cart to return them to their proper shelves.

As she worked methodically around the room, she picked up a stack of paperbacks. She went to place them on the trolley when something fluttered to the floor. She bent down and retrieved it, turning it over in her hand. It was a glossy brochure advertising The Halcyon Hot Springs and Retreat.

The picturesque landscape on the front cover stirred something in her. It was the mountains that intrigued her. She trailed her finger over the cool sleekness of the paper, outlining the gentle slope and curve of their peaks. As she did so, a shiver tickled the hairs on the back of her neck. In her hand, she held a photo of the exact mountain landscape she traveled past every night in her dreams.

She knew she'd never been to the Halcyon Hot Springs, but the landscape was the same as her dream of Rose Cottage. She sank down into the hard-backed chair.

"Lizzie?"

Startled, she shot out of the chair, knocking it backwards. She whirled around and snagged it before it clattered to the floor.

"Over here," she called out, slipping the brochure into the pocket of her cardigan. She peered out from around one of the stacks and spied Sister Mary standing in the doorway.

Like all the nuns who belonged to the Sisters of Mercy, she didn't wear a habit, but was dressed in modern if somewhat conservative garb. Her outfit was a grey tweed skirt, a white blouse, and a navy blue blazer. A large gold crucifix hung at her neck.

"There you are. I've been looking all over for you."

"I was just tidying up the library. Do they need my help in the kitchen?"

"Oh no, dear. There's a young lady who wants a word with you. She's waiting in the staff lounge."

Fear gripped her. If it was the police come to question her, she had no choice but to face the consequences of what she'd done to Richard. "Did she give her name?"

"No, but she did say that she has a message from someone named Gideon."

"Thank you," she said, holding herself back from tearing out of the library at a run.

As she walked briskly across the dining hall, she spotted Maria sitting with her mother. She was playing with her oatmeal rather than eating it. Waving a pudgy little hand, she gave Lizzie a sweet smile. She raised her hand to wave back when Carlotta looked up from her food and locked eyes with her. Lizzie's hand faltered in mid-air.

She looked from Carlotta to Maria, then waved and sent Maria a tender smile. Carlotta may not like her, but that wouldn't stop Lizzie from returning the little girl's affection. Her anger rose at Carlotta's ignorance. She couldn't fathom why some people chose to label something they didn't understand as a threat. Maria's only problem was a narrow-minded mother, not her gift of perception.

Her hand itched to send a blast of light at Carlotta and give her something to be afraid of. Instead, she stuck out her chin and marched into the employee lounge.

She found a young woman standing by a brand new red suitcase much fancier in design than Lizzie's drab utilitarian one. She stood at attention as if she was guarding whatever was in the case. Lizzie was sure the woman before her was a plainclothes policewoman. She certainly dressed like one, from the boxy black suit with huge shoulder pads to the sensible rubber-soled shoes. Her mousey brown hair was scraped back in a severe up-do. Her face was devoid of makeup, but her deep blue eyes showed intelligence and a shrewdness that made Lizzie's palms clammy.

"Hi, I'm Lizzie. I was told you wanted to see me."

"I know who you are. I've been fully updated on your brief. My name is Karen Watson." She pushed up the sleeve and turned her wrist so Lizzie could see her tattoo. "I was instructed to collect the rest of your things from your current residence and bring them here." She pointed to the cherry red case.

Lizzie relaxed her stance. This uptight woman wasn't a police officer but a member of the Order. "Sister Mary said you had a message from Gideon."

"Yes. He wanted you to have an update on the persons involved in last night's disturbance. The individual who is known to you as Miss Sweetie suffered a bruised larynx and has recovered fully. He has indicated he will be back at work here tomorrow."

Lizzie nodded, a wave of relief washing over her. She couldn't wait to see Miss Sweetie and thank him again for his courage.

"Madison Albright, apprentice to the Order, is still in our recovery unit. She suffered a dislocated left shoulder, a fractured left wrist, several broken ribs, a broken nose, and facial lacerations. She is healing well, but it will be at least a month before she can resume her training."

Lizzie could feel the blood draining out of her face as she listened to the litany of Madison's injuries. She was faint with a mixture of horror at what was done to her friend and relief that she was going to be okay. "When can I see her?"

"That's not possible. Miss Albright has indicated that she doesn't want any visitors at this time."

Lizzie felt the stone that had been pressing on her heart all day shift as Karen's words added another crushing boulder.

Karen continued to talk, but she was no longer listening. Madison still didn't want to see her. It wasn't until she heard Richard's name that she focused her attention back to Karen's words.

"He is still in a coma, but we are hopeful, with constant attention from our healers, he may come out of it. At this time, however, we cannot assess whether or not he's sustained any brain damage."

"And if he does pull through, what then? Will he be made to pay for what he did to Madison?"

"The director and the Council of Elders will decide how to deal with him when and if he ever awakens."

"But the police should be the ones to decide his fate, not the Order. He can't get away with what he did to her. He needs to be charged with assault." Her voice rose as she struggled to control her anger.

"And what should the police do about you?" Karen arched her eyebrow.

Lizzie glared at her. "It's not the same thing and you know it. I was trying to protect her."

"That may be true, but after you had him subdued, you went a little farther than was necessary. Do you realize that using so much of your power like that, you opened yourself up to being detected yet again by the Dark Presence? And because of you, we've had to position watchers outside the shelter."

"But Vivienne said because my energy and hers had blended, he wouldn't be able to track me."

"Whoever this person is, he's smart and we already know he's powerful, almost as powerful as you. More than likely, he's been monitoring the magick like we have and has picked up on your latest powerful blast. Don't you think he'd want to investigate it? Did you even think about the people you might have put at risk?" She took a deep breath. "I can't figure you out. Are you incredibly arrogant or just impossibly stupid?"

Lizzie clenched her hands at her side. She hated this woman, but even more, she hated the truth of what Karen had just said.

"And you've forgotten another important point," Karen continued. "How would you explain to the authorities how someone as tiny as you managed to overpower a one-hundred-and-ninety pound man high on cocaine and to inflict such severe injuries? Or would you rather Miss Sweetie take the fall instead?" She challenged Lizzie with a scathing look. Lizzie refused to answer. "At least you are loyal to your friends. So you see, the Order has done what was needed to ensure you and the members of the Order aren't exposed to the scrutiny of a police investigation."

"I appreciate you coming down here to tell me how my friends are doing and for delivering the rest of my things, but if there isn't anything else, I need to get back to work," she said through clenched teeth.

"Oh, there is one more thing and then I shall leave you to your duties." Karen stepped closer to her and with a quick, efficient movement, pulled out a business card from the inside of her suit jacket. "I've been assigned as your new guardian. This is my cell number. I assume you still have the phone the Order provided you with. Make sure you input the number in your directory."

Dumbfounded, Lizzie took the proffered card and held it by her fingertips as if it would burn her hand.

"I've been fully briefed on your situation and talents and your desire to have limited contact with your guardian. Rest assured, I will have no problem keeping to your request." Karen turned her back on her and made to leave.

Frantic, Lizzie struggled to find her voice just as Karen was stepping out the door. "They can't do this to him. Whatever impropriety they think he is guilty of, he didn't do anything. This is unfair. Gerald had no right to go behind Gideon's back telling tales to your stupid Order."

Karen stepped back over the threshold and turned to face Lizzie. She rested her hand on the door handle, her face inscrutable. "Although your devotion is touching," she said with a sneer, "Gerald didn't say anything, it was Gideon. And he knew in telling the Elders, he would no longer be your guardian. He knew exactly what would happen."

The floor was no longer solid under Lizzie's feet. The sensation of free falling was so strong Lizzie reached out her hand to a nearby chair to steady herself. She stared at Karen in disbelief.

Karen shot Lizzie a cruel smile then left, shutting the door with authority.

Furious, Lizzie ripped the business card in half and watched the two pieces flutter silently into the wastebasket.

Chapter Thirty-One

For the rest of the day, she moved through the shelter like a phantom, a grey wisp of smoke with no substance or purpose.

Her life had been one loss after another, but losing Madison, Gideon, and Vivienne all at once cut her to the quick. She knew Vivienne was lost to her even if she hadn't the courage to talk to her to find out for sure. Lizzie was responsible for her son's fall from grace; she doubted Vivienne would lend a sympathetic ear.

Those three had held her together, given her meaning and a sense she mattered. Her center couldn't hold without them. She had no one to cling to, no purpose other than her own, and with each passing moment, she had become less sure of what that was. Her life made no sense to her.

If Madison's and Gideon's rejection of her wasn't enough, Carlotta and Dorothy made it very clear they wanted nothing to do with her either.

Carlotta made no attempt to hide the fact she was actively avoiding Lizzie to the point of taking a dinner tray up to her room so Maria didn't have to eat in the dining room and risk being near to her.

When Dorothy and Lizzie's paths crossed during the day, Dorothy said nothing, just turned and walked in the opposite direction.

Retreating to the kitchen, Lizzie helped prepare for both lunch and dinner service and worked in the laundry between her kitchen duties.

During the busiest part of the early evening, she holed up in the library, knowing that the residents preferred to spend their time watching TV or conversing with each other. The children would be either in the games room or with the rest of the group in the TV room.

As she dusted books with a soft cloth and lovingly placed them back on the shelves, she pondered her unorthodox upbringing, allowing the questions that had long asked for her attention to come forth. Looking back on her life now, through the new lens of her recent experiences, created more questions than answers.

Did her mother seek sanctuary within the walls of the Abbey because she knew what she would be giving birth to? Or was it fate that had brought her there and was it the nuns who somehow knew what she was, even as a newborn? When the Abbey was finally rid of her, had the nuns prayed to their god that the magick placed on Lizzie's necklace would contain her evil, or did they even care now that she wasn't their problem anymore?

Why they decided to raise her behind their cloistered walls instead of sending her off to an orphanage when the Prioress had planned all along to make her leave when she turned eighteen made no sense. Had they struck some kind of bargain with her mother?

But what could Lizzie's birth mother possibly have used as a bargaining chip to make the Prioress agree to take in her baby? From what Lizzie knew, her mother showed up with only the clothes on her back and her books—the Austens she'd given to her daughter, and now they were lost forever. The only other thing of value Lizzie now wore around her neck.

Her hand crept to her neck, her fingers touching the stone resting at the base of her throat. She absently traced the intricate silver setting when Vivienne's voice broke through her rambling thoughts, and with it came a new and dreadful possibility.

"The color of the stone and the intricate silver filigree matches the description found in the archives, but the text mentions two strands of Dragon's Tears, twelve stones to be exact, that was part of the setting, whereas yours is just the cross. The setting could have been broken up sometime in the past, but we have no way of knowing."

She sat down hard on a nearby chair, not trusting her legs to keep her upright. Vivienne was right when she said that there was no way of knowing who had taken apart the stones or why the setting had been broken up. The only people who knew the answers were either dead or hidden behind the safety of their cloistered walls.

She thought about the remaining rubies in her possession. She'd been given six. Such beautiful stones, each one a deep blood red cut in the shape of teardrops. Dragon's tears.

It seemed preposterous, but the gooseflesh breaking out on her arms told her otherwise.

And the other half of the stones, were they given to the Prioress as a payoff for taking Lizzie in?

Her half, Lizzie realized with a sickening certainty, was the nuns' way of assuaging their guilt when they turned her out at the age of eighteen. They had kept their end of the bargain, raising her until she came of age then ensuring her financial wellbeing before washing their hands of her.

She had felt loved by Sister Collette. She was Lizzie's mother in all but name, but was that a lie too bought for the price of a handful of stones? Had she'd been mistaken all these years? She'd thought the gift of rubies from the sister was a gift of extravagant love.

When Sister Collette had presented Lizzie with the stones contained in a plain wooden box, she'd told Lizzie the gift was her legacy, but she wasn't to ask were they had come from. As Sister Collette pressed the box into Lizzie's hand, she instructed her to use them to secure her future. She had even given Lizzie Saul's name and phone number for the time when she would need to convert the stones to cash.

She knew Sister Collette, and any attempt on her part to try and wheedle the truth of where the stones came from would have been fruitless. She had also assumed the stones had been the sister's, something she'd brought into the nunnery from her former life.

Her mind bounced from question to question. Had the nuns know what and who she really was even as a child? Is that why they made her leave?

Pressing the heels of her hands into her eyes, she fought down her tears. Not knowing for certain if her speculation was right wouldn't make any difference. She knew full well what she was and what she was capable of. Richard's current condition was proof of her wickedness.

Only when she was certain the majority of the residents had been tucked up for the night, the building filled only with the soft sighs as the structure itself settled in, did she venture out of the quiet safety of the library.

Just the hallway lights remained on at night, dimmed down to a soft glow. As she passed by the nun assigned to the night desk, she looked over, waiting to give her a wave or a smile, but the nun was busy knitting pink yarn into something soft and comforting. She didn't look up from her clicking needles as Lizzie walked past.

If it weren't for the sound of her own footfalls as she crossed the dark dining room, she would have believed she truly had become a phantom. If she were to disappear tonight, would anyone notice or care?

She shut herself in the staff lounge for another restless night on the uncomfortable sofa. Sinking down into the unyielding futon, she contemplated her options.

She couldn't stay at the shelter indefinitely, and it was only because she knew there were guardians watching over the shelter that she felt it was okay to stay just one more night. She would remain at the shelter until Sweetie came in for his shift. She wanted to see him one more time. Until her apartment became available in a few weeks, she'd go back to the St. James.

And then what? She'd secured the lease on the apartment back when her focus had been on rebuilding Enchanted Garden.

Re-opening her shop seemed ridiculous now. She couldn't go back to that place in her life, not after what she'd done. The one thing she cared about only a few short days ago seemed frivolous and shallow.

She had had all she needed without even knowing it until it was no longer hers. For a fleeting moment, she'd had a taste of what it felt like to truly belong. She had been a member of a tribe that counted her as one of their own. Without them, what was the point of trying to move forward?

She had fueled herself throughout the day with her old friends, coffee, and sugar cubes. Exhausted and hungry, she shivered with tremors emanating from her core. Toeing off her shoes, she then curled her legs underneath her and huddled against the arm of the futon. As she crammed her freezing hands in the pockets of her cardigan to warm them, her fingertips touched something glossy in one of the pockets. Bewildered, she pulled out the brochure she had pocketed earlier in the day. The one she'd found stuffed between the pages of a paperback.

She turned it over in her hand, drawn again to the image of the mountains. A faint humming filled her head, growing in intensity until it became the susurration of ocean waves. The image in the brochure blurred and she surrendered to her tired eyes' inability to focus. The colors and the lines of the mountain range softened, taking on the texture of a Monet painting. Soft greens and blues blended and blurred into each other.

With a delicate sigh, she surrendered to the soothing resonance in her head that sounded like the steady heartbeat of a lover.

Chapter Thirty-Two

"Oh, hey, I didn't expect anyone to be here this early," said Evie, the morning cook, as she bustled into the staff lounge to hang up her purse and coat.

Lizzie jumped at the sound of the woman's voice. She whipped her head around and stared at her, dumbfounded. She blinked furiously as her brain tried to remember what she'd been doing curled up on the sofa in the staff lounge.

"What's the matter, cat got your tongue?" The older woman cackled.

Lizzie had no idea what the cook was laughing at as she struggled to clear the fog from her brain. She was about to ask her why she was showing up for the breakfast shift in the middle of the night when she glanced up at the clock on the wall. She snapped her mouth shut. It was five in the morning.

"You look like you've had a rough night. Man trouble? You don't have to answer that. I've seen that far off stare before and your eyes look like you've been crying all night. Well, whatever he said or did, it's not worth losing sleep over. Why don't you come join me in the kitchen and I'll make us a proper cup of coffee?"

Lizzie nodded, and that was enough for the cook. She finished buttoning up her whites and left Lizzie to join her later.

When she attempted to get off the couch, she couldn't move. Her legs, which were tucked underneath her, had lost all feeling. In her left hand, she still clutched the resort brochure. Like her legs, her hand was numb. Using her right hand, she yanked the crumpled brochure from her frozen grip and slowly pried her fingers open. She stuffed the brochure back into the pocket of her sweater.

It hurt when the blood began to flow down to her fingertips again. It started as pins and needles and blossomed into a red-hot surge of pain.

When she pulled her legs out from under her and the circulation returned, the burning sensation made her moan softly. By the time the pain subsided and she could walk without hobbling, she couldn't drum up the energy to have a proper shower, so she settled for a quick face wash, brushed her teeth, and ran a comb through her hair.

Thirty minutes later, she shuffled into the kitchen. She gratefully took the mug of steaming coffee the cook held out to her. Coffee would be just the thing to clear the cobwebs from her brain.

She took a gulp and almost spluttered the hot liquid all over the cook. It was laced with a hearty dose of brandy.

The cook raised her own mug and winked. "I told you a proper cup of coffee is just the thing to get you over your heartache."

"Yes, it's just what I needed. Thanks." She took a careful sip, this time letting the slow burn of the alcohol warm her cold insides.

"Just one cup, mind you, just to get the juices flowing." Evie took a sip from her mug and then turned back to the counter, breaking eggs into a large metal bowl.

As Lizzie left the kitchen, cradling her coffee, she noticed the box containing the faerie Maria had given her and the thank you card from Carlotta sitting on the counter. She turned the card over in her hand, saddened by the quick turnaround in Carlotta's feelings for her. She tucked the thank you card inside the box and took it with her back to the staff lounge.

She couldn't recall having any specific thoughts during the night, only the lullaby of waves filling her senses and a blanket of peace wrapping itself around her. She must have dozed off at some point, but if she had, the dream of her cottage hadn't found her last night.

Taking another sip of her brandy laced with a little coffee, she tried to clear her thoughts and figure out what she could do to fix what she'd broken, but nothing came to her.

She couldn't make Madison want to see her any more than she could make Gideon come back to her. Just as she couldn't make Carlotta understand she hadn't done anything to her daughter, that it was Maria who possessed the extraordinary gift of healing.

Her sorrow was sharp and brittle like ground glass underneath her skin. There was nothing she could do to change anything.

Placing the box carefully amongst the things in her suitcase, she transferred the clothes Karen had brought over in the bright red suitcase. She had no need for a brand new case, as everything she owned still fit in her old battered one. She'd donate it to the shelter so someone more deserving could have it.

* * * *

Lizzie spent most of the day avoiding people in the shelter. It wasn't as hard as she'd imagined. She sought out the day shift supervisor, Sister Anne, and asked to be assigned the least pleasant jobs that needed to be done.

Armed with a bucket of cleaning supplies and a mop, she scrubbed toilets, cleaned tubs and shower stalls, and washed floors in all the communal bathrooms on every floor of the shelter. She didn't stop for a break, not even when her rumbling stomach told her it was lunch or her back ached from bending over the tubs she was scrubbing.

It was almost three by the time she'd finished cleaning the last bathroom, just in time for Miss Sweetie to start his shift.

Stashing the mop and bucket in the supply closet, she rounded the corner to the kitchen. She ran into Miss Sweetie as he was coming out to the dining hall. She let out a muffled gasp as she bounced off his hard-muscled chest. Miss Sweetie instinctively wrapped his arms around her to steady her on her feet.

"Hey there, girl," he said, his voice a gravely whisper.

Around his neck was a pink paisley silk scarf tied to the side in a stylish knot. She glimpsed the shadow of bruises peeking out from the edges of the cheerful fabric.

She smiled up at him. He looked healthy. Except for the telltale bruising around his neck, he looked good, almost as if nothing bad had happened to him.

He gave her a warm smile back, a smile that extended all the way to his sea-green eyes.

"How are you feeling? I was worried about you. I'm so glad you're okay." Her words came out in a tumble, her nerves getting the better of her. She stood on her tiptoes and cupped his face gently in her hands.

"Wow, slow down. No need to get yourself all worked up. I'm fine."

She lowered her hands to his chest.

"My throat's a little sore, but nothing's broken. The doc said that should clear up in a bit, but in the meantime, I think it makes me sound kind of sexy, like Billy Holiday."

"Yes, it certainly does. But are you sure you're up to coming back to work? Shouldn't you take another day off and just rest?"

He shook his head and she noticed him wince before he could stop himself. "I'm fine."

"Thank you for what you did. You had no idea what kind of danger you were walking into and you did it just the same. You are very brave."

"So were you. When the burglar got the better of me and you smashed him over the head with that vase, I couldn't believe it. You knocked him out cold with just one swing. It was a good thing the police showed up before he came to."

Her mouth gaped. She was about to ask Miss Sweetie what he was talking about, but she caught herself in time.

"Now don't go looking all surprised. If anyone is a hero, it's you. It was your quick thinking that saved me and your friend. You are the brave one, and strong too. Remind me never to get on your bad side."

"Okay." She hoped her smile looked convincing. Her head was swimming and she felt like she was two steps behind in the conversation.

"Your friend, she's going to be okay?"

"Yes, her injuries are serious, but the doctor is certain she'll make a full recovery."

"That's good to hear. You aren't still staying at that place? Neither one of you should be living in a building with such crappy security."

"No, I spent the last few nights here. I'm getting my own apartment in a couple of weeks. Until then I'll be staying at the St. James."

He nodded his approval. He didn't wince that time.

"I don't think Madison will be going back there either."

"Good, good. Well, I should get back to work. I was just off to give Sister Beatrice the grocery order for next week."

"Yes, of course. I wanted to see how you were doing before I took my things to the hotel."

"Take care, Miss Lizzie." He engulfed her in a bear hug and, as he released her, he planted a kiss on her forehead. Immediately, he used his thumb to wipe off the shiny red imprint left by his lip gloss.

"See you on Tuesday," he croaked, his voice sounding harsher from the strain of talking.

"Until Tuesday then," she said, stepping out of his way to let him pass through the dining hall in search of Sister Beatrice. She watched his broad back, her vision blurring, as he disappeared down the hall.

Chapter Thirty-Three

She'd thought she would've been able to confide in Miss Sweetie. His reaction when he had first seen her had her believing she still had one friend left who had seen what she was capable of and still thought she was worthy of his affection.

When she realized the only reason he'd shown such concern and warmth toward her was because the Order had wiped his memory clean of what really happened, it destroyed the one thing that kept her from flying apart.

Her chest constricted and she couldn't breathe. She needed to get out of the shelter and into the fresh air to clear her head. She stumbled out into the street with only her cardigan to protect her from the brisk air.

All gone, all gone, all gone. The words thundered in her head as she walked blindly along the sidewalk. She couldn't stop the tears from coming.

She broke into a run. Her lungs burned, but she kept running, her tears stinging her cheeks. It wasn't until she careened off the shoulder of a passerby did she stop her frantic dash through the street.

She looked wildly around; for what, she wasn't sure. She couldn't outrun herself, and when she felt the familiar pressure building up inside her, she threw her head back and screamed in frustration. The pedestrians walking past her as she howled swerved out of her way, averting their eyes. No one stopped to ask her what was wrong, which was just as well because she wouldn't have been able to tell them anyway, and they wouldn't have believed her even if she could have.

Her anguished outburst had relieved the pressure, but it didn't bring her any clarity about what to do. Using the sleeve of her sweater, she swiped at her face, brushing away the tears and mucus.

I don't want to be here anymore, she thought, but she didn't know where else to go.

She turned in a circle, trying to figure out where to go. She had no idea where she'd ended up on her race through the streets. Looking up at the storefront where she'd stopped, her mouth fell open with disbelief. She was standing outside a travel agency.

She took a step toward the display window filled with posters of tropical travel destinations, but her gaze was riveted to one of the smaller poster boards advertising an all too familiar image.

"You've got to be kidding me." Pulling out the crumbled brochure in her cardigan pocket, she looked at it then back at the poster board advertising the same resort in the Kootenays.

She threw her head back and laughed. Her life was absurd, beyond absurd, but at least she knew what her next step would be.

She realized now the flaw in her desire to reopen her store, to go back to being what she was. She couldn't go back, only forward into the uncharted future. And she had to do it alone.

She had no one to go with her, her own actions had seen to that. And as much as Karen's words had enraged her, she knew if she had opened herself up yet again to detection from the Dark Presence, she needed to put as much distance as possible between herself and the people she loved.

She knew the stone cottage couldn't really exist, and the point of her traveling all the way to the other end of the country wasn't to find it. No, that wasn't what the dream had been trying to tell her. Finally, she understood the reason for the persistent dream; it wasn't a part of her past or her imagination but part of her future. Her subconscious had been telling all along what she needed to do and where she needed to do it, away from the people she held dear in a remote wilderness where she couldn't hurt another innocent soul.

Perhaps that had been the point of everything she'd been through. To get to this moment, to decide to take on whatever or whoever was after her. Everyone kept telling her how powerful she was, and soon, she would see if they were right. It would be just her and the Dark Presence.

She remembered Vivienne's words about destiny and how it seeks you out at any age. Maybe that is what she needed to accept; her life didn't lie with Gideon and his love or Madison and her friendship or Vivienne and her mentorship.

She'd always been on the outside of ordinary life, and the one she'd so carefully constructed with her shop had been an illusion too. She'd been marked at birth by her strangeness and her abilities. If the Dark Presence wanted her, perhaps it was because they shared something in common—a malevolence cut from the same flawed cloth.

But she wouldn't let that be her legacy. One way or another, she'd put an end to the threat even if that meant she was to be the sacrifice.

Squaring her shoulders, her nerves steady, she entered the travel agency and went toward her destiny.

Chapter Thirty-Four

As she sat in the cab heading to the airport, she realized although she couldn't change the way things had turned out, she could perform a few final acts of gratitude for the people she was leaving behind.

She could give the one thing she had an abundance of—money. Her whole life she'd guarded the rubies like a starving woman holding on to her last crust of bread. She'd mistakenly believed the financial security they represented was something worth fighting for. Without people to care about, to bring purpose and meaning to her life, money offered no comfort. There was only one thing worth risking everything for.

She pulled out the silver cell Gideon had given her and called her lawyer as the city center slipped past her through the cab window. As she explained to him what she wanted, Lizzie barely noticed the small corner of the city that had been her whole world disappear from view.

The few blocks she'd traversed for seventeen years were already behind her. Her village, surrounded by a vibrant and varied city that she had never really known or experienced, disappeared as she made another call, this time to Saul in the Diamond district to let him know that her lawyer would be in touch with him.

She was thankful several years earlier she'd given her lawyer authority to access the stones on her behalf. It being the weekend, she would have had to delay her travel plans in order to retrieve the stones herself and convert them into cash.

By the time the cabbie dropped her off at the airport departure's entrance, she'd managed to set her plans in motion, the execution of which she entrusted to her lawyer, her bank manager, and Saul.

She planned to have Carlotta's name on the rental agreement of the two-bedroom apartment she'd leased with the rent paid in full for a year.

She instructed her lawyer to draw up a bill of sale for the flower shop, and more importantly, leak the information to Penelope's lawyer that Lizzie was leaving town and closing up her business. Lizzie knew once Penelope felt she'd won the battle, she would stop delaying the release of the fire investigator's report.

She couldn't imagine his findings would indicate the cause of the fire to be anything other than faulty wiring or an accident of some kind. Once the building was released, Carlotta would be given the option to purchase the place for a dollar and given a sizable check to rebuild it. Or if she didn't want to own the shop, Lizzie had told her lawyer to sell the property and give the money from the sale to Carlotta.

For Miss Sweetie and The Sisters of Mercy, she would be giving them each a large check to do with as they pleased. These gifts would leave her with just one of the blood-red stones that had been her safety net and, in some ways, her albatross. One ruby was more than enough to cover her needs for the foreseeable future.

For the three people who she now thought of as her family, she would give them the only gift that mattered; she would use her powers to search out and destroy the Dark Presence.

After she'd checked her suitcase at the airline counter, she pulled out her cell one last time. There was one more thing she had to do before she boarded the plane.

"Good evening, concierge's desk, how may I help you?"

"Hello, Frank. It's Lizzie Bennet."

"Miss Bennet, what a pleasure to hear from you again. What can I do for you?"

"Actually, it's not me, but a young girl that is currently living at a women's shelter I volunteered at. She's only six years old, but she performed a hands-on healing on me that was very powerful. I think the Order may be able to assist her with her powers, especially as she gets older, and work with her mom to come to terms with her daughter's talent."

"It does sound like this little one may need our help and guidance, and the mother, too, of course. And which shelter are they currently staying at?"

"The Sisters of Mercy."

"And the mother's name?"

"Carlotta Jenkins."

"Splendid. I believe I have all the information needed. Rest assured that I will do my utmost to take care of this matter."

"Thank you, Frank. For everything."

"My pleasure, as always. And Miss Bennet…"

"Yes?"

"Do be careful."

"I will," she said, throwing up an energy block around her thoughts. "Take care." She disconnected the call before he could reply, her heart racing.

It was stupid of her not to have realized Frank possessed psychic abilities, especially considering who he really worked for.

She didn't want anyone to know where she was going. She hadn't even told her lawyer the specifics, only that she was going on a short vacation and she would be in touch with him when she'd had a chance to settle in. The last thing she wanted was to have the Order alerted to where she was headed. She prayed she'd blocked her thoughts from Frank in time.

Annoyed that she'd already jeopardized her plans before she'd even left the city, she hurriedly got in line at the security gates to board her flight.

It was a good lesson for her to remember. From this point on, she couldn't let her guard down, especially if she intended to be successful in her plans. She was going up against a force she knew nothing about, and she'd best remember another slip-up like that could be her undoing.

With grim determination, she set off up the boarding ramp and toward the destiny of her choosing with the dawning realization she had a lot of preparation and planning ahead of her if she wished to emerge from her scheme the victor.

Chapter Thirty-Five

Her flight to Revelstoke was enthralling. It was her first time on a plane, and despite the grave reason for her trip, she was enjoying the experience. The speed as the plane hurtled down the runway during takeoff made her heart leap into her throat, and the rumble of the engines vibrating through the cabin exhilarated her.

But once the plane leveled off to cruising altitude, there wasn't much to take her mind away from mulling over the events of the last few days. She had the row of seats to herself, as the flight was almost empty. The travel agent had been right, not many people wanted to vacation in the remote Kootenays in early spring.

She was flying at night and, even though she had a window seat, there was nothing but darkness outside the plane. When she glanced out the window, only her reflection stared back.

Pulling out a small notebook and pen from her purse, she set about making a list of the things she knew about the Dark Presence, the things she remembered from her previous encounters.

As she jotted down what it felt like, how she reacted each time she got too close to its energy, her mind kept wandering back to the night only a few days ago that had changed everything.

It was Gideon's face she saw. It was his strong hands holding hers she felt, and his lips brushing against hers that caused a rush of heat to her face even now, sitting alone on the plane.

She rubbed her fingertips against her lips to erase the tingling sensation. She wished she could rub away the memory of the look on his face when he pulled away from her. She wanted to erase the words he'd said.

She forced herself to focus on determining how to defeat something she wasn't sure how to beat. For the rest of the long flight, she poured through her memory for any little detail that could help her. While the few other passengers slept, Lizzie wrote a meticulous description of the ritual Vivienne taught her for her failed attempt at locating the Presence. She wanted to make sure she hadn't forgotten anything. Filling the pages of her notebook calmed her.

It was a little after four in the morning when her flight touched down. Her eyes burned from lack of sleep, her body running on autopilot. She was grateful that she'd taken the travel agent's advice and booked herself into the hotel next to the airport for the remainder of the night. The trancelike state she'd been in during her last night at the shelter hadn't provided any restorative benefits of even the few hours of real sleep she'd been running on for months. Now she was past the point of feeling anything but a drugged lethargy.

Hoping to grab a couple hours of shut-eye before heading off to the resort, she tried Vivienne's sleep draught as she slipped between the hotel's scratchy bed sheets, but it proved fruitless. The dream of Rose Cottage sought her out even in her exhaustion. She stirred awake in frustration after an hour of repeating the same journey up the curving driveway, stopping at the cottage door, and feeling the bitter disappointment of finding a door that would not yield to her efforts to get in.

After a breakfast of strong, sweet coffee, and armed with one for the road, Lizzie walked the few short blocks back to the airport to pick up the keys to her rental car from the Avis desk.

She drove the red Hyundai Accent the short distance to the ferry landing that would shuttle her across Ellis Lake. While she waited to board the small flatbed ferry, she pulled out the map and detailed instructions the clerk at the Avis desk had given her and spread them out on the passenger seat. Her rental car didn't come equipped with anything as fancy as GPS, but getting to her destination didn't look too complicated.

According to the map, the ferry would take her to Benevolent Bay, and from there she'd head West on Highway 6 for another two hours before she reached the resort. Seemed straightforward enough.

As the ferry chugged away from the landing and the pilot drew up the metal loading ramp, she got out of her car and stood by the railing. The handful of passengers sharing the ride remained in their vehicles.

She spied the other side of the lake even though they had just left the near shore. It wasn't as big as Lake Ontario, which at times, for all its beauty, looked to her as big and forbidding as the ocean. Ellis Lake seemed a more human-sized body of water. Its narrow, sinuous curves hugged the mountains as it meandered south.

A soft breeze coming off the water smelled of seaweed, fish, and diesel from the rumbling ferry engine. Only the slightest chill of the early morning brushed against her cheeks.

She thought of the greyness she'd left behind, the dirty snow banks and greasy slush still covering the city streets. Spring definitely came early to this part of the country.

Everywhere she looked, she was surrounded by mountains, their softly rounded summits bristling with the dark green of pine and cedar interspersed with the fresh green of new birch and cottonwood leaves.

She turned her face to the sun, luxuriating in the mild weather. There was a peace here amongst the gentle mountains and the untouched wilderness. It resonated low within her like a song calling her home.

When she thought about what she was attempting, it terrified her, but for the first time, instead of running away from the thing that scared her, she was meeting it head-on and on her terms.

Too soon, the ferry slowly banked left in preparation to dock at Benevolent Bay. Reluctantly, she got back in her car and waited her turn to disembark.

The highway leading to the resort was a single lane and although it was paved, it was littered with potholes. She noticed small clumps of snow lingering in the forest floor to the left of her vehicle where the spring sunshine had yet to penetrate.

She felt uneasy being alone on the road. Before her car had been repossessed, she had driven a fair amount and counted herself a more than competent driver, able to handle the aggressive Toronto drivers on the busy city streets.

Now, she white-knuckled the steering wheel as she negotiated the narrow, snaking road. To her right, the highway only had a two-foot gravel shoulder that dropped off steeply toward the lake.

Driving a nervous twenty kilometers below the speed limit, she scanned the trees on either side of the road, watching for deer waiting to dash out in front of her car. An eighteen-wheeler came up behind her at an alarming speed, the large grill of the truck filling her rearview mirror.

She fought down the urge to increase her speed to get him off her tail, and there wasn't room for her to pull over on the slim gravel shoulder. As the road dipped down and leveled out, the truck roared past her, throwing loose stones in its wake. A stone ricocheted off her windshield.

Instinctively, she wrenched the steering wheel to the right, spewing up a spray of gravel of her own as she hit the shoulder. Quickly correcting her steering, she brought the car safely back to the middle of her lane.

With her palms slick with sweat, she constantly checked her mirrors for approaching cars even though for the rest of the journey she was the only one on the road. By the time she turned down the road to the resort, her back and shoulders ached from sitting forward as she drove.

After checking in at the main hotel, a sprawling timber-framed building overlooking the lake, she followed a bellboy dressed in khakis and a dark green long-sleeved T-shirt back out to the parking lot. He loaded her two pieces of luggage onto the back of a strange-looking golf cart equipped with all-terrain tires. She left her rental car in the main parking lot with the three other vehicles parked there and climbed into the golf cart.

The bellboy chatted non-stop while he steered the cart up a dirt road only wide enough to accommodate the hotel vehicle. He informed her about the hours the hot springs were open, the hotel amenities, and what she could find for amusement in the little village an hour's drive from the resort.

She'd purposely booked the cabin farthest away from the main hotel. All ten of the cabins sprinkled around the hotel's grounds were named after the wildlife. Her cabin, The Osprey, came equipped with a small kitchenette, a king-sized bed, a stone fireplace, and a hot tub off the wraparound deck.

After the bellboy placed her suitcases on the floor by the foot of the enormous bed covered in a patchwork quilt of blues and greens, he toured her around the small cabin then stepped out onto the deck to instruct her on operating the hot tub.

She followed him back into the cabin where he stopped by the fireplace. A wrought iron bin, filled with neatly stacked logs, sat on the hearth of the fieldstone fireplace and a teepee of dry kindling was laid in the firebox waiting for a match. Lizzie declined the bellboy's offer to light a fire for her.

"If you need anything, just dial zero for the front desk, or if you want to order room service, hit nine. We have a small convenience store in the lobby of the hotel and there's a grocery store in the village if you needed to pick up a few things, but they're only open until six on Sundays."

Lizzie thanked him, fished out several twoonies from her purse, and handed them to the young man. He gave her a slight bow and left her alone.

She waited until he'd driven away and the high-pitched whine of the cart's engine grew faint before throwing open her suitcase. The spring air, although mild, was cooler underneath the forest canopy, and the ten-minute ride from the hotel to her cabin left her chilled.

The suitcase contained only her clothes. She hadn't packed her Raggedy Ann doll she'd had since childhood. She'd left it on Maria's bed in the shelter before leaving for her flight. The doll had been a comfort to her and she hoped it would be the same for Maria.

She dug out an extra pair of socks and a sweater then snapped the suitcase closed.

It was just approaching noon, and she wanted to explore the area around the cabin to see if she could find a suitable place for what she was planning.

Chapter Thirty-Six

After throwing on a heavy jacket for good measure, she ventured out into the forest surrounding her cabin. A Meadowlark trilled its flutelike song from somewhere in the distance as she picked her way cautiously across the springy, moss-covered ground and around fallen tree branches while trying to avoid stepping on pine cones the size of small pineapples.

All around her, the smell of cedar and wet earth enveloped her. The air was heavy with moisture, and droplets of water hung from the tips of the pine needles, catching the midday sun and making them sparkle in jewel-like colors of blue, red, and gold. In the darkest parts of the forest, small patches of hard, crusted snow dotted the ground.

She had only walked a few feet into the canopy of thick green boughs when she heard the loud, rhythmic beating of a drum. Her eardrums vibrated with every pulsing beat. Cocking her head, she closed her eyes to try to locate the direction of the sound, but it was coming from all around her. She covered her ears with her hands, and still the steady drumbeat continued.

She lowered her hands and opened her eyes, a sheepish grin spreading across her face. She glanced around to make sure she was alone and that no one had witnessed the fact she was creeping through the forest trying to locate the sound of her own heartbeat.

She leaned her back against the rough, deeply grooved bark of a hemlock, relaxing into the silence of her surroundings. Her cabin was far enough from the hotel and the highway that not even the sound of an occasional passing car could be heard.

It had been so long since she'd been in nature, not since her childhood. Even then, the sound of the church bells and the voices of the nuns singing their praises to God had punctured the quiet of her isolated upbringing.

Here, there was only the occasional sound of birds calling for a mate and the rapid-fire churring of squirrels high in the treetops. There were no blaring car horns, no human voices, or any of the hustle and bustle of city life. Even the air was devoid of the constant smell of pollution. She took in a deep lungful of sweet, cool air.

Sending her energy out a few feet from her physical body, she sensed the small creatures that made the forest their home, scurrying in the undergrowth, burrowing in the deadfall, or crouching silently behind the trees. Slowly, the energy signatures of the trees, and fiddleheads poking through the moss, wavered before her. The air filled with the swirling colors she associated with the Elementals; a kaleidoscope of soft, clear light danced amongst the trees, plants, and rocks of the woods.

She pushed off from the tree trunk and continued her survey around the cabin, feeling the life around her pulse and vibrate to the rhythm of her heart.

Before setting off further into the woods, she gathered up pinecones from the forest floor around her, tucking them into the front of her jacket for safekeeping until the front of her coat bulged out comically.

After thirty minutes of searching, she came upon a small clearing. At one time, a huge Western Cedar had grown in the center of the space judging by the size of the stump that remained. The severed trunk was about four feet high and had been cut cleanly across. The clearing created with the removal of the tree was no more than nine feet in diameter. The cedar must have been cut down during the fall because no new saplings had taken hold yet, and only the tender curled heads of ferns poking out of the needle-strewn ground vied for the space open to the sky. The overlapping branches of the surrounding trees created a curtain of green on all sides.

She walked the perimeter of the small nature-made circle and then stepped into its center. The ground was relatively flat. The area would suit her needs perfectly.

She retraced her steps back to her starting point, following the crooked trail of pinecones she'd dropped along the way. From where she'd dropped the first pinecone, she could easily see the outline of her cabin through the trees.

It had taken her a little over two hours to find the spot in the woods and an hour to head back to the cabin. As she entered her cabin, she realized despite her lack of sleep and food, she was energized.

She snatched her purse from the bed where she'd left it and walked the twenty minutes to the resort's parking lot where she'd left her car. Before she pulled out of the hotel parking lot, she quickly glanced at the map still sitting on the passenger seat. Highway 6 ran straight through the little village of Barton where she planned to pick up a few provisions for her short stay at the cabin. She couldn't be sure, but she'd hoped even a small town like Barton would have the particular shop she needed.

The village had only one main street, and the highway was renamed Broadway for the six blocks lined with the village's shops. The lakefront bordered one side of the shopping district; the houses of Barton's residents were scattered on the other side.

Lizzie parked at the grocery store and opted to walk the short distance down Broadway. She strolled down the cobbled walk, taking in the clapboard-sided storefronts, each painted whimsical shades of blues, pinks, yellows, and purples.

She passed a health food store, a bank, the local newspaper office, a wood fire pizzeria, a liquor store, a realty office, and a second-hand bookstore. A rather handsome white-sided, two story building with black trim contained the library.

As she ambled past the Broadway Beanery, the rich smell of coffee wafted from the interior as a customer stepped out on the street, luring her inside for a quick detour to pick up a large coffee to go.

She'd been right that even a village of two thousand people would have a hardware store, which she found at the other end of town. It was a small store with a low ceiling crammed from one end to the other with everything a customer could possible need and probably things they didn't. The store smelled of a mixture of rubber from the rows of black galoshes, kerosene, and cheap plastic from the inflatable pool animals hanging from the ceiling, ready for the summer vacationers to use them on the lake.

She browsed through the narrow aisles, filling a wire basket with items she'd jotted down on the list she'd made on the flight over. Satisfied with her purchases, Lizzie started back toward the grocery store when she spied a large wooden sandwich board painted violet with white lettering positioned by the health food store. *SpiritWood: New Age Baubles, Books, and Crystals* announced the sign. An arrow pointed toward a dead end street.

Curious as to what a New Age bauble was and feeling unusually lighthearted considering why she had come to the little mountain town, she turned down the street to investigate.

SpiritWood was situated in a converted two-story white Victorian. There was no front yard to speak of, the concrete stoop ending just before the public sidewalk. Instead of the traditional wrought iron railings, sinuous tree branches stripped of their bark and varnished to a high shine served the purpose. The door was propped open and she could hear the joyful rhythms of East Indian music floating into the street.

She climbed the stoop, her hand trailing over the silky curved wood of the banister, and stepped inside. The store was comprised of what would have been the front parlor of the old house, and every inch of space was filled with an interesting collection of fanciful and beautiful things. The store smelled heavily of patchouli.

Crystal sun catchers filled the two front windows, throwing rainbows across the wooden floor. To her left, two floor-to-ceiling bookcases were filled with books and CDs.

Carefully picking her way around low tables arranged with beeswax candles, stone Buddhas, hand-carved boxes, silk scarves in deep jewel colors, and brass Tibetan singing bowls, she kept her bag from the hardware store close to her body to avoid accidentally knocking into anything in the tiny space.

She wandered toward three glass curio cabinets at the back of the store near the cash counter. Each case overflowed with crystals and geodes of every shape, color, and size. Some were hand-cut into heart shapes and others into large smooth eggs. There were clear quartz crystals cut into small pendulums and colored ones polished into long wands. Others were left in their natural state, from the size of a pebble to ones as big as ostrich eggs.

Hanging in the doorway leading to the back of the store, a beaded curtain of cowrie shells swayed and clinked as the proprietor of the stored stepped through carrying a steaming mug.

He was in his early fifties and he wore what Lizzie was beginning to think of as the Barton uniform, as she'd seen several other locals attired in the same fashion—a plaid shirt tucked into faded blue jeans and scuffed work boots. The man had added his own personal touch to his outfit by wearing a khaki vest festooned with pockets in an array of sizes. He wore a fedora that looked like it had come from the wardrobe department of an

Indiana Jones movie. His white hair hung past his shoulders in straggly strands.

He gave her a broad smile, revealing tobacco-stained teeth. "Sorry, I didn't hear you come in. I was just making myself a cup of tea. Did you want one?" he asked, holding up his mug.

"That's very kind of you, but I think I'll pass. I was just heading to the grocery store when I saw your sign and decided to take a look around."

"Suit yourself." He smiled and took a sip of tea.

Lizzie glanced back at the curio cabinet, eyeing a cluster of large uncut quartz crystals on the bottom shelf. They were about twice the size of the ones Vivienne had placed around the hotel room during Lizzie's confinement.

When she'd drawn up her plans to confront the Dark Presence, she hadn't intended on using crystals for the ritual. Vivienne taught her intention and focus were the two most powerful tools she possessed, but as she looked at the crystals, she thought a little extra protection couldn't hurt.

"Did you want to take a look at those?"

"If you wouldn't mind."

He put his tea on the counter before retrieving a key from one of the smaller pockets on the front of his vest and unlocking the cabinet. Using both hands, he carefully lifted out the crystals one at a time and set them on the checkout counter. "With crystals, it's important to hold them, get a feel for their energy, and see if it matches your own." He stepped back, waiting for Lizzie to approach the counter.

Feeling self-conscious, she put her shopping bag and purse down by her feet and reached out to the first crystal. She could feel the vibration before her fingers touched its rough surface. Each of the four crystals gave off a strong pulsation, each one slightly different from the last. Their combined singing was potent but dissonant.

Without thinking, she rearranged them on the counter, putting them in an order that made sense to her. When she ran her hand over the tops of the stones in the new array, their energy felt stronger, more cohesive.

"I think I'll take these."

"All of them?"

"Yes, all of them," she said.

"Sure thing," the shopkeeper said, moving behind the till.

She had to dig out her old checkbook to pay when he informed her he only took cash or checks. It was a quaint notion that even in the twenty-first century there were still businesses that hadn't embraced the current technological advances in commerce.

"Are you a writer?" he asked as he looked over her check.

"No, not even close."

"Oh, I just figured with a name like Lizzie Bennet and the fact you're visiting our little area this early in the season, you gotta be a writer type. Only the artsy folk come out here this time of year. Not much to do except spend time in solitude and connect with the muse. Too cold to do much of anything else. Can't even fish right now with the lake being so rough."

"No," she reiterated. "I'm not an artist or a writer. Just someone who needed to take a break from city life." She picked up her purse and bag at her feet and took a step back from the counter.

Because of their weight, the shop owner put the four crystals wrapped in layers of tissue paper in two separate bags. When Lizzie went to lift them off the counter, she realized they were too heavy for her to carry them and the bags from the hardware store the four blocks back to her car.

"I have some more shopping to do and I left my car at the grocery store…"

"I'll just tuck these behind the counter and you can pick them up when you're done your shopping."

She thanked him and left the store to pick up a few provisions, including six boxes of sea salt. The grocery clerk gave her a strange look when she ran the boxes over the scanner, but didn't say anything aside from the standard "have a nice day" when she handed her the grocery bags.

After returning to SpiritWood to pick up her crystals, she headed back down the highway to her cabin. It wasn't until she was putting away her purchases that she found two extra things tucked into one of the SpiritWood bags.

They were a pair of cut crystals in the shape of wands about six inches long. One end of the wands were rounded, the other was polished to a sharp point. She held them up to the light, marveling at the colors. They were tri-colored, starting with a deep purple at the base, changing to an apple green in the middle, and fading to clear transparency at the top. A small card accompanied the wands.

Thought these may come in handy. They're fluorite crystals, good for protection against psychic attacks and negative energy. Take care, Gus.

She placed the fluorite wands on the nightstand next to the four pieces of quartz. She wondered whether Gus belonged to the Order, or if he was just being a thoughtful business owner to a patron who had just dropped a bundle in his store during the off-season. He had worn a long-sleeved shirt, so she hadn't been able to look for the telltale tattoo on his inner wrist.

If he was a member, he would inform the Order of her arrival to his sleepy little village. Either way, she was going ahead with her plans tomorrow night. She didn't want to delay and give herself time to succumb to her fear. The longer she took, the more chance she'd chicken out.

She would have gone ahead with her plans that very evening, but she was waiting for a fax from her lawyer. It would contain her amended will and confirmation that her gifts were being dispersed. Once she'd signed off on it and faxed it back using the hotel's machine, she would be able to do what she'd come here to accomplish, knowing that all of her affairs were in order.

She made dinner from the few items she bought at the grocery store—chicken soup, a thick slice of crusty white bread, and a cup of Earl Grey tea with honey. Placing everything on a tray, she took her meal outside on the deck. The chicken soup was from a can, but she'd never tasted anything so scrumptious, the fresh, yeasty bread a delight on her tongue.

When she finished her meal, she lingered on the deck, watching the day slowly give way to the coming night. She couldn't glimpse the lake from her cabin, but watching the sun dip behind the mountains, throwing up its blazing reds and oranges onto the canvas of the sky, was more than enough beauty for her. Only when full dark had fallen, the sky glittering in a dazzling display of stars, did the chilly air drive her shivering inside behind the warmth of the solid log walls of her cabin.

She built a fire in the hearth and after preparing for sleep, she slipped under the thick quilt, snuggling down in the extra comfort of the feather bed. She lay on her back watching the firelight flicker and dance on the ceiling.

She felt a peace settle over her like the comforting weight of the quilt she lay under. It was a curious sensation, unexpected but not unwelcome. She knew the choice she was making could and probably would end in her death, yet when she thought about what that would mean, she felt nothing but a deep and centered calm.

Her eyes grew heavy, and she finally succumbed to the irresistible draw of sleep, where she again walked the familiar driveway leading up to Rose Cottage.

Chapter Thirty-Seven

Even in the dream state, she was aware something was different, although nothing looked out of place. But as she traversed the long drive and made her way around the bend, she spied Vivienne sitting on the front porch stairs, her hands clasped loosely in her lap.

Even though she was dreaming, her heart sped up and a queasy uneasiness settled in her stomach. There was no doubt Vivienne would know what happened between her son and her and his subsequent resignation as her guardian. Lizzie slowed her approach to the cottage, steeling herself for Vivienne's disapproval.

Vivienne looked up as Lizzie approached, a quiet smile on her lips. The smile put Lizzie at ease.

Lizzie joined her on the steps. They faced each other, their knees only inches apart.

Vivienne looked out of place in the rustic setting, sitting on the stoop in a black and white Chanel jacket and skirt and black patent pumps.

"I'm not dreaming you, am I?"

Vivienne shook her head.

"Why are you here?"

"I had no other way of getting a hold of you. There's no cell service where you are."

"No, there isn't," Lizzie said, sticking out her chin.

"I suppose I could have activated the tracking device in your phone to find you, or I could have employed the talents of the seers, but you'd made it plain by your actions you didn't want to be followed."

"You're right, but if you're worried about me, don't be. I'm perfectly fine." A tracking device? The information surprised Lizzie. She'd assumed the Order only employed magickal means of dealing with their charges. She'd been foolish to think that they wouldn't use modern technology to fulfill their duty.

"You've become quite adept at blocking your thoughts," Vivienne continued. "Such natural talent you have but I still managed to catch a glimpse of what you intend to do."

Lizzie hadn't been as successful as she'd hoped in blocking her thoughts from her mentor. "So you've come here to talk me out of it?"

"No, if this is the course of action you believe is right, then I won't stop you."

She had no doubt if Vivienne wanted to thwart her plans, she could have. "So if you aren't going to stop me, why risk joining me here in this dream?"

"To let you know you don't have to do this alone. If you tell me where you are, I can join you. I'm so sorry I couldn't have been with you after you stopped Richard. But I can be now and if you tell me how to find you, I'll be there as soon as possible."

"Even after what I did to Richard, what I did to Gideon, why would you want to help me?"

Vivienne reached out and touched her hand. Even though she was dreaming, Lizzie felt the warmth and weight of Vivienne's hand on her own. The comfort she felt from the simple gesture brought tears to her eyes.

"Why are you always so quick to condemn yourself? You were reacting to a dangerous and violent situation. One you weren't trained to handle. You did what you needed to do to save your friends." Vivienne put her hand back in her lap and shifted slightly on the stoop. "And as far as my son goes, the choices he makes have nothing to do with me caring about your welfare."

Lizzie didn't need to delve deeper into her friend's energy to know she wasn't as dispassionate about what had happened with her son as she said she was.

"I never meant for him to break his vows. I never meant…"

"I know you didn't. What you feel for each other, that's between you and Gideon."

"He's no longer my guardian. But you know that already."

"Yes. A guardian must remain neutral with their charges for them to perform their duties. Gideon had no choice but to resign from his post and, as is expected, he has been placed on suspension from guarding anyone until the Elders decide his fate." Vivienne sighed and looked down at her loosely clasped hands in her lap. "The whole situation is more complicated than you realize. I suspect he broke his vow because of an unrealized desire, and his attraction to you may have been a convenient means to an end."

Her words stung and Lizzie struggled to keep her face neutral.

Vivienne looked up sharply. "No, Lizzie, I'm not saying what he feels for you is not genuine. But had he truly felt a calling to be a guardian, he could have resisted his feelings for you, or at the very least asked to be reassigned if he wanted to pursue a relationship with you."

"Then why did he choose to become a guardian in the first place?" Anger crept into her voice.

"That, I fear, may have more to do with pleasing me than I wish to admit. Even as a small child, he would spend hours poring over the old books in the Archives. But after his father's death, he abandoned his dream of becoming an Archivist to follow his father's path, not his own. And I did nothing to discourage him." Vivienne's voice grew fainter. "In fact, a part of me was pleased. As it has turned out, he is where he wanted to be all along. He has been reassigned to the Archives until his hearing with the Elders."

Up until now, Vivienne had always seemed so strong and self-assured. But now Lizzie saw Vivienne for who she was—just as human, complicated, and fallible as herself. Her anger toward her friend softened. "Will you tell Gideon despite how things turned out, I'm grateful for everything he's done for me?"

"No, you'll have to tell him yourself," she said with a gentle smile. "You have to make sure you come out of this alive and tell him yourself."

"I'm not doing this because I have a death wish, I really don't. But I have to do this alone. It's what I'm meant to do. In fact, it feels like this is what my whole life has been leading toward, and I intend to fulfill it no matter what happens."

"I see. When are you planning to go after it?"

"Tomorrow night."

"You've chosen well. It will be a new moon tomorrow. Very powerful for magick and drawing your power to its full potential."

"I hadn't realized that. Once I made up my mind to do this, I saw no reason to wait."

"I'll be praying for your success. We all will; everyone you've touched, everyone who cares about you. We will send thoughts of support and love."

"Thank you." Lizzie gazed around her, drinking in the serenity and beauty of her dream woods. "Vivienne, I think know what this place is," she said, still looking at the mountains and trees, excitement replacing her earlier trepidation at seeing Vivienne in her dream. "I know why I keep dreaming about this cottage, these woods." She turned to face Vivienne again. "Do you think spirits who have crossed over can send us guidance?"

"I do."

"I think this dream is a gift from my mother. She sent me a glimpse of these mountains, this general geographical location to show me the best place to confront the Dark Presence. I know you can't feel it because you aren't really here, but there is something extra special about the place where I'm staying. It's like the very energy of the trees, plants, and even the rocks are stronger here, more concentrated."

"Like an energy vortex."

"Yes, and I think I can use this vortex to my advantage to boost my powers."

"And the stone cottage? Did you find it where you are in the waking world?"

"No. I don't think the cottage exists in real life. I think it's what awaits me on the other side. Could heaven really look like this?"

"Yes, it could. I believe the afterlife is whatever it needs to be for each of us."

"I'd like to think that's true. If heaven is this place, then I won't fear death whenever it comes for me."

The two women sat in companionable silence, both looking out at the view. There was no sense of time passing as the sun remained constant in its position high above them. "It's almost time, isn't it? This dream will be ending soon."

"Yes, I must leave you now. Remember, Lizzie, you are loved. Let that carry you through and give you strength as you go forward."

"I will," she said.

Vivienne reached out her hand and placed her palm gently on her forehead. Lizzie closed her eyes.

"May the blessing of the Goddess be upon you, may her presence be with you always," Vivienne said.

"And with you," she replied.

When Lizzie opened her eyes, Vivienne and Rose Cottage were gone, replaced by the now familiar ceiling of her cabin. The morning light streamed through the windows, heralding the day.

Chapter Thirty-Eight

That evening, Lizzie walked through the forest, guided by the small, round, battery-operated lights she'd placed along the path to the clearing before nightfall. Vivienne had been right, it was a new moon and even with the bright light of the large Coleman lantern she held out before her, she wouldn't have been able to find the spot in the woods without the little lights pointing the way.

A knapsack, part of her purchase from the hardware store, slung over her shoulder contained the rest of the supplies she'd need for the ritual. The feeling of deep calm had persisted throughout the day as she went about her final preparations. As she picked her way through the thick carpet of needles, moving slowly and deliberately so as not to trip on fallen twigs or hidden stumps, she felt no fear.

Arriving at the small clearing, she set the lantern on the stump and began unpacking her knapsack, using the flat, rough surface of the severed tree as a makeshift altar. On it, she placed the quartz crystals, the fluorite wands, four thick, white pillar candles, four tin pie plates, a long-nosed butane BBQ lighter, and the several boxes of sea salt.

Pouring out the sea salt in a constant stream around the clearing, she focused her intention of creating a circle of power and protection. Even without moonlight, the salt circle gleamed an eerie white on the forest floor.

Next, she dripped a bit of melted wax on the four tin pie plates and secured the pillar candles to their crude bases. Each candle she placed on the ground in the position of the four directions, just inside the salt circle, keeping them unlit for the moment.

The four quartz chunks she placed in the four spaces between the candles in the order she had first put them in at Spiritwood. Even though she hadn't finished creating the protective circle or called the Elementals, she could already feel the strong vibrations traveling around the circle from crystal to crystal.

She grabbed the butane lighter from the altar and stood before the candle she'd placed to the east. Holding the lighter in her right hand, she lit the candle. Using her left hand, she drew the symbol in the air and called out to summon the first Elemental: East, home of Air and Sylph.

She continued around the circle in a clockwise fashion, lighting each candle, drawing the symbol in the air and summoning each Elemental in turn. As she beckoned to the spirits of air, fire, water, and earth, she softened her gaze so she could see the undulating mists begin to form as they heeded her call. She smiled broadly at the sight of her old friends. They added a great deal to her measure of calm and determination.

Satisfied with the drawing of the Corners and the protection of the circle, Lizzie stepped over to the tree altar and positioned herself so that she was facing east.

Before she completed the last steps, before she sought the Dark Presence, she undid the top two buttons on her coat to expose her neck. The chilly night air made the skin on her throat break out in goose flesh.

Reaching behind her, she fumbled with the clasp on her necklace. Finally managing to undo the chain, with careful hands, she slipped it from her neck and placed it tenderly on the tree stump.

She brushed her fingertips against her bare neck. Without the weight of her cross at her throat, she felt naked and exposed. But if her mother had placed a charm on her cross to absorb her excess magickal energy, she needed to remove it to allow her powers full rein.

With that same thought, she dug out Gideon's medicine bundle from her coat pocket and placed it next to her cross. She caressed the soft deerskin of the pouch before turning her attention back to the ritual.

She raised her hands and closed her eyes, preparing to send her energy up into the night sky when, to her left, outside the circle, a cedar branch swayed and creaked, startling her in an unexpected rush of fear. Her eyes snapped opened and she looked toward the direction of the sound.

The night was dead calm. Not even the faintest breeze disturbed the candle flames, which burned high and straight. They threw out a weak pool of light and she couldn't see into the deep gloom of the forest.

Raising the Coleman lantern in front of her, she stepped to the very edges of the salt circle to investigate. The light of the lantern picked up a gleam of six emeralds as the light reflected off the eyes of three large ravens roosting on a low branch. They made not a sound, their sharp, curved beaks shining in the lamplight she held aloft.

Lizzie smiled and gave them a nod. The three feathered creatures shifted on the branch; their feathers rustled like taffeta as they moved.

Their appearance didn't alarm her, not this time. She knew they were there to protect and watch over her as their brethren had done that day in the cemetery. She welcomed any extra support she could get, even from the silent black birds. As she made her way back to the center of the circle, she heard more movement in the trees ringing the little clearing. More sets of emerald eyes peered out from the dark.

Taking her place again at the altar, she raised her face to the night sky and drank in the sight of a thousand stars strewn across the black endless void. Holding a fluorite wand in each hand, she lifted her arms up in supplication and called out into the night.

"To the Goddess of the Triple Moon, the Maiden, the Mother, and the Crone, I ask for your guidance and protection for what I am about to do. Give me strength as I go forward to defeat the evil that has threatened me and the ones I love." A ripple of energy washed over her as she continued her prayer, her voice growing strong and clear. "Grant me the courage to see this through to the end. So mote it be."

As the last words left her lips, she closed her eyes and released her spirit into the night.

Chapter Thirty-Nine

Locating the Dark Presence that had dogged her for months, changed the course of her life, and brought her to the woods at midnight was easier than she anticipated. Whether it was the new moon, the energy of the land boosting her powers, removing her necklace, or a combination of the three, as her life force raced through the firmament, it was only seconds until she sensed the familiar darkness hovering near her.

Unlike her previous encounter, she didn't hesitate to send her energy directly toward it. From her altered perception, the Dark Presence appeared like a black mushroom cloud, its oily smoke continually moving up and curling over into itself, its darkness a result of it absorbing all the light from the space it occupied. At its very center, a dull red orb pulsed like a heart.

As she inched her energetic being closer, several tendrils uncoiled from the writhing mass reaching out for her. She zipped out of the way, but she wasn't fast enough and one of the tentacles of smoke brushed through her ethereal body. Its touch sent a biting cold burning into her and with it, a fear so sharp she felt it cut through her like a dagger.

Terror swirled to the core of her soul. Her rational mind screamed for her to leave, to get away as fast as she could. She fought the instinct to retreat. Instead, she pictured her energy streaming from where her hands should be, and with that thought, she sent two bolts of blue light at the mushroom cloud.

It recoiled instantly, only to reach out again with its thrashing tentacles with a speed so fast she had no time to get out of the way. The pain was worse this time and so was the fear and despair that overcame her. She struggled to free herself from its grasp while blasting it with her own energy.

The Dark Presence advanced toward her, hardly slowing in its progression forward even though she was focusing all her powers at the slithering vapor. It engulfed her, surrounding her within its oily gloom.

She'd never known fear as intense as what rolled over and through her as she was swallowed up by the entity. She was surrounded by a sharp-edged hate so intense that no light or hope existed within the dark being. Her determination faltered.

The energy pulsing through what she thought of as her hands weakened. She struggled to free herself from the confines of the miasma, but it was like moving in tar. The more she tried to pull away, the more viscous the air around her became, and the harder it was for her to move.

She could not believe that after all she'd been through, she was going to die without even causing the slightest damage to the cursed thing.

Gathering her energy to her center, she focused all of her reserves on remaining calm. She stopped blasting the entity with her energy and allowed the greasy blackness to press in even closer. Letting the panic and despair cascade over her, she did her best not to succumb to the feelings.

As she relaxed into the darkness around her, she unfurled her consciousness into the gloom, touching the texture of its soul. If the thing trying to kill her had a reasoning mind, she couldn't detect it. She felt only raw, powerful emotions of rage, misery, and viciousness, all aimed at her. She also sensed the creature was as ancient and timeless as the universe hanging serenely above them.

Touching its consciousness, she sensed no past or future, just a constant state of darkness. Its only desire was destruction of that which was its opposite.

As she allowed herself to become part of the darkness, she discovered its desire was not just to destroy whatever came across its path, but to go after her specifically. This thought form felt different than the overriding dark emotions she first picked up on. This information briefly confused her until she realized what she was sensing.

It was as Vivienne and Gideon had suspected. Someone had called up this demon to use as a weapon. Whoever was controlling it was using it like a madman would use a loaded gun.

Swiftly, she contracted her energy inwards and placed her attention on the pulsing red orb, watching it expand and contract like the beating of a malignant heart. When she sensed the air around her lighten just the slightest in response to her remaining motionless and small, she moved quickly.

Gathering her courage, she sent out a thin stream of energy, trying to get an impression of who was controlling the mass of evil. She found what she was looking for, a thread of energy that had a slightly different texture than the ancient evil enveloping her. The termination point of the thread ended in the angry red orb at the center of the mushroom cloud.

Acting quickly, she aimed a bright blast of her energy at the single tether of energy, sending it down and away from the entity and hopefully toward the person at the other end. As soon as she let loose the blast of light, the air constricted around her, trapping her. She floated helplessly in the void.

The thread remained intact. The despair she felt was hers alone and not a result of the dark entity. It hadn't worked.

So this is how it ends. I've failed yet again.

Then she saw it; a minute change like a ripple appeared in the energy thread. A sliver of hope coursed through her as she watched the cable of energy waver, then collapse in on itself. There was a vibrational disturbance akin to the sound of a brittle bone snapping as the thread vaporized.

The demon, now severed from its master, sent out waves of confused panic. The sticky murkiness eased up. Lizzie saw her opportunity. She struck out at the creature before it could regroup. Slipping into the very heart of it, she aimed herself for the middle of the menacing red sphere.

She only had time to register a defensive blast from the demon before she pushed her own energy outwards like a supernova. She could hear herself screaming in pain as the creature, realizing too late what she'd done, turned the full power of its rage on her. She struck back with her own anger, as hot and powerful as its own.

She was Kali, the Goddess of Destruction, sending out her own deadly energy like a thousand swords shredding her enemy's heart into ribbons. The pulsing crimson orb exploded, throwing out energy shrapnel that sparked and flared like fireworks, each bright point fizzling out to nothingness.

The destruction of its heart created a domino effect in the oily dark cloud as it began to double in on itself.

Lizzie tried to pull herself out of the avalanche of darkness as the creature writhed in its death throes, but she had nothing left. She couldn't move. She had no strength to get back to her body. Darkness narrowed her vision as the demon's energy continued to collapse around her until her consciousness let go. Silently, her spirit plummeted toward her earthly body below.

Chapter Forty

She was so annoyed. Why wouldn't Vivienne let her sleep? She heard Vivienne call her name again, insistently. Lizzie squeezed her eyes closed tighter and tried to roll over.

It couldn't be time to start her lessons already. She'd just gone to bed.

She was so tired. She just wanted to sleep a few more hours. She just wanted the water to stop dripping in her face. It was making it hard to go back to sleep.

"Lizzie, get up, child. You need to get yourself inside where it's warm."

Inside?

She struggled to open her eyes, but they hurt. Everything hurt, right down to the roots of her hair. A cold, hard rain pattered on her face and ran into her ears. She rolled on her side and regretted the motion as soon as she did it.

She groaned, fighting the urge to vomit from the pain. She cracked open her eyelids, squinting against the rosy light. From her viewpoint, all she could see was a carpet of dead pine needles. A fiddlehead bobbed near her nose, dipping and bending as the rain continued to pelt down from the sky. Everywhere she looked, everything was washed in a pink haze. The fern, the needles, the rocks all tinged pink.

She started to push herself up into a sitting position, using her hands as leverage, but stopped when white-hot pain exploded from both her hands. Using her forearms, being careful not to put any pressure on her damaged palms, she pushed herself upright and leaned back against the tree stump.

She was alone in the clearing. Well, almost alone. A soft rustling of wings brought her attention to the trees just outside the clearing. Raising her head caused the forest to spin drunkenly around her. She clamped her eyes shut, waiting for the vertigo to subside. Bile burned the back of her throat.

Slowly opening her eyes again, she was relieved to see her surroundings staying put. Being careful not to move her head, she raised her eyes to the trees. The boughs were thick with ravens. They huddled together, their heads bowed as rain dripped off the branches above them.

"Hey, guys, thanks for sticking around," she said, her voice coming out in a scratchy croak.

The largest of the ravens gave a low chortle followed by a deep *quork, quork* that echoed in the stillness of the morning. She tried to smile, but her face hurt too much to make the muscles work properly.

Carefully turning her hands over, exposing her palms to the rain, she winced. Once the rain washed away most of the blood, she could clearly see several deep lacerations running down the length of both her palms. A shard of one of the fluorite crystals was still embedded in the skin of her right hand. She pulled out the crystal sliver and had to press her hand to her chest to stop the freshet of blood.

As she waited for her hand to stop bleeding, she tried to link with Vivienne. She had urgent news to tell her. But she couldn't form the connection.

She was so tired. She could have sat against the tree trunk all day, even in the rain, but Vivienne was right when she'd whispered in her mind the words "get inside." She needed to get dry and clean her wounds. She needed to tell Vivienne what she had discovered about the location of the person who had sent the Dark Presence in her path.

Struggling to her knees, she pushed herself up, using the tree trunk for support. The pink-washed world turned grey. She lowered her head again until the urge to faint passed. Before leaving the circle of protection, she gingerly plucked up her necklace and the waterlogged medicine bundle, dropping them in her coat pocket.

As she stepped into the forest, a thundering sound shattered the silence of the rain-misted morning as hundreds of ravens simultaneously took flight.

She had to stop three times as she shuffled and stumbled her way back to the cabin, leaning against the trees for support, the pine resin sticking to her coat sleeves. Halfway to the cabin, she was forced to stop when her stomach finally rebelled and she retched painfully.

Sweet relief washed over her when she finally stepped inside the warmth and safety of the cabin. The desire to collapse on the bed and let sleep overtake her was so strong. She ignored it; she was getting good at ignoring her own pain. Leaning against the wall and dripping water on the wood floor, she grabbed the phone on the nightstand and called Vivienne.

At the sound of her friend's voice, she broke into tears.

Vivienne made soothing sounds until Lizzie's sobs turned into sniffles.

"Sorry, I don't know what came over me."

"Defeating a demon and a warlock all in one night can take an emotional toll, or so I've been told." She could hear the smile in Vivienne's voice.

"Yeah, I guess it does," she laughed, her voice sounding hoarse. "Since this is an unsecured phone, I'll try to be brief. The seers were right about California. The warlock is in Carmel, or what's left of him." Her tone turned serious.

"I'll send a team there as soon as I hang up."

"Vivienne...there's something else. His energy felt familiar. His signature was something I'd sensed before and I don't mean when the demon attacked in the past. That felt completely different. When I honed in on his energy string and sent a blast down it, I felt just him. His energy wasn't new to me."

"Do you think it's someone you've been in contact with?"

"No, that's the thing I can't figure out. I know for certain it's not someone from the Order or anyone I came in contact with at the shelter. I'll give it some more thought and let you know what I come up with." A small groan escaped her lips.

"Lizzie, tell me where you are. I know you're injured. Let me come and help you."

"Thanks, but I'll be okay. I just need to clean up and get some sleep. I'll call you later," she murmured, her energy flagging. She was so tired she hung up on Vivienne without waiting for her reply.

She lurched into the bathroom and immediately started shedding her damp, soiled clothes until she stood naked and shivering on the cold tiles. She dumped all of her things in the tub and changed into a white terry robe.

Her hands were still bleeding and she inadvertently left a red smear on the lapel of her robe. Turning the water on as hot as she could stand, she unwrapped a little bar of guest soap and diligently scrubbed away the blood and dirt from the abrasions as best she could. She gritted her teeth to stop from crying out.

Reaching for a hand towel, she looked up at her reflection for the first time and she let out a shriek of surprise. Tentatively, she leaned into the mirror. Her wet hair was plastered against her skull, needles and bits of moss stuck to her hair, she had bloody scratches on her cheeks and a dark smear of mud on her forehead, but it was her eyes that had shocked her when she looked at her own reflection. She looked demonic.

The whites of her eyes were red, blood red. That explained why even now everything she saw was washed in a soft pink light. She was seeing everything through a veil of her own blood.

Turning away from her alarming visage, she snagged two clean hand towels and wrapped her ravaged hands in them. Crawling into bed, she lay her dirty, battle-weary body down. Sleep took her in its gentle embrace before her head hit the pillow.

Chapter Forty-One

Lizzie stretched languidly beneath the heavy quilt. She'd been awake for hours, but had lain in bed luxuriating in the sheer pleasure of being alive. She'd slept dreamlessly and felt fully rested. She'd forgotten how that felt.

The rain had ceased while she'd been sleeping and now the cabin was bathed in the lemony sunshine of a perfect spring day. Everything in the cabin looked as it should. The pink wash obscuring her vision was gone. A robin sang outside her window.

Pulling her hands out from under the covers, she inspected her palms. During the night, the hand towels she'd wrapped around her wounds had come undone. She didn't need the makeshift bandages anyway, by the look of her hands. Her miraculous ability to heal meant the cuts had already closed over. All that was left of the bloody gashes were raised red lines of scar tissue.

She flexed her hands and found that they were stiff but not painful. She checked out the condition of the rest of her body by stretching her legs, her feet, and cautiously rolling her shoulders and neck. The agonizing pain she had experienced upon waking up in the forest was gone, leaving her with a mild soreness in her muscles. Nothing she couldn't handle.

The only real discomfort was the grinding pain of an empty stomach. She was starving. She thought about getting up and making a pot of coffee and hot buttered toast, but she snuggled down under the covers instead. She wanted to hold on to the moment as long as she could.

She was alive and the people she loved were safe. She'd killed the demon and she was still here. If what she'd done to Richard was any indication, she was certain the person who had summoned and controlled the demon was probably suffering a similar fate.

She could admit, now that she was lying safe and warm in her bed, she hadn't thought she'd survive. And now she had no idea what she was going to do with the rest of her life. She hadn't anticipated having to make that kind of decision. She found it immensely funny and laughed until tears streamed down her cheeks and her stomach muscles ached.

An insistent tapping on the window opposite her bed stopped her laughter and she sat up, trying to discover the source of the sound.

"Good morning," she said to the large raven perched on the windowsill. It tapped on the glass in response and turned its head so it could look at her with its dark, shiny eye. It tapped again. "Yes, I know. It's time to get up."

Throwing back the quilt, she climbed out of bed and padded over to the window. She raised the sash, fully expecting the raven to fly away, but it remained stationed at the window watching her every move.

"If you give me five minutes, I'll make you some breakfast. Toast with peanut butter suit you?"

The raven cocked its head and chortled deep in its throat.

Lizzie laughed. "I'll be right out with your breakfast." She threw on a pair of woolly socks before wandering over to the kitchen. She put a pot of coffee on to brew while she fixed toast for herself and her breakfast companion.

Rummaging through the few cupboards in the tiny kitchen, she found a small wooden tray and loaded it with a cup of strong black coffee and two slices of toast for each of them, liberally slathered in peanut butter. She carried the tray out the French doors and around to the back of the cabin where the raven waited patiently.

The back side of the cabin faced the woods, and a small wooden table and two chairs had been set up there. The raven had moved from the windowsill and stood on top of the table. The bird shuffled out of the way as she put the tray down and pulled out a chair for herself.

Placing one plate in front of the raven, she sipped her coffee while she watched him dig in. He used his claws as skillfully as hands, holding down the slice of toast while he ripped off bite-sized pieces with his sharp beak. Before she'd finished her first slice, he'd devoured everything on his plate.

The bird had a smear of peanut butter on his beak. She had a strange feeling if she handed him her paper napkin, he probably would have used it.

Instead, he waddled over to the edge of the table, his claws clicking on the wooden surface, and ran his beak over the side to remove the smear of peanut butter. He proceeded to preen himself on the far side of the table while Lizzie munched on her toast. When he finished preening, he looked over his shoulder at her, let out a caw that echoed into the forest, and with a mighty flap of his wings, he took off into the sky. As he flew off into the forest, a large tail feather floated down, spinning until it landed on the table in front of her.

She plucked it off the table and rolled the quill end between her fingers, watching the way the light made the black feather flash a dark iridescent green.

Although she had no idea what she was going to do with the rest of her life, she did know what needed to be done right away. The circle in the clearing needed to be disassembled and the Elementals released. Calling Vivienne back could wait until she could get to the village to call her on the secure cell.

Tucking the raven feather in the pocket of her robe, she gathered up the dirty breakfast dishes and headed back into the cabin.

She didn't think she could feel any better than she already did, but a shower and a change of clothes did just that. She was relieved to see that her eyes had healed as quickly as her hands. The whites of her eyes looked a bit jaundiced, giving her a slightly odd appearance, but nothing as disconcerting as when they had been filled with blood.

Before leaving for the circle, she dug out her necklace and medicine bundle from her coat pocket. She put her necklace back on, and laid the still damp medicine bundle on the nightstand to dry out.

Everything she'd worn that night was ruined. Her coat was covered in sticky pine resin and she had no desire to wear the other things ever again. She bunched all the soiled clothes in a black plastic garbage bag she found from a box under the kitchen sink.

Walking back to the clearing, everywhere she looked, she saw and felt the vibrancy of the plants and trees coming to life. As she stepped into the circle, she immediately began releasing the Elementals and closing the circle. She sent out her gratitude to the four directions, thanking them for their protection.

There was no need to scoop up the salt, as the rain had done the job dissolving it into the earth. She gathered up the spent candles, dumped out the water that had collected in the pie plates, picked up the soggy pieces of cardboard that had once been boxes of sea salt, and shoved all the paraphernalia in the sopping wet knapsack.

At first, she wasn't sure what to do about the quartz crystals, or what was left of them. Just like the fluorite ones that had shattered in her hands, all that was left of the solid chunks of quartz were small, broken pieces strewn about the forest floor.

Careful not to cut herself on the shards, she gathered up as many pieces as she could, placing them in a pile by the tree stump. Using her hands, she dug through the sandy soil until she had a small, deep hole. Before returning the pieces of crystal to the earth, she held her hands over the pile and sent them a blessing. She could no longer sense any vibrations coming from what was left of the crystals. The stones had been as much alive as she was and, with a pang of sadness, she placed them reverently in the earth and covered them with soil.

Sitting back on her haunches, she gingerly brushed the gritty soil from her hands. All she could sense in the clearing was an energy of peace and tranquility. A squirrel scampered across the ground and up a nearby tree, nattering at her the whole time.

She had survived her ordeal, but she hadn't done it alone. The prayers from her friends, the Elementals, the ravens, and even the crystals had come to her aid. She was not alone. She never had been, she just hadn't known it.

Returning to the cabin, she added the knapsack to the garbage bag full of ruined clothes. She lugged the bag to her car, tossing it in the back seat to dispose of it later.

The small breakfast she'd shared with the raven hadn't stayed with her very long. She was still famished and she went out in search of her second breakfast of the day.

As she walked through the resort's main building heading toward the restaurant, she glanced over at the reception desk where a brass desk calendar caught her eye. She stopped abruptly and walked over to the receptionist. "Is that the correct date?" she asked, pointing at the calendar.

The receptionist looked up from her computer screen and glanced over to the calendar. "Yes, it's Friday, April the third."

Friday.

Lizzie had slept for three days solid. Just like when she'd gone *In Between*, her body had needed three whole days to restore itself.

No wonder she was starving.

She was craving a huge plate of fried eggs, bacon, and hash browns, but when she stepped into the dimly lit cavernous dining lounge, her appetite faltered. The restaurant was empty. She turned on her heels and headed for town.

Sitting at a table with a wobbly leg, sipping strong, sweet coffee, Lizzie was pleased with her decision to come to the Broadway Beanery instead of eating alone. Her table was tucked into the corner by the kitchen and she had a perfect view of all the patrons in the tiny café. The place was packed, even for a weekday. There were several tables occupied by women who sat in small clutches nursing their coffee or tea and catching up on the village gossip. She smiled when she noticed a group of grey-haired men doing exactly the same thing.

Breakfast was served until eleven and she'd made it just in time to place her order. She devoured her plate of eggs, farmer's sausage, crispy hash browns, and buttered toast.

As she tucked into her food, she watched as the coffee shop slowly emptied out and a new set of patrons wandered through the door for lunch. The one waitress on duty was run off her feet scurrying from table to table refilling coffee, delivering orders, and clearing dishes.

Lizzie didn't linger over her breakfast. As soon as she was done, she left a healthy tip for the waitress and vacated her seat. Her table was snagged by a fortyish man wearing dusty work overalls and dirty steel-toed boots even before the harried waitress had a chance to clear the dirty dishes.

While she stood in line at the counter to pay her bill, she looked over a display of teapots and tins of loose tea neatly arranged on an antique sideboard. Hanging on the wall next to sideboard were several small handsomely made brooms—whisks, hand brooms, cobwebbers, shoe brushes, and hearth brooms.

She took a half a step out of the line to run her hand over the smooth, polished wood of the handle of the one hanging closest to her. She admired the intricately braided section where the bristles joined the handle.

"They definitely are unique, aren't they?" said the young man behind the counter. He had a goatee and sported a diamond stud in his right earlobe. His dark eyes reminded her of Gideon's and her heart tripped in her chest.

"Yes, they are," she replied. She was next in line to pay and quickly stepped up to the counter, handing over her bill.

"The guy that makes them has a studio just outside of town. It's called the Leaning Barn," the young man said as he tallied up her bill. "He's got more brooms than we have on display here and you can watch him make one. I know they're just brooms, but it's kinda cool. He even grows his own broomcorn for the bristles. If you're looking for something to do, it's worth checking out."

It sounded intriguing, and seeing as the only other thing she had on her agenda was to call Vivienne on her cell now that she was in town and could get a signal, she quickly asked for directions to the broom maker's studio.

The young man obliged her by sketching a quick map on a napkin, which he handed over to her with her change.

"Now remember, if you hit the bridge, you've gone too far and you'll have to drive another fifteen minutes before there's a place to turn around. After you see the sign for MacDonald Creek, you take the next right. There's a big boulder by the side of the road that looks like a lion if you look at it the right way. That's where the turnoff is to the studio."

She thanked him for the directions and headed back to her car. Digging out the silver phone from her purse, she dialed Vivienne's number.

While she listened to the phone ring, Lizzie turned in the driver's seat to watch an older woman walking her dog past the car. Her sudden movement caused a sharp pain in her back. She groaned just as Vivienne picked up.

"Lizzie, are you okay?" Vivienne asked, alarm in her voice.

"It's nothing, just a little residual tenderness. You know how it is with me, seems I just needed to sleep for three days straight and presto, I'm all good. Thanks for making sure I got back to the cabin safely."

"I hope you don't mind that I connected with you without your permission."

"God no, if anything I'm grateful." Talking with Vivienne felt almost like it had before that night with Gideon. Almost. There was still a stiffness between them that hadn't been there before. A small pain tugged at Lizzie's heart. "Any news on the warlock?"

"We dispatched a team to California as soon as you called me, but they just missed him. The seers picked up on his signature before he managed to cloak himself and they confirmed he's injured. Badly injured, by their account. For him to escape and cloak his signature in his current condition, he can't be working alone. But I'm confident we'll catch him. It's just a matter of time."

There was a moment of dead air on the line. Lizzie wanted to ask how Madison was doing. She wanted to know if Gideon had asked after her, but she couldn't form the words.

Vivienne broke the awkward silence first. "So, what do you plan to do now?"

"I don't have a clue and, strangely enough, I don't really care. I'm just going to take it one moment at a time. What that means for this moment is I'm off to see a man about a broom."

Vivienne laughed. "Sounds intriguing. Does he make two-seaters?"

"I'll make sure to ask," she said. "Vivienne—I'm staying at the Halcyon Resort in Barton, B.C. I guess there's no need for secrecy anymore."

"I hear the scenery is breathtaking in the mountains."

"It is. I have my cabin booked until next week. If you're not doing anything, you could come for a visit."

"I may take you up on the offer."

"I'd love it if you did. I'll call you later tonight."

After wishing each other well, Lizzie hung up, but still held the cell in her hand. With one touch, she could call Gideon. She wanted to share her triumph with him, which was as much his as it was hers but she couldn't reach out to him.

If what Vivienne had told her was true, that Gideon used her and her feelings for him so he wouldn't have to be a guardian anymore, she should feel betrayed. That he hadn't even tried to call her meant she should at least be angry. But all she felt was a sense of loss.

Alone in her car, thinking of him, she was surprised to discover what she missed wasn't Gideon's romantic affections but their friendship. They had been through so much together. He'd understood who she was and her need to feel a part of something. To belong.

Tucking her phone back in her purse, she looked over the directions to the Leaning Barn Gallery one more time. Forward was where her life now lay, not in the melancholy reflections of the past. Although she'd told Vivienne she didn't really care what she was going to do with her life, she realized that wasn't quite true.

Something new had been born inside her that night in the woods, something she just now perceived. She was curious to discover who she was in relation to no one but herself.

She shook her head. Had she birthed this new aspect of herself? Or had it been there all along, buried beneath the layers of fear and self-doubt?

She'd been given the gift of a second chance with her life. One she wouldn't squander on something that could never be. She trusted herself now and the guidance of her intuition. For now, her journey would be a solitary one, and for the first time, she looked forward to the discovery.

"Bring it on," she said, laughing at her own bravado. Squaring her shoulders, she drove off to find the Leaning Barn. The handwritten directions on the napkin seemed simple enough. Compared to what she'd been through, how difficult could it be?

Chapter Forty-Two

Lizzie pointed her car south on Broadway, going the opposite direction of the Halcyon, and zipped down the road to the edge of town where the main road turned back into Highway 6. She stayed on the highway as it snaked and climbed up and around the mountains.

As she drove along the narrow mountain road at a cautious eighty kilometers an hour, she rolled down her window to let in the fresh air. The noonday sun was a bright orb high in the bowl of the robin's egg blue sky. Sunlight winked off the surface of the lake to her right, making the water sparkle.

The rain that had pelted her three days ago as she lay cold and in pain had melted the remaining clumps of snow hidden in the shadows of the trees. Everywhere she looked, spring was bursting forth in its full glory, and the air was sweet with the smell of the rising sap from the cottonwood and willow trees.

Snapping her attention back to the road, she concentrated on looking for the turnoff. She'd been driving for twenty minutes and according to the squiggly blue lines on the hand-drawn map, she should be approaching the sign for MacDonald Creek at any moment.

From the treetops, a large bird burst out onto the road right in front of her car. She let out a startled shriek and slammed on the brakes as a flash of wings swooped over her car. She only had time to register the white of its feathered head and the bright yellow of sharp talons before the eagle disappeared from sight.

She thanked the Goddess there hadn't been anyone following behind her or her sudden braking would have surely resulted in a collision. Clutching the steering wheel, she leaned forward, craning her neck as she searched the sky for the eagle. It was nowhere in sight. With shaking hands, she slowly accelerated her car forward.

Just as she regained speed, the eagle reappeared, flying low and fast over her car from behind. With the driver's side window down, she heard the beat of its massive wings as it stirred the air in its path. Flying over the car, it proceeded straight down the middle of the road about ten feet off the ground.

Lizzie marveled at the size of the eagle's wingspan as it kept its course, following the center line on the road. And just as abruptly as it had appeared, the eagle swooped up into the sky, veering off in the direction of the lake. Out of the corner of her eye, she watched it disappear behind the treetops just as she drove across a bridge.

She pulled over onto the narrow gravel shoulder as soon as she crossed the wooden trestle, her heart pounding in her chest. There wasn't enough room to get her car completely off the road, but her curiosity overrode her caution.

It can't be. It just can't be.

Getting out of the car, she jogged back toward the bridge. Her mind wasn't playing tricks on her; she was standing on the same bridge from her Rose Cottage dream, right down to the wooden planks beneath her feet.

She gripped the handrail and gazed down the deep precipice below. A burbling stream danced over a bed of large boulders. The smell of water mingled with the biting scent of creosote drifting up from the bridge timbers under her feet. She turned away from the view below and looked down the road where she'd left the car.

Sprinting back to her vehicle, she pulled onto the road with confidence. She may have gotten lost looking for the broom maker, but she knew where she was going now, knew it like the beat of her own heart. Inching over the speed limit, she zipped down the highway until she spotted the familiar side road she'd traveled down for months in her dreams. Without hesitation, she turned her car down the gravel road.

The crystalline blue of the lake was straight ahead of her, but she didn't bother to take even a moment to enjoy the splendor. She turned east and stopped short of pulling up to the wrought iron gates blocking the driveway that was exactly where she knew it would be.

She was trembling with excitement, but she couldn't get out of the car. Digging through her purse, she yanked out her cell to call Vivienne, but there were no bars on the display. She'd forgotten there was no cell coverage outside the village. She threw the useless phone on the passenger seat.

"This is ridiculous," she said aloud, flinging open the car door and stepping out on the gravel road.

The dirt track was deserted. Her only companions on the lonely stretch of woods were the birds and squirrels. She hadn't passed any other cars or seen any cabins along the gravel road.

Tentatively, she approached the wrought iron gates. In her dream, they had been painted a bright glossy white. The gates before her had seen better days; rust had eaten away at the metal and the remaining paint was yellowed and flaking. A thick metal chain was wrapped around the two halves of the gate, secured by a shiny new padlock threaded through the ends.

She fingered the lock. Disappointment washed over her. It was so strong she could taste the bitterness in the back of her throat. In dreaming this place, it had become hers as much as she felt she belonged to it. It never occurred to her that someone may already call it home.

She rattled the gate, but there wasn't enough play for her to squeeze through and despite their decrepit appearance, they held fast to their mooring posts. If she wanted to see what awaited at the end of the driveway, she needed to find another way in.

A six-foot stone wall covered in weedy vines ran the width of the property. The rough stones of the wall provided convenient toeholds, making it easy to scale. She searched for a spot where the overgrown brambles were less dense. Pushing through the thicket of thorny branches, she placed her foot on a protruding stone and boosted herself awkwardly onto the top of the wall. She sat up, swinging her legs over the other side.

The ground on the other side of the wall looked just as neglected as the drive leading up to the gate. She knew she was trespassing and would have a hard time explaining what she was doing there. Before she chickened out, she pushed off the wall and dropped down the other side.

Instead of landing on soft ground, her foot hit something hard and smooth hidden under the thick vegetation and both her feet went out from under her. She let out a high-pitched squeal as she fell gracelessly on her rear end.

She sat on the damp earth, half expecting the occupant of the cottage to come down the driveway to investigate. When no one came down the lane demanding to know what she was doing there, she picked herself up and brushed off the leaves and needles stuck to her wet jeans.

Her foot had scraped back a mat of decaying leaves when she'd slid on the slick surface, revealing a bit of plywood painted red and white. She grasped the corner and pulled it free from the slimy leaves. It was a *For Sale* sign from the Barton Realty office. She recalled seeing the storefront on her first trip through town.

Wiping her muddy hands on her jeans, she hiked up the tree-lined lane, unsure if her wildly beating heart was due to anticipation or fear of what she might find at the end of the road.

She was rehearsing in her mind what she'd say if she found someone already living in the cottage when she stepped out of the trees.

Blinking back tears of delight, she followed the curved drive up to the house. Rose Cottage sat empty and forlorn. Her fear that the little house had already been claimed by someone else was unnecessary.

The stone house was deserted and by the looks of things, it had remained so for a very long time. A thick carpet from seasons of leaf and pine debris littered the front porch. The windows were obscured by grime and one of the shutters hung drunkenly from a single remaining hinge. The bright blue door of her dreams had faded to a pale grey.

She had to duck under the tangle of branches from the overgrown climbing roses as she mounted the porch steps. Their canes grew in a thick tangle, circling the porch's railings and pillars, even hanging down from the zinc gutters. The roses had just begun to leaf out, the buds not fully developed this early in the spring.

A thorn snagged her sweater. When she stopped on the steps to unhook herself, the unmistakable scent of roses wafted around her. She glanced up, locating the source of the smell. A delicate pink rose, it petals partially opened, hung just above her head. She raised herself on tiptoes and breathed in the intoxicating perfume.

There was no logical explanation as to how this fragile blossom could exist when the rest of the plant hadn't even budded out yet, but she was beyond needing logical reasons to explain away miracles.

Hers was a world where magick and the mundane coexisted, where the balance between darkness and light was continually shifting, where the only constant was change itself. Hers was a life that held as much pain as it did joy. And she was ready to live it fully.

Every molecule in her body hummed with delight as she faced the weathered door and turned the tarnished handle. The doorknob turned easily under her hand and with a rush of joy, she stepped over the threshold.

A gentle spring wind danced through the trees as Rose Cottage welcomed Lizzie home.

About the Author

"As a small child I dreamed of growing up to be a chestnut mare. I was terribly disappointed when I found out people couldn't magically transform into animals but I got over it by immersing myself in the world of fairy tales and thus began my lifelong passion for reading and make-believe."

Lora was born in the small town of Fort Saskatchewan, Alberta; the middle child of five girls. In 2006, she and her eldest sister moved to a hobby farm in the remote Kootenay area of British Columbia and for five years had several country adventures which included raising chickens and goats, encounters with wildlife and wrangling the neighbour's horses. Currently she lives in BC's Fraser Valley in a household of women spanning two generations of family with a collection of cats and a teacup Chihuahua affectionately known as Mexican Kitty.

Connect with Lora:

Website: http://loradeeprose.com/

Facebook: https://www.facebook.com/pages/Lora-Deeprose-Author/94913817417

Goodreads:

https://www.goodreads.com/author/show/2895248.Lora_Deeprose